THE LIES WE LIVE

MORGAN TAYLOR
GIESBRECHT

ISBN (paperback): 978-1-7386961-2-3
ISNB (ebook): 978-1-7386961-3-0

Printed in Canada

www.morgantaylorgiesbrecht.com

Contents

Historical Note

One of the beautiful things about story writing is blending fact with fiction, and this story you hold in your hands has its fair share of both.

Newhaven is a real town in East Sussex, England, and it did play an important role during the First World War. In fact, several of the places you will read about can be visited today, including the Promenade, Newhaven Baptist Church, Newhaven Town station, the Hope Inn, and the cemetery on Lewes (pronounced like *Lewis)* Road. However, despite the reality of these places, I have taken creative license to recreate the town as it appears in the book.

A topic of importance I will point out is the difference between MI5 and MI6.

- MI5 is the domestic branch of British Intelligence, also known as the Security Service during WW1. Referred to as MI5 or simply the Service in this book.
- MI6 is the foreign branch of British Intelligence and was known as the Secret Service during WW1. Referred to as the Secret Service in this book.

Both branches' performed important and fascinating work, but the systems and protocols in this book are heavily fictionalised.

As I performed research for this book, I found myself amazed at just how much was going on in the world during 1917–1918. Not only was World War I being fought on multiple fronts, but companies were founded, new laws passed, natural disasters occurred, books were written, and so much more. Through the pages of this story, I hope to bring a little bit of everyday history to life in the lives of the characters you meet along the way.

"My grief lies within,
And these external manners of lament
Are mere shadows of the unseen grief
That swells with silence in the tortur'd soul."
—William Shakespeare, *Richard II*

CHAPTER 1

Welcome to Newhaven

12 November 1917

LIFTING A TREMBLING hand to tuck a stubborn curl of chestnut hair beneath her hat for the fourth time, Clara Dankworth consulted the pendant watch hanging from her neck.

One more hour.

Clutching the edge of her seat, she braced herself as the afternoon train swayed around a sharp corner. Wistfully, she watched the blurring English countryside rush past her window. The South Downs of East Sussex were grey and bleak for mid-November, but then again, the whole world wore a shroud of gloom in the autumn of 1917. After three years of war, there was still no hope of an end in sight. She drummed her slender fingers against the worn cover of *Great Expectations* that lay unheeded in her lap. Coming back to England after a decade's absence should have been like coming home. But there was no home to come back to. Only broken dreams, tattered hopes, and shadowed memories.

Please, Lord, let Newhaven be different.

When the train finally pulled into the Newhaven Town

station, Clara waded carefully through the brimming aisle towards the exit. After a good deal of jostling and bumping, her feet found a firm footing on the platform of the dusky station. Snapping open her umbrella and clutching her valise in her free hand, she scanned the crowd in bewilderment as khaki-clad Tommies blurred her vision in every direction. *How am I supposed to find one man in a crowd this size?*

At a touch to her elbow, Clara whirled around, and a grey-haired porter tipped his hat politely. "Your luggage is right over there, miss."

"Thank you," she returned gratefully, letting out a breath she didn't know she had been holding.

"Someone here to meet you?"

"I hope so. I'm looking for Doctor Lindsey."

The porter pointed to the back of the station platform where a tall black-haired man stood leaning against a post, earnestly scanning the crowd.

Clara smiled. "Thank you, again."

"Welcome to Newhaven, miss," the porter replied with a crinkling smile under his moustache as he touched his hat and disappeared into the throng.

A cold, drizzling rain fell as Doctor Thomas Lindsey paced the covered portion of the wooden platform at the Newhaven Town station. The click of his oxfords echoed under each long stride. He glanced at the crinkled slip of paper in his hand for what had to be the twentieth time.

New assistant arriving on the afternoon train from London. 12 November. JC.

Thomas scowled at the familiar bold scrawl and stuffed the note in his overcoat pocket. His superior had given no name or description of the assistant he was sending. *How am I supposed to recognise him?* Running his long, slender fingers through his curly, black hair in an agitated fashion, Thomas continued pacing until a distant train whistle diverted his attention.

"Finally," he muttered, stopping abruptly and straightening his necktie. "The chap will have some explaining to do."

Thomas watched every passenger exit the train, growing more impatient with each one that walked past him unrecognised. Clearly, this was a waste of time. Chilled and frustrated, he spun on his heel to leave when a musical voice stopped him from behind.

"Doctor Lindsey, I presume?"

Whirling back around, Thomas sucked in a sharp breath as he came face to face with the tall, lithe woman in possession of the voice. Narrowing his eyes, he surveyed her from hat brim to boot top.

She was neither strikingly beautiful, nor remarkably plain. Rose tinged her pale cheeks from the biting wind. By proportion, her nose and mouth were rather small, making her expressive chocolate-brown eyes appear even larger. But it was the small white scar running above her left eyebrow that snagged his curiosity. The woman held herself with an air of dignity, and from her manner, he gathered she was responsible, practical, and quick-witted. But her voice? It held an unusual accent he couldn't place—English mixed with something else.

"Who's asking?" he asked skeptically, recovering from his initial surprise.

"Clara Dankworth, your new assistant."

Thomas's jaw fell slack, and he could not have been more astonished had the train station platform suddenly swallowed him up. *What in all of England was Crouthers thinking? I asked for an assistant, not a housekeeper.* Thomas mentally shook his fist at the portly, grizzled businessman with the bushy sideburns gracing garrulous cheeks and a halo of stringy grey hair, which poorly conveyed the image of a posh London businessman.

This must be payback for last month. Thomas couldn't deny he had disobeyed orders the previous month by being overly harsh and critical of Whittier, scaring the younger MI5 agent back to the safety of the Service headquarters in London. But it was hardly fair for Crouthers to retaliate by sending a girl when he had been expecting a man. *The British need competent agents to be successful, and so far Crouthers hasn't sent me a decent one.* He grimaced in disgust and disappointment.

When Thomas brought his eyes to rest on her face again, Clara lifted her chin slightly and held his gaze with determination in an unspoken staredown.

"You don't look anything like a nurse," Thomas scoffed, finally breaking the silence with the first thing that came to mind as he studied her appearance again critically.

"Nor you like a doctor." Her tone was polite, but he saw the daring flash in her shadowed eyes.

Thomas sighed. Regardless of whether he wanted her services or not, he couldn't just leave her. "You have luggage?" he asked wearily. When she pointed to the small, well-worn travel trunk to his left, he nodded. "Wait here." Leaving her alone, he darted towards a nearby porter, engaging his services with a few brief words. "Come along. My car is this way," Thomas called to Clara, leaving the porter to manoeuvre the trunk after them.

Once the travel trunk was loaded and the porter paid, Thomas held the door of the Model T open for Clara before he slid into the driver's seat. Neither said a word the entire way to the clinic. Thomas's mind raced with questions. He glanced at the young woman beside him, but she kept her head angled to study the passing scenery out the window and didn't seem inclined to break the silence. Sighing, he drummed his fingers against the steering wheel. Perhaps it was just as well.

~

Ten minutes later found them pulling up behind the Bridge Street Clinic. Clara glanced around her while Thomas unlocked the back door of the building. A small strip of grass had managed to survive around the doorstep, which in and of itself had a lovely view of the meandering River Ouse.

She followed him into the kitchen and then through an open door leading into a narrow hallway. Motioning her through, he opened the door directly across from the kitchen, revealing a moderately sized office. Two desks stood opposite each other, and a modest fire blazed in the grate. Several bookshelves lined the room, and the doctor's certificate hanging on the wall caught Clara's eye. *University of Leeds*, it read.

Thomas shrugged out of his overcoat and hung it on the hatstand, nodding for her to do the same. After she slipped out of her coat and unpinned her hat, the doctor pointed to a chair in front of his desk. "Sit."

So much for manners. Taking the offered seat cautiously, Clara inhaled a steadying breath as Thomas sat behind his desk and leaned his elbows on the edge, propping his chin on his clasped hands. Every nerve was taut as she waited for the onslaught of questions. She knew enough about this man to expect it.

"Miss Dankworth," he started, "what is the meaning of this?"

"You need an assistant. I am a nurse. Doesn't that suffice?" she returned lightly after a pause.

"Hardly," was the dry reply. "Why did Crouthers send you?"

Clara studied the man in front of her. Intelligence gleamed in his intense sapphire eyes, a lock of his curling dark hair falling stubbornly over his forehead. His face was pale, his firmly set jaw slightly squared, and his clean-shaven cleft chin had a determined tilt. But it was his accent that stood out to her. *There's a lilt not quite common to southern England. Perhaps—*

"Well?" Thomas demanded impatiently, interrupting her thoughts.

"He thought I would be sufficient. I have my nursing certificate and am sure you will find me quite capable," she answered elusively.

He snorted. "That doesn't answer the why."

"Haven't the faintest," she said, her shoulders tightening in frustration. "Trust me, I didn't volunteer for this position."

"I need a doctor with experience," Thomas muttered to himself, leaning back in his chair. "Of all the dastardly things he could do…" As his words trailed off, he rose abruptly and strode over to the far window overlooking Bridge Street, where despite the gloomy drizzle, a fog was rolling in. "He could have warned me. What am I supposed to do with you? You certainly can't stay here."

The weight of his words and his annoyance hung heavily in the room. Clara mentally pieced together his meaning before asking slowly, "Crouthers truly didn't tell you to expect me?"

"Gracious, no," the doctor exclaimed, spinning towards her. "If he had, I'd have told him not to send you at all."

She arched an eyebrow. "Touché." So far the doctor was living up to his reputation.

Stalking back to his desk, he plopped down in his chair again. With a cock of his head, he asked bluntly, "How old are you?"

"Twenty-one," she said with slight hesitation.

"Too young," was the decided response.

Clara smirked at the insinuation but said nothing. She knew the doctor was only twenty-six. However, she wasn't about to enlighten him as to what she knew of him—not yet anyways.

He frowned at her apparent humour. "Do you find this amusing, Miss Dankworth? This is no laughing matter, I assure you."

"Indeed it is not, and I now understand why your *five* previous assistants didn't last long. Not everyone can endure such *treatment*, Doctor," she said pointedly.

He ignored her and effectively changed the conversation as he snatched up the telephone receiver. "I'll see if the Forsythes can put you up." A moment later he said, "Hello? Mrs. Forsythe? Yes, this is Doctor Lindsey. Do you have a room available for my new assistant?" He shot a glance in Clara's direction, saying wryly, "Change of plans." Once he finished the call, he hung up. "Come along." He waved at her as he strode out of the room.

She rolled her eyes but followed. Apparently he was settling her affairs without asking for her input.

In the car, Clara dared to voice a question as they bumped down the street. "Where do the Forsythes live?"

"North end of Lewes Road. It's a fifteen-minute walk to the clinic."

Silence pervaded until the automobile stopped in front of a rustic red-brick farmhouse set back from the road by a large sprawling lawn and a low, grey stone fence, neighboured by small stone chapel and cemetery. The faded emerald hills of the distant, fog-covered downs were visible in the background. Clara smiled in awe at the charming place she would call *home*.

As she slid out of the car and approached the front gate, a deep bark startled her, and a St. Bernard appeared from around the corner of the house.

"Hush, Nana," Thomas scolded as he tugged Clara's trunk from the automobile.

The dog perched on her haunches and wagged her tail with uncertainty as her melting brown orbs glanced between the man she clearly knew and the woman she did not.

Clara unlatched the front gate slowly and held out her hand to the canine, who sniffed it cautiously, then gave it an approving lick.

"Unbelievable," Thomas muttered grumpily as they walked up the path to the front door where he rapped smartly.

The door was promptly opened by a short, amply waisted, motherly woman with a round face, greying red hair, and snapping brown eyes. "Och!" she exclaimed in surprise, her thick brogue betraying her Scottish roots. Quickly recovering herself, she ushered them into a spacious hallway. "Doctor, let that trunk be. Robbie and Alistair can send it upstairs later."

Thomas set down the awkwardly small trunk and straightened. "I must be on my way," he said with a polite nod at the woman. His eyes hardened slightly as he glanced at Clara. "I expect you tomorrow morning at 7:30 sharp, Miss Dankworth."

"I'll be there, Doctor," Clara assured him, her voice firm and resolute.

He gave the women a final nod of farewell before the front door clicked shut behind him.

"Come and have some tea, dearie. It's a *dreich* day," the woman gushed, bustling Clara into the parlour.

The small room was quaint but cosy. Faded braided rugs adorned the floor, and flowered curtains graced the windows. In addition to the sofa, there were several chairs, presumably for the many boarders who resided at the homey establishment. Several bookshelves lined the papered walls, and Clara smiled at the abundance of bric-a-brac scattered throughout the room.

Taking a seat on the sofa, a warm cup of tea was thrust into her hand within moments. She inhaled the soothing smell before taking a dainty draught.

"Where be me manners?" the woman exclaimed, dropping onto the sofa beside her. "I'm Mrs. Agnes Forsythe."

After Clara introduced herself, she ventured to ask, "I presume you weren't expecting me either?"

The Scotswoman hesitated. "An assistant, aye. But not a lass."

Clara sighed, shaking her head. "I'm not sure how this mess happened."

Mrs. Forsythe patted her knee. "Dinnae fret. We're grateful for all the medical help we can get. This town is too much for one man to handle with our regular doctors off fighting and all. If you were sent here, the Good Lord had a reason for it."

"I certainly hope so." Clara smiled faintly.

"His bark is worse than his bite."

Despite the weariness coursing through her veins, Clara smiled again and sipped her tea. "I don't believe in running from a challenge."

The older woman gave her an approving smile. "I certainly got that impression. You got gumption."

Clara's heart squeezed at that smile. It reminded her of another maternal smile bestowed on her so long ago. A smile she hadn't seen in years. Whatever happened in Newhaven, she was grateful for an ally in the motherly Mrs. Forsythe.

Thomas stormed into the clinic, slamming the kitchen door on his return from dropping Clara off at the boarding house. Mrs. Forsythe appeared to approve of her; even the silly dog liked her!

A curly red head popped out of the office door as the pictures in the hallway rattled on the walls. "Everything all right, Doc?" the youth asked with concern.

Thomas pushed past him and sank into his chair behind his desk. "Hardly, Robbie. What do you want?" he snapped. Everything was spinning out of control. The last thing he wanted was to make small talk with fifteen-year-old Robbie Forsythe, who was the proverbial sunshine on an otherwise rainy day and a friend to all the world.

"Message from Kasey." Robbie held out a slip of paper. As a crooked grin replaced the doctor's scowl, the young man perched on the edge of the empty desk, adding, "Good news?"

Thomas glanced at him and noticed the light dancing in the kind green eyes. "Yes. No reply."

Robbie nodded and studied the room curiously. "Where's the new assistant? I thought he was supposed to be here by now."

"*She* is."

Robbie blinked rapidly. "She?"

"Yes, she. You'll meet her at home. Your mother seems to like her, as does your dog." *Can't see why.* Thomas rummaged through the scattered paper on his desk. This mess with Clara had ruined his afternoon, and he still had work to do.

Robbie didn't take the hint. "You don't like her?"

Thomas paused at this question. He had seen nothing to dislike about Miss Clara Dankworth. She was polite and ladylike in every respect, with a flash of spirit—he could appreciate that. She just wasn't what he had sent for, and she unnerved him with her inquisitive eyes, uncanny intuition, and evident intelligence. "I didn't say that exactly," he clarified after several moments. "I just didn't send for a woman."

Robbie chuckled and flashed him a dimpled grin. "Count your blessings, not your problems, Doc."

Thomas scowled at the lanky youth, and Robbie chuckled again.

"Wait," Thomas called as his visitor moved to leave. Hurriedly opening his desk drawer for some stationery, he scribbled out a note.

Assistant arrived today. Why in all of England did you send her? Requesting replacement immediately. TL.

He tucked the paper in an envelope and handed it to Robbie. "For Crouthers in London."

Robbie hesitated before taking the note. "Are you sure you want to do this? He could have you fired—"

"If he wanted to fire me, he would have done it by now. We both know he cannot afford to lose me." *In more ways than one.*

"Just be careful, Doc," Robbie cautioned before disappearing into the hall.

Thomas leaned back in his chair, staring into the coal grate. His mind wandered back to his newly arrived assistant, and he reviewed the extent of their interaction. From the evident shadows in her eyes, he knew she had secrets lurking in her past... but then again, so did he.

Clara slowly circled the small bedroom she was to call her own. A cheery quilt of soft florals graced the brass-framed bed, contrasting prettily with the lightly patterned wallpaper. A bureau occupied one corner, and a small writing desk stood at the north window, overlooking the back lawn, the sprawling downs, and the next-door cemetery.

"Will it suit you?" Mrs. Forsythe asked from the doorway.

Clara smiled at her new landlady. "Very much so, thank you."

"I'll let you get settled in and cleaned up. Dinner's at six." With that cheery word, the door closed, and Clara found herself alone in her new room, in her new home, in a new town.

All alone.

Swallowing the lump in her throat and blinking back tears, she started unpacking her trunk. The image of another bustling harbour town thousands of miles away came to mind. Its lapping white-capped azure waves, salty sea breeze, and lighthouses standing sentry were vividly painted in her memory.

Clara shook her head. That life was long gone. Newhaven was home now.

Hopefully, it would last this time.

Dinner at the boarding house turned out to be a lively affair. The dining room was a large and cheery apartment with a long table. Mrs. Forsythe introduced Clara when she came in, and the young woman found herself subjected to half-a-dozen pleasant well wishes and curious inquiries. Overwhelmed by the hearty welcome, she answered with what she hoped were polite, intelligent replies and was quickly seated between a flaxen-haired young woman about her own age, who wore a gold wedding ring, and a curly, redheaded lad.

The young woman smiled brightly and whispered, "I'm so glad you've come. I'm Elizabeth Tilney, and that's Robbie Forsythe on your right."

Clara bequeathed a smile to them both before hungrily starting on the Scottish stew and biscuits before her. She said little during the meal but took the opportunity to study her companions, all the while picking up information from the conversations.

Alistair Forsythe ran the local grocery and welcomed Clara as warmly as his wife had done. Robbie, the youngest of the

Forsythes' five children, was the only one left at home. Elizabeth Tilney worked as a schoolteacher in the mornings and helped Mrs. Forsythe in the afternoons at the boarding house, along with volunteering at a local society supporting the war effort by wrapping bandages and knitting sweaters and socks. There were currently three other boarders staying with the Forsythes—a travelling mechanic and a barrister. The third, a telephone operator, wasn't present, as she was working the late shift at the telephone office.

After dinner, Elizabeth disappeared into the kitchen with Mrs. Forsythe, and Clara hesitated over following them.

"Need something, Miss Clara?" Robbie's voice beside her asked.

Clara glanced up into the grinning, freckled face of the tall, lanky young man. Curiously, he had no hint of a Scottish accent, quite unlike his parents. "I should like to help with the dishes. Would your mother take offence to that?"

Robbie beamed approvingly at her. "Not at all. She doesn't expect boarders to help, but help is never refused if genuinely offered. Go ahead."

Clara nodded her thanks and hurried into the kitchen, where she soon found an apron enveloped around her waist and her hands immersed in soapsuds while surrounded by the cheery chatter of Mrs. Forsythe and Elizabeth.

When the last of the dishes were washed, Mrs. Forsythe tugged the tea towel from Elizabeth's hand. "Lizzie, why don't you take Miss Dankworth to the parlour for a chat. I can finish up here now."

Clara smiled as she hung up the apron. "Please, call me Clara."

Mrs. Forsythe returned the smile and gave them both a gentle shove towards the door.

"What brings you to Newhaven?" Elizabeth asked curiously as they took a seat on the parlour sofa on the opposite end of the room from where Mr. Forsythe sat lodged in the throes of his newspaper.

When Clara explained her role as Thomas's assistant, Elizabeth's jaw dropped in an unladylike fashion, and she spluttered in astonishment.

Clara bit back a laugh. Clearly her job would astound most of the town's population. "How long have you lived in Newhaven, Mrs. Tilney?"

"Oh, call me Elizabeth. If we're going to be living under the same roof, we can dispense with the formalities. I've been here since the winter of '15." Her voice fell as she added, "My husband Aaron is a soldier in France, and the Forsythes are old friends of his."

Clara sobered at the all-too-common story. It seemed everyone had given up someone to the war effort. "You must miss him very much."

"I do, but there's plenty of work to do in the meantime. You know what the government says, 'Business as usual.'" Pasting on a brave face, Elizabeth launched into an animated explanation of her work as a schoolteacher and the many problems the school faced. Shortly after Newhaven's location had been declared a tactical advantage and issued as a military town, the Boys' School building had been converted into a military hospital for soldiers, leaving the boys to share the Girls' School for half-day double sessions.

Robbie's curly head popped in just then. "Am I interrupting, Miss Lizzie?"

"Of course not. Come in," Elizabeth invited.

The lad sauntered in, plopped into an easy chair across from Clara, and cocked his head to study her.

She grinned dubiously. "Do I pass muster for being the doctor's new assistant?"

He laughed heartily. "I think you're swell, and so does Nana. It's the doc who's not convinced."

"That man couldn't tell an angel from the Devil," Elizabeth muttered.

Clara raised an eyebrow at the comment, but the young woman didn't offer an explanation.

"He won't hurt you, Miss Clara," Robbie assured her. "He just... takes some getting used to, is all."

"Well, I intend to undertake the challenge."

"He certainly is that," Elizabeth added with a scoff.

Clara opened her mouth to inquire about the woman's meaning, but Robbie quickly cut her off by asking, "Where are you from?"

"All over really. I've travelled quite a bit." It was going to be hard to keep her tattered history straight in a small town, but in no case was she about to lie.

"Do you play piano, by any chance?" Elizabeth pressed hopefully, gesturing to the brown upright instrument on the other end of the room.

"I do."

"Will you play something for us?" Robbie begged, his green eyes shining.

Clara rose and moved to sit at the piano, reverently touching the aged keys. "Any favourites?" she asked, looking between the two smiling faces gathered around her.

"'Danny Boy,'" came from Robbie.

Three voices—Clara's soprano, Elizabeth's alto, and Robbie's tenor—joined the sweet Londonderry air that wafted through the parlour and into every corner of the cosy farmhouse. Mrs. Forsythe tiptoed in from the kitchen; the barrister and the mechanic came down the stairs; and Mr. Forsythe emerged from behind his paper. When the last strain of the Irish melody died away after the last line, hearty applause broke out.

"Beautiful," Mrs. Forsythe crooned as she wiped her eyes on the edge of her apron.

"Play us another," the travelling mechanic pleaded. His care-worn face lined with an expression of hope. Something all too rare those days.

Pivoting back to the piano, Clara played a steady stream of tunes from "Keep the Home Fires Burning" to "Loch Lomond." Everyone sat in rapt attention, sang heartily, or clapped in wild delight. When the clock struck nine, the group reluctantly broke up for the night.

As Clara brushed her hair before bed, she stared out the north window. Her thoughts centred on the little singing group. In the middle of a world at war, that homely parlour in a simple farmhouse on the coast of East Sussex had become a beacon of hope for them all.

CHAPTER 2

First Days

13 November

THE NEXT MORNING, as Thomas sat at his desk perusing the appointment book, the sharp ring of the doorbell shattered the silence. Sighing, he rose and, passing through the hall and the waiting room, opened the front door on Clara's polite smile. He tugged his pocket watch from his vest. Right on time.

"Good morning," she said, stepping into the waiting room. "What order of business first?"

Frustration rolled through him at the mention of *business*, and the strong urge for a cup of tea overwhelmed him. "The kitchen," he said bluntly, closing the door harder than necessary. In the kitchen, he poured two cups of the brew and handed one to her. "Let me show you around."

The office was directly across the hall with two examination rooms to the left. The space next to the kitchen was a supply room, and on the other side of the supply room was a small sitting room. The final doorway at the end of the hall revealed a staircase.

"There's two rooms upstairs. Mine and a spare. The spare is at your disposal when I'm out of town, and you are on call,"

Thomas explained. *Not that you'll be needing it once your replacement is sent.*

Clara merely nodded.

In the office, Thomas sat down at his desk and pointed to the second one across the room. "You may use that. There's writing material in the drawer. I have medical shipments arriving consistently, so I will leave the inventory and unpacking to your charge. While I'm out on house calls, you can take patient calls." He gestured to the telephone near his elbow before picking up the black notebook lying on the desk. "This is the appointment book. Make sure to mark appointments down immediately upon booking so we don't incur schedule problems. I expect to be handed a list of house call patients every morning. Also, I am managing Dr. Peterson's practice, so be sure you ask if they are his patient and make a note of it."

Clara nodded and moved towards her desk, trailing her fingers along the edge. "I am familiar with the nuances of locum protocol. I've worked with a locum doctor before."

"Very good. Doctor Peterson had a colleague, a Doctor Wilson, who perished overseas, and I bought his share of the practice. I presume you signed the necessary paperwork agreeing to the locum practice terms?" When she nodded, he continued. "Well then. The pay is nothing spectacular, but you'll receive your share at the beginning of every month." He glanced at her. "Payment for your... other services comes from London, and it's usually late." He steepled his fingers and pressed them to his lips before adding slowly, "I am willing to advance you a sum should the need ever arise." *Why in all England did I just offer that?*

Her cheeks tinged pink, but she said nothing as she gave another quick nod.

"Any other questions?"

"The nearest hospital is...?"

"Lewes. Twenty minutes north of here by car. Anything else? No? Then I leave you to handle what you can as long as you keep accurate records for anyone you treat." He cocked his head thoughtfully. "I neglected to ask yesterday, but how much experience *do* you have, Miss Dankworth?"

"I worked under a doctor for four years before attending nursing school. I have been a nurse for three years and am trained in anesthesia." Her voice swelled with a hint of pride.

He leaned back in his chair. He hated to admit it, but he was impressed. Anesthesia was usually only taught in medical school and rarely to nurses. For her to have the training meant she was either incredibly apt or had powerful connections... or both. "Very well," he said, rising from his seat. "I have my rounds to start. You can begin with organising the inventory in the supply room, as there's a shipment coming later this week. I'll be back by noon. Check the appointment book if you need to reach me in an emergency." With that, he caught up his black bag and stalked out of the office. Halfway through the kitchen, he halted and trudged back to the office. There was still one detail he hadn't covered. "Use the bicycle in the waiting room closet should you need it. I generally use the car for my rounds."

Finally alone, Clara heaved a sigh of relief and exhaustion. It was only eight o'clock in the morning, but that whirlwind of a Doctor Lindsey was enough to sap the energy out of anyone's aspirations. She stifled a groan as she trudged down the hall to the supply room to follow his "instructions." She scoffed silently. *More like orders.*

Opening the supply room door revealed the true state of Thomas's organisation system. The system, if it could even be called that, must be entirely his own. How the man managed to find anything in this mess was beyond her comprehension. She shook her head with a chuckle as she started rearranging the shelves of medications and bandages. *Since when do iodine and activated charcoal belong together?*

Humming softly to herself as she swept the floor, she caught the sound of the telephone ringing in the office. Hurrying down the hall, she snatched up the receiver and in her neat penmanship scheduled Harold Jones in an appointment slot for the next day. Smiling to herself, she felt a tinge of pleasure. Perhaps working for Thomas Lindsey might not be quite so bad as she expected. Then she sighed. Who was she fooling? He didn't want her here and would use any excuse to get rid of her. She would have to prove herself to him, and that looked to be no easy task.

That night, Thomas drove his Model T down Brighton Road, heading west of town towards the large estate of Colonel Arthur Jennings. Clara's first day had gone better than he had expected. The nurse was highly proficient in her work, and several patients had already praised her to him. In a town as small as Newhaven, there was no way to conceal the rapidly spreading news of her arrival. The whole town would know by morning if they didn't already.

He veered into a poplar-lined driveway and parked in front of the shadowy mansion. After storming past Kerridge, the Jenningses' elderly butler, Thomas stomped up the stairs and barged into the colonel's office without so much as a knock.

Colonel Jennings was a handsome man in his fifties with long salt-and-pepper hair curling just above his collar, sage green eyes that missed nothing, and a tall, strapping figure. He was a retired solicitor with army experience, who had changed his occupation to something more restful. Heading one of the branches of foreign intelligence in the War Office wouldn't have been Thomas's first choice of a more restful occupation, but the colonel's experience helped him excel at his work. Justice and common sense coursed through the colonel's veins, making Thomas prefer the man to Crouthers.

"I wondered when you would turn up," Jennings said amusedly from his easy chair across the room. "Tea?"

"What in all of England am I supposed to do?" Thomas complained, utterly ignoring the colonel's nicety. This wasn't a problem tea could fix. "Crouthers had the audacity to send her without the courtesy of even telling me."

"He can do as he sees fit; you know that."

"But we both know he was wrong. Surely you can't approve."

"Whether I approve or not matters very little. Besides, I haven't even met the woman. I can't form an opinion on her without doing so. Remember, Lindsey, I'm not in charge of your division."

"You aren't helping," Thomas snapped as he paced the room. Since the colonel worked for the Secret Service, not MI5, he didn't report to Crouthers, but Jennings had been working in Newhaven on his own mission. "We both know Crouthers sends me his most irritating agents for the sheer pleasure of annoying me."

"Maybe if you didn't cross him so much, you wouldn't be in this predicament... again."

"It's not my fault Whittier left!" Thomas was nearly shouting as he paused in his ceaseless circuit around the rug.

Instead of looking offended, Jennings gave the younger man a pointed stare. "The man preferred the risk of war compared to working with you."

Thomas bristled in frustration at the insinuation. But he knew from personal experience that arguing with the colonel was never productive, especially considering the man's background in law.

"Since you insist on running off your assistants—"

"If you must know," Thomas cut in, "half of them *chose* to leave England to risk their necks in the war, and the other half... requested a transfer of their own accord." He paused to take a breath. New agents brought risks. *Like what happened in...* He shook his head to shove away the unfinished thought, muttering, "I don't want her here."

A hint of a smile tugged at Jennings's mouth. "I do believe

you have finally met your match," he said with amusement, at which Thomas scowled vehemently.

~

14 November

Two days had passed since his new nurse's arrival in Newhaven, and Thomas hadn't yet heard from Crouthers. A few hours before closing time, Thomas asked Clara to stay on call while he had a meeting. He didn't feel the need to disclose *where* that meeting was.

He quickly boarded the afternoon train headed for London, intending to get to the bottom of the infuriating business mix-up. The three-hour trip sped by, and he soon found himself on the Victoria Station platform in the gathering dusk. Tipping his fedora to two ladies who passed him, he strode a few blocks northwest into Belgravia. Though primarily a posh residential district of Central London, there were a few streets lined with small shops.

Yanking open the door of a well-to-do bookstore, which doubled as a cover location for Crouthers's branch of the MI5 office, Thomas entered and found Walter Reed, Crouthers's secretary, at the front desk. Approaching the young man, he plopped his hat down on the counter.

Walter's sandy head snapped up and his hazel eyes darted a glance over his shoulder at the door leading into the back room. "We are about to close, sir."

After casually ensuring the shop was otherwise empty of customers, Thomas said quietly, "I need to see him immediately."

Walter nervously bit his lip. "I think he's been expecting you."

Thomas gave the secretary a nod and disappeared into the back. Weaving his way between crates and boxes, he ascended the stairs and knocked on the office door.

"Come in," growled a muffled voice from inside.

The door swung open upon a large, spacious office filled with shelves lined with books and files. Thick drapes covered the windows, and harsh gas lighting illuminated the room. Plush carpet cushioned his feet, and the air was filled with the scent of stale cigar smoke and a blueish haze.

"Ah, Lindsey, what a pleasant surprise," Crouthers purred from behind his fortress of a mahogany desk.

Pleasant indeed, Thomas scoffed inwardly. He surveyed the man—short and portly with a greying fringe around his ears and that knowing smile. "Sir," he ground out.

Crouthers motioned to a chair in front of his desk. "Sit."

Sitting, Thomas folded his hands, and taking a deep breath, he kept his voice steady. "I would like a replacement for my assistant."

"I sent you one."

"She won't suit."

"She'll have to. She is all that is available."

"For how long?"

"Until I decide to move her." A hard gleam entered Crouthers's dark eyes, reflecting in the faint lighting.

Thomas refused to be intimidated. "She's a hazard to the work."

"She's the best nurse in Sussex and a vital asset to the work in Newhaven. Your job is to collect the necessary information to implicate that German sympathiser, Edward Price. It's taken you long enough."

"I know how to do my job, but, sir—"

"Not another word, Lindsey," Crouthers growled. "Or I will have you removed for breach of orders. Don't think I haven't noticed your defiance." He jabbed a finger at Thomas accusingly. "You have given me plenty of opportunities to discharge you already."

Thomas swallowed back an angry retort that threatened to

escape, barely containing his inwardly raging persona. "We both know you can't get along without me." He was considered one of MI5's top agents, and they both knew it. He wet his lips, adding, "Besides, a few well-placed pieces of information about how you bribed your way into this office would do nicely."

Crouthers's face mottled purple. "You're bluffing," he spat.

Thomas smirked and pretended to study his fingernails. He was back in control now. "Do you really want to take the risk of finding out?"

As always, the words worked like a charm. "You dare threaten me?!" Crouthers hissed before falling into seething silence.

Thomas leaned back in his chair smugly. He had employed this tactic before, and it was no idle threat. He had the proof, and it provided him the necessary leverage to manage his overbearing superior. Looked like he would be getting a new assistant after all.

"I will ruin you one day, Lindsey; I swear." Crouthers's voice was cool and calculated. "Don't forget what I know about you. Clara Dankworth will stay."

Thomas's chair scraped against the carpet as he bolted up. "If something goes wrong in Newhaven because of her, just like it did with Sumpter in Folkestone, don't blame me. I won't be your scapegoat again. I have had enough of amateurs."

"Why, you impertinent—"

The rest of Crouthers's exclamation was cut off as Thomas slammed the door behind him with gusto. Hurrying down the stairs, he marched past Walter, who threw him a sympathetic grimace, and stormed out into the grey November shroud of fog that had fallen over Belgravia's streets.

The ride back to Newhaven dragged out, and in silent fury, Thomas rehearsed his conversation with Crouthers. If his boss thought he would sit by and let this inferior new agent from who knows where take over the Newhaven ring, Crouthers could think again. He shuddered as his thoughts drifted back to Folkestone. On an earlier mission, Sumpter, a new agent, had blown their cover, and a fellow colleague of Thomas's had paid the price with his life. He wouldn't let that happen again. Thomas scowled as he remembered Crouthers had called Clara an "asset." If he was required to work with her, he needed more information about her, and there was only one man for that job.

CHAPTER 3

Enlisting the Ferret

15 November

IN THE FAINT light of a misty dawn the next morning, Thomas drove a mile out of town to the Forsythes' house. A solitary lark sang overhead as a cool south wind blew off the English Channel, and Thomas shivered despite the warmth of his coat. At least it wasn't raining—yet. He parked near the front gate and marched up the path towards the brick farmhouse.

Mr. Forsythe answered Thomas's firm knock. "Morning, Doc." The burly man's green eyes crinkled in friendly welcome, much like his son's.

"Forsythe. I'm looking for Robbie."

"He's in the barn."

Thomas nodded his thanks and strode around the corner of the house to the barn in the back. He halted at the door when he heard voices.

"You do my chores better than I do, Miss Clara." Robbie's voice morphed into laughter, and Clara joined him with Nana's *woof* punctuating the concerto of merriment. "Susan taught me how to milk a cow," Robbie added quietly.

Thomas knew Susan Forsythe was a Red Cross nurse in

France and had been since the beginning of the war. She and Robbie were especially close, and her leaving had devastated the lad. Refusing to waste another minute eavesdropping, Thomas pushed into the barn. "Robbie?"

"Back here, Doc."

Thomas found them in the last stall where Robbie leaned against the stall door, patting Nana's head and watching Clara milk Bossy with expert fingers.

Clara spared him a quick glance but continued her work.

Robbie flashed him a grin. "What do you need?"

"A private word."

"Go on, I'll finish up," Clara said.

"Thanks, Miss Clara. Come on, Doc." He whistled for Nana, and the dog trotted obediently after her master. Outside, Robbie waited expectantly as Thomas tugged an envelope out of his pocket.

"For Richard. I'm sure you know how to contact him."

"Right-o." Robbie pocketed the letter and scampered away with his dog on his heels. "No, Nana, stay." He bent down and whispered something to the canine, who plopped down and sighed.

Thomas shook his head. That dog had more personality than some people he knew.

Clara pushed open the barn door as Robbie disappeared around the corner of the house. "Something wrong, Doctor?" she asked, setting down her milk pail and studying him intently. Her chestnut tresses were plaited and wrapped around her head like a coronet—she looked like a regular milkmaid.

Thomas fought the urge to squirm under her inquisitive gaze. "Just fine," he muttered.

Picking up her pail, she started back towards the house. "I'll be along shortly," she called over her shoulder. "Come along, Nana."

Thomas watched her walk away with Nana trotting beside her, then shook his head incredulously before turning on his heel to leave. Somehow his nurse was also a British spy and resident milkmaid—what a morning.

At the unwelcome click of heels Thomas knew only too well, he snapped the newspaper open in front of his face, creating a barrier between him and the door. Maybe she would go away... maybe...

He heard the office door squeak open and a bright voice call, "Thomas?"

No such luck. He bit back a groan but didn't lower the paper. "What do you want?"

The top half of the periodical suddenly folded backwards, revealing a blonde woman. He grimaced as she leaned across his desk towards him. Where was Clara anyway? Surely she should have been here by now. Then he could have avoided this ambush. The woman couldn't take a hint. He snatched the paper away from her. "Spit it out, Mitchell. I don't have time for this."

"Thomas, don't be so hasty," the silken voice pleaded. "Dinner tonight?"

He growled in response. Any attempt at words would have been a disaster. Patience wasn't exactly his strong suit, and whatever miniscule amount he possessed had dissipated the minute she walked through the door.

A discreet clearing of the throat diverted his attention to the doorway as Clara slipped into the room. "Ah, Miss Dankworth, you're here," Thomas stated the obvious, jumping up in relief. "I am sure you two know each other."

A pout sprouted on the blonde's dainty rosebud mouth. "We've met."

Clara smiled politely. "Nice to see you again, Lena."

Lena Mitchell was the telephone operator staying at the boarding house. The young woman was close to Thomas's age, aloof, with icy blue eyes, prominent cheekbones, and a flawless complexion.

"If you'll excuse us, Miss Mitchell, we have a very busy morning," Thomas said with feigned politeness.

Lena sniffed, and her heels clicked as she vanished down the hall. Thomas sighed in relief as the front door slammed shut behind her.

"You don't like her, I take it. It's not like we are all that busy," Clara stated with a pointed look.

Thomas only shrugged and added to himself, *She's not the only one.*

Later that evening, the comfortable fire in the grate burned low as Thomas pored over the day's records. His hand curled comfortably around his cup of hot tea, and he let its warmth seep through his chilled frame as the clock struck eleven. His pen scrawled methodically across the page when a knock sounded on the kitchen door across the hall.

The door opened on a tall figure in a black reefer coat and fedora.

"Glad you came, Richard," Thomas said, ushering the man inside.

The men shook hands before the stranger removed his hat, revealing a crop of brown hair. "Anything for an old friend."

"We can talk in the office." He handed Richard a cup of tea, and Richard helped himself to the sugar bowl.

The two men retreated to Thomas's office, where Richard tossed his coat over the back of a chair and loosened his necktie before taking a seat. Thomas sat down across from him at his desk.

"What's going on for you to call me all the way from Nottingham?" Richard asked good-naturedly before taking a swig of his tea.

"I never know where you are," Thomas challenged with an amused look. "I'm surprised you came this fast."

"Trick of the trade." Richard shrugged with a smile. "Now to business."

"I need you to look into an agent," Thomas said with what he hoped was only casual interest.

Richard knew him too well to be fooled. "Who this time and why?"

Thomas cringed. He hated that Richard could read him like that, but what did he expect when they had been friends for nearly fifteen years? "My new assistant."

"I heard about that. Who did Crouthers send this time? Williams? Finley?"

"Clara Dankworth."

Richard choked on his mouthful of tea. "A woman? He must be desperate."

"No more desperate than I am to get rid of her," Thomas snarled.

Richard set his cup down on the desk. "What do you want to know?"

"Anything you can find on her. She's as tight lipped as they come."

"Can you give me anything to go on?" Richard asked, pulling a small pencil and pad of paper from the breast pocket of his suit jacket.

Thomas let out a puff of air thoughtfully. "She's twenty-one years old. Been a nurse for three years. Doesn't sound fully British. Robbie said she didn't answer where she was from, just that she's travelled around a lot. Oh, and she has stellar cow-milking abilities."

Richard rolled his eyes and chuckled at Thomas's sarcasm.

"And Crouthers refused to have her removed," Thomas added with a frown.

"You asked?"

"I wrote a note and went to London. Crouthers said she's an asset. If I *must* work with her, I don't want any surprises."

Richard nodded and drained his cup. "Did you see where her nursing certificate was from?"

"The Nightingale Training School for Nurses in London, but

I wouldn't place much stock in that." Thomas thought of his own certificate on the wall. Though it listed a medical school in Leeds as his alma mater, the real certificate hidden upstairs told quite a different story of a school in the heart of London. All part of an agent's life. Nothing was ever what it seemed. He drew out his wallet but frowned when Richard held up his hand.

"No charge. I'll call in a favour sometime, then we'll be even." Richard tucked his notes away before rising and heading for the door.

"Richard."

The man turned at his name.

"Completely confidential."

"For you, always, my friend," and with that Richard slipped out into the hall.

A moment later Thomas heard the kitchen door click, and he knew his visitor was gone.

CHAPTER 4

Sunday Revelations

18 November

RARE WINTER SUNSHINE PEEKED through Clara's bedroom window on Sunday morning. Groaning, she rolled over, pulling the pillow over her head. She had been out on a call with Thomas till late last night—or was it earlier this morning? It couldn't possibly be time to get up yet. A tap came at the door a few minutes later.

"Are you coming with us to church this morning, dearie?" Mrs. Forsythe's muffled voice asked through the door.

Clara paused before answering. Thomas had mentioned something about his only attending services once a month, so the other three Sundays were hers to do with as she pleased. Today was one of those days, and it was her first Sunday in Newhaven. She lifted the pillow off her head and forced her protesting limbs to climb out of bed as she called out an affirmative to her landlady.

Half an hour later, she met Robbie coming out of his room across the hall, looking quite a different sight from his usual rough and tumble self. His cowlick and curls had been tamed, and he wore a white collared shirt and brown suit jacket. Clara stifled a grin and greeted him warmly before they headed downstairs to the dining room. Helping herself to a bowl of porridge, she thumbed through the pages of the latest paper, dripping with news of France's newly elected prime minister, Georges Clemenceau.

The Forsythes attended the red-brick Newhaven Baptist Church in the centre of town. Sliding into the pew between Elizabeth and Robbie, Clara stole a glance around curiously. Everyone she had met was friendly and highly intrigued by her status as Thomas's assistant.

Robbie nudged her with his elbow. "Things getting better with the doc?" he whispered.

"Hardly," she whispered dryly. It had been six days, but Thomas was as frosty as ever.

"Just give him a chance."

He's had more than a few chances already.

Elizabeth shushed him from Clara's left, and Robbie flashed an apologetic grin as the offertory music started. "Sorry, Miss Lizzie."

Clara listened intently to every word of the pastor's sermon. The Psalm 23 text was familiar but comforting, especially in times like these. As the congregation bowed their heads in prayer at the end, she added her own silent petition.

Lord, I'm frustrated and just want to go home. Give me the strength to see this mission through to the end. Shine Your light in this darkness.

Her head snapped up as Elizabeth's elbow dug into her ribs. The last hymn had already begun. Hastily, she took the offered half of Robbie's hymnbook as she felt her face redden.

After the service, Clara left with Elizabeth, leaving Mr. and Mrs. Forsythe chatting with another couple and Robbie laughing with a lad near his own age. She had heard Robbie mention his name. *Sam, wasn't it?*

"What happened back there?" Elizabeth asked as they walked arm in arm up Church Street.

Clara stifled a yawn and inwardly groaned, wanting nothing more than a nap. "I was praying myself and didn't hear the amen."

Elizabeth chuckled and chattered amiably as the two ambled quickly up the street. The sun had ducked behind grey clouds high overhead, and the threat of rain loomed as a possibility. As they rounded a corner, Elizabeth bumped into a tall man in a navy overcoat. "I'm sorry, sir, I..." she stammered before her eyes narrowed. "Oh, it's you."

Thomas bowed stiffly. "Mrs. Tilney."

"Doctor Lindsey," Elizabeth returned coolly and tugged Clara's elbow as she marched down the street away from him.

"Are you hurt?" Clara asked.

"No."

"Then whatever is the matter?"

"It's that... that... infuriating man," Elizabeth sputtered, her cheeks stained red with indignation.

Clara extracted herself from her friend's grasp and paused. "I don't understand. What did he do?"

Elizabeth sighed, and her rigid posture softened as her shoulders drooped. "He is the best of friends with my brother Richard and sister Maranda, but he and I never got along. Tempers flew and... well, we both said things we shouldn't have. After all these years, I never imagined we would be living in the same town."

"Can't you just make up?"

"He hasn't asked my pardon."

"Have you asked his?"

"Not till he asks first."

Neither woman said a word for the remainder of the walk. Upon their return to the boarding house, Elizabeth started up the stairs to her room.

"Lizzie," Clara said softly.

Elizabeth stopped but didn't turn to meet her friend's gaze.

"Just remember that sometimes in life it's more important to be happy than it is to be right."

The flaxen head nodded before fleeing up the stairs.

Willing her own tired feet up the well-worn wooden staircase, Clara opened her bedroom door and collapsed onto the bed in an unceremonious heap. She thought of her own tense relationship with Thomas Lindsey. He was a hard man to understand. Maybe she should take some of her own advice.

Later in the afternoon, the sky cleared, enticing Clara out of her room for a stroll down to the Newhaven Promenade. Muted winter sunshine sparkled on the azure water of the English Channel, and a gentle breeze teased the hair curling around her temples. Running her hand along the cold metal railing, she inhaled the salty air. To her left, the distant white chalk cliffs of Seaford Head gleamed in the light. To her right, at the end of the long breakwater stood a lighthouse, standing sentry against the lingering shadows and threatening darkness. She shuddered to remember how many ships had met their end crossing the Channel as her gaze wandered towards the barely visible distant shores of France. German U-boats patrolled beneath the waters. No captain was ever guaranteed that his next voyage across the Channel wouldn't be his last.

Uneven footsteps behind her signalled she had company, and a friendly voice with an Irish lilt interrupted her thoughts. "Afternoon to you, missy. You must be the good doctor's new assistant."

Clara smiled up at the white-haired and bearded old man beside her. "Clara Dankworth. How did you know, sir?"

The old man chuckled amusedly. "You've caused quite the stir in these parts," he said, a smile crinkling the edges of his twinkling blue eyes. "I'm Captain Kasey Grahame; pleased to meet you at last."

Clara shook the strong, calloused hand he offered to her. She recognised the name from a whispered conversation she had with Robbie. The Irish-American sea captain chartered supply ships across the Channel with the help of his grand-nephew Kavan.

"Beautiful, isn't it?" Kasey asked, motioning to the water before them.

"Almost enough to make me forget all about this war."

They chatted for several minutes about the war, their jobs, and several other mundane subjects. All the while, the frothy waves of the Channel lapped against the base of the promenade's retaining walls below them. Above, the distant drone of patrol aeroplanes hummed on their lookout for German submarines in the Channel. Once, Newhaven had been a sleepy town, but after the military had seized its harbour due to its proximity to France, the small town had two fears—a direct German attack and espionage.

At last, Kasey sighed. "I must be off now, but I saw you out here and wanted to offer my greetings. Don't stay out too late. My leg tells me there's a storm brewing, despite all this sunshiny weather," and he patted his left leg in emphasis.

Clara smiled and assured him she would be on her way to the evening service shortly. Kasey tipped his hat to her and started back towards town. As she watched him leave, she cocked her head curiously at the subtle limp in his gait on the left side and wondered what injury had caused the lasting effect.

After the church service that evening, Pastor Henderson stopped Clara at the door. "I had a favour to ask you," the elderly man rasped.

"Of course."

"Forsythe told me of your musical finesse. Would you be willing to play at our soldier canteens sometime? They're small affairs. Just a little taste of home for the soldiers who pass through here on their way to Seaford and Folkestone, you know."

"I would be delighted, Pastor."

He wrung her hand gratefully. "God bless you."

～

Several hours later, Thomas waited in the shadows of the Newhaven Harbour. The day's sunshine had melted into a foggy night, and the threat of rain whispered in the air. A tall, grizzled man with a slight limp approached him, calmly smoking his pipe.

Slipping from the shadows, Thomas extended his hand to Kasey. "That will kill you, you know."

The old man shook the offered hand. "Can't teach an old dog new tricks, lad. Let me be, and I'll take my chances."

Thomas rolled his eyes. "Any news?"

"Nothing yet. I'll be sailing again tomorrow. Have anything for me to take over?" In addition to chartering ships, Kasey smuggled information the Secret Service and MI5 required from the Continent. One would hardly expect the weather-beaten old gentleman to be a first-rate contrabandist.

Thomas shook his head. "Not till I hear from 045. Thanks, Kasey," and he turned to leave.

"I met that girl of yours," Kasey said in low tones.

Thomas's eyebrows flew up in alarm as he whirled to face the captain. "My girl? Is that the talk around town? She's not mine."

Kasey chuckled, and Thomas growled. The old sea captain had more than his fair share of romantic notions.

"She's a nice thing, lad; don't run her off like the others."

Thomas noted the gleam of mischief in the sea captain's eyes and grimaced. "Take your oar out, old man; you're meddling."

"The liberty of old age," Kasey countered as his face bloomed into a full-blown grin.

Rolling his eyes, Thomas shook his head.

Kasey chuckled again and shook hands with the doctor before strolling towards the inner harbour where his flat was.

Thomas stared after him. Clara Dankworth—the nurse, his assistant—was now *his* girl? What *was* this town coming to? Balling his fists, he marched back to Bridge Street, insulted at the very notion. Maybe sleep would help him forget the appalling gossip he knew was even now being whispered about behind closed doors and friendly faces.

CHAPTER 5

The Piper Comes to Town

19 November

KASEY'S PREDICTION of a storm proved true as Monday morning arrived, and Clara trudged towards the post office, huddling under her umbrella and dodging mud puddles that threatened to spoil her skirt. In her free hand, she clutched the letters Mrs. Forsythe had asked her to post. Running a gloved finger over the postmark, she sighed. They were destined for the Western Front. The Forsythes had given two sons and two daughters to the war effort. Every day they thanked God their children were still alive. But for how long would that last?

After leaving the precious missives in the hands of the young postmistress, Clara wove her way through the wet streets. She arrived at the clinic several minutes later and hurriedly set the kettle on to boil. Thankfully, the overnight storm had eased into a misting drizzle, leaving her only moderately damp from her walk. Stomping footsteps overhead startled her, and she hurried out into the hallway.

"Are you well, Doctor?" she called from the foot of the stairs. She heard a door click open.

"Fine. I'll be down presently," Thomas called before the door clicked shut again.

Fifteen minutes later, he clomped into the kitchen and accepted the cup of tea Clara handed him. Dark circles rimmed his eyes, and his black curls were tousled. From the looks of him, she doubted he had slept at all last night.

"You're early," he said as he dropped into a chair at the table.

"I went to the post office first."

"We don't send messages through the post!" he cried, starting up in alarm and upsetting his tea.

She rolled her eyes. "They were Mrs. Forsythe's letters. I'm not so daft as that," she retorted as she mopped up the mess.

Thomas sank back into the chair and rubbed his forehead. "My apologies."

"Crouthers said you would inform me about the situation we're dealing with here. I have been in town nearly a week now and should like to know what's going on." She shot him a pointed look. "And as we don't send messages through the post, I should like to be informed as to the location of the drop box, assuming there is one." Sarcasm laced her tone, and she crossed her arms expectantly.

Thomas stalled, taking a long swig of tea. "In time. Medical business first," and he jumped up, disappearing down the hall.

The front door slammed minutes later, and Clara knew he was gone. She sighed heavily. While she loved her job as a nurse, she had been sent to Newhaven for another purpose, and she wanted to accomplish it as quickly as possible.

Not long after Thomas's departure, a businessman from across town came in with a shoulder injury that needed a sling, followed by a little boy with a four-inch gash on his leg in need of stitches. She had barely finished making a stack of sandwiches for lunch when the telephone rang.

"Is the doctor there?" an anxious voice asked as she picked up the receiver.

"No, he's out, but I'm the nurse. Can I help you?"

"I'm Maggie Andrews. It's my daughter-in-law, Mary. Her baby's coming."

"What is your address, Mrs. Andrews?" Clara scribbled down the information. "I'm on my way."

Leaving a hastily scrawled note on Thomas's desk, she snatched her black bag and dashed to the kitchen. This was a matter she could handle. Shoving the sandwiches into the icebox, she hurried outside and was soon pedaling down the cobblestone street, heading south.

Her knock on the small flat's door was promptly answered by a middle-aged woman with a pensive face. "This way," the woman said as she led Clara to a small back bedroom where a young woman lay on the bed.

Clara spoke soothingly to the mother-to-be, who wasn't much older than she was. "You're doing wonderful, love."

"Have you done this before?" the elder Mrs. Andrews asked, eyeing her skeptically.

"Plenty of times," Clara reassured her with a smile. "I'll need some hot water."

Three hours later a high-pitched cry burst through the small back bedroom, and Clara laughed happily as she laid the infant in the new mother's waiting arms. "You've got a beautiful baby boy."

Mary's tired face was beautified with a smile and shining eyes. "Isn't he perfect, Mother?"

The older woman's face showed she fervently agreed with the sentiment as she knelt beside the bed.

"Do you have a name picked out?" Clara asked.

Mary smiled up at her. "Joseph William. Joseph after his father, William after mine."

A lump stuck in Clara's throat, and she blinked back tears. "It's perfect," she choked out, and turned her back on the happy picture.

"Your daddy will be so proud of you," Mary murmured to the bundle in her arms.

Clara left the flat shortly afterwards, promising that she or the doctor would call tomorrow. A crushing weight rested on her heart, and instead of pedaling back to the clinic, she sought refuge on the Newhaven Promenade. Grey clouds loomed overhead, threatening another downpour, and choppy waves from the Channel lashed the rocky retaining wall below. Standing with her back to Castle Hill, upon which Newhaven Fort sat high above her, she tugged a silver filigree cross set with sapphires from the front of her dress and clutched it tightly. A gift from her parents many years prior.

"Why did they have to leave me alone, Lord?" she whispered.

The eerie howl of the autumnal wind whistling around her and the crashing of waves were her only answer. Her shoulders slumped as she slipped the cross back into its hiding place. Mounting the bicycle, she glanced over her shoulder to look out over the Channel once more.

"You'll be proud of your little wife and son," she whispered to a soldier far away on the front. Then, to the sky, she added, "I hope they would be proud of me, too, Lord."

Clara hadn't returned by the time Thomas arrived back at the clinic. He read her note and helped himself to several sandwiches. Retreating to the silence of his office, he drummed his slender fingers on the smooth desktop thoughtfully. His conversation with Clara earlier rang through his mind: he really should tell her what was going on. It was his duty to. *Why hadn't Crouthers simply filled her in? If only—* The doorbell interrupted his thoughts, and he sighed.

To his surprise, he found Lena on the doorstep, and without a word of invitation from him, she bounded into the waiting room.

"Why are you here?" he asked slowly, closing the door and studying her in bewilderment.

She raised an eyebrow. "You left a message for me in the drop box earlier asking for my help."

Right. "About that—"

"Anything for the right price."

He rolled his eyes. "So you keep reminding me. I want you to search Miss Dankworth's room during dinner for any information about her you can find. I'll keep her occupied here. Be finished by eight o'clock, and I'll meet you on the west beach at 10:15 tonight."

She tapped her chin saucily as if thinking about it. "Very well. Until tonight," and she sauntered out the door.

Thomas let out a puff of air. He had employed others to search for information in the past. Why did it feel so wrong now? Shoving aside the guilt, he hurried back to the office and skimmed through the appointment book. Five minutes before the next patient.

At 4:30 that afternoon, Thomas found Clara in the kitchen, stirring something on the stove. "Ah, Miss Dankworth, would you be able to stay late this evening?" he asked breezily.

She didn't look at him as she continued her work. "For what?"

"It's about time I showed you how to do the books and records for the practice. You know, dividing the clinic income between Doctor Peterson's practice and mine." When Clara said nothing but swivelled to stare at him with the spoon suspended mid-air in astonishment, he added, "May I count on your assistance? We should be done by eight o'clock."

She shrugged and leaned slightly to taste the soup. "You're in charge."

He didn't miss the suspicious tone of her voice. "Excellent," was all he managed before ducking out of the kitchen and back to the safety of the examination room to deal with his patient's physical ailments, which were much easier to remedy than personal matters. If she resented being here as much as *he* resented her being here, it just might be enough to convince Crouthers to send a replacement.

Thomas paced the rocky shore of the beach in the inky shroud of the late-autumnal night. It was going on half-past ten, and the guards above his head on Castle Hill had already retired. No one would know of his meeting. A soft tread behind him caught his ear, and he instinctively reached for the Webley at his hip.

"Don't shoot, Doctor, or you'll never know what I learned," a feminine voice chided merrily as a blonde head became faintly visible in the silvered moonlight.

"Hush," he scolded. "Your voice carries. What did you find?"

"Nothing."

Thomas's voice raised in pitch. "Nothing?"

"I checked everywhere. There was nothing."

He growled. "Impossible. I refuse to be outwitted by a nurse from who knows where. She'll have to slip up sometime. Are you sure you put everything back as it was?"

Lena crossed her arms and tossed her head saucily. "Do you really have to ask?"

He rolled his eyes. "Forget it. Sorry I put you up to it."

"I chose to do it, Lindsey. I could have said no."

Thomas flashed her an inscrutable grin. "And we both know that wouldn't have been the first time. I've already asked Crouthers to send someone else."

She blinked in surprise. "She's only been here a week."

"I've got Richard on her, too," Thomas added, ignoring her.

"He succeeds where no one else can. Now for payment," and Lena held out her hand.

"I don't pay for no information."

"I risked my neck for you, Thomas Lindsey. Pay up or I'll inform Crouthers of what you're doing," she dared with fire in her icy blue eyes.

Thomas fished a small stack of bank notes from his trouser pocket and handed them to her. "Never took you for the blackmailing type, Miss Mitchell."

"Nice doing business with you, Doctor." She tossed him a grin before ambling up the rocky coast and disappearing into the dark shroud of night.

Thomas balled his fists and watched the lighthouse beacon flash in the distance before turning his back on the light and strolling up the coastline towards town. He had a meeting with Jennings at the manor.

The colonel was buried in paperwork at his desk when Thomas knocked and poked his head inside. "What did you want me for, Jennings?"

Jennings motioned him to a chair and flicked a note across the desk to him. "This letter was intercepted from Detweiler."

Thomas snatched up the letter and scanned it with a frown. "The Piper's come to Newhaven? I wasn't expecting this turn of events."

And from the deep-creased grimace on the colonel's face, neither was he.

For the last three years of the war, MI5 and the Secret Service had an inside leak they had been unable to identify. Everything pointed to a double agent German spy, simply referred to as The Piper, on the loose in England but with no clear indication of his whereabouts or identity.

Thomas cocked his head. "I may have a lead, sir."

This caught Jennings's attention.

"Miss Dankworth."

The colonel snorted. "Just because you're upset about her being sent here doesn't implicate her."

"But—"

"I don't want theories, Lindsey; I want facts. Find out her alibi and confirm it. And don't forget, The Piper is my jurisdiction. While you're at it, I want to meet this woman."

Thomas saw himself out and retreated to the clinic, but sleep was elusive that night as he tossed restlessly back and forth in bed. Finally, getting up, he lit a lamp and lifted two tattered, faded blue hair ribbons from the top drawer of the dresser. Perched on the edge of the bed, he studied them in the dim light; frequent rubbing had begun to fray the edges—his last link to home.

An image flashed through his mind of a little girl who shared his own dark curls and sapphire eyes.

"Remember me," she whispered with a shining tear on her cheek.

Always. He made a motion to wipe away the tear, but the picture faded. "I'll make it up to you. I promise," he whispered, returning the ribbons to the drawer. Snuffing out the lamp, he fell into an uneasy sleep haunted by images of heathered hills and the tear-stained face of a little girl.

CHAPTER 6

Midnight Meeting

20 November

THE FOLLOWING EVENING, Clara plaited her long hair into a braid and blew out the kerosene lamp. Crawling under the freezing sheets, she tugged the quilt up to her chin and shivered. It had been a long day at the clinic, and while she was growing accustomed to Thomas's taciturn moods, he had been especially irritable today. She was almost asleep when something hit the window with a *ting*. Bolting upright, she listened intently. Silence. Certain she must have imagined it, she lay back down, but it came again a minute later. Sighing in frustration, she threw on her dressing gown, yanked back the curtains, and poked her head out the window into the bitterly cold night air. She shivered and glanced down to find Thomas standing below, scowling up at her with his arms akimbo and Nana at his side.

"What are you doing?" she hissed.

"The better question is what are *you* doing, Miss Dankworth?"

"Going to bed like a sensible person. Unlike you."

"We have a meeting tonight." He pulled out his pocket watch

and examined it in the faint moonlight. "And we're going to be late at this rate."

"You never told me."

He shrugged. "It was last minute. Regardless, be quick and come down."

Clara snapped the window shut and closed the curtains. For a moment, she was tempted to return to her warm covers, but knowing Thomas would just throw rocks at the window again if she wasn't quick, it didn't seem worth it.

Reaching for her shirtwaist, she felt the chain of the silver cross tangle in her braid. It had slipped from under her dressing gown collar when she leaned out the window. Inwardly groaning, she prayed Thomas hadn't seen it. Slipping into a skirt and tucking in her shirtwaist, she hurriedly wrapped a scarf around her neck and donned her coat, buttoning it up as she tiptoed down the stairs.

Clara didn't dare put on her shoes until she was at the front door. Thankfully, the ancient hinges didn't creak in the damp air as she stepped outside. Shuddering at the blast of frigid air, she rubbed her eyes as she joined Thomas at the front gate. Then she stifled a groan—of all things, she had forgotten her hat. What sensible woman forgot her hat? Apparently ones awakened from their near-sleeping state by maniac doctors who spoke in cryptic riddles.

"The car's down the road a ways," Thomas whispered in answer to her raised eyebrow.

Neither said a word as they walked the short distance to the Model T. Once in the automobile, they travelled for ten minutes until Thomas detoured to the right. At the end of the long, poplar-lined lane stood a majestic house with marble columns and a wrap-around portico nestled between two oaks amid a sweeping lawn.

"Where are we?" Clara's brow furrowed as she stared at the house.

"Colonel Jennings's estate. Come along."

Her face remained impassive, but an icy hand gripped her stomach. Light from a single window shone on the second storey. The butler answered Thomas's light tap, and they were ushered inside.

The grandiosity of the house caught Clara's breath. Velvet carpet cushioned the floor, and a crystal chandelier hung overhead. She trailed her fingers over the polished oak handrail as she followed Thomas upstairs. A gallery of paintings graced the prettily papered walls, and she craned her neck to take it all in, feeling uncomfortably out of place among the finery.

Thomas seemed to know exactly where he was going and soon rapped on a large wooden door at the end of the hall. Without waiting for an answer, he turned the knob and motioned for Clara to enter. Her eyes widened at the vast assortment of books housed on a myriad of bookshelves; it had been years since she had seen a home library so grand.

Colonel Jennings sat in an easy chair reading a newspaper. "Thank you for coming…" The man faltered as his sage eyes landed on Clara, and he quickly rose to his feet.

Clara advanced and offered her hand. "You must be Colonel Jennings. Clara Dankworth. Pleased to make your acquaintance, sir."

Jennings bowed stiffly and squeezed her extended hand, appearing rather unnerved.

Thomas stared curiously at the exchange.

"Miss Dankworth," Jennings mused absently before recovering himself. "Please have a seat."

Clara accepted the offered seat and waited.

"How much have you told her?" Jennings asked, posing the question to Thomas, who stood leaning against the mantle in abject indifference.

"Nothing."

"Did you do as I said?"

"Her alibi is impeccable with six witnesses," Thomas admitted, his voice heavy with reluctance.

Jennings gave him a hard look. "As I said, she's not our man. Or woman, as it may well be."

Clara bristled as the men's talk flew above her head as if she weren't present. If it was Thomas's single goal to annoy her, he was succeeding. As he tread past her to approach the sofa opposite her, she stuck her foot out, tripping him.

Thomas flailed, grasping the air in vain before he careened face-first into the sofa cushions. Rubbing his nose as he jumped up, he shot Clara a withering glare.

She met his gaze with mock sincerity. "Oh, my apologies, I didn't realise you were aware of my presence."

Straightening his jacket and cuffs, Thomas flashed Jennings an apparent plea for intervention.

However, the colonel's mouth twitched in an unexpressed smile while his eyes crinkled in merriment. Evidently, he wasn't about to address the situation.

"Point taken, Miss Dankworth," Thomas ground out before plopping down on the sofa. He rubbed his nose again, likely smarting from the fabric burn. "Women," he muttered under his breath.

Clara bit back a smile as Jennings skillfully manoeuvred the conversation and carefully explained about The Piper and his recent visit to Newhaven.

"And you assumed it was me," Clara concluded.

"Precautionary, I assure you."

"Should you need further proof, sir, I assure you I can clearly prove I am innocent of fraternising with the enemy."

"No further proof is needed."

Clara stole a glance at Thomas and saw immediately he wasn't convinced of her innocence or impressed by Jennings's assurances.

Jennings also noticed the look and repeated, "No further proof. Are we clear, Lindsey?"

Thomas only shrugged and studied the firelight.

"Sir, if I may be so bold, might I ask a few questions? The doctor has been reluctant to share information."

Jennings once again shot Thomas a disparaging glance before giving Clara an encouraging smile. "Of course, my dear."

"First, why am I here? It can't be to infiltrate The Piper, whoever he is, if you have only just discovered his connection to Newhaven."

"Quite right. Edward Price is the reason."

"And he would be?"

"Only the most prominent member in town and our banker," Thomas cut in sarcastically.

Jennings ignored the comment and continued, "He appears to be a German sympathiser with a connection to Germany. Particularly a Herr Anton Detweiler, a high-ranking official in the German government."

Clara nodded knowingly. "I have heard of Detweiler. So, we are looking for proof of the connection?"

"Precisely. Up until now, The Piper wasn't the main problem here. But now, everything's changed."

"As a banker, what do you expect him to have done? Wired money to Germany? If so, wouldn't it be best to check his records?"

"It's not as easy as that, and he's a slippery man with friends in high places. He's bought off more people than I would care to admit," Jennings said with a scowl.

The Piper? Clara mused to herself as Jennings addressed a question to Thomas. She grasped at memories but came up empty. The name sounded vaguely familiar—important even—but why?

~

21 November

The next morning, Clara skirted around a puddle as she hurried down High Street. She was running late and could well imagine Thomas's solemn lecture on the importance of punctuality. She barely contained a snort; as if the man wasn't ever late himself. She nodded to several passersby as she rounded the corner onto Bridge Street.

"Miss Dankworth!" A masculine voice bellowed from behind her.

Startled, she spun around and faced the broad man about her height as he approached.

"Forgive the liberty, but I have heard so much about you. Edward Price, at your service. It's a pleasure," and he caught up her hand, kissing it gallantly.

She barely contained a shudder at the man's overt overtures. He was nearly as old as Jennings. *This* was the man they were supposed to be watching? She pasted on a polite smile. "I have heard of you as well, Mr. Price."

"Do me the honour of accepting a dinner invitation at my home tonight? Say six o'clock?" His voice was loud, drawing the attention of several pedestrians in the vicinity. Clara felt her cheeks burn as he continued, "It is the least I can do to welcome the town's newest medical professional. Such an important role, I assure you." He flashed her a rather condescending smile.

Though her mind whirled and her heart plummeted to her shoes, she dipped her chin in deference. "The honour would be mine, sir." A moment later, she was once again hurrying towards the clinic. "Doctor Lindsey, I—oh!" She stopped in surprise as she burst into the office and found Thomas at his desk and a young girl sitting in front of it.

The girl, who looked to be fifteen or sixteen, jumped up from her seat in alarm. She was a petite girl with a unique shade of strawberry blonde hair that was tucked up in a loose knot at her neck. Her creamy skin accented her bright, emerald eyes. However, her shoulders were hunched, and as Clara took a step closer, she realised the girl suffered from a hunchback condition.

"It's all right, Emily. She is... one of us," Thomas assured the girl, who relaxed visibly.

Clara nearly smirked. How much did that admission cost him?

"Miss Dankworth, this is Miss Emily Price."

"Any relation to Edward Price?"

Emily gave her a tight smile. "His daughter."

Clara's mouth formed a small *o*. "Indeed? Then I shall have the pleasure of your company tonight."

Emily's eyes widened. "Father invited you to dinner? And you accepted?"

"Yes."

Thomas shot to his feet. "You have been in town for barely two weeks, and you were invited to dinner?" He huffed. "Not even Lena was that good. You're definitely going."

She stiffened. "I can manage my social affairs without your interference, thank you."

"And I want a detailed report afterwards," he continued as if he hadn't heard her. Returning his focus to Emily, he added, "Are you sure that's all you heard?" He was evidently referring to the conversation before Clara interrupted.

"Absolutely, Doctor. I wish I had more."

"It's fine, but let me know if you hear anything else."

Emily thanked him and smiled at Clara. "See you tonight," was all she said before disappearing out of the office.

"What did I miss?" Clara asked in confusion after she was certain the girl was gone.

"Emily is an informant for me."

"She actually spies on her father?"

Thomas sent her a wry glance. "As do we. But it's hardly spying, and he is involved in illegal dealings. There's no loss of love between them, I assure you."

"Aren't there rules about involving civilians in political matters?"

Thomas shrugged. "I'm sure there are, but I wouldn't know. Just because the rules are there, doesn't mean they have to be followed."

But isn't that the purpose of a rule? She shook her head in disbelief. "Do you honestly operate under that principle?"

"Works for me," he said with an accompanying smirk.

~

22 November

Thomas peppered Clara with questions about the Prices when she arrived at the clinic the following morning. "Well, how was it? I can't imagine how you managed to secure the invitation in the first place, but what did you learn? Do speak up."

She appeared to not have heard him until she plopped down at her desk. "It was fine."

"Fine? That's it?!"

But try as he might, Thomas couldn't pry another word from her. Snatching up his bag, he noisily left the office and stormed across town. At the crossroads leading down to the harbour, he stumbled upon Emily and a young man. He tipped his hat to her and studied her companion intently. "I don't believe we have met."

"Nay, sir, but I know of you."

"This is Sam Johnson; he runs some of our errands," Emily explained.

The name jogged Thomas's memory. "You're a friend of Robbie Forsythe, are you not?"

Sam grinned. "Aye, sir."

"Mmmm..." Thomas mused before adding, "Might I have a word with Miss Price?" Surely she would be more agreeable to his questions than Clara had been.

Sam bobbed his head and scurried ahead out of earshot.

"How was dinner?"

"Fine."

Seriously? He clenched his jaw. Were all women this exasperating? "More than a one-word report, please."

"There is nothing *to* report," Emily insisted. "Father was as charming as he could be, Miss Clara admirably deflected his egregious overtures, and that was that." A smile crept across her face. "I rather like her."

Thomas groaned inwardly. "Obliged, Miss Emily." Nodding to her, he strode away to pay his next call. All he could do was shake his head. What was it about Clara that attracted people to her? The Forsythes, Elizabeth, Robbie, Kasey, Nana the dog even, and now Emily had all become infatuated with his new nurse, it seemed. Unbelievable.

CHAPTER 7

Memories of Home

27 November

THOMAS GLANCED at the calendar on the office wall. How was it almost December? Rubbing his forehead, he fingered the list Clara had left for him. He gulped the last mouthful of his now tepid tea as he mused over it absently. Setting the cup on his desk, he slipped into his coat and picked up his black bag. "I'm off, Miss Dankworth," he called, unsure of her whereabouts.

"Take an umbrella. It's a soaking mess out there," came her muffled reply from the supply room. She popped her head out the next minute as if to make sure he listened to her suggestion.

Thomas smirked as he popped the umbrella open over his head and set off down Bridge Street. Usually he took the automobile, but today of all days, it had decided to act up and was in the hands of a mechanic. Thomas spent the morning checking on the Andrewses' baby; sending the McIntyre boy to the chemist with a new prescription for his grandmother; checking on the farmer who had experienced a run-in with an axe; and comforting a young widow's son who had recurring panic attacks and begging to see his daddy.

As he trudged back towards the clinic, a numb weariness

seeped deep into his being. A steady drizzle had been falling all morning, and a bone-chilling wind was blowing inland from the Channel. Shivering, he tugged his coat closer around his thin frame. His mind wandered across the greyness of the Channel. The Third Battle of Ypres had ended barely two weeks earlier once the Canadians Corps captured Passchendaele, but losses had been heavy on both sides. Today the wind kept him from hearing the distant clamour of fighting, but on a still day, the noise of battle from war-torn France was a part of life for the people of Newhaven. Shuddering, he found himself on the back doorstep of the clinic.

Inside the warmth of the kitchen, he could almost put the thoughts of war behind him. Almost. Sighing, he poured himself a steaming cup of tea and mopped up the water he had trailed in.

Clara entered the kitchen and gave him a tentative smile. "Soup's hot," she offered, moving to pull two bowls from the cupboard.

Thomas sank wearily into a kitchen chair and watched her dish up the soup. "Thank you," he said as she placed the bowl in front of him, curls of steam floating up towards him.

She gave a small nod and seated herself across from him with her own bowl. Her head dipped in silent prayer before she took a mouthful of soup.

He watched her silently. How long had it been since he prayed over a meal? Since he had prayed at all? He gave his head a little shake. Now was not the time to linger on the past.

"Something's bothering you, Doctor." It was a statement, not a question.

He avoided her steady gaze as he blew on a spoonful of his soup. "Just thinking about the war." He could tell she was unsatisfied with his answer, but he wasn't in the mood for a lengthy discussion—theological or otherwise—and they finished the rest of the meal in silence.

After seeing his last patient for the day, Thomas locked the front door. Trudging back to the office, he found Clara with her coat already on, waiting for him.

"Mrs. Forsythe called and invited you to come for dinner."

Managing his meals hadn't been the original deal, but after one taste of his cooking attempts, Clara had tactfully taken over. He didn't mind; it was one less thing for him to have to remember. "I'll be there," was all he said, and she took the words as a dismissal.

Once he was alone, Thomas laid his head down on his desk for several minutes. The memory of a curly-haired little girl laughing merrily danced before him. His head snapped up, and she disappeared. He groaned and dropped his head again, feeling utterly alone and miserable. And yet, company was the last thing he wanted.

An hour later he knocked on the Forsythes' front door, which Elizabeth promptly answered. Grimacing, he pasted on a polite smile. "Good evening, Mrs. Tilney. Mrs. Forsythe asked me to dinner."

She raised a skeptical eyebrow. "I see," she said in a tone that clearly said she didn't. Although she held the door with one hand, she made no motion to let him enter.

Clara and Robbie descended the stairs that moment and noticed the arrangement at the door. "Play nice, Lizzie, and let the doc in," Robbie called.

Elizabeth glanced over her shoulder at the youth, then, placing a hand on her hip, she stepped back to let Thomas pass. As he moved through the doorway, she stuck her small foot out and tripped him.

Groping for the wall to regain his balance, Thomas clawed back a string of angry words unfit to be spoken in a lady's hearing... or at all for that matter. He glared at her as she slammed the front door harder than was necessary, stalked down the hall, and disappeared into the kitchen. Elizabeth Morgan Tilney would be the death of him.

"Sorry, Doc," Robbie apologised as Thomas hung up his coat and hat. "You know how she gets."

"I should be used to it by now," Thomas grumbled before giving the boy a friendly slap on the shoulder. He ignored Clara's bewildered stare and moved into the parlour to greet Mr. Forsythe.

After one of Mrs. Forsythe's hearty meals, the little boarding house family migrated into the parlour. Since that first night when Clara had played the piano, gathering around to sing and listen in the evenings had become something of a tradition. Although Clara, Elizabeth, and Lena were the only permanent residents of the boarding house, temporary boarders arrived frequently, and most were eager to join in on an evening of music. Tonight was no exception.

Clara settled on the piano bench, and looking around the group, asked, "Whose night is it to pick?"

"Your choice, Doc," Mr. Forsythe announced.

All eyes riveted to Thomas, who fumbled with the cuff of his navy cable-knit sweater. Robbie had coerced him into staying past dinner against his better judgment.

"We haven't stumped her yet, so don't be shy," Robbie encouraged, grinning impishly at the doctor's evident discomfort.

Thomas sighed. No sense prolonging the inevitable. "'Keep the Home Fires Burning.'"

Clara turned back to the instrument and let her fingers dance over the keys.

As everyone sang along, Thomas found himself humming and his mind wandering as he listened to the piano's gentle cadence. Clara's fingers glided up the keys just as expertly as they had milked the cow, and the thought made him grin. As he mused over the familiar words of the song—of soldiers far away, of family on the home front, and most of all, of a longing for home—for one brief moment, an intense feeling of *hiraeth* overcame him as he let himself dream of a place he had not dared dream of in years. *Home.* The little cottage surrounded by heathered hills and nestled at the mouth of a winding river hundreds of miles away. He shook himself from his reverie as the song ended.

More songs were rapidly requested. Robbie propped his elbow on the piano top and sang heartily. Twice he flashed Thomas a teasing grin.

When the clock struck nine, Clara nodded at Elizabeth, and they both started singing "Auld Lang Syne" as Clara's fingers drifted across the keys. The rest of the group joined in solemnly until the last notes died away.

Soon after, Thomas rose and thanked his host and hostess for the evening before taking his leave.

Robbie followed him to the door but stopped him before he could leave. "You all right, Doc?"

Thomas nodded. *Just fighting nightmares.* That was nothing new.

"What did you think of the music?"

"It was... fine," Thomas conceded with a half shrug.

"She's a swell girl, Doc," was Robbie's next serious remark. "Give her a chance."

"We'll see. Good night."

Thomas slipped out the door, and Nana trotted after him to the front gate, where he paused and stroked her silky head. As he glanced back at the farmhouse, light shone from the windows, warming the cold late-autumn night. He tugged his sweater closer as a shiver passed through his slim frame, but the shiver penetrated deeper than the comfort of the cashmere sweater. It was on nights like this he was faced with the crushing reality of how alone he truly was. Nana nudged his hand with her damp nose, reminding him of her presence. Poor consolation. Sighing, he gave her a final pat before starting down Lewes Road towards town, and the last twinkling light from the boarding house vanished behind him.

CHAPTER 8

The Ferret Returns

29 November

THOMAS STOOD in the examination room cleaning implements after the clinic was closed for the day. He had sent Clara home and now whistled softly to himself, looking forward to a quiet evening. *Maybe.*

"Thomas."

With a startled cry, he whirled around to face the voice behind him and dropped a handful of implements to the floor. "So much for knocking, Richard," he growled, stooping to pick up the mess.

His friend's green eyes gleamed with hidden foreboding. "It's urgent."

Thomas dumped the implements in the sink and washed his hands. He would deal with them later. "Out with it then," he returned impatiently as he snatched up a towel to dry his hands.

"I followed a lead on Clara."

Thomas locked his gaze with his friend's in silence as he grimaced and braced himself for the worst.

"A nurse from a hospital in Rotterdam disappeared about a year ago, and no one knows where."

Thomas's eyebrows flew upwards. He knew Richard was

good at finding out obscure pieces of information, but this was surprisingly fast and detailed, even for him. "And what makes you think it's her?"

"The woman went by Colette Gibson. There are no passenger steamer records between England and the continent for anyone by that name."

Smuggled in or alias. "Did you find anything on her?"

"I'm working on a few leads, but she might be the one we've been looking for."

"The Piper? Jennings already cleared her, and she had an alibi."

Richard studied Thomas. "But you aren't convinced, my friend."

Thomas dipped his head to admit he wasn't, adding, "Keep looking."

"Will do. You still want her replaced?"

Hesitating momentarily, Thomas steepled his fingers and pressed them against his lips, considering the matter. Was replacing her the right decision? While she wasn't what he anticipated, she had proven herself capable. But... no, he wouldn't let matters cloud his judgment. He had to see things through. "More than anything."

Richard raised an eyebrow as if hearing the reluctance in his friend's voice. "No promises, but I'll see what I can do."

The minutes slipped by as Thomas stood leaning against the counter, staring at the floorboards as if in a trance. If Colette Gibson was indeed Clara Dankworth... what would it all mean? There was more to this woman than met the eye, but how far would he have to look to find the truth?

~

30 November

Dense fog covered the cobblestone street that dreary last day of November. Clara hugged her coat closer as she skirted yet another puddle. She hadn't bothered with her mackintosh, but it really was too bad she had forgotten to don her galoshes. Her shoes would be soaked in no time.

Upon reaching the backstep of the clinic, she entered quietly through the kitchen door. The room was empty, but a fire blazed warmly in the stove and the tea kettle puffed off curling fingers of steam. Removing her sopping shoes, she set them to dry by the stove and wiggled out of her coat. She halted in the middle of pouring two cups of tea as a faint stream of whispering through the wall from the supply room caught her ear. Her damp stockinged feet padded silently across the worn floorboards, and she pressed her ear to the wall.

Straining to listen, she could make out two men's voices. One belonged to Thomas, but the second one, she didn't recognize.

"A yw hi'n amau unrhyw beth," said the unknown voice.

Does she suspect anything? Clara's eyes burned, and a lump lodged in her throat. Her heart thumped at the sound. Welsh. How long had it been since she had heard it? Thomas's oddly familiar lilt suddenly clicked in her mind. He was a Welshman. She started to pull away when she heard Thomas's voice say her name. Willing her heart to stop its incessant pounding, she remained with her ear to the wall, mentally translating the words.

"Not yet. But it's only a matter of time. She's quicker than anyone else Crouthers has sent before. That doesn't make it easy."

"He said he doesn't want to hear another word from you about a replacement. I heard him say she's more valuable to the ring here than you, Thomas."

She cringed as a fist slammed one of the shelves and hoped nothing was broken.

"What I get for all these years of service," Thomas growled.

"Watch your back, my friend," the voice cautioned.

The men stirred in the next room, and she hastened away from the wall. Finishing pouring the tea, she poked her head into the hall and called loudly, "Tea's ready, Doctor."

"I'll be out presently. Start on the records," was Thomas's muffled reply.

Clara furrowed her brow as she carried the tea to the office. She had suspected Thomas was hiding something from her, and the other man's admission of her worth scared her. If someone found out who she really was... *Impossible.* Shaking her head, she refused to finish the thought and attacked the stack of patient records they were behind on.

When Thomas joined her minutes later, he held up her shoes. Clara's face flushed as she stood up to take them. Thomas flashed her an uneasy smile and settled at his desk with his cup. Footsteps in the hall creaked, and Clara knew the second man was making his exit. Opening her mouth to inquire if he had seen a patient this morning, she thought better of it and said nothing while she continued scribbling away furiously. There was no need to indicate how much she knew. Not yet.

CHAPTER 9

One Woman's War

7 December

CLARA CAREFULLY OPENED the first box of newly arrived medical supplies and began cataloguing the inventory in the supply room. The door was ajar, and she could hear Thomas on the telephone in the office. As she rummaged through the box, the click of the telephone receiver sounded across the hall followed by a soft *thud*. She paused to identify the sound—must be the newspaper. Footsteps in the hall signalled Thomas was retrieving it.

Several minutes later, Thomas's voice sounded from the doorway. "Read this, Miss Dankworth." He shoved the newspaper towards her with a furrowed brow. "Happened yesterday."

She straightened and studied his rigid form and concerned face. Glancing at the headline, the blood drained from her face, and her heart dropped to her shoes. In bold letters, it read: HALIFAX WRECKED. With shaking hands, she snatched the paper and skimmed the article. Half the city in flames. Thousands dead. Those missing or buried in debris beyond count. Germans in Halifax to be arrested.

"A terrible thing," Thomas mused quietly.

"Indeed." Clara's mouth was as dry as the cotton bandages she had unpacked. Shoving the periodical back in the doctor's direction, she stumbled past him and hurried down the hall to the office. She couldn't let him see how much it affected her.

Robbie's lank form was perched on her desk as she entered, and he jumped up.

So much for privacy. She dropped into her desk chair as her legs threatened to give out.

"I didn't hear you come in," Thomas said to Robbie as he joined them, throwing down the paper on his desk.

Robbie frowned and glanced between the two grim faces. "What's wrong?"

"Have a look." Thomas motioned to the paper.

The boy snatched it up, reading softly, "'Halifax harbour explodes, killing hundreds and wounding thousands.' Doc... that's awful."

Clara wanted to plug her ears. Scream. Tear the paper in shreds. But she remained ramrod straight as she sat at her desk, only her hands trembling slightly as she rummaged through some paperwork. She had seen the questions in Thomas's eyes, but she wasn't about to answer them. Not now. Not ever.

In the days that followed, emotions ran high. It was natural to want to blame the Germans. After all, the world was at war, and German submarines had made it to the mouth of the Halifax harbour in the past. But the Germans weren't to blame. Two ships from France and Norway had collided with one another. With the French ship loaded with explosives, an explosion had been inevitable.

News of the explosion continued filling the papers days after the tragedy as the casualty rate climbed and journalists reported on the travesty in detail. From the crumbled city, to the woman with a half pane of glass sticking out of her back due to the blast. It was sensationally horrendous.

The afternoon of the tenth was painfully slow. From the doorway of the examination room, Thomas sipped his tea and perused the newspaper while Clara cleaned implements at the sink. The gentle pitter-patter of rain plunked rhythmically on the window.

"The British captured Jerusalem," he commented casually.

"Brilliant."

"Don't sound so enthusiastic."

A crash from the sink made him jump. Scalpels littered the floor, and Clara hurriedly scooped them up and dumped them in the sink. He set his cup and paper down on the counter and sprang to her side.

"I'm sorry." Her cheeks flamed.

He grabbed her hands, examining for any cuts from the scalpels. "You're bleeding."

"I'll be fine. I'm just tired." She snatched her hands from his grip and shrank away.

Thomas held her gaze and probed the depths of the brown eyes intently but immediately saw she would say no more on the subject. He wondered how the news of Halifax had shaken her this much. And why. "Take the rest of the afternoon off. Doctor's orders, and I must be obeyed." He sent her a reassuring smile and nodded towards the door. "Just be sure you clean those cuts."

She whispered her thanks before fleeing the room but not before Thomas heard the tears in her voice.

Instead of returning to the boarding house, Clara's feet dragged her to the Newhaven Promenade. Resting her elbows on the railing, she buried her head in her hands. Gunfire echoed across the Channel despite the gentle murmur of rain and winter waves rippling against the retaining wall below her. "I can't keep running, Lord. I'm worried, and if something happened to them…" she whispered into her fingers.

A warm hand touched her shoulder. "What's wrong, missy?" Kasey asked soothingly.

Clara masked her face with a smile. "Just tired."

The blue eyes studied her from beneath bushy white eyebrows, and her gaze fell. The kind Irish captain could hardly miss the telltale signs of pale cheeks and sleep-deprived eyes.

"Go rest then. It's too stormy to be out here today."

As she pivoted to obey his orders, Kasey's voice stopped her. "I know it's not much, but remember, you'll always have a friend in Kasey Grahame."

Swallowing back tears, she flung her arms around the captain in an impulsive hug, inhaling the comforting smell of sweet tobacco and sea spray lingering on his coat. When she pulled away, she threw a wave over her shoulder. Dropping proper decorum, she lifted her skirt hem and bolted towards town. Maybe if she ran fast enough, she could forget the horrible knot in her stomach. Forget the nightmare. Forget the past. But it didn't seem likely.

Twenty minutes later, she clicked the front door of the boarding house shut. Pausing to lean her head against the cool wood of the door, she inhaled its musty scent as the clock in the parlour chimed four o'clock. Starting up the stairs, she flinched as the third stair creaked, and Mrs. Forsythe's voice called from the parlour.

"Is that you, lassie?"

"Yes, ma'am." She really needed to remember to avoid that third step.

"Come here for a moment, will you?"

Clara descended the stairs and ducked into the parlour. Mr. Forsythe reclined in his easy chair, studying his newspaper, while his wife's knitting needles clicked softly as she rocked in her rocker, perusing the contents of a letter in her lap. Probably from one of her children on the front. The warm glow from the fire in the grate clothed the room in a gentle ambiance and was a welcome contrast to the gloom outside.

"Sit a moment." Mrs. Forsythe nodded at the sofa.

Clara took the offered seat and studied the couple curiously. "Is something the matter?" she queried.

Mr. Forsythe gave his wife a nod, and the woman said frankly, "We couldn't help noticing how down you've been ever since you came. Anything we can do to help you?"

Clara shook her head. "There's a war going on; that's enough to discourage anyone."

"My dear, you're shouldering a burden much bigger than Germany by my reckoning," Mr. Forsythe returned with concern in his green eyes.

Clara's gaze dropped to her lap, and she twisted her skirt absently with her fingers. Her heart froze—torn between trusting the people she cared about and fearing the living nightmare she could not escape. "I can't say," she murmured.

"Can't or won't?" probed Mrs. Forsythe gently.

Clara bit her lip. "I'll be fine. Really. Thank you for your concern," she added firmly before fleeing the room and leaving the Scottish couple to look after her in perturbed silence. *I'm fine.* Two simple words that created the biggest lie she told herself. The reality was, she was anything *but* fine.

She didn't go down to dinner. She couldn't stomach the thought of food. At seven o'clock, she shrugged into her coat and pedaled towards town. There was only one person who could end her prolonged agony. It would be a risk, but she was willing to take it. She needed answers. The rain had stopped, and the cold air stung her face, but she pressed on until she was riding up the poplar-lined lane of the Jenningses' estate.

Kerridge answered her ring and ushered her into the parlour. "I will inform the colonel of your presence," he said with a bow.

Clara leaned back in the easy chair and studied the lavish room filled with every pleasure and comfort money could afford.

"Miss Dankworth, is something the matter?" Jennings asked in immediate concern as he appeared in the doorway.

She took a deep breath. "Did you see the newspaper? About Halifax?"

Recognition flashed through the sage eyes. "I did."

"Are my—" she paused, scrambling for the right word "—contacts safe?"

"I received a telegram this morning and have it on good authority that they are safe, yes."

Thank You, Lord! Relief rushed through Clara's frame, and she sagged back in her chair. "It has taken every power of my self-control to keep away from the post office."

"Your secret is safe with me," Jennings said in a low tone.

"Thank you, sir," she whispered. "It's good to see you again."

He flashed her a paternal smile. "It's been far too long. Whatever you need, you know you have only to ask."

Thomas summoned unwilling feet to the harbour. The rain had let up, but a trip into the damp night was still the last thing he wanted. He hesitated at the door of a small flat before rapping softly. The door creaked as Kasey's face came into view.

"Come in, lad," Kasey's warm hand on his shoulder pulled him indoors.

Thomas seated himself in front of the fire without a word and accepted the tea from Kasey's weathered hand. "Robbie said you wanted to see me." Thomas slowly took a sip of the steaming hot liquid. He held it in his mouth for a moment, relishing the rich flavour.

Kasey settled in the chair across from the younger man with a cup of coffee. "Good news from France."

Thomas straightened. "From 045?"

Kasey nodded thoughtfully.

"When will she come?"

"I'll fetch her tomorrow and send Robbie with word of the meeting place."

"This might be our break, Kasey." He smiled with satisfaction, but the captain remained in serious thought.

"Have you been good to that little nurse of yours?" Kasey questioned frankly.

Thomas groaned. "She's not mine, Kasey."

"She's your assistant. That makes her yours."

"Contrary to popular opinion, I am not a monster," Thomas muttered, scowling into the fire.

"Then what was she doing at the promenade looking as miserable as a leprechaun with a toothache this stormy afternoon?"

"I sent her home to rest. She said she was tired."

Kasey sipped his coffee slowly and methodically.

Just like the man, Thomas thought. He and the Irish-American sea captain had met up in 1912 when they first joined MI5, but Kasey had never lost his methodic ways, his romantic notions, or his genuine care for those around him.

"We're in a war, Kasey. It's not easy on anyone."

Kasey didn't answer immediately. "That little lady is fighting something bigger than any war in France, lad. Mark my words. Bigger than any war in France."

CHAPTER 10

Canteen Shadows

14 December

"ARE YOU READY FOR TONIGHT?" Robbie asked Clara as she scribbled out the next day's house calls.

"Ready for what?" Thomas asked from the doorway, and two pairs of eyes swivelled in his direction.

"Miss Clara's playing at the canteen. It's Friday. Remember, Doc?" Robbie grinned as he hopped off his perch on Thomas's desk.

Thomas shot him a sharp look, but the lad just laughed and slapped the doctor's shoulder on his way out the door.

Clara cocked an eyebrow at the exchange. "What was that about?"

Thomas gave a blasé wave of his hand. "Nothing worth mentioning. You may leave early if you like."

She handed him the finished list. "Thank you. There's leftover soup warming on the stove."

He fingered the list as she donned her hat and coat, picked up her black bag, and disappeared into the kitchen.

"You really should go, Doc." Robbie poked his head back into the room.

Thomas flinched. He thought the lad had gone. "Robert Forsythe, if I hear one more word from you about this, I—"

The lad raised his hands in surrender. "Message received, Doc." But his merry green eyes twinkled otherwise.

The basement hall at Newhaven Baptist Church was nearly bursting at the seams that night. Clara wiped her damp palms on the skirt of her rose-coloured dress as she waited for Pastor Henderson to call her to the front. Uniformed men of all ages mingled about the spacious room, laughing and enjoying the food and service provided by several of the local volunteer ladies' societies. The room smelled of fresh coffee and doughnuts.

"If I could have your attention, gentlemen," the pastor announced from the front platform, and a reverent hush fell over the room. "For those new among us, I would like to introduce you to our musician, Miss Clara Dankworth. Give her a hand in welcome."

Applause overwhelmed the room as Clara took her place and smiled brightly at all the expectant faces before her. Tucking her violin under her chin, she began a stirring rendition of "It's a Long Way to Tipperary."

Voices bellowed out around the room, and couples paired off for dancing. Clara tapped her toe in rhythm. Drawing the bow over the strings, she silently thanked her persistent sister for making her take music lessons all those years ago. The rest of the evening passed quickly as Clara played as many tunes as she could think of, including some special requests from the soldiers.

At nine o'clock, Pastor Henderson gave her the signal that the night was drawing to a close. Nodding, she closed her eyes as she drew the violin bow over the strings in the tune of "Auld Lang Syne." Sweetly, the old Scottish ballad sang out, joined by the rich, solemn voices of the men in khaki before her. It was the farewell song. When the last notes died away, applause thundered around her. Sudden exhaustion rolled over her, and Robbie caught her elbow, leading her through the crowd. Hands reached out from every direction to shake hers, and many hearty thanks were shouted from across the hall. When the church doors closed behind her, Clara inhaled deeply and closed her eyes.

"You all right, Miss Clara?" Robbie asked, laying a hand on her shoulder in concern.

"It's not fair, Robbie. They're so young," she lamented softly as they strolled along the dark, deserted street. The youthful face of more than one soldier was seared in her memory—so full of hope and excitement, so utterly unprepared for the enormity of the task that lay before them across the Channel.

Robbie didn't answer immediately, but when he did, his tone was thoughtful. "But if not them, then who?"

Thomas glanced at the feminine scrawl on the slip of paper Robbie had brought him earlier from the docks. He paced in the shadow of the South Downs on the east side of town. East Newhaven was mostly warehouses, docks, and train depots. Few people lived or wandered out to the downs in the direction of Seaford, which housed a Canadian military training base. He checked his watch uneasily. He would wait five more minutes. Running his fingers through his curls, he sighed. She was always late; why should tonight be any different? A slight shadow soon appeared in view to his left. He squinted as it approached.

"*Bonsoir, Docteur. Comment ça va?*"

Thomas frowned in the darkness. "You know I don't understand French, Chantelle."

Soft, girlish laughter emerged from the hood, which slipped back slightly, revealing a rich mass of brown curls, hazel eyes, and an impish, heart-shaped face that was twisted into an amused smile. "All's well." She reached inside her cloak and handed him an envelope.

"Are you still safe in Boulogne?" he asked, tucking the envelope in his overcoat pocket.

Chantelle shrugged. "As safe as possible in the middle of a war."

"I want you to be careful. No unnecessary risks."

The girl rolled her eyes and dramatically laid a hand over her heart. "When have I ever taken unnecessary risks?"

"Always."

She chuckled. "I'm going to Paris. Send anything you need to Matheson; he will know how to contact me."

"I would prefer not to hear you were killed in front of a firing squad," he whispered fiercely.

The girl's noble face sobered immediately as she caught the veiled warning. "You won't, Thomas. God is with us." She touched the rosary beads hanging around her neck.

"The enemy thinks so, too," he muttered.

"Have some faith. You will see me soon. *Au revoir*."

"Wait," Thomas called after her, and Chantelle glanced at him over her shoulder. "If for whatever reason I can't meet you, I'll send my assistant, Clara Dankworth. You can send information through her."

"Kasey told me you didn't trust her." Chantelle's eyes held a dare as she stared at him in the fading moonlight.

He hedged. "It seems I have to."

"Very well. *Bonne nuit*."

"How did I end up mothering a little French girl in the first place?" Thomas muttered as he watched the shadow melt away into the night. And had he really just said he trusted Clara Dankworth? Mentally cursing his abominable tongue, he took one more look at the distant downs before starting back towards town. He wondered ruefully how the canteen had gone. Maybe he would go someday. But in light of the ribbing he would take from Robbie about it, perhaps not.

CHAPTER 11

Blue Ribbons

17 December

ON A SLOW MONDAY AFTERNOON, Clara glanced up from her newspaper as sharp footsteps echoed in the hallway.

"Thomas!" a shrill voice called just before Lena bounded into the office.

Thomas paid no attention to the woman and continued scribbling away at records.

"Oh, Clara, I didn't see you there. Reading the newspaper, are we? It's such a bore. I much prefer *Vogue*," Lena offered, twirling her strand of pearls around her finger. Turning her attention to Thomas, she batted her eyelashes. "Are you busy? There's a dance tonight."

"I have work to do, Miss Mitchell, and I believe you do as well. You need brains as well as looks."

Clara smothered a snicker. Ever since Thomas had told her Lena Mitchell was an agent, she had taken to watching the woman closely. All Lena seemed to do was flirt, read *Vogue*, and shop—in that order.

"You never do anything but work. Lighten up," the blonde

whined, and Clara rolled her eyes in disgust at the woman's overt flirting.

Thomas gave Lena an inscrutable grin. "You're not the first to tell me that."

"You are the most exasperating man!"

"You're not the first to tell me that, either."

Lena scowled at him and flounced out of the room, slamming the door behind her.

"Has she been in the Service long?" Clara questioned as Thomas returned to his paperwork.

"Three years, I think. Why?"

She paused to choose her words carefully. "She's an interesting woman."

Thomas snorted. "If by interesting you mean strong-willed, independent, and annoying, I don't think those words quite do her justice."

~

18 December

Clara strolled down High Street with Thomas's weekly supply of groceries in her arms. With Christmas only a week away, Newhaven buzzed with the energy of the holiday spirit. Carolers sang on street corners, a light dusting of snow blanketed the downs, and many packages found their way to and from loved ones on distant shores.

Back at the clinic, Clara checked the clock as she shuffled the groceries away. It was nearly time to close. She paused at the window as a group of Boy Scouts marched down the street singing. Opening the window to hear better, she waved to them as they passed. Their faces lit up when they saw her, and the tune they were singing broke off abruptly.

"Happy Christmas!" she called, smiling.

They grinned and waved back. "Happy Christmas, Miss

Clara!” Starting back down the street, they bellowed out to their hearts’ content:

> *“I saw three ships come sailing in*
> *On Christmas Day, on Christmas Day;*
> *I saw three ships come sailing in*
> *On Christmas Day in the morning.”*

For a harbour town, it was quite the fitting song. Clara chuckled then closed the window. Despite the surrounding sadness, there was still joy to be found.

“I do believe you have bewitched this town.”

She spun around to find Thomas leaning against the door frame, watching her curiously with a twinkle in his eye. She had been in town a month and still couldn’t figure this man out. He could be charming one moment or a complete monster the next. She cocked an eyebrow at him, unsure if it was a compliment or veiled sarcasm. “Hardly. You’re the one who charms everyone with that incorrigible grin of yours.”

The incorrigible grin beamed at her. “I have no idea what you are talking about.”

“Did they train you to do that when you joined the Service?”

Thomas chuckled. “You are something else, Miss Dankworth.”

19 December

The next morning, Clara bustled into the office only to find the room empty. A flash of colour on the floor near the doctor’s desk caught her eye. Stooping to retrieve the object, Clara carefully fingered the tattered, frayed edges of the dull blue hair ribbons. A little girl’s hair ribbons. *Why would...?*

"Why do you have these?" she asked as Thomas's dark curly head appeared in the doorway.

His sapphire eyes kindled as they landed on the ribbons in her hands. Crossing the room, he snatched them from her and stuffed them into his trouser pocket. "None of your business."

She frowned as questions swirled in her mind. Could he have a little girl? Given his age, it wasn't impossible.

He eyed her sharply. "It's not what you're thinking. Leave well enough alone, Miss Dankworth," and with those hasty words, he fled the room, leaving Clara to stare after him in bewilderment. The phone rang shortly thereafter, interrupting her thoughtful daze.

"Clara, can you bring the groceries I ordered from the store? Robbie's out, and I'm fit to be tied," Elizabeth's breathless voice asked over the line.

Clara managed a weak laugh; leave it to Elizabeth to be dramatic. "I'll be there shortly," she assured her friend before hanging up. "I'll be back," she called to Thomas, unsure of where he had disappeared to. When she received no answer, she shrugged and plunged out into the crisp winter morning, still mulling over the doctor's touchy reaction to the ribbons. Though he was prone to overreact at times, there was something more to those ribbons than just an overreaction; though just what, she couldn't be certain. She absently touched the hidden necklace at her throat—she might have more in common with the doctor than either of them realised.

CHAPTER 12

Merryn

20 December

AFTER THE EVENING PARLOUR SINGING, Clara sat comfortably on the rug in her room carefully stitching yet another patch on her well-worn woollen coat. An assessment of her funds earlier hadn't revealed enough for a new coat, and Thomas's words had proved true about a delay in her payment coming from London. Knotting the thread and snipping the tail, she clutched the garment close and drew up her knees, absently stroking the thinning fabric under her fingers. She hadn't expected to be a world traveller when she received it as a Christmas present four years ago. The thought brought a fond smile to her face. How different life had been then. Before the war... before the threats... A knock on the door snapped her out of reminiscing.

At her "come in," Robbie's curly head poked inside. "Doc's downstairs asking for you."

She clambered to her feet. "I'll be right there."

"I'm sorry to call so late, Miss Dankworth," Thomas apologised with a bow as she joined him in the parlour, and Robbie hovered in the doorway.

She waved off the apology. "How may I be of service?"

Thomas cleared his throat and said in a low tone, "We are to meet with Jennings at midnight."

"We?"

"You, Robbie, and I. Lena is working the night shift. You'll have to dress warmly, as we will be cycling. Robbie knows where we are to meet. Don't be late." He bowed again, and the front door shut a moment later.

"Meet me out back at 11:30," Robbie whispered from the door frame.

In his small room above the clinic, Thomas yanked his sweater over his head before holstering his two Webleys—one at his hip and the other at his shoulder. Shrugging into his overcoat, he picked up his pocket watch from the dresser. It would take twenty minutes to cycle to the manor.

Dense fog hovered over the deserted streets. Thomas's fingers ached through his gloves from the dampness as he pedaled through the silence of Brighton Road. Stopping at a clump of trees, he paused and gave three soft whistles. Three whistles answered back from the treeline, and Robbie and Clara emerged from the shadows. The trio guided their bicycles up the winding lane hedged with poplar trees.

Kerridge ushered them into the library where Jennings intently paced the carpeted floor; the oil lamps bathed him in golden light, reflecting off his salt-and-pepper hair. He motioned for them to sit. Thomas claimed an easy chair, while Clara dropped down on the sofa with Robbie leaning on the back of it.

Jennings halted his pacing. "We intercepted a transmission last night."

"From the Germans?" Thomas leaned forward.

Jennings nodded. "Something about a messenger by the name of Merryn being sent to England, presumably here. I did some checking, and the name hasn't been intercepted through the postal system, which means we have no other leads on where or whom Merryn is connected to. We have no detailed information about the arrival—date or location."

"Logically, it would make sense for him to come through a different harbour and catch the train," Clara mused.

Thomas whipped his head to stare at her, and she flushed as if suddenly realising she had spoken aloud. He steepled his fingers together and pressed them to his lips. *Of course.* It was brilliant. Why hadn't he thought of it? "Folkestone is the prominent port, and with thousands of refugees coming through, it would be a good cover and impossible to catch him."

From Clara's startled expression, he knew she was surprised at his support for her idea. But that was neither here nor there. They had a mission and a task to complete, regardless of whose idea it was.

Jennings nodded in agreement.

"Are you any closer to identifying The Piper or nabbing Price?" came from the sofa back.

"Neither. What new information do you have for me?" Jennings asked sharply.

Robbie shook his head, and Thomas fiddled with the cuff of his knitted sweater.

"Lindsey?"

The information from Emily flashed through Thomas's mind, but he wasn't ready to disclose it quite yet, so he shook his head in the negative. He caught the raised eyebrow Clara directed at him, but he ignored it. His business was his business alone.

"Gentlemen, must I remind you of the importance of—"

"We know the stakes, Jennings," Thomas interrupted curtly. "But neither a rogue agent nor a two-timing banker tends to slip up easily. It takes time."

Jennings snorted. "Time? We've been at this for over three years."

"You said The Piper travelled *to* Newhaven."

Thomas and Jennings both turned at the sound of Clara's voice.

"That could imply then that he travels around, conveniently throwing us off his trail. Going a step further, The Piper may actually have others working for him as a ruse while he is in a different part of England." She shifted in apparent discomfort as all three men stared.

"Possible, Miss Dankworth, but perhaps, not probable," Thomas returned.

"'When you have eliminated the impossible, whatever remains, *however improbable*, must be the truth,'" Clara said sagely.

From her expression, Thomas knew she was quoting but couldn't place the source.

Jennings sighed heavily, seeming to age before their very eyes. "You drive a compelling argument, Miss Dankworth. I'm open to any possibility, however improbable, at this point. Romania's fallen, and rumour has it Russia will be next."

An hour later, Clara slipped through the boarding house door, and Thomas grabbed Robbie's elbow before he could follow her.

"What's up, Doc?"

"I need you to go to London tomorrow. Give this to Walter." He fished a note out of his coat pocket. "Don't let Crouthers see you."

"Are you sure about this?" Robbie asked with evident concern.

"As sure as I am of anything," was the confident reply.

The note asked the young secretary to check the files for a Colette Gibson. Thomas wanted to find out if the missing nurse from Rotterdam was indeed Clara. The mousy secretary never dared breathe a word in complaint to his bully employer, but he seemed to admire Thomas's maverick spirit and didn't hesitate to help him when possible.

"And don't breathe a word to anyone."

"Mum's the word, Doc." Robbie shrugged and disappeared behind the door, leaving Thomas alone to ride back to the clinic. Again, for the second time in the last few weeks, an empty hole stung his heart as he realised in the numbing winter wind the depths of his loneliness.

~

23 December

"What do you have for me?" Thomas whispered urgently to Robbie as they stood behind the Forsythe barn in the rapidly falling twilight.

Robbie thrust an envelope at the doctor. "From Walter."

Thomas fought the urge to tear the missive open then and there, but he didn't want Robbie knowing the nature of the content. Shaking hands with the boy and whispering his thanks, Thomas quickly drove down Lewes Road towards the clinic.

Once in the safety of his office, he slit the envelope and tore out the message. His brows furrowed as he read. Rotterdam nurse Colette Gibson had become Caroline Maxwell and had been transferred to work for a doctor in Folkestone. His frown deepened; there was no name given of the doctor. But a smile quickly replaced the frown as he saw the next entry. Caroline had then been transferred again—to Newhaven. Walter had confirmed his suspicions—Clara was indeed the missing Colette Gibson. Strange that Richard hadn't found it out before he did. When it came to ferreting information, Richard Morgan was second to none.

Questions swirled in Thomas's mind, but a single one rose to the forefront. *Why?*

CHAPTER 13

New Information

24 December

IN THE WEEKS leading up to Christmas, the boarding house had buzzed with a perpetual flurry of preparations for the holidays. Loving packages and letters were sent to the front, the parlour was trimmed in garlands, and the tree shone brightly in the corner with its paper snowflakes and homemade decorations. A lovely woodsy smell permeated the house, and more than once, one of its inhabitants would stop in the parlour doorway to observe the festive room and simply smile.

"Don't forget to ask the doctor and the Grahames for Christmas dinner," Mrs. Forsythe called after Clara on Christmas Eve. Since only the three young women would be staying on through the holidays, the Scottish landlady had insisted on inviting company to fill the house. Even though Christmas wasn't widely celebrated in Scotland, the Forsythes had adopted the custom when they moved to England shortly before Robbie was born and lived by the philosophy that the more company, the merrier. Clara had never met a more welcoming, hospitable family.

As she strolled towards the clinic, the crisp air stung her nose, and she adjusted the scarf more securely around her neck. She exchanged many calls of greetings and Christmas wishes as she went. Mounting the clinic steps, a lump formed in her throat as she paused to survey the busy street. Newhaven, with all its concern of a direct German invasion and infiltration spies, had accepted her with open arms as one of their own.

Setting the kettle to boil, Clara quietly hummed Christmas carols in the kitchen. When she entered the office five minutes later, she nearly dropped the tea she carried at the sight of a stranger sitting behind Thomas's desk. "Goodness!" she cried.

The stranger shot to his feet. "My apologies, Miss Dankworth."

Clara set the tea down and eyed the man intensely. There was something familiar about him that she couldn't place. "Who are you, sir? And why are you here?"

"Richard Morgan," the stranger offered smoothly with his hand outstretched, completely ignoring her last question.

"Lizzie's brother?"

"The same."

She swallowed hard but shook his hand. She recognised his voice. He was the Welshman Thomas had met with in the supply room all those weeks back.

"Pleased to meet you," she offered politely, attempting to hold back her internal agitation. She fought the urge to squirm under the scrutinising gaze of her companion, whose brown hair was slicked back and shone in the pale sunlight filling the room. After a moment, she gestured to the cups. "Tea?"

"No, thank you. Is the doctor in?"

"I heard him upstairs a moment ago. He should be down presently."

Clattering footsteps echoed in the hall, confirming her words, and Thomas appeared in the office doorway. He frowned at the picture in front of him. "What are you doing here, Morgan?"

"Is that any way to greet an old friend?" Richard asked with a reproachful smile.

Thomas folded his arms over his chest and narrowed his gaze on the man. "Will you excuse us a moment, nurse?"

Clara nodded and carried her tea out of the room. She paused in the hallway after clicking the door shut. Eavesdropping had never been so tempting.

"My question stands," Thomas whispered fiercely after the door shut, and Clara's retreating footsteps disappeared towards the supply room. "Why are you here?"

"I came with information."

"In broad daylight? You must be daft."

Richard only shrugged and handed him an envelope from his pocket.

Thomas snatched it and tossed it in the middle drawer of the desk before locking it.

"Don't you want to see it?"

"Not with her just outside the door. Really, Richard, of all the foolish things—"

"Easy, Lindsey," Richard warned. "Besides, Lizzie talks about her all the time. Thought it was time I met her."

"Well, you met her. Now, please, go, and for goodness's sakes, don't come back in such a manner," Thomas whispered desperately.

"No promises, Doc." Richard smiled placidly, disappearing out of the room before Thomas could respond.

Clara returned a moment later, still cradling her cup of tea. "Friend of yours?" she asked, sitting down at her desk.

"None of your business," Thomas snapped as he snatched up his black bag and stalked out of the room. How could a perfectly good morning have gone south so quickly?

Clara scrubbed the examination room at closing time, listening to Mrs. McIntyre drone on about her terrible ailments to Thomas in the waiting room. With a chuckle, she dried her hands and poked her head out the doorway to watch the exchange.

"Yes, yes, Mrs. McIntyre. I'm sure this medicine will help you feel better. Have a happy Christmas." Thomas smiled politely, scandalising the older woman as he practically pushed her out the front door, hung the "Closed" sign behind her, and locked the door.

Clara chortled from her vantage point in the hallway. "I thought she'd never leave." Mrs. McIntyre had quite the reputation around town as a hypochondriac.

He let out a breath and raked his fingers through his hair. "Nor did I. First, it's her stomach, then her shoulder, then her back. I declare—"

"You grumble about her complaints, but you know she sings your praises with the same breath, and you like that, don't you?"

He did not reply to the charge, but the twitching at the corners of his mouth affirmed her accusation.

"Incorrigible rogue," she muttered, but her tone was teasing, earning her a grin from the doctor. "Mrs. Forsythe is hoping you will come to Christmas dinner tomorrow."

"Yes, of course. Give her my thanks." Thomas nodded, stepping past Clara and marching into the office.

She followed and said lightly, "If that's all for today, I'll be on my way."

"Certainly." His voice was distant as he thumbed through a stack of files on his desk.

Buttoning her coat and pinning on her hat, she turned to leave when Thomas's voice stopped her. "Miss Dankworth, Happy Christmas." He held out an envelope to her.

She accepted it and tilted her head in question. When he didn't offer an explanation, she simply said, "Happy Christmas, Doctor." Pausing at the door, she added, "Will you be at the Christmas Eve service tonight?"

"I'm not a total heathen," he returned dryly, rolling his eyes.

Later, as she climbed the boarding house stairs to change her dress for the evening, Clara tore open the envelope with shaking hands. Several pound notes and a slip of paper with a bold scrawl tumbled out.

Happy Christmas. T. Lindsey.

She smiled. The letter was like the man—quick and to the point—but she was grateful. The extra pounds would serve her well in the coming days.

After Clara left the clinic, Thomas locked the office door and removed the envelope from Richard out of his middle desk drawer. He held it gingerly between his fingers, and his stomach gnawed as he considered what might be inside. Sighing, he slipped out a single paper and read.

Clara Dankworth. Nurse in Brussels from 1914-15. Worked with Edith Cavell. Moved to Rotterdam in November 1915. Connection to Switzerland in December 1916. Transferred to Dr. Greshem in Folkestone April 1917. Received nurse's training in Toronto, Ontario. Other known aliases are Caroline Maxwell and Colette Gibson. Previous history undisclosed.

Thomas settled back in his chair and let the paper flutter to the ground. He blinked rapidly as his brain rapidly began assimilating the facts and mentally mapping out their connotations. His thought-pattern resembled a spider's web—intricate and precise. This was far more information than he had dared hope for.

Rotterdam was not only home to a central spy ring for the British at Cummings Station, but also for the French and Germans. Edith Cavell was executed by the Germans for alleged treason in October '15. Thomas wasn't familiar with Dr. Greshem, though he had done a stint in Folkestone himself earlier in 1917. He and Clara had just missed crossing paths. Switzerland was neutral territory, but there were several French and British agents operating in Geneva. But training in Toronto? Clara may not be British after all, but then what of her accent? It was certainly British but hinted of something else. *Not American. Perhaps Canadian?* He shook his head. Too many things still didn't add up.

Shoving the paper back in his desk, Thomas donned his coat and stormed out into the lightly falling snow in the dusky shadows of nightfall. A short jaunt down to the promenade would clear his head. He would get answers, but not till after Christmas. A twinge of guilt shot through him as the little girl with blue eyes frowned at him worriedly in his mind's eye.

"Just one more time. I promise," he whispered in the stillness as he stared out into the misty darkness hovering over the Channel, the light at the end of the breakwater sharing its cheer. He couldn't tear himself away from the gloominess; it was a tangible picture of what he felt inside himself. Clanging bells cut through his reverie, and he groaned. Late for church. Talk about irreverent, especially when he had made such a point of his going to Clara. He dashed northward, abandoning the gloom. Perhaps he would make it in time for the sermon at least.

CHAPTER 14

Happy Christmas

CLARA CLUTCHED her violin's neck nervously as she waited for the cue from Pastor Henderson to begin playing. The church was packed that Christmas Eve night. Though the ladies from various local volunteer societies had decorated the sanctuary festively with candles and garlands, an air of mourning lingered throughout the room, tempering the gaiety, as the absence of loved ones far from home was keenly felt. It was the fourth Christmas of the war, but would it be the last?

Clara's eyes misted as she looked out on the congregation, and at the pastor's nod, she drew her bow across the strings in the first few notes of "Silent Night." She closed her eyes and swayed gently to the music's cadence as voices joined her accompaniment. After a few more Christmas hymns, she slid into the Forsythes' pew between Robbie and Elizabeth. The former flashed an approving smile at her, and the latter squeezed her trembling hand.

Pastor Henderson spoke on the birth of Jesus so many years ago, born to Mary under less than ideal circumstances. His warm, raspy voice reminded them of the love God has for all in sending His Son down to earth.

"God shines," he said, clutching the edges of his pulpit. "In the midst of our greatest darkness, God has always shone His light."

A shuffling behind her made Clara glance over her shoulder just as Thomas slid into the pew behind her. She cocked an eyebrow at him. Late to a Christmas service?

He skittishly met her gaze before focusing on the pastor.

Elizabeth nudged her, and Clara whipped back around to face the front, half ashamed.

"On that day, all those years ago, the Son of God was born in a stable. Born knowing He would die, and yet loving us enough to do it. A humble birth to humble parents, the news of His birth was sung of angels and proclaimed by shepherds. Love in its truest form involves sacrifice." The old man of sturdy Sussex stock paused. "Tonight, we remember the coming of our Lord. Our hearts are heavy with the absence of our loved ones and the war being fought beyond our shores. But let us not forget the power of that night and what it still means to the world. Because that night changed our world forever."

After Pastor Henderson's closing prayer, a reverent silence fell over the congregation. Until, in his deep voice, Mr. Forsythe started to sing:

"O come, let us adore Him..."

Mrs. Forsythe's low alto joined her husband's voice, and the rest of the church followed their lead. Elizabeth squeezed Clara's hand as they sang, and Clara sucked in a shuddering breath, suddenly overcome with a joy she could not express and a sorrow she could not deny.

Later that night in the solitude of her room, Clara sank onto the rug beside her bed and stared out the window into the shadowy night. Reaching up to her nightstand, her fingers grasped her Bible, and she settled it on her lap. Her heart throbbed with fullness as she stroked the thin, well-worn pages.

Her mind replayed the words from Pastor Henderson's message. *Love in its truest form involves sacrifice.* As for light... she could use a good dose of it right about now. A tear dripped off the tip of her nose as she clasped her hands and bowed her aching head to thank the Lord for this most cherished Christmas gift.

Christmas was a quiet affair for Thomas. It had been for years. Slowly sipping his tea after the Christmas Eve service, he stood at the office window surveying the shadowy, tranquil street. Everyone would be at home with their families and thinking about loved ones far away on the front. Everyone but him. Grateful for the next day's dinner invitation from the Forsythes, he swallowed the painful reminder. Friends, though he had but few, were a blessing, of course, but a poor substitute for family. Shaking his head at the thought, he abandoned the cup of tea in the kitchen and headed upstairs for bed, only to toss restlessly until sleep mercifully claimed him.

But an unbidden image haunted his lonely mind. A smiling little girl of ten with long, thick, curly black hair. Sparkling blue eyes. Dimples that deepened with her smile. She beckoned to him and offered her hand. He stretched out his own hand to take hers, but as suddenly as she came, she disappeared.

Thomas's eyes snapped open, and he bolted upright. He shook his head to clear the mental picture. It was all a dream. Just another dream. But it had been so vivid... so... so... He scrubbed his hands over his face as a tear rolled off the tip of his nose, chased by several more, and for the first time in years, he let himself utter her name. "Oh, Bryn." A deep moan of anguish escaped through suppressed lips as he buried his head in his pillow and begged morning to come.

When dawn did finally arrive, he felt no better as he drank his tea in solitude. He thought of Kasey and Kavan. Richard and Elizabeth. The Forsythes and Clara. *What would it feel like to not be alone? To be together.* He nearly choked on the rising lump in his throat and shoved the unwelcome thoughts aside. There would be no Christmas gifts. There never was. Except for perhaps a single package from Wales, but even that hadn't arrived. *Must be the effects of wartime.*

He tried to interest himself in the volume of Sherlock Holmes stories Clara had left behind, but his mind refused to focus on the words. After rereading the same paragraph six times, he tossed the book aside in disgust. He almost wished the phone would ring with an emergency—anything to get his mind off the haunting sense of isolation crushing him. Retreating to his desk, he retrieved out a sheet of writing paper and began to write.

Dear Maranda and Donovan,

Thomas tapped his finger on the desk, unsure of what to write next, when knocking sounded at the kitchen door. He dropped his pen and rushed to answer it, nearly giddy with the possibility of a diversion, not stopping to think why a patient would be knocking on his back door. The door swung open upon a petite young woman, barely five feet tall, and a giant, redheaded man. Thomas's jaw dropped in incredulity.

"Happy Christmas, Doc," the man said with a broad grin on his jovial face as he enveloped the astonished doctor into a bear hug.

"Donovan, I... What's going on?" Thomas spluttered.

"May we come in?" the woman asked, smiling.

Thomas ushered them into the kitchen and quickly put on the kettle. Surveying the couple, he shook his head as if expecting them to vanish in a dream. Just like Bryn.

"We're real, Thomas," the woman spoke again and hugged him tightly to prove it.

A vision of the little dream girl flashed before his eyes, and he gripped the small woman. As a sudden thought crossed his mind, he jolted back. "Did something happen to her, Maranda? Is that why—?"

"She's fine, Thomas; they both are. We just didn't want you to be alone this Christmas," Maranda said, gently patting his cheek.

Her words took the starch out of him as he sank weakly into a nearby chair, dazed as he watched his friend take over the making of the tea. He couldn't believe they had travelled all the way from Wales just to make sure he wasn't alone. It was... touching.

Donovan Byrne was a broad-shouldered man, standing at the impressive height of six feet six inches, with a grin that seemed to fill the room as he fumbled with the tea kettle. His red hair held a rugged windblown look, indicating his frequent exposure to the elements. A natural talker, his green eyes sparkled as his booming laughter echoed in the kitchen. Although the Irishman was six years the doctor's senior, the two had been friends for more than twelve years.

Maranda was a petite young woman of nineteen, and she wore her dark curly hair pulled back in a ribbon that matched her eyes. She was quieter in nature than her husband of two years but every bit as friendly. Though Richard and Elizabeth's younger sister, she was unlike her siblings in many ways.

"I've been invited to dinner at the Forsythes; would you both come?" Thomas said at last when there was a pause in the conversation.

Maranda set a steaming cup of tea in front of him. "We wouldn't want to impose..."

"Elizabeth and Richard are both coming."

The young woman's eyes sparkled at the mention of her older siblings, and Donovan said with a chuckle, "We'll be there, Doc."

"Oh, and I nearly forgot. Here." Maranda held out a brown paper package to Thomas.

Accepting it with a smile, he untied the string, already knowing what was inside. He reverently ran his fingers over the cable stitches of two new navy cashmere sweaters. Swallowing hard, he cleared his throat. "Thank you," he whispered softly with a contented sigh. "I look forward to this every year."

CHAPTER 15

New Year's

31 December

THE WEEK after Christmas was quiet at the clinic. Thomas tended to a handful of house calls and appointments, while new medicine shipments occupied Clara, but the days dragged painfully. Fog shrouded Newhaven all week long, dampening the jovial holiday spirit. However, when the fog lifted on New Year's Eve, church bells tolled, and the community lined High Street to sing in the New Year.

Thomas pedalled along Lewes Road towards the north end of town in the bitter cold to avoid the celebration mayhem. Silent stars twinkled overhead, and a gentle hush fell over the landscape as he passed the cemetery beside the boarding house. Ahead lay the downs. Veering off the road to a grassy bank on his right, he dropped his bicycle, climbed to the hillcrest, and inhaled the night air. The gurgle of the River Ouse, a dark thread snaking across the shadowy landscape, and the metallic twang of church bells echoed softly in the distance behind him. He fixed his gaze on the northwest horizon. Hundreds of miles over those grassy rolling hills lay home.

The pealing bells ceased. The echoes died away. It was midnight.

Thomas stood transfixed for several minutes before carefully descending the hill. It was time to return home. Or at least to the place he called *home* for now. The rushing, frigid air stung his face. *God, if You really are there, let 1918 be different.* His heart murmured the prayer all the way back to Newhaven. Had he really just prayed?

The clinic was dark as he mounted the back steps. He hesitated as the door handle turned without resistance under his grasp —he clearly remembered locking it before he left. Drawing out his Webley from his hip holster, he flicked on his torch as he entered and kept his back against the wall. A movement caught his attention on the right. Wheeling the gun to cover it, he found himself staring down the barrel of a Ruby pistol held by a cloaked figure.

"Chantelle?" he choked.

"*Bonjour*, Doctor," the phantom returned with a smile in her voice as she holstered her gun, Thomas doing the same before lighting a lamp to chase away the shadows.

"What are you doing here? It's not safe."

Chantelle lowered her hood and her curls tumbled around her slim shoulders. "Everyone's occupied with the New Year. I've been waiting for ages. Do tell me you were out celebrating."

Thomas set the tea kettle on the stove, eager for something warm to thaw the damp chill in his bones. "You know me better than that."

She scowled. "You're hopeless, Lindsey."

"And you're reckless, my dear."

With a toss of her head that reminded him of Lena, Chantelle countered, "Someone has to be."

He stepped closer to her and laid firm hands on her shoulders. "But not sixteen-year-old French girls."

"I'm not a child!"

He crossed his arms. "No," he drawled patiently, "but I still need you to be safe."

"You care that much?" Her hazel eyes softened ever so slightly.

"I care enough to have you replaced if you keep taking these foolish risks."

She raised her chin indignantly, and Thomas chucked it good-naturedly with his knuckle. "And you know I would. You've eluded capture, escaped from gaol, and survived a shipwreck. You won't be lucky forever." When she showed no signs of backing down, he gentled his tone. "I made a promise to your father to keep you safe, and I intend to keep it."

Immediately, the girl dropped her gaze and stood silently analysing his words. "Very well, sir. I shall be more careful—for your sake."

Pounding sounded on the kitchen door, and terror sprang into Chantelle's eyes. Thomas shoved her into the hall, whispering, "Out the front door. Wait for me at Kasey's."

She drew up her hood and vanished.

Once Thomas heard the front door click a moment later, he opened the kitchen door and found Richard on the step. Thomas ushered him into the warm kitchen. "What are you doing here? Take a chair."

Richard accepted the offered seat as Thomas poured two cups of tea from the now whistling kettle. "I saw your light on."

Thomas inwardly winced. He should have remembered to draw the curtains before he left and certainly before lighting the lamp while Chantelle was there. At least she hadn't been visible from her position. He gave himself a mental shake; with all that was at stake, he couldn't afford to be careless.

"I leave later this morning," Richard continued, seeming not to notice Thomas's silence. "Need anything before I go?"

Thomas set a cup in front of Richard and shook his head. Opening the cupboard, he wondered what to offer his friend. Though Richard protested he wasn't hungry, Thomas knew otherwise from the man's unusually gaunt frame. Richard was notorious for forgetting to take time for meals. Much like Thomas himself. Pulling out a cream tart Clara had left for him in the icebox, he cut two slices and handed one to Richard. Taking a bite of his own piece, Thomas sat down across from his friend and sipped his tea. The warm liquid seeped through his chilled frame and the tart sweetened his otherwise dismal evening.

"Did you look at that envelope I brought?" Richard asked between bites.

"I did." Thomas knew this conversation had been coming; he was only surprised it had taken Richard this long to seek him out for it.

"And?"

"It's still not much to go on."

"Face it; she could very well be The Piper."

Thomas pursed his lips and knit his brows thoughtfully. There was no logical reason for Clara to be The Piper, and the information didn't line up. Especially considering their last meeting with Jennings. She was hiding something, but that didn't mean she was guilty. The only way to find out was to prove the point. "Can you delay your trip till tomorrow?"

Richard frowned. "What do you have in mind?"

"Clara mentioned something about galavanting down to the beach this morning to watch the sunrise. Dawn of the new year or some such nonsense. See if you can get anything out of her."

"Can't see me having more success than you."

Thomas waved his hand. "You're the brother of her best friend. If Elizabeth has vouched for you, she might open up."

"Leave my sister out of this. I don't want her hurt," Richard replied darkly.

Thomas didn't argue. Elizabeth was one subject he and Richard would never agree upon, so he changed tactics. "Fine. If she *is* The Piper and we don't know that till too late because of you, don't blame me." His chair groaned as he coolly shoved himself away from the table and stalked over to the sink, waiting for the weight of his words to take effect. The only man who hated failure more than he did was Richard Morgan.

"Fine. I'll do it," Richard muttered, rising. "It's a good thing I consider you a friend, Lindsey, because someday you're going to get yourself into a mess that neither of us can fix."

Thomas leaned against the counter triumphantly, and he raised an eyebrow over the rim of his cup. "I hardly think so."

Richard left soon after, and as the church bells rang one o'clock, Thomas tapped softly on Kasey's front door. The captain answered the knock, his eyes bleary with weariness and his limp much more pronounced than usual as he ushered Thomas inside.

Thomas grimaced as he watched the old captain. "Sorry about this, Kasey. We'll make it quick."

Kasey waved his concern off as Chantelle made her appearance from a side room. She handed Thomas an envelope and plopped down next to him on the sofa.

Thomas scanned the note furiously. "You can't be serious? How did they know about Simms's location?"

Chantelle grimaced. "Someone called Merryn had met with him, and the next thing we know, he's dead. I need another identity card sent to Boulogne."

"I'll go and see Alaina tomorrow." Thomas rubbed his forehead. "She owes me a favour."

"And you were worried about *my* unnecessary risks," she muttered.

"We've got a dead agent and a stolen message. Did Simms hint at what he found out before he died?"

"Not a word. Any ideas as to The Piper's identity yet?"

Thomas shook his head. "It might be an agent outside of Newhaven with an accomplice inside, but we haven't been able to pin it to anyone specifically yet."

Chantelle squeezed his hand. "God has not abandoned us. We'll make it, Thomas. Anything else you want me to look into?"

"Any information you can find on who this Merryn is and..."

Thomas hesitated. "The failed '05 Calais mission under William Melville, if you have a chance."

She frowned. "How is that related?"

"Consider it a personal favour."

She shrugged, and Kasey whispered something to her before she slipped out the door. No doubt where she was to meet Kavan so he could steal her back to France before daybreak. Channel crossings were as difficult as they were dangerous with the threat of German U-boats. Smuggling a French spy in and out of England only made things more complicated.

Thomas stared vacantly into the hearth fire. He glanced up as a strong, fatherly hand clasped his shoulder.

"Have faith, lad," the captain's gentle cadence whispered.

"I'm afraid I'm fresh out."

"You've got to let go of the past or you'll never be able to embrace the future."

Thomas laughed bitterly. "The past is all I have left."

CHAPTER 16

The Birthday Surprise

1 January 1918

BEFORE THE SUN WAS UP, Clara slipped out of the boarding house and strolled down to the beachfront. It was low tide, so she ambled over the rocky quay to the strip of sand between the rocks and the waves. Sea spray misted over her as the wind whipped her skirt about her ankles. A golden thread laced across the eastern sky, heralding the first dawn of the new year. A promise of new beginnings, new hopes.

"Good morning to you," a smooth voice called behind her.

She glanced over her shoulder and smiled politely. "Mr. Morgan."

"Would it be too forward of me to request to join your company?"

Truthfully, she craved solitude at that moment, but instead she gave a half-hearted wave of her hand. "Be my guest."

He offered her his arm, and she accepted it reluctantly. Richard Morgan was suave and polished. Too much so for her comfort. They wandered in awkward silence for several moments before he asked, "How are you enjoying Newhaven?"

She shrugged nonchalantly. "It's charming."

"What do you like best?"

She had to hand it to the man—he was pleasant and subtle, but his conversation with Thomas all those weeks back had put her on edge about him. Halting her steps, she removed her hand from his arm. "I know what you're doing, and it's not worth your time. I would advise you not to interfere in my business unless you have a death wish."

Richard's eyebrows raised in surprise. "Is that a threat, Miss Dankworth? I thought we could be considered friends."

Clara met her companion's gaze with calm assurance, but there was something in his emerald depths. A lurking shadow. "I never threaten, but it is a warning, and I believe you already know too much."

~

2 January

The next morning, Thomas entered the supply room, fumbling with his cravat that refused to tie properly. "Could you stay on call tonight? I have a meeting and won't be back till tomorrow," he asked, tugging the offending piece of fabric again in dissatisfaction.

Clara glanced up curiously from the shelves. "Of course." She grinned as she watched him. "Do you want some help?"

"No," he growled.

She chuckled and continued marking inventory with a shake of her head.

"There," Thomas triumphed a minute later, satisfied with his tie at last, adding as he sauntered out the door, "I'll call to check in at eight this evening from the Midland Hotel in Derby."

"Tell the lady I say hello," Clara called teasingly after him.

Thomas stopped dead in his tracks and whirled around with a fierce frown. "I didn't say what I was doing."

"You didn't have to. You are in your Sunday suit jacket and

best cravat on a Wednesday morning. You aren't taking your bag, which means it isn't a medical case. My staying on call overnight indicates you are heading out of town. Plus, your shoes are polished, and you combed your hair instead of running your fingers through it as you usually do."

Thomas's jaw hung slack, and he blinked in astonishment when she finished her Holmes-like harangue. Did nothing escape the woman's notice? He felt his face flush as he muttered, "Why did I even bother?" before escaping down the hall away from Clara's merry laughter.

At the ticket window, Thomas drummed his fingers along the counter impatiently. Everything around him reflected the toil of the war. Worn paint. Scuffed floors. Several men in uniforms waiting for the Seaford and Folkestone trains.

The brunette at the counter had clearly stayed up too late on New Year's to be well rested enough to be pleasant for an early morning shift. Yawning, she handed him a ticket. "Due in fifteen minutes. Next!"

Thomas gave her a nod and plopped down on a nearby bench to peruse the day-old newspaper. A headline on the third page caught his eye.

Ten years since the tragic death of Parliament member Joseph Cromwell and his family at their home, Hollyside Manor, in Colchester.

Frowning, he skimmed the article. Joseph Cromwell had been a prominent Member of Parliament for nearly three decades when he, his wife Marian, his youngest daughter Clarissa, and their butler were mysteriously found dead one night. No charges were ever laid due to lack of suspects. Thomas shook his head disgustedly and tucked the paper in his inner coat pocket as a train whistle shrilled in the distance.

When he reached Derby several hours later, he stopped to use the public telephone. "Reverend Moore," he told the operator.

A moment later, a young woman's voice floated across the line. "Hello?"

"Guess who?" he teased.

The woman laughed. "What do you need, Lindsey?"

"Have dinner with me at our café in ten minutes?"

"Time me," and the line fell silent.

Thomas chuckled and started down the street. At the aforesaid café, he secured a table and waited. Flushed and breathless, a young woman with rich brown eyes, a riot of shoulder-length copper curls, and bright red lips plopped into the chair across from him.

He consulted his pocket watch. "Nine minutes and thirty-seven seconds."

"You doubted I would make it," she accused.

Thomas handed her a glass of water. "Never, Alaina, but as always, you forgot your hat."

She rolled her eyes, and water dribbled down her chin as she drank eagerly. Letting out a loud sigh, she dabbed her chin with her napkin and flashed him a grin. Surveying his polished appearance, she groaned. "You could have at least warned me to change my dress," and she quickly pulled out a compact mirror and tube of lipstick from her handbag.

Thomas chuckled amiably. "You look fine. Happy Birthday, *fy ffrind*."

Realisation shone in Alaina's eyes, and she beamed at him as she tucked her cosmetics away. After the waiter took their orders, she crossed her arms on the table's edge and whispered, "How's your new assistant?"

Thomas frowned at her curiously. "You know about her?"

"Of course, I do. I did her paperwork."

"Anything you can share with me?"

"No can do. You know the rules. What's she like? I never met her."

Thomas sighed and offered her a brief character sketch of Clara Dankworth, filled with several complaints.

"Ah, I see she hasn't fallen for your charm, and that's what's bothering you."

"You think I'm charming?" Thomas feigned innocence.

She snorted. "You are when you choose to be, and your charm can make anyone do anything for you."

"Even you?"

Her soft eyes locked on his as she sobered instantly. "You know the extent of what I would do for you."

Live and die were the unspoken words, but Thomas heard them just the same.

After a moment's pause, Alaina sipped her water again and smiled, changing the subject. "She'll be good for you."

"Whose side are you on?

She gave her riot of curls a shake. "It's not a matter of sides. It's a matter of heart, but surely you didn't come all the way to Derby to complain about Clara Dankworth and have supper with me?"

"What if I did?"

"Liar," she accused saucily.

He grinned. "You haven't changed."

"Neither have you, you old scoundrel. Now, what do you need this time?"

He put on an offended air. "When have I ever asked you for anything?"

Alaina's eyes danced mischievously over the rim of her teacup. "Only every time you come to see me."

"I can't be that bad."

"You are, and you know it."

"Chantelle needs a new identity card."

"Kell's orders?"

Thomas raised an eyebrow at the mention of MI5's leader. "Off record; you know she's not on the payroll."

"Lindsey—"

"Come, Alaina, help a chap out."

Her jawline softened, and he saw her defenses dropping. "It would mean a lot to me, you know. Please."

She sighed. "Only for you."

"There's a dear. Send them to me, and I'll get them across the Channel. If anything comes of it, I'll take responsibility."

She grinned ruefully. "Nice to know you have my back."

"Always," he replied softly.

When they were finished, Thomas paid for their meal and escorted Alaina back to the parsonage, where she boarded with the elderly minister and his wife.

"It was good to see you, even if it was only to help you out of a scrape... again," she said with a sad smile.

Thomas flashed her a grin and tried handing her a small stack of banknotes, but she shoved them away. "Keep them. I don't want your money."

"Thank you. And remember, I'll take responsibility if anything happens."

Alaina studied him seriously. "You say that every time. I certainly hope you never have to." She stood on tiptoe and kissed his cheek.

So do I, Thomas thought as he left her and hurried to his hotel for the night, absently rubbing away the lipstick smudge.

In the quiet evening hours, Clara carefully dusted the bookshelves in the office. She loved studying the volumes; many were old favourites, but a few titles were new to her. Reaching up to dust the top shelf, her fingers brushed against an oilcloth bundle. Pulling it down, she unwrapped it. There was a file inside. When it fell open, a gasp escaped her lips as she stared at a picture of herself. Judging by the white cap that hid her chestnut hair and the white uniform she wore, it was the picture taken in Brussels when she first worked under Edith Cavell.

She dropped into Thomas's desk chair to peruse the

remaining contents of the file. In addition to the photograph, she found records of her trip from Halifax to Brussels. Her nursing certificate. Several notes written in two types of penmanship, neither of which she recognised. The last things she noticed were several entries made in Thomas's scrawling hand.

Reads Holmes, Dickens, Austen, and the Illustrated London News.
Strong interest in politics and social reforms.
Twenty-one years of age.
Spent time in Brussels, Rotterdam, Switzerland, and Folkestone before coming to Newhaven.

Clara's eyes burned as she read the brief account of her life. Why would Thomas have a file on her? And more importantly, how had he managed to find out so much?—though it was very little, to be sure. Most of his scrawled notes were snippets of conversations from the last two months.

A glance at her watch told her he was late in calling. Lifting the telephone receiver, she asked the operator for the Midland Hotel in Derby. She had every intention of inquiring about the secret file. All these weeks, she had thought they were moving past their mutual distrust of each other and settling into a comfortable routine. How wrong she had been.

Thomas was perched on the edge of his bed about to retire for the night when his room phone rang. Wearily easing himself up, he crossed the room to answer it, and Clara's voice came over the line.

"What's wrong?" he asked in alarm.

"You said you'd call an hour ago." Her voice was frigid and distant.

He grimaced. "Sorry about that. I was... occupied."

"You obviously made it to Derby."

"Yes, and I'll be back in the morning as promised." Silence. "Miss Dankworth, are you well?"

"Would you give me an honest answer if I asked you something?"

"I think you know the extent of what I would do for you," he returned lightly, his words mirroring Alaina's from earlier in the evening.

"Why do you have a hidden file on me?"

The words felt like a swift blow to his stomach. That was the last question he had imagined her asking. Shoving the sick feeling aside, he cleared his throat. "How did you find it?"

"That's beside the point. I want to know why you have been looking into me." Her voice held a fire he had never heard before. When he didn't reply, she added, "Because you didn't trust me?"

"Not exactly," he protested weakly.

"Because you didn't want me interfering with your plans?"

Thomas inwardly groaned. Why did she have so much uncanny insight? "Something like that," he said slowly, keeping his voice steady.

"Since you never told me your plans, I see little harm of that."

"To your credit, you gave me very little information."

He heard her snort. "That's why you put your... your... *minions* on me? You're not the man I thought you were."

Her voice lowered a few decibels with the last words, and then the line fell dead. She had hung up.

Setting the phone back on the receiver, Thomas groaned and flopped down on the bed. Nothing had been this complicated until Clara Dankworth stepped off the train in Newhaven. He had never met a more insightful, intelligent, inscrutable, and yet intriguing woman. And never had he felt so guilty for doing his job.

CHAPTER 17

A Dinner Invitation

7 January

AT FIVE O'CLOCK, Clara straightened the supply shelves one last time. Thomas was due back at any moment from an emergency call to an accident near the train station. Hopefully he would bring the mail back with him. Moving to the office, she tidied the loose papers on her desk and placed the list of tomorrow's house calls on Thomas's. Pausing at the window, she glanced out expectantly into the dark street. Through the grey dusk and drizzling rain, an umbrella came into focus. She snatched a navy sweater off the hatstand and hurried to fetch a towel from the examination room.

In the dry safety of the waiting room, rivers of water ran from Thomas's shoes and umbrella as he emerged from its cover. Clara tossed the towel over his head, and he cried out in surprise.

"Dry off," she said crisply. "I'd rather not mop the whole floor again."

Thomas tousled his hair with the towel and then mopped up

the small puddle he had created before shedding his wet coat. It had been five days since the incident in Derby and things were still frigid between them. He couldn't blame her—he had betrayed a tremendous portion of her trust.

"Worst weather yet," was his muffled remark as he tugged the navy cashmere sweater she handed him over his head. She said nothing, and they retreated mutely to the office.

"Any mail?" she questioned from the doorway as he sat down at his desk.

"A dinner invitation from Colonel Jennings with orders to attend for business purposes."

Clara coughed. "I beg your pardon?"

"'Doctor Lindsey and Miss Dankworth,'" Thomas read the invitation amusedly.

She arched an eyebrow at him. "I will have to regretfully decline."

"Do you have a good excuse, nurse?" he asked in a daring tone.

She straightened. "Always."

"I'm replying immediately." He picked up his pen to carry out his threat. He wanted to laugh—anything to break the palpable tension—but wisely held himself in check. "I thought all young ladies enjoyed parties," he added lightly.

"I detest them."

"Surely they can't be that bad. When did you last attend one?"

"It was—" Clara stopped herself from finishing the sentence and a faraway look crept over her face. "A long time ago," she finished lamely.

Thomas made a mental note of her hesitation when a thought struck him. "Is it the matter of dress that concerns you?"

His words brought her focus back to him, and she shook her head. "No, I have something that could suit with a little work."

"It's all settled then. This Saturday I'll be by the boarding house in the car to fetch you at quarter to seven if that suits you."

"Fine," was Clara's terse reply as she fiercely jabbed her hatpin in place.

He smirked. "Take an umbrella; you'll need it," he offered, looking over the smartly written list she had left him.

She availed herself of the offer and then paused at the door. "You do intend to go then?"

"Of course, the order was to you as well as to me," he returned, not looking up.

"You have not always taken so well to orders and have had no qualms in breaking them in the past."

This made Thomas glance up at her. "Touché."

"Good evening, Doctor," and with a snap of the umbrella, she was gone.

In her room later that evening, Clara opened her travelling trunk and lifted out a large tissue-wrapped package. Unwrapping it with reverent fingers, the emerald silk brushed coolly against her skin. She smiled absently as she stroked the fabric between thumb and forefinger—it had been years since she had worn anything this fine. Holding it against herself and peering into the small mirror, she sighed at the number of alterations that would be necessary to bring it up to the current fashion. She had told Thomas it needed a little work. More accurately, it needed a miracle. Perhaps Elizabeth and Mrs. Forsythe would help; she knew both to be excellent seamstresses.

The two women were delighted when Clara asked them. The Scotswoman ran an expert eye over the dress on the bed. "We'll shorten the hem and add the material to the sleeves."

"And add a little lace to the neckline," Elizabeth added. Mrs. Forsythe gave an approving nod.

Clara smiled at the women's enthusiasm. As little as she wanted to attend the party, it was a relief to see the two women so excited about a project.

Elizabeth held out the dress to Clara. "Why don't you try it on now so we can start right away?"

"Are you sure you don't mind?"

"Not in the slightest, lassie. It's been a long time since I've had anything this pretty to work on," Mrs. Forsythe assured her as her broad face crinkled into a smile.

Clara quickly slipped into the silk dress and spent the next half hour being turned about, poked, and prodded as the two seamstresses discussed their vision for the dress.

9 January

Upon returning from a late house call, Thomas found Clara filing patient records. Weariness plagued him to the core as he dropped his bag on the chair and shuffled towards his desk. He glanced at the clock; it was already past eleven.

"The Prices' housekeeper, Mrs. Landis, called while you were out. She wants you to check on Emily. She's been running a fever all day. I volunteered to go, but she said Emily was insistent you take the call." Clara met his gaze. "I can stay till you come back."

Thomas sighed and wearily retrieved his bag again, leaving the room without a word. As he stepped out the kitchen door into the night air, he debated between the car and the bicycle. Deciding a ride in the open air might improve his mental state, he opted for the bicycle and pedaled southwest towards the Price estate.

Hyde, the butler, met him at the door and ushered him upstairs to Emily's room. The girl reclined against a heap of pillows, her cheeks flushed, and her eyes closed as Mrs. Landis hovered near the bed.

"Emily," Thomas said softly as he approached the girl.

"Doctor?" her voice croaked as her green eyes fluttered open a crack.

Opening his bag, he retrieved a thermometer and slipped it under Emily's tongue. "Quite a high fever you have," he commented as he read the reading. After examining her throat and listening to her lungs, Thomas smiled reassuringly. "Seems to be a touch of the flu, but it's nothing a bit of rest and plenty of liquids won't fix."

"Are you sure?" Mrs. Landis pressed, and Thomas saw the deep concern in the matronly woman's eyes.

"Very sure. Would you fetch some weak tea for her?"

Emily moaned, and Thomas turned back to the bed as Mrs. Landis scurried out of the room. "Is there something you're not telling me, Emily?"

"Father had a visitor," she whispered hoarsely. "An Irishman. Father called him Fallamhan. Also, he's attending the colonel's party this Saturday. Father is, I mean."

The message put Thomas on immediate alert, but he smiled at the invalid. "Thank you for telling me. Now rest up, and Miss Dankworth or I will stop in tomorrow."

As he pedaled back towards Bridge Street, Emily's message replayed in his mind. He offered Clara an absent good-bye and trudged upstairs to retire for the night. Price's presence at the party could provide the perfect opportunity, but he needed help.

An opportunity presented itself the next afternoon when he found Clara washing implements in the sink. From his position in the doorway, he informed her of the situation and his solution.

"You want to break into the Price house? While he's at Jennings's?" Clara spluttered as she whirled around. "Surely you jest."

Thomas scowled at her hands, dripping water all over the floor. "Surely I don't."

"You're supposed to obey the rules, you know."

"What rules?" Thomas deadpanned. "I would rather die as I am than live according to someone else's rules."

"Even God's?"

"I'm afraid I haven't much use for or faith in the Almighty, at present."

Clara sighed as she caught up a towel to dry her hands and faced the doctor. "That's what I thought. You're on your own. I'm not breaking the law for you."

"Miss Dankworth, it's the only way."

"Doing the wrong thing for the right cause doesn't justify the means. Come up with something within the legal parameters, then we can talk."

Thomas crossed his arms impatiently and huffed his frustration. "Do you have a better plan?" He instantly regretted asking that question as he saw the gleam in Clara's eyes.

"We will attend the party as planned, and you can *talk* to Emily later."

"I can't involve civilians."

"That's rich coming from you. I've lost count of how many you've involved already. Emily included."

She had backed him into a corner, and they both knew it. But he wasn't about to give it up. If she wouldn't help him, he would find another way. He always did.

~

12 January

Despite Clara's concern that the dress would never satisfy the vision of the seamstresses, the last seam was sewn and the last bit of lace added when Saturday evening came.

Elizabeth expertly twisted Clara's long chestnut hair into a beautiful chignon and added some curls. "You look absolutely stunning!"

"Only because you worked wonders, Lizzie."

"Poppycock!" Elizabeth laughed. "There! It's done, and you look positively splendid!"

A tap on the door interrupted Clara's reply. "The doctor's here and waiting," Mrs. Forsythe called through the door.

"You go down first. I'll follow in a moment," Clara said softly. She shut the door and knelt beside the trunk after Elizabeth tripped out of the room. Touching a small notch on the inside, a panel opened from the false bottom. Hastily snatching up a necklace case from the hidden compartment, she closed the panel quickly and locked the trunk. Opening the small jewellery case, she lifted out a string of pearls and clasped them around her neck. She caught her reflection in the mirror and gave herself a small smile. It was time.

Thomas glanced at the parlour clock and tapped his foot impatiently as he waited perched on the sofa's edge. Clara was two minutes late.

"Easy, Doc," Robbie whispered from across the room.

He shot the boy a glare. "There's nothing wrong with me."

Robbie chuckled and flashed him a knowing grin.

Rolling his eyes with a stifled groan, Thomas rose and strolled to the window. A gentle rustling noise behind him caused him to turn around. *Finally...* He felt his jaw slacken and his eyes blink blankly.

Robbie snickered then beamed at Clara as he bowed. "You look grand, Miss Clara."

Somehow, the word *grand* didn't seem to go far enough to describe the emerald silk vision before him. Thomas tugged at his cravat, which suddenly felt too tight. Recovering himself, he sent a stern glance to the young miscreant, then bowed politely to Clara. "Shall we go, Miss Dankworth?"

Clara rested her hand on his offered arm, and he led her to the door, but not before he caught sight of Elizabeth's mischievous grin from where she sat on the stairway. He silently groaned. What *was* this town coming to?

Kerridge met them at the front door of the Jenningses' estate and ushered them inside. The house glowed with light, and a sea of voices murmured around them. After taking their coats, the butler led them to the drawing room where he announced them by name for the company.

Colonel Jennings introduced his wife, Hannah, who greeted them warmly. "Keep your ears and eyes open. Price is here," Jennings whispered as an aside before Hannah drew him away to welcome another newcomer.

Thomas twitched, and Clara nudged him, mimicking Robbie's voice. "Easy, Doc." He scowled slightly, but she only smiled.

"We're keeping our finger on the pulse of society. It isn't hard." With those words, she floated off to a group of ladies in the corner and was soon chatting merrily.

Mingling in society was far from his forte, but Thomas reluctantly followed her example and joined a group of men, only to fidget uncomfortably more than he spoke. When dinner was announced, he firmly clasped Clara's elbow and guided her to the dining room.

"Was it that hard?" she whispered lightly as he took a seat beside her.

"Don't ask," he retorted between gritted teeth.

Clara rolled her eyes and shifted her attention to her plate and the gentleman on her right. Talk centered around Prime Minister David Lloyd George's recent stirring speech, outlining the country's war aims and conditions for peace.

Halfway through the meal, Kerridge, the butler, announced an urgent call had come for the doctor. Rising, Thomas graciously thanked his hosts and apologised for the inconvenience before hurrying out of the room.

~

Thomas crept across the spacious lawn of the Price estate towards the trellis on the east side. Careful to hide any footprints in the damp garden soil, he slowly began his ascent of the ancient woodwork, earnestly hoping it would support his weight. At the top, he tapped softly on the windowpane, and Emily shoved the curtain aside a moment later to open the window. Pulling himself in, he shut the window behind him and swept the curtain closed to hide the light. He had successfully made it into Price's study without Clara's help.

"Thank you for your assistance," Thomas said to Emily. "Can you stand guard outside the door?"

As the clock struck nine, Emily took up her position, and Thomas dug through Price's desk. At first, he found only ordinary items. An inkwell, an address list, and stationery paper. Balling his fists in frustration, he knelt on the plush carpet and felt underneath the desk for any hidden catches. Nothing.

Thomas surveyed the room with a critical eye. *If I were a German sympathiser, where would I hide information I didn't want to fall into the wrong hands?* He smirked ruefully. *I would burn it, and I would never get caught.* The thought jogged his mind as his eye caught the expansive gun display behind the desk. Rummaging through the desk drawer for a key, Thomas carefully inserted one into the lock and to his amazement, found that it opened. Running his gaze along the impressive line of firearms, he narrowed in on a pistol in the middle—he recognised it as German-made. Carefully removing it from its position, he peered down the barrel and with the help of a pencil, recovered a paper scrap from inside. He studied it intently in the faint lamplight. Half of it was smudged beyond recognition, but he could still make out parts of the message. It was addressed to Edward Price.

Proceed as planned—don't send money directly—arms shipment—Wicklow—

Thomas peered intently at the missive but couldn't make out the date. *A German arms shipment heading for Ireland, but when?* He continued reading.

Fallamhan will receive shipment—sending Merryn—Sincerely, Anton Detweiler.

Fallamhan and Merryn were still relatively new names to Thomas, having only heard of them recently, but he was all too familiar with Detweiler, the powerful German government official Price was in cahoots with. Hurriedly scribbling down a copy of the message, Thomas shoved his copy into his trouser pocket and the original back in the pistol barrel. Emily slipped in just as he was locking the gun cabinet.

"You have to go. Father's back early. Hurry!"

Thomas scanned the office and ensured he had left it in decent enough order. Throwing the window open, he thanked Emily, scurried down the trellis, and darted across the lawn without a backwards glance.

The last of the guests had gone, and Thomas had yet to return to the Jenningses' estate. The colonel was oblivious to the real reason for the doctor's sudden departure and offered for the chauffeur to take Clara home. She was too exhausted to refuse, and her head ached from the seventeen hairpins scraping her scalp, which Lizzie had placed with surgical-like precision.

The parlour clock struck eleven as she crept in at the front door, followed by the ringing of the telephone. She answered it quickly to avoid waking the rest of the house.

It was Thomas. "My apologies for not explaining anything earlier and failing to return for you."

"How was your *emergency*?" She was too tired to censor the sarcasm lacing her words. While she had been surprised by Thomas accompanying her to the party instead of breaking in as he had planned, it hadn't taken her long to realise her mistake. His *medical emergency* had really been a *political emergency*. The man was mad.

"All's well that ends well," and from the tone of his voice, she knew he had found whatever he was looking for. "Again, my apologies. Oh, and Miss Dankworth? You looked well tonight."

She hesitated.

"The compliment was sincerely meant. Simply accept it. I'll see you first thing on Monday," and the line went dead.

Dazed, Clara hung up with a growing sense of annoyance tempered with curiosity, all the while hoping that with whatever evidence Thomas had procured, the case with Price would be wrapped up soon—very soon.

CHAPTER 18

Face from the Past

14 January

THOMAS STROLLED DOWN to the harbour at twilight to see Kasey. The old sea captain stood smoking his pipe as he leaned against the rail on the promenade overlooking the Channel. The strong, golden light from the lighthouse at the end of the breakwater swung lazily, flinging its friendly rays far into the distance.

"Any news?" Thomas asked in a low voice after greeting his friend.

"Chantelle wasn't there."

Thomas froze. He couldn't have heard the words correctly. "What did you say?"

"I waited as long as I could; she never showed. I had to shove off without her."

Thomas's legs shook, and he sagged heavily against the rail. "She's never missed."

"I know. That's what worries me."

He groaned and balled his fists, horror gripping his heart. "She promised to be careful." His voice fell to a whisper, "You know what they did to Gabrielle Petit." He shuddered at the thought of the girl facing her death in front of a firing squad

"Pray it isn't that, lad."

Thomas snorted. "Pray? Doesn't seem to do much good. If God let something happen to her, I—"

"You're not the Almighty, Thomas. You're only a man," Kasey interrupted firmly. "You can't control Him, and He doesn't answer to mere mortals." His voice softened. "If the Good Lord allowed her to be taken, He had a reason. I know you think you can run your own life, but His hands are far more capable than yours, son."

Thomas's jaw tightened, but he remained silent. Once, he might have agreed with the man's words, but that day had long passed. Too much hurt lay behind him, too much was at stake ahead.

Kasey squeezed his shoulder and left him alone in the deepening darkness with only the winking light for company. It was then that Thomas realised he had forgotten to ask Kasey if he knew anything about Fallamhan.

Several hours later, Thomas hunched over his desk, poring over the package of papers Chantelle had sent through Kasey the week prior to her disappearance. The lights were low, and the curtains drawn for the night. A knock on the kitchen door shattered the stillness. Growling with frustration, Thomas swept the papers into the middle drawer and stomped to the kitchen. With his hand on the gun near his hip, he opened the door a crack.

A short man stood on the top step with cat-like eyes reflecting in the low light from the kitchen. He wore a dark trench coat and bowler hat tilted low over his face. "Good evening, Doctor," the voice purred.

A shiver passed down Thomas's spine at the sound, but he kept his voice level. "What do you want?"

"I have information you may be interested in."

"Doubtful."

"I was sent by a mutual friend of ours."

Mutual friend? If the man truly had information, there were only two possible senders—Crouthers or Richard. Information from the latter would be welcome, but from the former, not so much. Thomas held back a sigh and cautiously let the man enter, still keeping his hand on his gun. The stranger removed his hat and laid it on the table, helping himself to a chair. Thomas sat across from him and stared intently at the newcomer, whose blond hair shone in the dim light, and his eyes held a malice Thomas couldn't understand.

"Your name?" Thomas broke the silence.

"Konrad Reynolds."

He didn't recognise it. "What information do you have that I could possibly want?"

"Does the name Colette Gibson mean anything to you?" Reynolds leaned forward conspiratorially as he watched for Thomas's reaction.

Thomas kept his face impassive. "Should it? There's no one in town by that name."

"Don't be coy, Doctor. We both know who she is, and I'm here to warn you about her."

"And why would I need warning?"

"She's using you."

Thomas snorted. "I beg your pardon?"

"She's an intelligent woman. She uses her charm to get information out of even the best of our agents. That's why she was sent from Rotterdam, you know."

Thomas stared at the man. Clara was friendly, genuine, and without a double motive, but he was curious about the man's information. "What do you know about it?"

"She was sent back to England on probation for fraternising with the enemy."

The room began to spin before Thomas's eyes. This was not what he had expected. "You can't be serious. What proof do you have?"

Reynolds slid a photograph across the table. "Have a look."

Leisurely, Thomas lifted the image and ran a critical eye over it. It was Clara side by side with a young man. "Am I supposed to be impressed?"

"The inscription on the back."

Thomas flipped the photo. The script was unfamiliar, but the words were clear: *Colette Gibson and Franz Zimmerman.* His lip curled at the name, and acid burned at the back of his throat. Zimmerman had been a double agent for the Germans and the British... until he went rogue. He had cost more than one agent their life, including Thomas's former partner in Folkestone. *If Sumpter had just kept his mouth shut—* Thomas clenched his teeth till his jaw ached. "She's The Piper?" he ground out.

"Seems to be. Don't feel too badly; you're not the first to have been fooled. You're working with the best."

Anger simmered in Thomas's chest as he steepled his fingers. Originally Franz had been suspected of being The Piper, but since the leak continued after his capture and execution, no one believed it was him. *Something doesn't line up, and as much as I hate to admit it, Jennings is rarely wrong when it comes to character. Clara had an alibi. How could—?* Snapping back to the conversation, Thomas asked, "Who sent you? Crouthers? For what purpose?"

The man tilted his head in apparent admission. "Needed solid proof against her, and he hoped you would get it out of her before she got too much out of you." Reynolds's mouth twisted into a smirk. "After all, aren't you one of the best yourself?" he taunted.

More likely another way to irritate me, Thomas thought with an inner eye roll. But what if Reynolds was right? Thomas *had* commissioned Richard for information. His friend had seemed to think Clara had a connection to The Piper, while Jennings vehemently discredited the theory. Jennings had also forbidden Thomas to dig for information. If he went to him now, Jennings would know the doctor had once again disregarded his instructions—a fatal mistake.

As if reading his victim's inner turmoil, a smug, twisted smile touched Reynolds's mouth as he stood to leave. "No charge for the information, Doctor. Goodnight."

Thomas barely heard the door close. All he heard was a confused pounding in his own ears. He slammed his fist on the table, but the smarting in his hand wouldn't drown out the warring confusion in his heart. Why had she *really* come?

Clara awoke to a clink on her window. Groaning and still half asleep, she wrapped her dressing gown around her and raised the window. Rubbing her eyes, she poked her head out, only to find Thomas glaring up at her with fire in his eyes. *Not again.* "What's going on? Is there an emergency?" She stifled a yawn.

"I believe you know, Miss Dankworth," he stated coolly. "I received notice this evening that you were sent back to England on probation for your connection to *Franz Zimmerman*."

Clara frowned and rubbed her eyes again. She had to be dreaming. "Are you daft? I wasn't sent back on probation. Who told you that?"

"Does it matter?"

"Yes. Because if his name was Konrad Reynolds, he's lying."

He paused, seemingly confused. "Why should I believe that? How do I know you aren't lying to me?" He crossed his arms. "Jennings is convinced you aren't The Piper, but I am not. I saw the picture."

"Upon my honour, there's a reasonable explanation for all this. You must believe me."

"Prove it."

She rubbed her temples as she could feel a headache coming on. "It's not that simple."

"But you admit to being in Rotterdam, *Colette Gibson*."

Clara cringed, and her temper flared. How had he found out? Reynolds, no doubt. *That two-timing, double-crossing...!* "Of course, I admit to being there—I was one of the hospital's head nurses!"

Thomas sneered and whirled away. "I don't believe a word of it," he threw back at her before disappearing into the night.

All hope of sleeping fled as Clara slammed the window and sank down on the edge of her bed with a hurt and angry heart. Pressing her fingers to her throbbing temples, she fought to regain her bearings, suddenly feeling helpless and utterly betrayed.

Her enemy was after her for reasons she could only imagine. Crouthers had sent her here when it was the last place she had wanted to go. Thomas seemed to have interests of his own for her stay here. And now he dashed cold water over her head with that ridiculous story. Oh, why hadn't she just told him who Reynolds really was? About her connection to Franz? She had been just as shocked as the rest when she found out he had turned rogue. *Not like Thomas would have believed me,* she thought bitterly.

"You're a fool, Clara Dankworth," she whispered. "Lord, I can't do this anymore. I just want to go home." Flinging herself face first into her pillow, she dissolved into a storm of pent-up tears. Anger, betrayal, and confusion coursed through her veins and found a release. An hour later, she finally found rest from the exhaustion and a weary heart. For now, sleep was the best medicine.

～

15 January

Before dawn, Clara slipped out the front door, valise in hand, setting out towards the train station. Mist hung low over the streets, and the cobblestones clicked softly under her heels, but not a soul stirred.

Thirty minutes later, she reached the train station and purchased a ticket to London. As she waited for the train, she reflected on the note she had left at the boarding house. Hopefully, the Forsythes would understand. Her anger had cooled overnight, but betrayal's painful sting still barbed her heart when she thought of Thomas's hasty words. The rest of the trip was lost on her as she fumbled about in a daze, but somehow managed to find herself at the Victoria Station and on her way into Belgravia. When she reached the bookshop, courage failed her at the door. Breathing a prayer that her boss would be reasonable, Clara bustled in at the front door.

Walter sat in his usual place behind the desk. He glanced up as she approached him, and his pale face puckered. "What are you doing here, Miss Clara?" he whispered, his eyes darting nervously around the empty store.

"I came to see Mr. Crouthers. Is he in?" Clara returned calmly.

"He's in, but he won't be happy to see you."

She bestowed a reassuring smile on the young man. "I'll take my chances, Walter; thank you," and she marched into the back room and up the stairs. At the office door, she gave a light rap, which was returned with a gruff, "Come in."

Clara wrinkled her nose as she entered the smoke-filled office and firmly shut the door behind her.

"What are you doing here?" Crouthers questioned.

Slowly, she approached the intimidating man behind his large desk. "I'm here on business."

"Your business is in Newhaven," Crouthers growled.

"Not anymore. I am requesting an immediate transfer, or else I leave the Service immediately and return home."

Crouthers's dark eyes narrowed to mere slits, his face florid with indignation. "Think you can order me around, you arrogant little hussy! You will do no such thing. You will go back to Newhaven this minute if I have to drag you there myself. And don't let me hear such balderdash from you again."

Startled at being so addressed by the man, Clara's spine stiffened. "After sending Reynolds to Lindsey to make him distrust me as some sort of sordid joke, I'll do no such thing."

She flinched as Crouthers brought a fist down on the desk with a roar. "Silence!"

Never had she seen him so angry... especially with her. He was a little rough around the edges but always courteous enough.

Crouthers withdrew paper and a pen from his desk and wrote in silence for several moments. Jamming the missive in an envelope, he rose and thrust it towards Clara. "Deliver this to Lindsey when you arrive. I'll hear about it if you don't." Grabbing her arm, he dragged her across the room. "As for my reasons, they are mine, and mine alone. You would do well to remember that." He shoved her out the door, slamming it behind her.

Clara trudged down the stairs and past Walter. Her arm ached from Crouthers's grip, and her shoulders slumped as she wove her way through Belgravia towards the train station. Her hands were tied. She had to return. Something was eating at Crouthers; he had never treated her so poorly in the past. Sniffing back tears, she straightened suddenly. "Fine. I'll play his game," she muttered. "And win it, too."

Once back in Newhaven, she marched to the boarding house and received many anxious inquiries as to the meaning of her rather cryptic note that morning. Brushing these off as gently as she could, she apologised for the undue concern and set off for the clinic. Pausing on the back step, she swallowed her pride and opened the door.

Thomas was in the office when she entered, and he stared at her with asperity, leaning back in his chair. "Well?" he asked after an uncomfortable silence.

Clara handed him the note from Crouthers. "Before you read it, however, I apologise for getting angry with you last night."

Thomas stared at her and cocked his head, the fire dying in his eyes. "How much did it gall you to say that?"

She grimaced and lowered her gaze. "More than I would care to admit. But I was wrong and hope you will forgive me."

"Apology accepted," Thomas returned hesitantly and ripped open the note.

Clara retreated to the kitchen while he read and helped herself to a cup of tea to calm the rapid beating in her heart. He hadn't apologised to her and still didn't appear to believe her, but perhaps the note would change his mind. She wrinkled her nose at the thought. Nothing changed Thomas Lindsey's mind unless he decided to change it. The stubborn man.

Thomas joined her in the kitchen several minutes later with the missive in hand. "You are to stay."

She turned on him sharply. "Not my choice," she muttered.

"It seems there was a misunderstanding. Crouthers cleared your name. My apologies." He shifted uncomfortably.

"Accepted," she returned with a brief nod.

Thomas left on his rounds, leaving Clara to see to several patients at the clinic, but once again, the easy camaraderie they had previously shared lay scattered in the dust at their feet.

CHAPTER 19

Trial by Poison

24 January

THOMAS CAUGHT a cab down to the harbour to meet
Kavan Grahame. The young Irishman worked with Kasey in the
shipping and contraband information business, but Kasey had
dropped a hint or two about Kavan serving more in a messenger
role. Thomas wasn't opposed to the idea—Kasey was after all
pushing seventy-five—but he needed to conduct a little reconnais-
sance on Kavan first.

The Hope Inn bustled with evening patrons as Thomas and
Kavan entered. Scores of uniformed men lined the tables, and the
waitresses kept their steins full. Jazz music crooned softly from the
gramophone in the corner as the pair claimed a secluded table
near the front window.

"What can I get for you, gentlemen?"

Thomas glanced up at the brunette waitress to whom the
tinkling voice belonged. "I don't suppose you have tea?"

The waitress wrinkled her nose. "Fresh out."

Thomas sighed heavily. "Coffee then."

"Make it two," Kavan added.

"You got it, darling." The young woman gave him a flirtatious wink.

Thomas rolled his eyes as she disappeared, only to return momentarily with the two cups of coffee.

Kavan flicked her a coin. "Thanks."

The woman's eyes gleamed as she caught it. She glanced at Thomas, but he lowered his eyes to the rim of his mug. The last thing he needed to deal with was a coquettish waitress. Shrugging, she tripped over to the next table.

"I need to know a few things about you, Kavan," Thomas said in low tones.

Kavan's forehead creased in a pensive frown, and he fortified himself with a long draught of coffee. "What did Kasey tell you about me?"

"Nothing more than you're his great-nephew, twenty-eight, and came from Courtmacsherry, Ireland. He vouches for you, and that's good enough for me. But is there anything else I should know?"

The wrinkles deepened in Kavan's forehead. "I wouldn't tell everyone this, but I feel I owe it to you if we're going to be working together." Discreetly, he rolled up his right sleeve, exposing a simple three-cornered Celtic knot tattooed on the inside of his forearm.

Thomas recognised the symbol as the Triquetra. The Trinity knot. Donovan had a larger, more elaborate one on his forearm. He braced himself for what was coming next.

Kavan's voice dropped to a husky whisper. "I was an Irish rebel."

Though somewhat prepared, Thomas still had to check a vocal exclamation of surprise, but then he cocked his head and whispered, "Was?"

The Irishman tugged his sleeve back down. "I was part of the Easter Rising back in '16, but I gave it up when I came to work with Kasey. My Irish heritage is enough to keep most people from getting involved with me even before getting into the rebellion part."

Thomas leaned back in his chair and studied Kavan intently. His ebony hair, frank blue eyes, and fair skin were trademarks of the Irish. A jagged scar ran from his chin to his ear along his left jawline. Broad shoulders showed he was used to hard work, and he had an honest gleam in his eyes that begged for understanding. Thomas had always prided himself on his instincts about a person. Well, except when it came to Clara. She threw him off at every turn, but he felt confident about Kavan. "Glad to have you aboard, Kavan Grahame," he said with a smile and extended his hand to the man.

Gratitude flickered in the blue eyes as the Irishman gave Thomas a firm handshake. "I won't let you down, Doc."

"I'm counting on that." As Thomas reached inside his pocket for the missive to France, his fingers brushed against the paper scrap from the night of the break-in. Pulling it out, he slid it across the table. "Does this name mean anything to you?"

Kavan's eyes widened as he read. "Fallamhan is the name of a leader in the Irish rebellion. A powerful man. I never saw or met him, but I heard stories aplenty. The name means 'leader,' and he's that to be sure."

Thomas's voice was hardly above a whisper as he asked, "Do you know anything about an arms shipment from Germany heading for Wicklow?"

Kavan slowly shook his head. "It was talked of when I was in Dublin last, but nothing ever came of it that I knew of."

After Kavan departed, Thomas remained at the table, mulling over the man's confession and information. He hailed the waitress for another cup of coffee and observed the dark, quiet street through the nearby window. Halfway through his second cup of coffee, he felt his jaw begin to tighten. An adverse reaction to the coffee, no doubt; he hated the stuff. But then his legs twitched in agitation. This was no mere reaction.

Rising calmly without drawing attention to himself, he

dropped a few coins on the table. The frigid January air slapped his face as he stumbled out of the public house. The road was nearly deserted this time of night, but he pressed northward and soon flagged a cabby. Barking out orders to the clinic, he fell back against the seat as the cab lurched into motion.

By the time he reached his destination seven minutes later, his legs were stiff and his breathing raspier with each breath as he struggled to unlock the front door. Snatching activated charcoal, tannic acid, and a bottle of ipecac from the shelves in the supply room, Thomas staggered up the stairs. He was running out of time.

~

25 January

The following morning, Clara tried the kitchen door and found it locked. She knocked and waited. No answer. Slipping the key Thomas had previously given her from her handbag, she unlocked the door and cautiously entered. No lights were on, and the rooms were quiet.

"Doctor Lindsey?" she called.

No answer.

Checking all the downstairs rooms, the doctor was nowhere to be found. She hesitated at the foot of the stairs. "Doctor Lindsey?" she called up the stairway.

Silence.

Timidly mounting the stairs, she paused at Thomas's door before knocking. A faint moan came from within. Poking her head in, she noticed the room was dark apart from the light that had been left on in the adjoining washroom. She wrinkled her nose at a sour smell.

Another groan came from the open washroom door. Clara peeked in and cried out in alarm as Thomas lay sprawled out on the floor. She sprang to his side and gently touched his shoulder.

He groaned again. No fever, she concluded as she felt his forehead. Her eye caught three medicine bottles on the counter, and she snatched them up. One nearly empty bottle of ipecac, a jar of tannic acid, and a container of activated charcoal. That combination could only mean one thing. Poison.

"Doctor, can you hear me?" she asked.

Thomas grunted unintelligibly.

Clara flew to the bedroom phone and rang the boarding house asking for Robbie to come immediately. Quickly, she snatched her stethoscope from her bag and placed the end against Thomas's chest, listening intently. "Breathing is shallow. Pulse is a bit weak," she muttered. At least he was still alive. Carefully avoiding the vomit, she positioned him more comfortably to prevent aspiration in case he retched again.

Five minutes later, Robbie clattered up the steps and caught sight of the still form. "Is he... dead?"

"Not yet. Help me."

Together, they lifted Thomas onto the bed, and Clara dashed down to the supply room for rags and vinegar to clean up the mess, while Robbie got Thomas into clean pyjamas. As Clara scoured the washroom, Robbie kept watch next to Thomas.

"What happened, Miss Clara?" the lad asked softly.

"Poison, I'm guessing. We'll have to wait and see what the doctor can tell us. I'm going to open the clinic. Can you keep an eye on him?"

When she came back a few minutes later, Thomas was groggy but awake.

"Easy, Doc," Robbie said as he pushed Thomas down gently when he tried to sit up.

"What happened?" Thomas whispered hoarsely.

Clara stood behind Robbie's chair. "We were hoping you could tell us that."

Thomas blinked slowly. "Coffee at Hope Inn." He shuddered with a moan.

"Whatever they used was strong; good sense in using the

ipecac, tannic acid, and charcoal." Clara nodded approvingly. "But you're going to be out for a few days."

"Can't. Must—"

"Hush. Get some sleep," she instructed, adding to Robbie, "I'll be back to check on him shortly." She stopped at the door and pointed her finger at the patient. "You had better listen and behave yourself, Doctor."

Too weak to argue, Thomas only nodded.

Clara popped in and out of the darkened bedroom all day in between patients, and Robbie kept a vigilant watch over Thomas while she was out. At suppertime, she brought up a plate of sandwiches for her and Robbie, a bowl of broth for Thomas, and hot chocolate for them all.

"Any ideas on how it happened last night, Doc?" Robbie asked between bites.

Thomas swallowed the spoonful of broth Clara offered him. "I went to the Hope Inn to see Kavan. I started to feel sick about an hour later."

This was the longest sentence he had gotten out all day. When the broth was finished, Clara held the mug of cocoa to his lips. The warm liquid sensation running down his throat relaxed him visibly.

"Any idea what the poison was, Miss Clara?" Robbie asked.

"Based on the symptoms, just short of a lethal dose of strychnine is my best guess."

"How comforting," Thomas muttered as his head drooped, and Clara helped him lie down.

"Who was your waitress?" she asked.

"Hazel Whyte." His voice slurred with exhaustion.

"Don't worry, Doc; we'll take care of you," Robbie reassured him.

Thomas mumbled his thanks before his eyes fluttered shut.

~

26 January

"No, don't go!" Thomas protested feebly. His mind looped as he fought against the poison coursing through his veins.

Clara stood beside his bed, her face sombre but determined as she uttered the fateful words. "Good-bye, Thomas."

"No!" he cried, his hands fumbling in vain to catch her hand as she drifted away from him. Then all was darkness.

Thomas shot up in bed drenched in sweat, his breathing laboured. A dream. Only a dream. But would Clara really leave? After how he had treated her, he couldn't blame her if she did. He laid back down, trying to steady his breathing and avoid waking Robbie, who was fast asleep in the easy chair beside the bed.

Later that morning, when Clara came to check on him between patients, Thomas decided to broach the topic casually. "Do you wish to leave Newhaven, Miss Dankworth?"

"Yes, I wish to leave but not until I have finished my job." She hesitated slightly. "And it's Clara, Doctor. I would say we are past the time for formalities."

"And you're certain you wouldn't leave before?" Thomas pressed. He knew his insistence sounded ridiculous, but he had to be certain. Would she walk out on him when it mattered most? All this poison business had addled his brain.

Her wide eyes betrayed her bewilderment. "What's gotten into you?"

Running his fingers through his curls, Thomas reclined against his pillow, muttering, "Nothing. Merely wondering. One can never be too sure about their assistants these days."

"Or their employers, it seems," she added quietly.

Despite his grumbling, Clara remained firm in her insistence that he take a few days off, but while she was with a patient that afternoon, he lifted himself shakily from the bed and padded to the washroom. He ran his hand along his chin as he studied his reflection in the mirror. Dark stubble covered his chin and jaw.

After lathering up his face, he reached for his razor. With one unsteady stroke, blood trickled down his chin.

"Of all the…" he muttered in frustration.

A smart knock came on the bedroom door, and Clara popped her head in. "Doctor?"

He growled. *Perfect timing.* "In here," he called weakly, grabbing the counter's edge as a dizzy spell hit him.

Clara's eyes flew open at the sight of blood and shaving cream, and she snatched the razor out of his hand with a cry of dismay. "What were you thinking?"

"I'm not fond of a beard." He tried to smile but swayed again.

She clutched his elbow and marched him to the easy chair Robbie had occupied.

He sat down, too weak to protest.

Once he was settled, she snatched up the telephone receiver and asked for the boarding house. "Mrs. Forsythe, can you send Robbie over? The doctor's being belligerent again."

Thomas grinned weakly. "Can't blame a fellow for trying."

"The sooner the better. He's downright unmanageable." Clara sighed before hanging up. "You have a death wish, Lindsey."

He chuckled to himself. She had picked up on using his last name when she was especially annoyed with him, and he rather liked it.

"You could have slit your throat," she continued.

"But I didn't."

"Not this time, you mean."

He shrugged. "What's a chap to do?"

"Have patience or ask for help."

"Don't fancy either, ma'am."

"So I've gathered. Now sit still so I can finish the job."

Thomas lifted a hand in protest, but Clara pointed the razor at him. "I have the blade, Lindsey. You are in no position to negotiate."

"Are you sure this is necessary?"

She grinned at him. "You have two choices—no shave, or me."

"Not much of a choice," he grumbled. "I suppose you'll have to do."

"Don't fret. This isn't my first time." She tipped his chin up.

"Wait," he said, nudging her hand aside. He hated being vulnerable, but with the razor in her possession, he thought it best to clear the air. "About what happened with Crouthers, I—"

"Let bygones be bygones. I forgave you, and though we have had a rather tumultuous start, I propose a truce... for the sake of the mission."

A wry smile slipped across his face. "I'm amenable to that," and he held out his hand to her.

She shook the offered hand, and then, smiling reassuringly at him, she ran the blade down his cheek. After several minutes, she gave him a towel to wipe his face and applied the aftershave. Pointing to the bed, she added, "Nurse's orders."

Her warm hand braced his elbow as he took an unsteady step. "Easy," she murmured. With strict instructions for him not to move until Robbie came, she started to leave the room, assuring him she would be back to check on him after the next patient.

"Clara," he whispered, and she turned at her name in surprise. "Thank you."

Thomas ran a hand over his chin once she was gone. She had done a good job. Did he just call her Clara? She hadn't given him leave to use her Christian name. Or had she? Oh, why did his mind have to do such abominable things... Another dizzy spell hit him, and he clenched his eyes shut as the world swam, derailing his train of thought. Perhaps he would remember later. Rolling over with a groan, he fell fast asleep, nearly oblivious to Robbie's arrival minutes a short time later.

Dose of Patience

28 January

BY MONDAY, after four days of bedrest, Thomas was back on his feet and itching to get to work. Clara handed him his patient list with a warning to be careful and to take it easy. Thomas flashed her a charming grin and assured her he would, but the shadow didn't leave her eyes as she watched him leave.

Thomas drove around town for appointments from East Side to Brighton Street and then down to the inner harbour. On his way back to the clinic, he popped in to see Kasey.

"Heard you had a close call, lad. Glad to see you back up." The relief was evident on the captain's weathered, friendly face as he slapped Thomas's shoulder companionably.

"Clara kept me down for a few days to make sure."

"Smart lass." The captain nodded approvingly.

"You would take her side."

Kasey gave him a knowing look. "You know she was right to do it. You'd have done the same thing. Now, what brings you down here at this time?"

"Any more news from France?"

Kasey shook his head. "Still nothing. Matheson has been out of contact with her. There's no telling where she's gone to."

"Tell him to make finding her whereabouts his top priority."

The captain studied him. "Even over the '05 disaster?"

Thomas hesitated. Matheson didn't know about Thomas's personal mission, but Kasey did. "Yes," he said finally with more conviction than he felt.

"I leave tonight. Kavan will make sure he knows."

Thomas shook hands with Kasey and drove back to Bridge Street. Clara was in the kitchen stirring a pot on the stove when he slipped inside.

Planting her hands on her hips, she glared fiercely at him. "That's not what I call taking it easy, Lindsey."

Thomas cringed at her tone. Definitely upset. "Whatever do you mean?" he asked innocently.

She cocked an eyebrow.

He sighed. She wasn't going to buy his act of innocence. "I stopped to see Kasey. I hadn't seen him in a week."

"You should have called him or sent someone for him then," she countered, shaking her spoon at him, adding, "But you don't have patience and don't like to ask for help."

He grinned impishly.

She glowered at him and added under her breath, "You're going to kill yourself one of these days. Oh wait, someone else nearly did."

He fled into the office and found Robbie waiting. The boy shoved a message into his hands, and Thomas read it before slamming his fist on the desk.

"What is it?" Robbie questioned. Thomas showed him the paper, and the lad frowned. "Can't read a word, Doc. What language is that?"

"No idea. Who sent it?"

"483."

Alaina. But she knew he didn't understand foreign languages. Why did she send it then? Unless...

Clara appeared in the doorway and stared at their puzzled faces. "Something wrong?"

"Doc got a message in a strange language," Robbie explained before Thomas could stop him.

"May I see?" She held out her hand.

Thomas hesitated, but Robbie snatched it from him and handed it to her.

Clara scanned it curiously. Going to her desk, she pulled out a sheet of paper and scribbled a few lines.

Robbie nudged Thomas in wide-eyed admiration as she handed him the translation.

Safe in Switzerland. Package on raid following. Inform Matheson of safety.

"It's Swiss, and it sounds like good news," Clara affirmed.

"How did you do that?" Thomas spluttered.

She smiled ruefully. "I inherited my love of language from my father."

"How many languages do you know?" Robbie questioned.

"Five fluently, but I have dabbled in others."

Thomas shook his head incredulously, finding it hard to eliminate the silly grin on his face.

"Glad to be of service, gentlemen." Clara retreated to the door.

"What did you inherit from your mother?" Thomas called after her.

She turned, flashing him a teasing smile. "The patience to deal with people like you."

Robbie howled as Clara disappeared down the hall while Thomas tried hard but failed miserably to hide his amusement.

～

29 January

Kasey sauntered into the clinic, cradling a clumsily bandaged hand, and Clara ushered him into the examination room with Thomas on her heels.

"What happened?" Thomas asked, washing his hands at the sink.

"Knife slipped while I was doing some unpacking."

Clara clucked her tongue as she took her turn washing her hands.

"Some slip." Thomas whistled. "Iodine and stitches for you."

Clara arranged the implements on a tray, and Kasey winced as Thomas cleaned the gnarled hand with the iodine.

"That hurts more than the knife did," the captain muttered through clenched teeth, but he declined something to dull the pain before stitching.

Thomas's deft fingers sutured the wound as quickly as he dared, and Clara carefully wrapped it in fresh gauze.

"Keep it clean," Thomas instructed. "And come see me the day after tomorrow."

"Will do," Kasey agreed, standing up.

"And no using knives from now on. You'll come in here without a leg next," Thomas said in mock sternness.

The captain's eyes twinkled as he pulled a package from under his coat. "Thought you'd be happy to have this, lad."

Thomas snatched at it.

"From France?" Clara questioned, looking over his shoulder.

"Yes," he whispered incredulously.

"Still want me to keep away from those knives?" Kasey asked smugly.

Thomas sighed in defeat. "Guess not. Just be more careful next time, or I will have you replaced."

Kasey shot Thomas an amused look, and his eyes crinkled in merriment. "We both know you'd never do it."

Thomas waited until Clara had left for the day before opening the package Kasey had brought. His hands trembled as he loosened the strings. A black folder lay inside along with several sheets of paper. A note in Chantelle's looping script lay on top.

1905 Calais mission notes. Attached photograph is of the contact. No evidence from the site was recovered. Still looking. Staying safe, don't worry. Tu me manques, mon ami. Dieu te benisse [I miss you, my friend. God bless you]. *CD.*

Thomas stuffed the note in the middle desk drawer and thumbed through the papers. The photograph fell out, and his heart leapt at the sight. *Da.* He could hardly believe it.

But who was the other man with him? Thomas rubbed his forehead. He had seen that man's face before. *The newspaper.* Scouring the middle drawer, he pulled out the paper from the train station and flipped to the Cromwell account. Comparing pictures, there was no doubt. The contact was Joseph Cromwell. He scrawled out a hasty reply to Chantelle.

Package received. Send more information when available. Contact in photograph is Joseph Cromwell, former Member of Parliament murdered 10 years ago. Follow leads on him. Glad you are staying safe. You forget I don't know French, fy ffrind. TL.

Thomas grinned at the note. Nothing like a little bit of Welsh to keep them even.

CHAPTER 21

Called to London

30 January

CLARA TWISTED and pinned her hair into a low chignon as she got ready in the morning. Tucking her blouse into her skirt waistband, she snatched up her black bag and dashed down the stairs. She was already running late.

At the front door, Lena stopped her and shoved an envelope into her hand. "This was wedged in the door," she tossed over her shoulder as she hurried up the stairs.

Clara stared at the disappearing woman in surprise before glancing down at the missive in her hand. Except for her payment from London, which didn't come to the boarding house, she never received mail. She had no one to write to her. With a sigh, she buttoned her coat and plunged into the crisp January morning air. Opening the envelope as she headed towards town, the typewritten note suddenly halted her feet.

You have been found out. It is only a matter of time before it's too late.

Shoving the paper into her coat pocket, she clenched her trembling hands. How could she have been found out? Only five people knew her secret—and three of them were dead. Her heart continued its rapid staccato as she entered the clinic ten minutes later. Water sloshed out of the kettle, and the cups clinked loudly as she tried to prepare the morning tea. Willing her hands to steady themselves, she mopped up her mess in frustration.

"Good morning," Thomas called cheerily as he entered the kitchen.

"Can't see what's so good about it," she muttered through gritted teeth. Her hand shook as she shoved a cup of tea at him.

He frowned as he took it. "Is something the matter?"

She turned away from him. She wouldn't—couldn't—involve him. "Nothing that concerns you."

"Try me," he encouraged gently. "We did agree to trust each other."

Swallowing a scorching mouthful of tea, she weighed her options. Telling him would be a danger but hiding the truth could cause even more problems. The paper weighed heavily in her pocket. Slowly rotating to face him, she watched the concern clouding his sapphire eyes. Could she possibly trust him with this?

Thomas frowned as he watched the struggle etch across Clara's ashen face. Cupping her elbow, he led her to a seat at the table before sitting down opposite her.

She traced the grain of the table in an agitated fashion with her forefinger and kept her eyes averted.

"Clara, please."

Her shoulders sagged as her defences dissolved, and she retrieved a crumpled paper from her pocket, scooting it across the table to him.

He scanned it quickly and glanced at her. "Where did you get this?" His frown deepened as she explained the morning's events, and he stroked his chin absently. "Have you received threats like this before?"

She nodded slowly and fingered the dainty handle of her teacup.

"You're hiding something." It was a statement, not a question. Thomas leaned back in his chair. "I can't help if I don't know what I'm up against."

"You would be a dead man within a week if I told you." Her eyes flickered with the fear of a hunted animal before she squeezed them shut with a shudder.

"Well, you certainly aren't safe here," Thomas murmured, rising and pacing the floor absently.

"I'm not safe anywhere."

"You should at least be armed or..." The rest of his sentence fell off as he pivoted and found himself staring down the barrel of a derringer. His heart stopped, and a flash of annoyance drummed inside of him. He was getting a little tired of having guns waved about in his face. "It seems I have underestimated you... again," he conceded respectfully as she holstered the pistol somewhere within a hidden recess of her skirt pocket. "But you are still in danger, as is anyone connected to you. I would suggest writing Crouthers immediately."

She nodded and moved towards the doorway. "I trust I shan't regret putting you in confidence of this matter, Doctor."

Thomas stilled as he met her gaze steadily. Gone was the usual wariness, and instead he read the mix of hinted warning and hopeful pleading. She was trying to trust him. He swallowed hard. "I trust you won't," he returned with a bow before she disappeared into the adjoining room.

Later that afternoon, on his way back to the clinic from a house call, Thomas caught a glimpse of Lena exiting the telephone office. Weaving through the busy street, he called to her, but she kept walking without acknowledging him.

"Why didn't you stop?" he asked breathlessly when at last he caught up to her. Her gait was faster than he had expected.

"Why should I?" the woman sniffed.

He grabbed her elbow. "Whatever's going on, I need your help."

She snatched her arm out of his grip. "Why should I help you?"

Couldn't the woman be reasonable and answer his question without a question for once? "Because this affects you as much as anyone. Clara told me about the note you gave her this morning. Did you see who left it?"

Lena smoothed the front of her dress, uninterested. "No. I found it with her name on it and gave it to her. That's all I know."

Thomas studied her shrewdly but detected no hint of a lie. "Very well. Sorry to have bothered you."

"You had best stay away from her. She's nothing but trouble," Lena called over her shoulder as she turned on her heel and sauntered away.

"I'm beginning to get that impression," he muttered as he retraced his steps towards Bridge Street. He had a German spy on the loose, a nurse who attracted no end of trouble, and no new information on Price or the Calais mission. Things couldn't get much worse.

~

31 January

Clara carefully copied out the following day's house calls. The clock chimed; it was nearly closing time. Ever since the post had arrived several minutes ago, Thomas had reclined in his chair, perusing his latest missive, seemingly unbothered by her presence. A sudden slam made her pen jog mid-stroke. Looking up, she noticed Thomas's balled fist and his eyes shooting darts at the paper in his hand from under furrowed brows.

"What is it?" she asked casually.

"Call to London tonight," he growled in reply.

"And what's the matter with that?"

Thomas glared at her but said nothing. Turning back to his note, he raked long fingers through his dark hair.

Shrugging, Clara resumed her task. If he didn't want to share information, she wasn't about to press him for it.

"Of all the..." he muttered and then fell silent for several minutes. "Clara, I am in need of a favour," he asked politely.

She glanced up at the request and waited for him to continue.

"I have an urgent appointment tonight that I need you to keep. There will be a knock on the back door at midnight. Let the messenger in and give them this envelope." He retrieved an envelope from his middle desk drawer and crossed the room, extending it to her.

"I haven't agreed to this yet," she returned pointedly, ignoring his outstretched hand.

Thomas's hand dropped to his side, and he inhaled deeply. "Please. I can't describe the importance of this."

"Who is the messenger?" She frowned at his hesitation. "I won't do it without a name."

He growled in defeat. "Chantelle Delvaux, but you must not breathe her name to anyone."

"Delvaux? That's French."

"Not a word," he reiterated fiercely as he shoved the envelope at her.

She tucked it in her skirt pocket. "As you wish. Anything else?"

"She will likely have an envelope of her own for you. I must ask you to guard it with your life." Thomas retreated to his desk.

"You have my word, but if it's so important, what makes you think she'll give it to me? She doesn't even know me."

He paused, apparently scrambling for the right words. "Trust me, she will. She knows... about you."

"She does?"

"Yes. Now, remember, midnight and not a word." He slammed the middle drawer shut and locked it. "Leave the list on my desk. I'll be back as soon as I can," he instructed as he moved to leave.

"Very well. For your sake, I hope all goes well in London," Clara called after him.

Thomas paused at the door and glanced back at her. A dull light had settled in his eyes where there was once life and vigour. He looked much older than his twenty-six years, and for the moment seemed to lose his cocky aura. "Thank you. As do I," he said quietly. Hesitating, he studied her momentarily. "I'm sorry I dragged you into this," and then he was gone.

Clara stared at the door where he had stood moments before, unsure of his meaning. Swallowing back her questions, she rose and locked up the clinic, being careful to slide the deadbolt on both doors.

Returning to the kitchen, she lit the oil lamp on the table and tugged the curtains closed. Golden light danced through the room, chasing away the shadows. She sighed and boiled the kettle for tea. Chantelle's visit was still hours away, but Clara mused curiously over the significance of it. The fact that Chantelle was French gave her a clue—she was an overseas agent.

The hours ticked past slowly. Clara maintained her post at the table, sipping her tea, reading *Emma*, and keeping her pearl-handled derringer within arm's reach on the tabletop. Her pulse skittered as the office clock echoed through the silence—midnight. Rising slowly, she caught up the pistol and touched her skirt pocket where Thomas's note rested. Drawing in a deep breath, she crept over to the door and waited. The silence roared in her ears as she vainly tried to still her racing heart. With every nerve taut, gun at the ready, she waited. The last strokes of midnight faded into oblivion, and there was no knock. Nothing but silence. Was something wrong? Had Thomas been mistaken? No. She must wait. Chantelle Delvaux, whoever she was, *would* come.

Five minutes ebbed past before a soft tap came on the door. Swallowing hard and white-knuckling the double-shot derringer, Clara quietly slid the deadbolt and inched the door open. A small, dark-cloaked figure stood on the steps. Quickly, she opened the door further, ushering the messenger inside and locking the door again. Only once she turned to face her visitor did Chantelle remove her hood, revealing a mess of curly brown locks and intelligent hazel eyes on an impish face.

"Chantelle Delvaux?" Clara whispered.

The girl gave a barely perceivable nod and looked around the kitchen. "You must be Clara Dankworth."

"I am."

"Where's Thomas?"

"London. He left this for you." Clara slipped the envelope from her skirt pocket and held it out to the French girl.

Chantelle pocketed it and handed Clara one in return. "Give that to the doctor when he returns. Nice doing business with you."

"Wait," Clara whispered as Chantelle made a motion to leave. "How did you know me? And why do you trust me?"

Chantelle hesitated with her hand on the doorknob, but she met Clara's gaze with understanding in her glowing eyes. "Thomas told me you could be trusted in his absence. But don't tell him I told you that."

Clara smiled faintly. So, he did trust her after all. She reached to shake Chantelle's hand. "I wish we could have met under better circumstances. *Que Dieu soit toujours avec vous* [may God always be with you]."

A sparkle lit in Chantelle's eye as she heard her native tongue. In a whisper, she added, "*Je vous souhaite la même* [I wish you the same]." Smiling, she slipped out the door and vanished into the swirling grey fog.

~

The impromptu call to London left Thomas on edge as he hailed a cab to catch the evening train. He carefully reviewed his work of the last few months as the cab clattered over the bridge towards the station. Being summoned to the office usually meant a reprimand, but he wasn't guilty of any breaches of service—at least, not recently. Nothing made sense. He hadn't been summoned in months. *Unless...* He quickly dismissed the thought before finishing it. If this had anything to do with Clara or Chantelle, he would be in over his head—and he knew it. Pushing aside the possibility as he boarded the train, he settled into a seat uneasily. Best not to borrow trouble, and he wasn't about to let Crouthers see he was rattled.

Thomas sauntered into the Belgravia bookshop with more confidence than he felt and stormed past Walter at the front desk. Marching up the stairs, he barged into Crouthers's office with little more than a knock.

Crouthers sat comfortably at his desk, smoking his cigar and reading his paper.

"What is this all about?" Thomas snapped. "It's a little late for social calls."

A slow, sinister smile spread across the man's portly face as he set down his paper and observed the younger man in front of him. "Whatever do you mean, Doctor?"

Thomas tilted his head without speaking a word, in no mood to play mental games with his superior. His foot tapped impatiently.

Crouthers's smile faded, his dark eyes smoldering. "Why are you threatening my agent?"

"I beg your pardon?" Thomas exclaimed indignantly.

Crouthers flicked a note across the desk to him. "You really thought I'd believe this?"

Thomas scanned the page quickly. It was Clara's report about the threatening message she had received. He slid it back across the desk to his boss. "I had nothing to do with it. The note was delivered to Miss Dankworth, and Miss Dankworth showed it to me."

"I know your game, Lindsey, and I don't approve of it. If I hear of one more misstep on your part, you're out. And don't think I won't do it. I can ruin you and everyone you care about."

Thomas stared hard at the man. "You know nothing of my business, and where Miss Dankworth is concerned, she was all your idea. Remember that." Slamming the door behind him, he clambered down the stairs.

"Didn't go too well?" Walter asked sympathetically.

Thomas shot Walter a scalding glance, and if looks could kill, Walter would have been a dead man. Without stopping to reply, Thomas stormed out of the office into the winter night in the direction of the train station, inwardly seething.

After boarding the train, Thomas watched the darkness rushing past his window. The lulling motion relaxed him into a doze. When he woke up, he checked his watch: midnight. Chantelle should be at the clinic now or, knowing her penchant for lateness, within a few minutes. He should have mentioned the possibility of her tardiness to Clara; too late now. He hoped for good news. It had been far too long since he had received any.

Arriving back at the clinic, he found Richard waiting in the kitchen. Thomas scowled at him. "What do you want?" he snapped, too upset to deal with visitors.

"I sent Clara home. What happened to you?"

Pouring himself a cup of tea without offering Richard any, Thomas plopped down at the table still trembling with rage. "He accused me of threatening her!" he half shouted.

"Keep it down," Richard warned. "What are we talking about?" A frown crossed Richard's handsome features as Thomas explained the threatening note Clara had received and his consequential summons to London. "You're in over your head now," was his only comment.

"All these years and this is what I get," Thomas growled. He set his cup down too hard, and tea sloshed over the side.

"I've never seen you like this before."

"My position has never been jeopardised to this extent."

"Are you jealous?" Richard asked cautiously.

Thomas said nothing. *Jealous? Of course not. Only furious over false accusations.* The thought struck him—maybe he had an idea on how Clara felt when he had accused her after Reynolds's visit several weeks earlier. He cringed. He had been an utter brute.

"Be careful, my friend," was Richard's solemn parting.

CHAPTER 22

One More Chance

7 February

A WEEK LATER, Thomas left for Derby to see Alaina, and Clara promised she would handle everything in his absence. After catching the morning train, he disembarked at the Derby station shortly before noon. Weaving his way through the crowded streets, he called at the bank, asking for Alaina.

The young woman at the counter frowned curiously at his request. "Miss Huntington quit three days ago."

"Did she say where she went?" he inquired sharply.

The young woman shook her head.

Thomas thanked her and hurried to catch a cab that could take him across town to the parsonage. Mrs. Moore was also no help and told him that Alaina had left them two days prior with no information on where she was going next. Thomas searched all over town for the next several hours but found no sign of the copper-headed young woman. Locating a public telephone, he asked the operator for the Bridge Street Clinic.

Clara's voice came across the line a moment later. "I was wondering if you would call. I have someone here to speak with you."

"Listen, Clara, it'll have to wait. The contact I was looking for is gone and—"

A laughing voice floated through the receiver. "I'm right here, you silly boy."

"Alaina! You're in Newhaven? I've been all over Derby in a state looking for you! What happened?"

"A long story I would rather tell you in person, but it's all gone wrong. And I came to Newhaven for some advice."

"I'll be down on the next train."

Arriving at the clinic several hours later, Thomas found Alaina and Clara chatting merrily in the kitchen as if they had been friends all their lives instead of merely a few short hours.

"Alaina, what happened?" he asked abruptly.

The woman raised an expressive eyebrow. "Hello to you too. I am well; thank you for asking."

He grimaced and rubbed the back of his neck, chagrinned. "My apologies. Hello, Miss Huntington and Miss Dankworth. Now, what are you doing here?"

"We'll get to that. Is there somewhere I can stay in town?"

Clara bit her lip thoughtfully. "The boarding house is full right now, but Mrs. Jennings mentioned wanting company. I'm sure they would be willing to have you."

Thomas nodded in agreement.

"Then all I need is a job." Alaina beamed.

"Price said he needed another teller," Clara suggested.

"How do you possibly know all this?" Thomas asked in disbelief.

Clara shrugged. "I know who to talk to, and he mentioned it over dinner last week. I thought I had mentioned it."

"No, you failed to disclose that detail. The last agent we had under Price didn't last a week, but it might be worth another try." He paused. "Now, why are you here, Alaina?"

Her hand snaked up to rub her left elbow nervously as she glanced everywhere but at him. "Crouthers fired me."

"On what grounds?"

"None he shared with me," Alaina said with a shrug. "Simply dismissed me and said my services were no longer required."

He did it to spite me. He's one of the only ones who knows about my connection to Alaina. A connection that, if public knowledge, would endanger both their lives. Thomas was seething by this point. "Let me go talk to him. I—"

"No." Alaina's tone bode no argument. "It won't work this time; he said so himself. I barely managed to keep him from sacking you, too. Walter told me you had one more chance," she added. "You've made it this far, and I don't want you to fail because of me, so I didn't put up a fuss. Don't ruin it."

Silence fell over the kitchen.

"*Thank you* doesn't seem the right thing to say," Thomas said at last, rubbing the back of his neck again.

"Forget it, you rascal. I'm here now, though."

"Would Jennings take her?" Clara said in an aside to Thomas.

He tilted his head in consideration of the suggestion. It was possible, especially since the colonel worked for the Secret Service and didn't report to Crouthers. "We might as well find out," Thomas muttered to himself as he left the room to ring Jennings.

The colonel and his wife were more than happy to welcome Alaina as their guest. When the trio arrived twenty minutes later, Kerridge ushered them inside, informing them the Jenningses were waiting in the parlour.

Colonel and Hannah Jennings received their guests warmly, and Alaina was soon settled into one of the spare rooms upstairs. After bidding Hannah and Alaina goodbye, Clara and Thomas prepared to leave, while Jennings saw them to the door.

"Clara heard Price is looking for a teller," Thomas said in a low tone. "Might be a good opportunity to get someone on the inside. I know Kent didn't work out, but Alaina's far more competent than he was." He had already explained Alaina's situation to Jennings and felt confident the man would approve her.

Jennings paused to consider the idea. Nodding slowly, he

agreed. "After Clara's last bit of intel, she might be what we need to break this case."

~

8 February

Thomas stood at the sink cleaning implements after a long day. Everything that could have gone wrong that day seemed to. He hoped for a quiet evening tonight to recoup. Maybe he could...

"Thomas?" a soft voice called, interrupting his mental train. "Can we talk?"

Turning, he was surprised to see Alaina standing hesitantly at the open door of the exam room—and wearing her hat, no less. What a feat. She was usually such a forgetful young woman. Perhaps, fashion-conscious Hannah Jennings would be a good influence on her.

"Of course." Thomas dried his hands and abandoned the remaining implements in the sink. He would deal with them later. Motioning her through the door, he led the way to the office and offered her a chair. After she availed herself of the seat, he leaned against the edge of his desk in front of her, waiting for her to begin.

She didn't say a word. Only rubbed her left elbow—her nervous tic.

Thomas studied the pale face that was usually bright and cheerful. "What's the matter?" he asked quietly. No answer. "Alaina, look at me."

The bent head rose slowly, and her soft, brown eyes, shining with unshed tears, met his.

Thomas's forehead puckered slightly. "What is it?"

"Colonel Jennings told me what you did. I can't let you sacrifice your career to save mine," she burst out.

"Seems to me it was in repayment of a debt. You sacrificed your career for me, you remember."

"That's different."

"How?"

Thomas hid a grin as Alaina paused to assemble her argument. "You only had one chance left, and I wasn't about to ruin it for you. This operation needs you; they don't need me."

"That's not true. You have gotten me out of more than one scrape."

"I can't accept it. I won't be the destruction of you, Thomas, and I know it could happen. Crouthers knows about us. He—"

"You won't be the destruction of me," he interrupted, holding up his hand. "You are a necessary part of this operation. Trust me, Alaina."

Appreciation shone in the young woman's eyes as she smiled at him.

Thomas winked at her. "It will be nice to work with you again, but you know what this means? Same cover as our last mission together in Sheffield."

"Very well. You can take me to dinner to make it official," and with that she rose and kissed his cheek.

He scowled at her as he rubbed away the kiss. "Not with the lipstick. It's a hideous colour."

Alaina only laughed.

~

9 February

Thomas whistled softly as he trudged up the long lane to the Jenningses' estate. A bitter, early, February wind moaned as it travelled through the grounds, and he wrapped his coat closer to his thin frame. Kerridge answered his ring at the door.

"Is Miss Huntington in?" Thomas asked as the butler ushered him into the parlour.

"Yes, sir. She will be down presently," the butler assured him and then disappeared from the room.

Settling back on the sofa to wait for Alaina, his eyes travelled the length of the room, taking in its richness.

"Well?" a voice asked from the doorway, snagging his attention. Alaina stood with her arms crossed and an annoyed look on her face.

He jumped up politely. "You called," he said with a shrug.

"You're early."

He glanced at the grandfather clock across the room and winced. He was nearly an hour earlier than the time she had specified. "Sorry about that. I was in between patients and didn't check the time. I can come back—" He moved as if to go.

"Don't be a goose. You're here now. Sit." Alaina plopped down on the other end of the sofa. "I have the information you were looking for."

Thomas straightened rapidly. "On Cromwell?"

She nodded and handed him a small folder. "It's all I got before Crouthers dismissed me, but there's quite a bit there. "The unsolved murder of one of the most prominent Members of Parliament in his time, along with his family, created quite the sensation."

Fingering the bulging folder, he frowned. "Save me some time and fill me in on the highlights, would you?"

"He was born in Colchester in 1858 and was the only child of his parents. He married his wife in 1880, and they had three children: Charles, Catherine, and Clarissa. He was a Member of Parliament from 1888 till his death in 1908."

He frowned and leaned forward as she paused. "Do go on."

"As I'm sure you remember, Parliament was in major upheaval during those years with the Boer War, Irish Home Rule, the Irish Crown Jewel theft, and the Entente Cordiale. Joseph Cromwell was an influential social reformer and was said to be dangerously persuasive."

"Anything else?"

"There's more in the folder, but that's all I remember offhand. From the sounds of it, he was a wonderful man.

Though, dangerous to the political world, it would seem. And you're already familiar with the details of the murder."

Thomas let out a thoughtful huff and stroked his chin.

"Does any of that help?" Alaina asked, cocking her head.

Shaking himself from his reverie, he smiled at her. "Very much so, thank you. Though I apologise if retrieving it cost you your job."

She shrugged nonchalantly. "Glad to be of service. Anything else you need?"

"No, this is quite sufficient at present."

"Then," she said, rising from her seat, "I must be going. There's a canteen tonight, and I don't want to be late. How do I look?" She twirled, making her green gingham dress balloon around her ankles. When Thomas only shrugged, she rolled her eyes. "Come on, give a girl a compliment."

He bristled uncomfortably and gave her a once-over. "You look fine."

"Coming from you, I suppose that will have to do."

"Why are you going to the canteen?"

"To serve coffee."

"Not to dance?" he teased.

She grimaced. "You very well know I don't dance, Lindsey."

"How would I know that? Well, I suppose my broken toes might be the answer to that." She smacked his shoulder, but he continued mischievously, "Then there was that one time—"

Her hands flew up to cover her ears. "Don't you dare start!" she shouted over her shoulder as she stalked out of the room.

CHAPTER 23

Middle of a War

17 February

THOMAS STOOD PERUSING the newspaper in the kitchen while sipping his coffee absently. The newly imposed food rations had forcibly curbed his tea habit, reducing him to cocoa and coffee with tea only on very special occasions. He frowned at the reminder and flipped the page. Dover had been shelled by a German submarine the previous night. His frown deepened as he took another sip of his coffee. He set it down with disgust. Tonight, it wasn't worth finishing.

A pounding on the door interrupted his thoughts. Hurriedly setting aside his paper, Thomas threw open the door and a breathless Robbie tumbled clumsily inside out of the drizzling rain. Thomas grabbed the boy's shoulder and gave him a shake. "What's wrong?" he asked in alarm.

Robbie shoved a slip of paper into Thomas's hands, his breathing too laboured for words.

Thomas tore open the envelope and scanned the brief missive. His knees went weak, and he slumped into a nearby chair.

"Kasey said it was urgent. How bad is it?" Robbie gasped.

Thomas's vision blurred and his mouth moved, but no words came out.

Robbie shook him by the shoulder. "Doc?"

Thomas blinked several times before meeting Robbie's gaze. "They captured her. Chantelle Delvaux is in gaol." *Again.*

He fairly flew down to the harbour, where he found Kasey at his flat, looking as sick as Thomas felt. "Is it true?" he demanded.

Kasey nodded slowly. "Matheson sent it himself."

Thomas's fists balled, and he thumped one against the door frame. "I told her to be careful. Why couldn't she listen?"

"She knew the risks, and even with being careful, there is never any assurance of safety. You know that," Kasey maintained quietly.

"I don't want her to be a martyr or a war hero," Thomas flared. "She's just a child. Captain Durand entrusted her to my care and now look what's happened." His voice cracked. "I can't fail again."

"She's a young woman with a mind of her own. You've done the best you could; Durand would be proud."

Thomas sank into a chair, burying his head in his hands. "What am I going to do with that girl?"

"There's still hope."

Thomas glanced at the old captain. He suddenly looked older and weaker in the dying firelight. This war was making old men out of them all. Thomas wasn't ready for that. "If you find out she died in front of a firing squad, don't tell me unless I ask you." He shuddered. "And even then... I don't think I can handle another loss right now."

The captain laid a comforting hand on Thomas's shoulder. "You have my word, lad."

Thomas was in a sore mood when Alaina dropped by the clinic later that evening. Helping herself to a cup of coffee, she seated herself at Clara's desk. He had already told her in as few words as possible about Chantelle's disappearance, but he didn't want to discuss it further. He grumbled about the coffee, her lipstick, and whatever else came to mind.

"Spill, Lindsey. You're making the evening miserable," she finally exclaimed. "And it's more than the news from France. What's bothering you?"

Thomas studied Alaina carefully before commenting. "Clara has a secret I can't sort out." That wasn't exactly what was bothering him at the moment, but he wasn't about to tell Alaina that. He needed to distract her from pressing him... and perhaps distract himself.

"You seem to have a few yourself." Alaina's eyes danced in merriment, and a grin lit her face.

"That's beside the point."

"Is it?"

"It is," he assured her.

"What is the point, Thomas?"

"Oh, stop being rhetorical and try being sensible for once," he snapped, but he did pause to consider her words. What was the point? What *if* Clara had a secret? Alaina was right—he did as well. Frowning, Thomas slumped lower in his chair.

Unfazed by his outbreaks, Alaina propped her chin on her hand and mused conspiratorially, "Some secrets hold the fate of nations."

"And desperate ones have ruined the best of agents," he countered.

It was Alaina's turn to shrug. "I don't know about hers, but, Thomas, think about it. We all have secrets, and some of those secrets are going to affect the fate of the nation. Secrets are necessary in our line of work. We're fighting for justice and freedom. We are in the middle of a war."

Thomas stared at her. "How do you do that?"

"Do what?"

"Put me in my place like that." He ran his fingers through his hair. "It's uncanny."

At Thomas's assessment, Alaina grinned. "Someone's got to." Twirling a loose lock of her hair around her finger, she asked hesitatingly, "Do you think Clara suspects the truth about us?"

He snorted. "No. She thinks you're my sweetheart."

Alaina laughed heartily and threw a crumpled sheet of paper at him, which bounced off his shoulder. "Not on your life. When should we enlighten her?"

"When the time is right but not yet. Maybe when this case is done."

"That could be years."

"Not if I have anything to say about it."

"Promise you won't tell her unless I'm there. I want to see her face."

Thomas shrugged. It didn't matter to him where or how Clara found out the truth, as long as it wasn't anytime in the immediate future. It was still too dangerous. "If you insist." Count on Alaina to keep life interesting.

CHAPTER 24

Promise

28 February

KASEY STOPPED by the clinic and left a whispered message for Thomas to meet him at his flat that night. Accustomed to such summons, Thomas set out after dark in the direction of the harbour without question. When the captain ushered him inside, Thomas didn't notice anything out of the ordinary. That was, until Kasey called softly, "Come on out."

A side door swung open on a petite figure with a mass of curly brown hair and... Thomas's jaw fell open as the figure charged him and flung her arms around him, nearly bowling him over.

"You're alive?" he stammered as he patted Chantelle's shoulder and then pushed her away from him slightly to investigate her face incredulously in the dim light.

Chantelle's eyes sparkled as she flashed him her impish grin. "Of course."

"How did you get out of gaol?" Thomas questioned as they moved to the sofa, and Kasey stood smiling in a shadowy corner.

"Well..." Chantelle drew the word out, tilting her shapely head and lifting her shoulders.

"On second thought, never mind. I probably don't want to know," Thomas returned dryly.

"Coward," Chantelle dared in a whisper.

"Brighton."

Chantelle scowled fiercely as she crossed her arms, muttering, "You don't play fair."

"Chantelle, we had to assume the worst. I want to know what happened."

"Same thing that happened to Gabrielle Petit. A German agent pretended to be on our side, and I got caught where I wasn't supposed to be."

Thomas's gaze narrowed on her face, and he reached out a finger to tip up her chin, angling it towards the firelight for a better look.

Chantelle stiffened and shoved his hand aside but not before he saw the dusky bruising around her left eye.

"What did they do?" he demanded in quiet indignation.

She shrugged again and avoided meeting his eyes. "You know how questioning works. I didn't say I escaped unscathed. All that matters is that I talked my way out of this one, too. With a little outside help from Matheson."

"I'm sure you had no problem with that," he muttered, and Chantelle's elbow dug into his ribs. He absently stroked the worn fabric of the sofa with a finger as his stomach twisted. He could guess what the imprisonment and escape had cost her. "Behave yourself, girlie, or I will send you away. I have every intention of doing it now," he warned, and Chantelle straightened up. He went on, "I already told Kasey I don't want you to be a martyr or a war hero. Sending you to your great-aunt in Brighton is looking better and better."

"Lindsey," Chantelle hissed angrily.

"You disobeyed orders."

"And you haven't?"

"We aren't talking about me."

"I was being careful. It just... happened."

Thomas surveyed her in silence for several minutes. At last, he sighed. "Very well. I won't send you away." He laid a heavy hand on her shoulder. "But you still have to be careful."

Chantelle's face lit up in the dusky light of the room. "I will. I promise."

Thomas nodded and dropped his head to his hands with a sigh of relief, running his fingers through his hair.

"I'm sorry I'm so much trouble," she whispered guiltily.

He glanced up with a rueful smile and chucked her chin gently. "You're not trouble, Chantelle. I'd just like to keep you *out* of trouble."

She gave him a quick hug and then turned to Kasey. "I'd best be going." As her hand touched the doorknob, the girl turned back to Thomas's still hunched figure on the sofa. He felt as if the strength to hold himself upright had fled. "*Au revoir*, Thomas. I'll be back soon," she whispered.

Thomas gave her a faint nod without moving to look at her. He couldn't bear to see her leave. The next moment a *whoosh* of cold air flew in the door, telling him she was gone.

1 March

Thomas waltzed into the Newhaven bank and scanned the tellers' faces. He smiled at the sight of Alaina on the left. "Good afternoon, miss," he said as he approached her.

Alaina's head bobbed up, and her signature red lips parted in a wide smile. "How may I help you, sir?"

Thomas leaned against the counter and said softly, "What would it take to convince you to grab a cup of tea with a Welsh boy at the café?"

"I'll get my coat." She disappeared for a moment before reappearing in a brown woollen number and daintily accepting Thomas's offered arm.

They did not speak until they were comfortably seated in the warm, spacious café a few doors down from the bank.

Alaina sipped her tea, her lipstick leaving a telltale sign on the cup rim. "Spill it, Lindsey. What do you need? You would only ask me out if you needed something."

Thomas laid a hand on his heart. "Your accusations wound me."

Alaina snorted. "Like anyone could do that."

"You never know. But truth be told, I do need some information. I need you to see if you can get a glimpse at Price's personal ledgers. I want to know if they look legitimate."

She nodded slowly. "I'll see what I can do."

Shadow of the Past

2 March

AS CLARA STROLLED ALONG High Street after work towards the place she called *home*, she sighed with mixed satisfaction. Victory for the Allies in Kermanshah and Jericho pervaded the papers. Young Donnie Kirke's arm wasn't broken, only sprained, despite taking a nasty tumble off a ladder while playing pirates with his younger sister. Jennings had information on another intercepted transmission about Merryn. And yet news of the sinking of a British armed merchant cruiser, the HMS *Calgarian*, had reached the town only days after the sinking of the British hospital ship *Glenart Castle* in the Bristol Channel. Victory never seemed to come without devastating loss.

Passing a small alleyway as she turned onto Lewes Road, rough hands suddenly grabbed her from behind and yanked her into the shadows. A hand clamped over her mouth, muffling her scream.

"Is that any way to treat an old friend?" the voice purred.

Reynolds. Clara cringed and struggled in vain against the vice-like grip of the man she knew only too well.

"Crouthers sent me, so behave yourself," the voice whispered in her ear.

She fell limp at the name, and the hand left her mouth. "What do you want?" she hissed in angry terror.

"Information."

She stifled a grimace at the hot breath in her face. "Get it yourself. I can't help you."

A slap connected with her cheek and echoed off the stone walls. She bit back a cry as her cheek stung more than it should have as his ornamental ring scratched her skin. She aimed a swift kick at her captor's knee, but another slap disorientated her focus.

"Wrong answer, Miss Dankworth." The cat-like eyes gleamed in the fading light.

"Unhand me, sir," she demanded with icy fury.

"The information."

"No." She bit her lip against the pain shooting through her arms from his tight grip. She would have bruises for certain, and her arms were pinned in a manner making it impossible to reach her hidden derringer or her hatpin.

A sharp pang sliced through her face, followed by a third blow, and she tasted blood as she crumpled to the ground. Before Reynolds could get in another swing, Clara's hands shot up, and grasping both her hatpin and derringer, she lunged towards her attacker.

Reynolds leapt backwards out of reach of her pin, but he was still within reach of her pistol.

Equal portions of rage and terror raced through Clara's veins as she aimed the pistol at her attacker. She was a crack shot, and they both knew it. At that moment, shooting him held great appeal, but it would not solve her problem, only multiple it. Besides, wounding him would blow her cover and her past if he needed medical attention. Not to mention the police would look unkindly on a woman shooting a man, regardless of her story.

He sent her a taunting glare as if daring her to pull the trigger.

"You've been warned, Miss Dankworth," he hissed before retreating from the alley and disappearing around the corner.

Clara touched her face and felt a warm, sticky liquid trickling down her cheek. Her lip, too, was bleeding and her eye ached. Mustering up her courage, she limped out of the alley, keeping both her weapons in her hand just in case Reynolds was still lurking around.

Nana barked as Clara slipped in at the front gate of the boarding house. Hoping to avoid a scene, she crept around to the back door and tiptoed through the hall towards the stairs.

"Clara, is that you?" Elizabeth called from the parlour as the stairs squeaked under Clara's light tread.

That dastardly third step! It always squeaked at the wrong moment. She grimaced through her swollen lip. "Yes."

"Come here for a moment, will you?"

Clara hesitated, but a gasp echoed through the parlour as she poked her head in on the Forsythes and Elizabeth.

"Goodness, what happened to you, lassie?" Mrs. Forsythe cried, springing out of her seat.

Clara waved them off. "Nothing important."

Mrs. Forsythe rushed to the kitchen for water while Elizabeth made her sit down on the sofa. Clara cradled her head in her hands as the world spun around her. It was a wonder she had made it home. Mrs. Forsythe bathed her face while Mr. Forsythe instructed Robbie to call for the doctor immediately.

"She might need stitches," Mr. Forsythe called as Robbie dove out of the room and down the hallway. Facing Clara, he added indignantly, "How did this happen?"

"Wait till the doctor comes, love, then she only has to talk once," Mrs. Forsythe murmured to her husband as Clara tried to answer. "We should call the police."

"No!" The word shot out of Clara's mouth, and she winced at her intensity. "No police. Please."

The Forsythes exchanged a startled glace. "But, love—" Mrs. Forsythe said.

"Promise me you won't call them. I mean it," Clara begged. When the couple finally nodded, albeit with evident reluctance, she shut her eyes and leaned back heavily into the sofa cushions.

Thomas noisily rushed into the room five minutes later. "What happened?" When his eyes met hers, he scowled fiercely. "Who did this?"

"I got into a fight," she mumbled through her swollen lips, lightly wincing at the effort.

Pulling iodine from his bag, Thomas started cleaning the cuts. "You'll need two stitches on your cheek. Your lip will be fine, but you'll have a nice shiner come morning."

"Lovely," she muttered, wincing from the pain, but his gentleness surprised her. This was a different side of the brusque man she knew.

After the stitches, Thomas closed his bag and leaned forward in his chair expectantly. "Well?" When she didn't say anything, he added, "You certainly didn't do this to yourself."

"We want to help you, lass," Mr. Forsythe encouraged as Clara swallowed and studied the concerned audience with her good eye.

"I can't say," she said slowly.

The room fell silent until Robbie growled, "I'd happily bash his face if you tell me who he is, Miss Clara." His green eyes blazed with fierce anger as he clenched his fists.

Clara smiled weakly but gave her head a gentle shake. The kindly meant sentiment warmed her heart, and tears pricked her eyes.

Thomas sighed as he rose. "To bed, and don't you dare try to come in tomorrow. I'll cover for you and come by to check on you before church."

Her face hurt too much to argue so instead she let Elizabeth and Robbie help her up the stairs.

～

Thomas handed a bottle of aspirin to Mrs. Forsythe. "She'll be needing a few of these."

"Should I report it to the police, Lindsey?" Mr. Forsythe asked quietly as he showed the doctor to the door. "She made quite a fuss when the missus suggested it earlier."

Thomas pursed his lips thoughtfully. "I would like to, but we don't have the identity of the man to go on, and I doubt Clara will tell us who he is. Just keep a close eye on her for a while and don't let her go off alone if it can be helped. I'll do the same."

The fresh air fanned Thomas's angry features as he stepped outside. He heartily echoed Robbie's sentiment: he would like to bash that man's face, whoever he was.

Clara protested that she was fine when Thomas checked on her the following morning, and he begrudgingly agreed she could come back to work on Monday.

"Before I go, I would like to hear that story," he said in low tones, casting a glance over his shoulder at the open door. They didn't have much time before the Forsythes would be leaving for church and letting Clara rest. "Who did this?"

"Do you remember the man who came to town in January to persuade you I was working with the enemy? Well, it was him."

"Reynolds did this?" Thomas's eyebrows flew upwards as fire danced through his veins.

Clara nodded. "I met him on the Continent. He was working at Cummings Station in Rotterdam. When he asked me to marry him a year and a half ago, I said no. That was one of the reasons I left Rotterdam when I did."

"You'll have to keep talking, Clara; I'm not following." Thomas rubbed his forehead in an attempt to smooth out the crease. "This is more than a jilted man's revenge."

"He wanted information I couldn't give him."

Thomas studied her closely. "On what?"

"He didn't say, but I know him well enough to imagine. He's dangerous."

Thomas picked up his bag. "Will you let me alert the police?"

"He's probably left town already."

"Better safe than not." He stalled at the door. "What exactly happened?"

As Clara reluctantly recounted the previous night, an approving smile tugged at Thomas's mouth at the mention of the hatpin. "I will never underestimate you again. Well done."

The following morning, Clara returned to work, where her stitches and black eye created quite a titter among the day's patients.

"Hardly respectable for a lady," one woman whispered to another.

"I assure you, ladies, Miss Dankworth is not to blame for this mess," Thomas chided, overhearing them.

"Of course not, Doctor," the woman returned quickly.

Clara laughed good-naturedly when Thomas told her about it later as they worked on records. "Can't say I blame them."

Thomas studied her face. The stitches were healing nicely, but her eye and jaw were a mess of purple and blue bruises.

"I look forward to the day when I can get out of this," she murmured.

He grinned at her. "Don't give up yet."

"I'm not a quitter, Doctor."

"Of course you aren't. You're the only assistant still here after five months."

She chuckled. "Since I told you about the fight, will you tell me about... oh, I don't know. The ribbons?"

Thomas immediately hedged. "No. It doesn't concern you."

Clara smiled as she slipped on her coat, finished for the day. "I'll get it out of you someday, Lindsey."

He rolled his eyes. "Brave woman." A soft chuckle escaped his lips as the door clicked a moment later.

CHAPTER 26

No Small Tempest

11 March

IN BETWEEN PATIENTS, Clara rummaged through Thomas's desk drawers, searching for a patient's file. The middle drawer, which she knew was always locked, surprised her by opening under her touch. Glancing at the door, she listened. Thomas's lilting voice was still coming from the exam room. A little peek surely wouldn't hurt.

Swallowing the uneasy feeling in her chest, Clara thumbed through several papers. A collection of white feathers was tucked between a few sheets. She frowned, knowing them to be symbols of cowardice. Why in all of England would Thomas have kept them? She shook her head; she would never understand the man. A newspaper clipping caught her attention. Something about the Cromwell murders. She shoved the clipping aside and snatched up the picture that lay below it. Clara jumped as the door swung open, letting in a blue gingham–clad figure.

"Snooping, are we?" Lena asked with a smirk.

"Merely searching for a patient file."

Lena crossed the room and plucked the picture from Clara's hand. She examined it with obvious interest.

Clara snatched the photo back. "You will have to excuse me, Lena; I'm very busy."

The blonde sniffed haughtily, and the slam of the office door rattled the pictures on the walls. Clara sank into the desk chair. Lena was one of the most spoiled, flirtatious, and self-absorbed individuals she had ever met. She shook her head; what had the young woman been coming into the office for in the first place?

Thomas's head popped into the room several minutes later. "Was that Lena?"

"You heard?"

"The whole waiting room did."

Clara groaned. "Perfect."

Thomas's eyes narrowed at the picture in her hand, and he crossed his arms. "Looking for something?" he asked coolly.

Clara dropped the picture in the drawer and closed it. "Gerald Bennett's file."

Thomas crossed to the desk and extracted the file from a stack beside the telephone and handed it to her. "We'll talk about this later," was all he said between tight lips before disappearing back through the doorway.

After his last appointment, Thomas rejoined her in the office to finish the day's records.

Clara slipped on her coat, preparing to leave. "Where did you get that picture?" she asked quietly as she hesitated at the door.

"Why does it matter?" he said, refusing to look at her.

"Forget the why. I need to know," she insisted firmly.

He glanced at her, embers smoldering in the depths of his gaze. "Government property."

"Who are those men?"

"None of your business."

"But—"

"No." Thomas's voice rose several decibels.

Silence fell over the office. "Someday you'll get yourself into a problem you can't solve. Why don't you let people help you while they can?" She kept her voice cool and even, moving into the hallway towards the kitchen door.

"You're wrong, you know," he hollered after her. "I'm just fine on my own. Always have been, always will be!"

She stiffened as the words struck her like arrows. Pausing, she remained with her back to him as she lifted her chin and kept her voice level, though it was laced with anger. "According to you, I'm always wrong."

~

Thomas blinked as she disappeared, and the kitchen door slammed a moment later, signaling her departure. Leaning back in his chair, he let out a long breath, only to jump at the sight of Alaina standing in the doorway. He hadn't heard her come in.

"I can't believe you said that." Alaina crossed her arms, clearly displeased.

"It's rude to eavesdrop."

She ignored him. "You've changed. All this scheming and distrust. I hardly know you anymore. Do you even know yourself?"

"Don't you start on me now. People change, times change, you need to change with them," he snapped.

She said nothing for several moments. Just stared at him with fire in her brown eyes and a stubborn tilt of her chin that mirrored his own. At last, she said in a low, clear voice, "I have never had anything but your well-being in mind. My coming to Newhaven was clearly a mistake. I should have never come," and she turned on her heel to leave.

Thomas's voice stopped her. "You don't mean that."

As she glanced over her shoulder at him, Thomas saw a shadow had replaced the spark in her eyes, and with a tinge of sadness in her voice, she replied, "Actually, I think I do."

He stared at the vacant doorway long after she had left, her accusations whirling in his mind. *I hardly know you anymore. Do you even know yourself?* Beneath the lies and without the aliases? That wasn't a question he was ready to answer.

~

The meeting with Jennings later that night proved awkward. Upon seeing Thomas, Clara gave him a perfunctory nod but otherwise said nothing to him the rest of the evening. Alaina, too, appeared to be put out with the doctor, and Clara read the hurt expression on her face. If Jennings picked up on the tension, which Clara had no doubt he did—the man saw everything—, he made no mention of it. *Smart man.* After the meeting, Clara politely declined Thomas's offered ride home, pointing out she had ridden her bicycle.

"Dare I ask what this is about?" Jennings asked with concern in his sage eyes after the doctor had taken his leave.

"He's a hard man to work with. I thought I had him figured out," Clara said, rubbing her forehead. She could feel a headache coming on. "Do you have any inkling on why Crouthers assigned me to work with him?"

Jennings shook his head. "Thomas Lindsey is a visionary and one of the best agents MI5 has. But in the eight months he has been in Newhaven, you are his sixth assistant. I imagine Crouthers was running out of options, and like Thomas, you are one of the best."

"I hardly think so."

"You did good work in Rotterdam. I never understood why you wanted a transfer from foreign to domestic affairs."

"Do I need a reason?"

Jennings's eyes crinkled in a smile. "I know you well enough to know you wouldn't have left without one, my dear."

Clara shrugged and leaned back in her easy chair with a sigh. "You know about Cate?" When he nodded solemnly, she added hoarsely, "After her death, they found me. Or maybe they never lost me and were just biding their time. I don't know. But it was like a warning."

"More threats?"

She nodded. "I just wish I knew who from."

"We're still working on that."

"Do you think I could just quit and go home?" she asked suddenly.

Jennings chuckled, but there was a sadness in his face. "It's not that simple, and I know that's not what you want. Hang in there a little longer."

"Does... my contact know where I am?"

"Only that you are safe and nothing more, and that is how I intend to keep it, according to your wishes."

Clara thanked the colonel and bade him goodnight. She found Alaina waiting for her down the hallway near the staircase. "Is something wrong?" she asked the young woman.

"I'm sorry my cousin is so awful," Alaina said, offering an apologetic grimace.

Clara felt her jaw drop. "Cousin? Thomas?"

Alaina looped her arm through Clara's and led her down the stairs. "Yes, cousin. I wasn't going to tell you yet, but I think it's time you knew. Although, I must ask you not to tell anyone; it isn't exactly safe for our connection to be known. I'm sure it's no surprise to you that Thomas has made his fair share of enemies."

"I... of course," Clara spluttered.

Alaina sighed. "Thomas has been my hero since I was ten years old." Her eyes went soft. "But he's changed. He's not the Thomas I used to know."

"Cousins," Clara marvelled, shaking her head as they reached the bottom of the stairs. "I can see the resemblance now. I thought you two were a couple; you seem close."

"It's an act we use when we work together. We are close, just not in that way. I couldn't marry him if I wanted to, and trust me, right now, I definitely do not."

Clara almost laughed at Alaina's blunt words. "Why are you telling me this now?"

Alaina smiled at her approvingly. "You don't run from problems. And from what Jennings told me, you are Thomas's longest-lasting assistant. I believe that says a great deal about your character. You're good for him, and you don't let him walk all over you."

Clara huffed. "It's complicated."

"Oh, I know. Thomas complains about you all the time. That's what caught my attention. He didn't do that about any of the others." She paused. "Despite his flaws, Thomas is a good man, and trust me, I've known heaps of bad ones. For years I've been praying that God would send someone to shake up his carefully constructed world." Her gaze dropped to the floor as she whispered to herself, "Before his house of cards completely destroys him."

Despite her skepticism, Clara inwardly winced. She knew the feeling. "And you think that's me?"

"I still believe in miracles." Alaina hugged Clara, adding in a low tone, "Don't tell Thomas I told you about us. He's not ready for that yet. Goodnight."

CHAPTER 27

Love and War

12 March

FROM THE OFFICE, THOMAS HEARD A "HELLO?" in the waiting room. He was surprised to find Emily Price standing nervously in the middle of the room. Her arms crossed across her front as if for protection, but he knew better. The lovely girl suffered from a hunchback condition and was embarrassed by her appearance. He remembered overhearing cruel remarks whispered about her more than once.

He greeted her warmly with a smile. "I don't recall your name on my appointment list today."

"Oh, I'm not here for an appointment," she quickly clarified. "I thought you might be interested in this." She pulled a paper scrap from her skirt pocket.

Reading it quickly, Thomas's forehead puckered. "Where did you find this?"

"In the rubbish pile. Or rather beside the rubbish pile at work."

"Do you recognise the writing?"

Emily nodded. "Hazel's fella. He comes to the Hope Inn often."

"Do you know his name? What does he look like?"

Rubbing her nose in concentration, Emily recalled the facts. "His name is Sean. Don't know his last name. He's about your height. Blue eyes, auburn hair, and a beard. He works on the docks and has an accent like that friend of yours with the scar on his jaw."

"Kavan Grahame?"

She nodded, and Thomas smiled at her thoroughness. Tilting his head, he asked, "Could you do something for me?"

"Of course."

"Wait here a moment." He hurried to his office and dashed out a quick note to Kavan. Returning to the waiting room, Thomas entrusted the missive to Emily. "Kavan should be in tonight. You work the night shift?"

She nodded.

"Good. Give this to him without anyone noticing and come to me directly if you learn anything more about this Sean fellow."

Emily promised to follow his instructions to the letter. At the door, the girl hesitated, and Thomas caught a glimpse of hollow fear in her eyes when she turned back to face him. "Should I be concerned, Doctor Lindsey? Does this have anything to do with my father?"

Thomas flashed her a reassuring smile. "Say nothing of this except to Kavan or myself, and you'll be just fine, my dear."

Nodding and smiling her thanks, the stooped figure disappeared out the door.

The smile on his face faded as Thomas watched her retreating figure through the window. He knew Emily's mother had died several years ago, before he had come to Newhaven. Her banker father was not only Thomas's main reason for being in town, but also one of the most influential, selfish, and wealthy men in the area. However, Thomas well knew there was a vast difference between being rich in gold and being rich in love, and as rich as Price was in the former, he was certainly destitute in the latter.

~

18 March

Thomas received word from Kasey through Robbie that Chantelle would be arriving from France that night. The familiar hazel eyes gleamed in the moonlight as Thomas approached their meeting place at the cemetery on Lewes Road.

He laid a hand on the girl's shoulder. "Any infraction of rules?"

Chantelle tossed her head. "Never, sir."

"Pretty little liar," he muttered.

"I was careful as promised."

"Good, because the threat still stands. One slip up, and I send you to your great-aunt in Brighton."

Her glare shot daggers at him, but he met them steadily. At last, her eyes softened. "Please don't do that."

"I won't yet, and I don't want to, but I have to keep my promise to your father. That means you have to be careful."

Snatching up his hands in hers, Chantelle pleaded, "I will; just don't send me back."

Thomas squeezed her hands. "As long as we understand each other."

"Perfectly."

"Good. Now what do you have for me?"

"German news. I caught a conversation from Detweiler to The Piper on the wireless. They were talking about your assistant."

"Clara? What did they say?"

"Didn't make much sense. Something about papers, a murder, and an alliance."

Thomas frowned. This was new information. Papers and an alliance could be related to Price, but a murder? Something wasn't right. "Are you sure they were talking about Clara?"

"Positive. Also, the name Merryn came up again but no details."

If The Piper and Detweiler were talking *about* Clara, that proved beyond a doubt she wasn't the rogue agent. He had no doubts now, though the possibility had lingered in the back of his mind.

Chantelle studied Thomas's grave face. "She's quite charming."

"Who?"

"Clara, of course. And she knows French."

"She must be perfect in your eyes then."

Chantelle grinned. "Nearly."

"Where did the transmission come from?"

"I wrote down the coordinates." She handed him a scrap of paper.

Thomas studied them carefully. "Don't know them offhand. I'll have to look into them. Much obliged." As Chantelle nodded and turned to leave, he called after her softly, "Don't forget."

She flashed him an appreciative smile. "I know, I know, be careful. I always am, Thomas."

Thomas knocked firmly on the boarding house door five minutes later, and Robbie's cheery face appeared in answer.

"Come on in, Doc," the boy offered.

"No time. I need you to take these coordinates to Jennings. I want to know the location when he's finished."

Robbie snatched the slip of paper Thomas held out to him. "Right-o. Just tell Mum I'm off," and the boy dashed off into the night.

Thomas poked his head into the parlor and informed Mrs. Forsythe of Robbie's departure. The Scotswoman nodded knowingly, and Thomas took his leave.

The phone rang as he entered his office fifteen minutes later. "Doctor Lindsey; how may I help you?" he answered.

"What's this all about?" the voice asked fiercely. Jennings.

"Did you get the coordinates figured out?" Thomas asked pleasantly.

"Yes. What I want to know is—"

"Good," Thomas interrupted. "I'm on my way. I'll explain when I get there. Send Robbie home."

Ten minutes later, Thomas brushed past Kerridge, the butler, at the door and hurried up the stairs into Jennings's office. The older man stood staring meditatively into the fire.

"Sir," Thomas said politely.

Jennings frowned at him. "What were those coordinates?"

Thomas took a deep breath. "From France. An agent there intercepted a message over the wireless between The Piper and Detweiler. Those were the coordinates they originated from."

"Don't act without permission next time," Jennings growled.

Though Thomas chafed under the rebuke, he wisely said nothing.

"Detweiler was in Rotterdam, and the Piper was in Canterbury."

Thomas frowned. "None of us were out of town that night."

Sage eyes locked on Thomas's. "Seems to me Clara might have been right after all. The Piper is on the outside and pinning it on Newhaven."

"He would have to have someone on the inside then."

"Face the facts, Lindsey. I want an alibi from the whole division."

"Clara and I were at the clinic that day. I can't answer for Kasey, Robbie, or Lena."

Jennings's gaze returned to the fire. "I'm putting this whole division on probation."

"Excuse me? Last I checked we answered to Crouthers," Thomas countered coldly.

Jennings ignored him. "The Piper is my business. Nothing happens here without my oversight."

"Didn't think anything did," Thomas muttered.

Jennings strode over to his desk and wrote in silence for

several minutes before handing Thomas an envelope. "Take this to Robbie for the Secret Service headquarters in London. There will be a reply."

Thomas accepted the missive for the foreign intelligence department and moved to leave, but Jennings stopped him by holding out another envelope. "This one goes to Crouthers. I need them delivered tomorrow night."

A strange knot twisted in Thomas's stomach as he stalked out of the room. As he mulled over the words later that night, he hoped Jennings hadn't just made a terrible mistake.

CHAPTER 28

Tell No Tales

20 March

TWO DAYS LATER, Thomas wrinkled his nose as he caught a whiff of the coffee Clara set down on his desk. He eyed the black liquid suspiciously.

"Add milk and sugar," Clara suggested. She knew the curbing of his tea habits due to rationing had soured his mood.

He scowled. "I doubt the taste could possibly be improved."

"You do it with your tea. There's no difference."

"Of course there is." He watched her take a sip from her own cup. "How you drink it, I shall never understand."

"Then don't drink it."

"I won't," and he shoved away the offensive cup. "I would rather have tea."

"You know we're out."

He dropped his fist wearily on the desktop. "I hate this war."

"You must have a better reason for hating the war than tea rations," Clara chided, rolling her eyes at the doctor's overt childishness on the topic. She knew he had been up most of the night and was clearly running on little sleep. The air had cleared between the two of them since their argument the week before, but only after Thomas had apologised. In his own awkward way.

Moving toward her desk, she crouched and distastefully held up a grungy old piece of plumage. "Why the white feathers? I find them on the floor every so often, and I noticed them in your desk drawer."

Thomas eyed it gravely. "As a reminder that no matter what anyone says, I am no coward."

Coward? No, indeed. Borderline lunatic? Perhaps.

"I received my first one in London six weeks after the war started," he continued.

"Seems like a strange item to attach value to."

He shrugged. "A colleague unlawfully disposed of my collection of death threats, so white feathers seemed safe enough."

She stared at him. Had it been anyone else she would have assumed they were joking. But this being Thomas Lindsey, there was probably more truth in his words than she wanted to believe. "You kept death threats?"

He grinned. "Proof that none of them ever worked."

She shook her head slowly as a wave of dizziness rolled over her. If she had doubted it before, she was certain of it now—Thomas Lindsey was mad. Or at least as close to mad as a ridiculously intelligent and sane man could get. The telephone rang, interrupting any further argument as she snatched it up. "Nurse Clara."

"Have you seen Robbie?" Mrs. Forsythe's anxious voice asked, her Scottish brogue growing thicker with concern.

"Not since yesterday afternoon; why?"

"I can't find him anywhere. No one's seen him."

"I'll ask Thomas and be right over," Clara promised before hanging up the receiver. "Have you seen Robbie?" she asked, glancing at the doctor.

"Last night. He stopped in on his way home from London. Why?"

"Mrs. Forsythe said she can't find him, and no one's seen

him." She moved towards the door. "You're sure he went to London yesterday?"

"Yes, of course." He followed her into the kitchen, adding in a worried tone, "Let's go."

Quickly locking up the clinic, they hurried to the automobile and sped towards Lewes Road. Clara was out of the car almost before Thomas had fully come to a stop in front of the boarding house. They burst through the front door and found the Forsythes in the parlour with a constable.

"Any news?" Clara asked.

Mrs. Forsythe shook her head. "Nothing yet, lass."

"Have you checked with the Grahames at the harbour?" Thomas suggested.

"I checked with them both. They haven't seen him," Mr. Forsythe returned wearily.

"How about Alaina or the Jennings?" Clara added.

Again, Mrs. Forsythe shook her head. "Not there either."

"When did you last see him, miss?" the constable asked Clara.

"Yesterday afternoon at the clinic." She paused in thought. "It would have been about four o'clock."

"And you, Doctor?" the constable addressed Thomas.

"Eleven o'clock last night. He popped by the clinic on his way home from the train station. He went to London yesterday afternoon."

"Between four and eleven?" the constable clarified.

Thomas nodded, and the grandfather clock chimed across the room, echoing softly.

"I need to use your phone," the constable said to Mr. Forsythe.

While the constable stepped into the hall to ring ahead to London, Clara restlessly fiddled with a pleat in her skirt. Seven hours was plenty of time to travel to London and back. It was only a fifteen-minute walk between the clinic and the boarding house, so he couldn't have gotten home any later than 11:20 even if he was dawdling, as was often his nature. She had been awake at that time; she had heard the parlour clock strike half-past eleven and hadn't heard the door click or a creak on the stairs. That left two options: either he came home later and went out at an unearthly hour this morning, or worst of all, he never made it home at all.

I have to do something. Jumping up from her seat, she headed towards the back door. Footsteps behind her signalled Thomas on her heels. Near the doorstep lay Nana. Her chocolate eyes stared at her visitors pleadingly as she whimpered softly. Clara stooped to pat the dog's head, whispering, "We'll find him. Don't you worry." She marched across the yard to the barn. Her bicycle was in the corner, and Robbie's was right next to it. "He couldn't have gone far on foot," she commented.

Thomas nodded as he mounted it. "Let's go." He followed her out of the barn and up Lewes Road. "Why are we going north? There's nothing between here and Piddinghoe. Heading back to town would be our best chance."

"I have a hunch," was all Clara said as she turned onto the path leading into the local cemetery. Dismounting, she dropped her bicycle and hurried towards the far corner.

Thomas grabbed her elbow. "Can you please stop for a minute and explain yourself in a rational manner? I don't want to waste valuable time on a rabbit trail."

A flicker of hurt cut through her heart as she looked at him, but she said quietly, "Robbie showed me a special place here in the cemetery that Susan showed him. You can see a spectacular view of the downs. He often comes here to think. Besides, we were talking about heather the other day, and he said that corner had the best patch. He promised to bring me some."

Thomas nodded solemnly and motioned with his hand. "Lead on."

The northwest corner was empty. Clara sighed and prayed silently, *Lord, You know exactly where Robbie is. Please keep him safe and help us find him.*

"Where now?" Thomas asked quietly. "Back towards town?"

She shrugged. "Might as well." Pausing, she cupped her hands around her mouth and shouted, "Robbie!" Her voice echoed slightly off the downs, but there was no answer. Shaking her head, she started down another path.

"Clara, town is this way!" Thomas hollered after Clara's swiftly retreating form, but she didn't turn around.

As a light sprinkle began to fall, he groaned and jogged back towards the entrance where they had left their bicycles. They would be soaked in no time. He contemplated where else Robbie Forsythe may have run off to. Maybe he should try the train station and make sure the boy hadn't doubled back to London early this morning. Or perhaps—

A piercing scream from Clara's direction shattered the rest of his thoughts.

Dashing across the grassy lawn which was growing slick with rain, Thomas sprinted back in the direction he had seen her go. As he hurried down a row of tombstones, Clara had her back to him. "What in all of England—" But the words died in his throat as he looked over her shoulder, and a sickening sight met his eyes.

It was Robbie, lying on the grass with his face towards heaven amid the headstones. Gently pushing past Clara, Thomas sank to his knees and probed the boy's neck for a pulse, half hoping for a miracle. Nothing. Thomas was vaguely aware of the rustle of skirts beside him as Clara knelt and ran her hand over the red curly locks. Silent sobs rocked her back and forth in the rain.

The formerly bright green eyes were now dull and fixed unmoving on the grey sky. Blood soaked the lad's shirt front and coat, pooling on the grass beneath him. Robbie's blood-stained hand lay limp on his chest, as if he had clutched it as he fell. A heart shot. Thomas checked his watch; it was 8:30 in the morning. Judging by the stiffness of the body, he reckoned Robbie had been dead for about nine hours, which would put the time of death at less than an hour after the boy left the clinic the night before. Apart from the killer, Thomas had been the last one to have seen Robbie Forsythe alive.

He heard Clara flee, weeping. She would alert the police. A bloodied scrap of paper lay in Robbie's other hand. Thomas snatched at it. It was typewritten, and despite the drizzle, it was dry.

First warning. Dead men tell no tales.

Thomas's stomach roiled at the words, and his anger blazed. The sound of sobbing woke him from his reverie as he realised it was coming from his own voice. Robbie was gone. The fury welled up in his chest and found vent in a soul-wrenching roar that echoed through the stillness of the falling rain. So much for a miracle. The world had suddenly become very bleak, and he was completely powerless to change it.

~

24 March

Thomas sought out Jennings the day before the funeral and found the older man in his library, staring into the fire, his face as if turned to stone.

"What do you want, Lindsey?" Jennings asked without turning to look at his visitor.

Thomas blinked in surprise at the tone of the man's voice—hollow and almost lifeless, so unlike the stalwart colonel of only days ago. "There was no reply from London found on the body."

Jennings slowly pivoted to face the doctor. "Are you certain?"

Thomas nodded and held out the warning note he had found. "Sir, I think we can both agree this was no accident. That message was intercepted."

"The Piper," Jennings spat, followed by a curse.

Thomas waited in respectful silence as the colonel began to pace the floor restlessly. Double-crossing and espionage were one thing, but the cold-blooded murder of a sixteen-year-old messenger boy was quite another. Thomas's jaw tightened with suppressed anger of his own as he tried to shake the mental image of finding the boy's body in the cemetery. He was a doctor; he had seen death countless times, but none had ever shaken him to this magnitude, and from the look on the colonel's face, he knew the man felt the same way.

"He couldn't have known about the message. No one did." Jennings said at last. When Thomas hesitated, the colonel added, "Speak up, man."

"Maybe it wasn't the message they were after."

Jennings stopped pacing and met Thomas's gaze. "Keep talking."

"We have established that The Piper is someone on the inside, be it of your division or mine. Robbie went to both the Secret Service headquarters and Crouthers's office that evening. He could have heard something."

Jennings frowned. "Then why didn't he tell you when he saw you later that night?"

"He probably didn't know what he heard or saw was of any importance. Or he thought it could wait till morning." Thomas shrugged with a hopelessness that threatened to break him. "I wish I knew."

After the funeral on the twenty-fifth, the reality of the situation sank in like a dead weight, burning a hole in the hearts left behind. The police had conducted an inquest, but there were no suspects, no witnesses, and no answers. The note had been right —dead men tell no tales.

The next few weeks were endured in a state of numb silence. Easter was a somber affair. Days blurred together. Meals were neglected. Sleep was beyond question. War had come in a tangible way to the home front. News of the Spring Offensive launched by the Germans and the shelling of Paris only sank their hearts lower. March stretched into April, and the spring breezes arrived with the blooming of crocuses, bluebells, and purple orchids. The promise of new life was painfully poignant against the backdrop of such intense heartbreak.

On the first Saturday in April, Thomas sat Clara down in the office after she assigned the wrong dosage of medicine, which he thankfully caught before she sent it to the chemist.

"You haven't slept in weeks, have you?" he asked quietly, her sorrowful, sleep-deprived eyes mirroring what he knew was the same look on his own face.

She blinked at him blankly. "I don't remember. Too many nightmares," was all she whispered.

He reached out and gently touched her shoulder. The strong, unflappable woman was beginning to crumble. But she couldn't. Not yet. "The war won't last forever. You'll make it."

"I'm not so sure anymore."

"For now, you need sleep. I'm going to send you home."

"No, please don't," she begged in a frenzy, her eyes flashing in panic.

He sighed. They couldn't keep going on like this. "I have to. Don't worry, Clara; I'll get you through this."

"Don't make promises you can't keep," she whispered. Regarding him with a smile full of pity and eyes full of regret, she slipped from the room.

His mind mulled over the sickening circumstances. An innocent boy was dead because of their work for freedom. Robbie had paid the ultimate price, leaving those behind to pick up the pieces. Thomas's thoughts wandered to the ribbons hidden in his room, and he clenched his jaw. "I will get justice for you; I swear it," he muttered.

In the wake of Clara's absence, Thomas heard a familiar voice echo through his mind—a voice he hadn't heard in thirteen years.

Trust in the Lord with all your heart and lean not on your own understanding. In all your ways acknowledge Him and He shall direct your paths. Surrender is the only way to success, my son.

Shoving the voice aside, Thomas angrily flipped through the stack of already organised files on his desk. God had done precious little for him. Thomas Lindsey was in charge of his own life, and he was leaving nothing to chance.

Later in the afternoon, Thomas drove out to the boarding house to check on Clara.

A red-eyed Mrs. Forsythe answered his firm knock. Her usually cheerful face faltered with a smile, and she lifted a hand to her mouth to muffled a sob.

"I'm so sorry," he said hoarsely.

The woman reached out to him and pulled him into a motherly embrace, clinging to him for dear life while silent sobs shook her frame.

Thomas swallowed hard and willed the moisture out of his own eyes. It had been two weeks since Robbie's passing. Would the pain ever stop? From his previous experience, no. Sorrow went right on aching. There were some wounds time could never heal.

When Mrs. Forsythe stepped away, she dabbed her eyes with her apron. "That boy thought the world of you. You were good for him."

Thomas's throat constricted, and he dipped his chin in a nod to hide the moisture threatening to escape his lashes. *He was good for me, too.*

"You're here to see Clara, I know. Poor thing." Mrs. Forsythe sniffled. "She's out back with Nana."

"Obliged." Thomas squeezed the woman's shoulder before slipping around the side of the house. True enough, there was Clara on the back step with Nana's head in her lap.

"Come on, Nana, you have to eat," Clara coaxed.

Thomas heard her voice crack, but Nana made no motion of interest in the dish Clara held. "Can't say it looks appetising," he said quietly as he approached and eased himself down on the step beside her. His nose scrunched at the soggy-looking mess of bread and beef broth.

Clara glared at him and slammed the dish down, making Nana jump. "You aren't helping."

He said nothing but watched as she threaded her fingers into Nana's thick fur. At least she hadn't thrown the dish at him. She held her shoulders rigid and yet she trembled. He read the telltale signs of sleepless nights from the dark half-moons under her eyes. "I sent you home to rest," he said softly.

"Can't. I have to keep busy." Her voice was tight. "I don't want to remember."

He sighed. "I know."

In silence, they sat facing the cemetery, which was draped in a mockery of budding spring foliage. It was alive but full of death. Something of beauty had become foreboding. A hollow shell of what used to be.

At last, Thomas stood and held out his hand. "Come. You need to rest."

"Don't make me."

Something in her upturned face threatened to shatter him. The anguished look of terror in her eyes. He knew the signs of living a nightmare. He had seen them often enough in himself.

Swallowing hard, he whispered, "I have to," and gently he tugged her to her feet.

She stumbled slightly, and he steadied her elbow before leading her inside.

Elizabeth intercepted them in the hall and followed them up the stairs.

Clara perched on the edge of her bed with Elizabeth beside her, while Thomas drew the curtains.

"You'll be all right," he heard Elizabeth whisper softly. Clara only dropped her head into her hands with a shudder.

Opening his bag, Thomas mixed a few drops of a laudanum tincture into some water and crouched down to eye level with Clara. He handed her the cup. "Drink this."

Clara's terror-stricken eyes met his. "Please, no," she whispered.

"It's for your own good," he soothed, but the fear didn't leave her face. "Do you trust me?" He held her gaze with as much gentleness and sincerity as he could muster. He knew how hard this was on her, on him, on the Forsythes, on everyone. Robbie and Clara had shared a special bond; one that had been cruelly broken. Finally, she lifted the cup to her lips with shaking hands and drank the medicine.

"Now, to bed. I'll be back to check on you later," he instructed kindly, leaving her in Elizabeth's care.

In the privacy of his car, Thomas slammed his fist against the steering wheel and grit his teeth. His eyes fixed unseeingly on the cemetery next door. *It's all my fault. I should have never recruited him. Should have never let him put himself in harm's way.* "We'll find whoever did this," he whispered hoarsely as a scalding tear rolled down his cheek. "I promise."

∼

9 April

Several days later, Clara inhaled the salty air hanging over the Channel and listened as the waves crashed against the lower wall of the promenade. Her tears were spent and her heart sore. In her hand, she clutched a crumpled sprig of heather from the cemetery, and her mind wandered back several weeks.

Clara and Robbie perched on a large flat rock in the northwest corner of the cemetery overlooking the downs.

"This is my favourite spot," Robbie said happily. "Susan showed it to me. She liked to come here to think; now it's my thinking spot."

"You must really miss her."

Robbie nodded and then slowly tugged a small, ragged book from the inside pocket of his jacket. It was a copy of Peter Pan. *"Susan gave this to me for my eighth birthday. It's just a kid's story but..." He shrugged, and the tips of his ears reddened. "It makes me feel closer to her. Probably sounds silly."*

Clara smiled gently. "Not at all. Stories remind us that there is hope in the darkness. They sing the songs of truth and light back to us when our hearts have forgotten. They remind us of who we are and where we are going. That isn't just a story; it's a memory."

Robbie's green eyes shone with unshed tears of appreciation. "I promised her I would be brave until she came home, so she would be proud of me."

Reaching out, Clara covered one of his hands with hers. "She's proud of you already, Robbie."

"How do you know?"

She squeezed his hand. Despite his sixteen years, there was still something of a little boy inside of him. "Because I know I am proud of you."

Clara covered her mouth to smother a sob. That had been a week before his death. The sound of a limping gait caught her attention from behind.

"I'm sorry, missy," Kasey said softly, placing a hand on her shoulder.

She nodded as a fresh supply of tears threatened to fall. "He was only a boy. Why... why did God let it happen?" she whispered.

"I don't know," Kasey said huskily. "There's a powerful amount of evil in this world, and it breaks the Good Lord's heart even more than it breaks ours. But that's why we have hope. Hope that this world isn't our final home. Hope that there is more to this life than tears and darkness. Hope isn't a thing. Hope is Jesus. As for His purpose, there are some things we will never understand this side of eternity."

"Robbie said something like that to me a little while before he... he..." Clara couldn't give utterance to the word.

"You can say it. He died, but he's alive in a place with no tears, pain, or regrets."

"I believe that. I really do, but everything is..." She waved her hand in the air in the helpless gesture. "Broken in pieces."

Kasey hugged her. "I know the feeling."

As the rough wool of the captain's overcoat tickled her cheek and the aromatic smell of tobacco and sea spray filled her nose, Clara remembered that nearly forty-five years ago, Kasey had lost his wife, Molly, and daughter, Charlotte, to consumption. The loss had hurt him badly enough that the man hadn't stepped foot in Ireland since.

"My little girl was like you. You've always reminded me of the granddaughter I never had," he whispered wistfully, his blue eyes shining in memory.

Clara half-smiled up at him. "And you, the grandfather I never knew."

Kasey squeezed her hand and steadily gazed out over the Channel. "Just remember, we don't mourn as those who have no hope. Robbie knew where he was going. He knew the risks, and he accepted them. Let him go and leave him in God's hands."

Kasey's words echoed through Clara's mind that night as she fought to fall asleep. *Let him go and leave him in God's hands.* She would never forget him, but she could release the pain to her Saviour and commit Robbie to Him, too. After all, God loved Robbie even more than she did. Peace washed over her heart, and for the first time since she had seen that grey, lifeless body lying in the cemetery three weeks ago, Clara fell asleep without the haunting dreams and fears to torment her.

CHAPTER 29

When Tomorrow Came

19 April

THOMAS HURRIED to answer the ring at the door. It was after hours, but injuries and emergencies had little respect or concept of time. Swinging the front door open revealed the fashionably dressed figure of a young girl, hardly more than twelve or thirteen, cradling her left hand. He ushered her into the examination room for a closer look.

"What happened, Miss...?"

"Fletcher. Josephine Fletcher," the girl replied with gentle dignity. "I tripped."

Thomas probed the swollen wrist. It wasn't broken, only sprained, but the deep one-inch gash on the back of her hand needed stitches. He was careful to clean the area to prevent infection before he sutured the wound closed. Straightening after wrapping the injury, he studied his patient with intense interest.

Josephine had said nothing as he worked, but the pain was evident by the creases in her broad forehead and the pallor in her round cheeks. She had a prominent and pointed nose, her hair was the colour of bronzed gold, and her eyes were an unusual shade of deep violet.

"Where are your parents?" he asked.

"Dead." A glimmer flashed through her eyes.

For an instant, Thomas deciphered it as sorrow, but could it be more than that? Was it fear?

"They perished in the shipwreck of the SS *California* last year. I am travelling alone to visit my aunt in Hastings, but I stopped here for the night."

"My condolences. Where are you travelling from?"

"Cornwall."

Giving himself a mental shake for the interrogation, Thomas smiled at her. "A pleasure to have met you, Miss Fletcher, despite the unfortunate circumstances."

"Likewise, Doctor..."

"Lindsey." He shook hands with the girl and showed her to the door. "Allow me to escort you back to your hotel. Where are you staying?"

"The Bridge Hotel on High Street." Josephine took his offered arm with an air of surprise, clearly not having expected the courteous offer.

They walked in companionable silence down the deserted High Street until they reached the warmly lit hotel.

"Come and see me tomorrow if you have any trouble with your arm," Thomas said politely as he opened the door for the girl.

Josephine nodded. "Thank you, Doctor."

With a bow, Thomas left her and retreated down the cobbled street in the direction of Bridge Street. His thoughts focused on his late-night patient. There was something more to her than she let on, but he couldn't put his finger on it. All he could do was hope that she would show up tomorrow.

But somehow, he had a feeling she wouldn't.

~

20 April

Thomas told Clara about Josephine the next morning, in case the young girl came in while he was out on house calls, and Clara promised to keep an eye out for her. When he returned, the mysterious Miss Fletcher had not made an appearance. Indeed, by the end of the day, he was convinced she would not.

Clara stayed late at the clinic to cover for him while he took an emergency call at the harbour. The clock struck ten when he finally pushed open the kitchen door and dropped his bag on the table.

"Quiet night," Clara said, poking her head in the open doorway.

Thomas rubbed his forehead and helped himself to a hot cup of cocoa. "Good."

A soft knock came on the door behind him. Doctor and nurse frowned; patients came in at the front door, not the back.

With his hand on his hip holster, Thomas eased the door open and found himself staring into the violet eyes of Josephine Fletcher. "Miss Fletcher, come in. This is my assistant—"

"Clara Dankworth, I know," Josephine said quietly, keeping her eyes trained on the worn floorboards, as he closed the door behind her.

"How could you...? Ohhhh." Clara's voice held a note of realisation. "You must be Merryn."

Thomas stared at Clara as if she had lost her mind, but his jaw dropped when the girl stole a glance at him and nodded. Recovering himself, he demanded, "Who are you? Who are you truly?"

Josephine trembled visibly as she hugged her arms across her chest, clutching her coat sleeves. She looked so small, so lost. With great effort, she kept her voice steady. "Lotta. Lotta Detweiler."

"Detweiler!" Thomas roared.

"Thomas, don't shout," Clara admonished as the girl shrank away from him. Approaching Lotta, she laid a hand on her shoulder and said softly, "As in Herr Anton Detweiler?"

Lotta nodded. "He is my uncle. Please, he forced me here. I didn't want to come."

Thomas frowned. "Keep talking."

"I was sent to retrieve this from Edward Price," and Lotta slipped an oilcloth package from beneath her red cloak. "And I am supposed to return to Germany with it. Without it, I won't be allowed back into the country."

"Can your uncle really prohibit you from entering the border?" Thomas cut in.

"You have no idea how much he is capable of. He... he can do anything."

"Why are you telling us this?" Clara asked slowly.

"Because I don't want to be arrested." Lotta hesitated. "I should like to strike a bargain with you."

"Go on," Clara urged gently, seeming to ignore the withering glare Thomas shot at her.

"I'll give you the package, if you'll let me go and never say a word about my identity to anyone until the end of the war."

Thomas snorted. "So you can return to Germany and continue to help the enemy? I think not."

"No, sir, I don't want to go back; I can't. I love Germany, and it's my home, but you aren't like the English folk I was taught to hate. You were kind, Doctor Lindsey; much kinder than I deserved. At least, yesterday you were. Now, please, will you?" Lotta begged, her violet eyes flickering with the terror of a hunted animal. She clearly knew far too much fear for one so young.

Thomas and Clara shared a long look. To risk this was to risk everything. They needed that information desperately, and this could be the only way to get it. Or, it could be a trap.

Receiving a slight nod of affirmation from Clara, Thomas said at last, "Deal, but on one condition."

"Name it."

"If we can't tell anyone about this, neither can you."

Lotta nodded in solemn agreement. "You have my word and my thanks."

Thomas crossed his arms. "How much of your story was a lie? You have a very convincing Cornish accent."

Lotta coloured. "My parents are dead. They were silenced for disagreeing with the German government years ago. That's why I live with my uncle, but he threatened me with the same fate if I didn't help him. I was scared."

"And the accent?" Clara pressed.

"My parents and I used to spend time in Cornwall at St. Merryn's parish every summer. I picked up the accent to blend in."

Thomas had to hand it to the girl. She was clever, level-headed, and in the process of outsmarting her uncle. Suddenly, he asked, "Lotta, who is The Piper?"

"The Pied Piper of Hamelin?" the girl asked slowly in evident confusion.

Thomas rolled his eyes. She was either an incredibly apt liar or telling the truth. "No, the double agent in England."

Realisation flashed across Lotta's face. "I don't know who he is or what his name is, only that he's Irish."

Irish? That was a new piece of information. And valuable. Thomas stroked his chin as he tried to add the new detail to what he already knew about the elusive spy.

"What do they want?" Clara asked.

"Power and money. It's all wrapped up in someone they call The Pawn, and they're getting desperate."

"Do you know who The Pawn is, or how much time we have before they do... well, whatever it is they have planned?" was Thomas's next question.

Lotta shook her head.

Thomas let out a puff of air. "How about Fallamhan? Do you know anything about him?"

"No, sir, but there might be something in the package."

Clara opened her handbag, which lay on the table, and drew out a stack of pounds—enough for a passenger ship's fare—and gave the girl a warm hug. "Be safe wherever you end up, and God be with you, Lotta."

"Thank you." Lotta smiled with tears in her eyes. *"Auf Wiedersehen."*

Neither doctor nor nurse said a word after Lotta Detweiler slipped out of the kitchen into the black recesses of the night. The oilcloth package lay unheeded on the table before them, reminding them of the decision they had just made.

Clara broached the silence. "Did we—?"

"We did." Thomas stared vacantly at the package. "How are we going to explain this?"

"Haven't the faintest," Clara murmured, adding under her breath, "I hope we didn't just make a terrible mistake."

Thomas ran his fingers through his hair and dropped his gaze to the worn floorboards. *So do I.*

"Where did you get this?" Jennings exclaimed in utter astonishment when Thomas brought the package to him half an hour later, as the doctor had decided to complete this mission alone.

"It was intercepted," Thomas said simply. *That's the truth.* Truth? He nearly snorted. Never had he been concerned about stretching facts if it suited his needs before. Why did it feel so necessary to be truthful now?

"And the messenger?"

"Escaped." *Also the truth.* Clara must really be rubbing off on him.

"Was it Merryn?"

"Possibly."

Jennings stroked his chin and paced the velvet carpet of his office.

Thomas sat in rigid silence, earnestly hoping his superior would not press further on the subject.

When the colonel finally ceased his pacing, he studied the younger man curiously with his probing, sage eyes. "This was the break we needed," he said at length. "We have some names and dates. We still need the evidence to tie Price to the Germans so we can take him into custody... but, well done."

CHAPTER 30

When All was Lost

30 April

THOMAS RUBBED HIS ACHING FOREHEAD. He couldn't believe tomorrow was the first of May. He needed to finish up his patient records so he could send Mrs. Peterson her husband's portion of the clinic's fees. The phone rang, and he stifled a groan. The last thing he wanted at that moment was an emergency call. Lifting the receiver, he was astonished to hear Mrs. Landis, the Prices' housekeeper, on the other end, sobbing.

"Whatever is the matter?" he asked in alarm.

"Please come immediately," she said, strain evident in her tone.

"I'm on my way." Slamming down the earpiece, he snatched up his bag and dashed out the door.

Driving as fast as he dared, he hurriedly pulled up in front of the wealthy banker's house and was startled to find the place swarming with police. After parking, he brushed past Hyde, the butler, and found Emily sitting in the parlour with Mrs. Landis. The girl's face was ashen, and her hands trembled where they lay in her lap.

Thomas touched her shoulder gently to avoid alarming her. "What happened?"

The vacant eyes glanced up at him and began to pool. "Father, he... they said... he's..." No further intelligible words came out as the girl dissolved into another fit of tears.

Thomas's mind raced to piece together the fragments of information. Something had happened to Edward Price, something horrific enough to make his daughter weep. With the police involved and no Price in sight, his stomach flopped. Reaching his own conclusions, he was sure he could finish the end of Emily's sentence. "I'm going to talk to the inspector. I'll be back shortly," he said soothingly before hurrying from the room, leaving her with the housekeeper. He found the tall, greying inspector upstairs outside Price's office. "What's going on? Mrs. Landis called me."

Inspector Ashely nodded in acknowledgement of his presence. Shadows lingered in his grey eyes as he motioned towards the office door. "Price is dead. I would appreciate it if you could give us an approximation on how long he has been so."

Thomas sighed inwardly at the confirmation of his suspicions. "How?"

"Apparent suicide," Ashely stated grimly as he held the door open for Thomas.

Marching into the room, Thomas found the desk lamp lit, and the dead man sprawled out on the floor near the window. The same window Thomas had snuck through nearly five months earlier. "Anything suspicious or moved?" he questioned as he knelt beside the limp figure.

Ashely shook his head in the negative.

A splattering of blood had seeped into the carpet by the man's head. Thomas touched the wound gingerly and rubbed his fingers —the blood was dry, the black soot from the gun's discharge easily rubbing off. *The gun wasn't pressed against his head but within close contact.* After a thorough examination, Thomas straightened as his eyes darted around the room. He moved to inspect the window and looked out thoughtfully. It was unlocked. "'Something is rotten in the state of Denmark,'" he muttered to himself before turning to the inspector. He frowned. When had he started quoting Shakespeare?

"Well?" Ashely pressed expectantly.

Thomas checked his pocket watch. It was ten o'clock. "I am going to approximate about six hours ago. Who found him?"

"Miss Emily tried the door earlier this evening, but it was locked from the inside. Hyde broke the door down about an hour ago and found him. Poor bloke."

"Yes," Thomas mused, unsure if the man's sympathies were directed at the butler or the victim. He pointed to the pistol lying near Price's hand. "Is that the weapon?"

"Appears to be." Ashely motioned to the gun cabinet on the opposite side of the room. "From his collection. German-made if I'm not mistaken."

Thomas recognised it as the same gun which held the message he had found the night he broke in. Something wasn't adding up. "Did no one hear the shot?"

Ashely shook his head. "Miss Emily, Mrs. Landis, and Hyde were all out. Price was alone in the house minus the servants downstairs in the kitchen, but all of them claim they heard nothing."

"Did you check below the window? It was unlocked," Thomas asked casually.

Ashely scoffed. "We're on the second storey, and the only way up is that rickety old trellis. It couldn't hold a child, let alone a grown man. Besides, there's no evidence of murder. It's a straight-forward suicide."

Thomas didn't press the window issue any further. It wouldn't put him in a good light to mention that he had made it up and down the trellis just fine. Not that Ashely needed to know that. He decided it was time to make his exit. "I'll let you resume your investigation. I must see to Miss Emily."

Emily was in much the same state as he had left her earlier, and she agreed to his suggestion of staying with Alaina at the Jenningses' house that night. After he dropped the girl off and gave her a sedative, Jennings pulled him aside to his office, where Thomas gave him a brief sketch of the events.

"Poor girl," Jennings mused. "This doesn't bode well for us. Price still had information we needed, and dead men tell no tales."

Thomas remained deep in thought as he drove back to the clinic. Jennings was right—it was bad timing—but there was more. Of one thing he was perfectly certain: Edward Price hadn't committed suicide. It was clearly murder.

"Murder? Are you sure?" Clara asked in disbelief when he told her about the night's events the following morning.

"Positive. It was meant to look like suicide, but there are too many little things that say otherwise."

"Such as?"

"The window was unlocked, and there's a trellis. I've climbed it before, but there are no footprints on the ground."

"But the door was locked from the inside."

"He didn't want to be disturbed; it's his practice. Furthermore, the gun wound is all wrong. Price was right-handed, but the bullet entered on the left. Plus, there's no powder evidence on Price's hands, and there would be if he had pulled the trigger."

Clara stared at him in amazed silence. "Did you tell the inspector?"

"No, Ashely saw what the murderer wanted him to see, but the apparent isn't always the truth. Besides, there is no evidence to point to the identity of the killer, so that won't help him. It is probably the best for the town since Robbie..." He didn't need to finish his sentence. Both were still keenly aware of the unsolved murder not even a month and a half earlier. He cleared his throat and shifted uncomfortably.

Clara took a deep breath. "How about Jennings?"

"I told him last night, and he agreed. We'll keep it quiet for now but be on the lookout."

"But shouldn't the town know there's a murderer on the loose?"

Thomas shook his head. "We would risk tipping off the enemy. As far as he knows, the police consider it a suicide. Jennings said for now we'll keep it that way."

"A man is dead. It just seems wrong—"

Thomas cut her off with a huff. "There's not much we can do about that now. He may have been an enemy, but he still had information we needed. Besides, this was Jennings's order. What I want to know is who killed him and why. Something tells me we're not the only ones who wanted information from Edward Price."

Clara cocked her head thoughtfully. "What about Lotta's package?"

"Meaning?"

"If Detweiler found out Lotta didn't return with the package, maybe he assumed Price had double-crossed him? Sent someone to confront him and things escalated?"

Thomas shrugged, but the implication of her words was not lost on him. There was a chance their decision may have been the indirect cause of Price's murder.

CHAPTER 31

Foreign Accounts

7 May

"THOMAS, DO YOU HAVE A MOMENT?" Alaina asked from the office doorway.

"For you, always." Pushing aside his paperwork, Thomas gave her an expectant look as she sat down across from him.

"I was able to look through Price's books."

Thomas raised an eyebrow. It had only been a week since Price's death, but with the banker out of the way, Alaina had easier access to the man's paperwork. "And?"

"They are impeccable."

"Is that a good thing or a bad thing?"

"If he is..." She bit her lip. "If he was guilty of all we assume, it means there would have to be another set of books somewhere."

Thomas frowned thoughtfully. "Can you tell anything by the bank set?"

She shook her head. "Do you think Emily would let us in to have a look around her father's office?"

"You think he kept them at the house?"

She shrugged. "Why not? He didn't expect anyone to be suspicious of him."

"See, I told you we needed you around here. I'll give her a ring and ask."

Though still shaken from the past week's events, Emily was willing to be of assistance, and it was arranged for Thomas to meet her and Alaina at the Price estate at eight o'clock that night.

Thomas shivered in the damp night air and stamped his feet as he waited for the young women to arrive. He pondered what they might find inside. Last he had heard, Ashely was still ruling Price's death a suicide, though the division was collectively convinced it was murder. Clara and Thomas were certain it had to do with Lotta, but, true to their word, they hadn't mentioned that suspicion to Jennings.

In the dim light, Thomas saw two heads bob up the driveway —one wearing a hat, the other without. He shook his head with a smirk. Alaina couldn't remember her hat to save her life, excepting Sunday mornings, but he attributed that to Hannah Jennings's good influence.

The two young women met him on the front porch, and Emily rang the doorbell. Hyde opened the door, ushering them inside, and Emily politely answered his commonplace inquiries before leading her friends upstairs.

Inside Price's office, little had changed. Emily locked the door behind them to prevent any interruption, and the trio spread out in search of the books.

"Is Clara on call tonight?" Alaina asked curiously, as if suddenly realising the nurse's missing presence.

"Mmmhmm," Thomas murmured as he thumbed through several volumes on the bookshelves.

Emily surprised her companions by discovering a hidden compartment in the wooden slats lining the lower half of the walls near the easy chair in the corner.

Thomas reached into the gaping cavity and groped blindly for anything that might be hidden there. He started when his fingers brushed a cool metallic box. "I need a light," he said urgently.

Alaina pressed a torch she found in the desk drawer into his hand.

Shining the light into the hole revealed a small, compact safe. "We need a key."

"I saw a key ring in the desk," Alaina said, springing back to the oak desk and rummaging through the drawers. She tossed him a set of keys. "Try these."

None of them worked.

The trio sprawled out and searched the room again. They rifled through every drawer, shelf, and box, but no more keys emerged. Emily dropped into an easy chair with a weary, frustrated sigh. Alaina perched on the desk, frowning intently at the carpet. Thomas raked his fingers through his curls and paced the floor. Suddenly, he stopped and stared intently at the painting on the wall. It was a landscape portrait of a mist-covered mountain range.

Emily noticed his keen interest in the artwork. "Do you like it?"

Thomas didn't acknowledge the question as he approached the painting. The best-kept secrets were always hidden in plain sight. Price had hidden a message in the barrel of his German pistol; why not a German painting? Smirking, Thomas thought of his own picture on the wall, and the secrets it hid. Clever minds just might think alike. The secret of the safe lay in the picture—somewhere. Probing the frame, he found a tiny catch and pressed it. A piece of the frame slid aside, revealing a cubbyhole with a key inside. He held it up in triumph for his companions to see, and both girls bolted upright in astonishment.

"How did you—?" Alaina spluttered.

Thomas gave a blasé wave of his hand. "A replica of *The Giant Mountains* by German painter Caspar David Friedrich. Not much to figure out." He wasn't about to spill his own secrets just to explain someone else's. Crouching before the yawning hole again, Thomas felt for the safe. "Hold the light, won't you?" he said to Alaina, and the young woman obliged, allowing him to see what he was doing.

The key slid into the lock perfectly and the safe's door swung open, revealing several books. Thomas handed them to Alaina and waited for her to peruse them. Experience had taught him she could detect fake records from real ones in a matter of minutes, and he wasn't disappointed.

A smile lit up Alaina's face, and her brown eyes danced in success. "These are the real ones."

"What do they say?" Emily asked curiously.

"I'll need some time to fully analyse them."

After tidying up the study and relocking the safe, Thomas drove the young women back to the Jenningses' estate. With a promise from Alaina to keep him informed as to her progress, he drove back to the clinic to relieve Clara, who had just returned from a call.

The following afternoon, Alaina called the clinic asking for Thomas to swing round to the Jenningses' house immediately. Clara took the message and passed it onto the doctor, stressing the urgency in Alaina's voice.

Thomas hurried out to his car and sped towards the colonel's. Alaina met him at the front door, dragging him outside for a stroll in the garden so they could speak in private.

Extracting his sleeve from her grip, Thomas said, "I doubt you called me here just for a stroll. What's going on?"

"The accounts. I cracked the code." Alaina's eyes shone, not with the success of the previous night, but with a new gleam of horror. "They're foreign accounts, Thomas."

Thomas's lungs deflated as he stared at his cousin. A gentle breeze toyed with his curls, and he rubbed his forehead. "Foreign accounts?"

Alaina nodded. "You need to find out exactly what Price's foreign connections were. There's a notice about a sum of money that is to be wired out on the tenth of May."

"That's only two days away. Where to?"

"I'm still working on that, but I need to know where it's coming from first."

"I'll ask Emily," Thomas said in a flat tone, dreading the coming conversation.

"She's at the grocery."

He nodded and left the garden. The drive into town seemed to take longer than usual with his impatience, but he soon found himself in front of the Forsythes' grocery. Emily was stepping out the door as he parked.

"Care for a ride?" he called through the open window.

She flashed him a tired smile and availed herself of his offer. He caught her studying him curiously as they drove through town. "Is something wrong, Doctor?"

"I was hoping to ask you a few questions." At the girl's encouraging nod, he continued, "Where was your mother from?"

A shadow flickered through her green eyes. "Hartford, Connecticut."

"Can you tell me about her family?"

"She was an only child, but her parents are still living in the family home, though they are quite advanced in years now."

"When was the last time you visited America?"

"A little more than a year before Mother died. The summer of 1913."

"Did your father accompany you?"

"He did."

"Was there anything unusual about that trip?"

Emily pondered for a moment before shaking her head slowly. "No, not overly unusual. My parents had several business meetings to attend and—"

"Both of them?"

"Yes. My mother inherited several businesses and properties in both Hartford and Philadelphia."

Philadelphia? A light clicked in Thomas's mind. "Did that trip change anything in your family?"

"Mother and Father had an argument, over what I don't

know, but that was all. Life continued as it had until..." Emily's voice fell to a whisper. "The day of the accident."

They continued driving in silence for some minutes. Thomas knew of the accident she spoke of. Myra Evans Price had been one of ten fatalities in the Ilford rail crash on New Year's Day, 1915, when two passenger trains collided at a London station.

"Thank you for your help, Emily," he said as they reached the manor.

She offered a weak smile, appearing far older than her sixteen years. "No, Doctor, thank you. I appreciate what you're doing."

Leaving her with Mrs. Jennings in the parlour, Thomas inquired as to Alaina's location and learned she was upstairs in the library. Darting up the stairs, two at a time, he burst into the library, where he found her huddled over the bank ledgers. Her pen was poised over a sheet of paper, and she was clearly taking notes.

"Find anything?" she asked without looking up as Thomas perched on the edge of the desk she sat at.

"Philadelphia, Pennsylvania or Hartford, Connecticut. I'm leaning towards the former."

Alaina glanced at him, her face lined with worry. "Good work. We need to talk to Jennings."

They found the colonel in his study, buried under paperwork and in a less than jovial mood.

Thomas hastily filled Jennings in on the morning conversation with Emily. "You will remember Alaina found a discrepancy in the books, and I suspected foreign accounts."

"I don't want speculation," Jennings interrupted.

"Sir, we found the original ledgers, and they have proof of foreign accounts," Alaina added. "I just didn't know where they originated from."

"I talked to Emily this morning, and I think we have the answer. Myra Evans Price, an American multimillionaire with dealings in both Hartford and Philadelphia."

"And there is a notice in the original ledger about a sum of money to be wired out of the account two days from now," Alaina added.

Jennings sat in abject silence, taking in the information, his sage eyes smoldering with thoughtfulness.

"Do you realise how much money is involved?" Thomas pressed after several moments of the colonel's silence.

"I can imagine."

"Is there any way we can stop the transfer?" Alaina asked practically.

"Unfortunately, it's not that simple," Jennings said, rising from his chair to pace the length of the room. "And where is this money being wired? To Germany? That's an obvious move, even for Price."

Alaina shook her head. "Another account here, in England."

This was news to Thomas, and he wondered how she had found that piece of information out so quickly.

Jennings halted. Alarm etched across his strong features. "Where?" he demanded fiercely.

"Colchester."

The colonel let out a slow breath that seemed to deflate him. "This is more serious than I thought."

"Wait, now that Colchester is involved, you're suddenly concerned?" Thomas cut in. "I don't understand you, Jennings."

"I, too, have interests to protect in the British Isles." Jennings's face seemed to age right before their eyes. "Trust me when I say that this whole war is now at stake. I'm going to London; I'll send a wire to America and see what comes back. We have to stop that transfer."

CHAPTER 32

Attempted Murder

10 May

DELICATE FLORAL PERFUMES, mixed with the gentle pungency of the distant sea, danced through the morning air. Light spring breezes teased the sheets Clara and Elizabeth were hanging on the clothesline and whispered among the pine trees in the next-door cemetery.

"Beautiful weather," Clara mused contentedly. After seven months in Newhaven, spring was her favourite season so far.

"Mmmhmm," Elizabeth affirmed absently.

Clara glanced at her friend in concern. She had learned from Mrs. Forsythe that today was Elizabeth's wedding anniversary. "Hand me that corner, will you?" she asked.

Together, the women wrestled another wet sheet onto the line. Elizabeth suddenly squealed and dropped her end. Half the sheet slipped off the line onto the grass.

"What in all of England?!" Clara cried in consternation, snatching at the wet shroud that fell on her as she looked for where Elizabeth had rushed off to.

Then she saw her.

Sobbing, Elizabeth clung to a tall man in uniform who stood

in the yard with his arm in a sling and his other wrapped around her waist. A discarded crutch lay unheeded on the grass.

Tears pricked Clara's eyes, and her hand flew to her mouth as joy bubbled up inside her. Aaron Tilney had made it home at last. Wounded, yes, but he was alive. Thank God, he was alive.

The boarding house buzzed with triumph over Aaron's arrival. He told them how after catching shrapnel in both his arm and his leg, his commander sent him home since he was unable to hold a gun. Elizabeth clung to her husband's hand all evening, as if letting him go would cause him to vanish. A soft light danced in her grey eyes, and her cheeks flushed radiant with rapture.

Before retiring for the night, Clara whispered to Elizabeth, "Not all stories have a happy ending, but I'm glad yours did, Lizzie. I truly am."

Thomas pored over the file from Alaina in the soft glow from the lamp in his office. Sipping his cup of tea—rations be hanged—he jotted down a few notes from his reading. He still had the Cromwell clipping from the paper, but the photograph was missing. He had questioned Clara on its whereabouts, but she hadn't been into his desk since the day Lena had interrupted her. The piece of furniture was always locked; how could someone have taken it without his noticing? He frowned as he scratched down another note, trying to refocus his mind, when a frantic banging on the front door jogged his pen. Sweeping the paper into the middle drawer, he hurried to the door and found Kasey standing on the step with an unconscious, dripping-wet Alaina cradled in his arms.

Thomas's heart dropped to his boots. "Bring her in here," he instructed, leading them swiftly to the examination room.

Kasey laid the limp form down gently on the exam table, and Thomas quickly took over. With deft, probing fingers, he determined no broken bones or external injuries, with the exception of the rapidly growing lump on the back of her head and a swollen elbow.

"What happened, Kasey?" Thomas demanded, pulling out his stethoscope and trying to listen to his patient's breathing instead of the staccato of his own heartbeat.

"Don't rightly know. Kavan didn't have time to say much. Only that when he fished her out of the water near the docks and pumped the water out of her, she wasn't conscious."

Thomas growled and gently shook the woman's good arm. "Don't you dare think of leaving me, Alaina Huntington, or I will never forgive you." He added to Kasey, "Call Clara and ask her to come."

"Lad, I don't know anything about those newfangled gadgets."

Biting back an impatient retort, Thomas explained the process as simply and as quickly as possible, while Kasey reluctantly did his bidding. Within minutes, Thomas sighed with relief. Clara was on her way. He set aside the stethoscope once he was convinced of Alaina's steady, albeit shallow, breathing and a stable pulse. "How did she get in the water? Did Kavan see anything?"

"He didn't see what happened, just was near enough to hear the splash and fish her out right away. He's searching the docks now to see if anyone else saw anything."

"What was she doing down there?"

"You'd have to ask her that, lad."

Thomas thanked the captain for his help as Clara arrived. A frown puckered her brow when Thomas explained what happened. After helping move Alaina upstairs to the spare room, Kasey slipped out.

"What was she doing there in the first place?" Clara questioned as Thomas handed her a navy sweater for Alaina to wear. He had pulled one of the new ones from Maranda out of the closet.

"Wish I knew," Thomas replied with a frown of consternation before hurrying out of the room as a thought struck him. He needed answers.

In the office, he quickly rang the Hope Inn and was relieved when Emily answered. "Emily, it's Doctor Lindsey. Was Sean in tonight?"

He could barely hear her quiet "No, sir" over the background noise. He thanked her before hanging up, then paced the office for several minutes deep in thought. If Sean wasn't in, could he have had something to do with this?

Clara's voice floated down the stairs, interrupting him several minutes later. "Thomas, she's awake."

Taking the stairs two at a time, he found Alaina propped up amongst the pillows with his navy sweater pulled over a borrowed nightshirt. Her face was ashen against the brilliance of her damp, copper curls and her eyes were wide in shock. A weak smile sprang to her lips as he took a seat on the edge of the bed.

"Are you all right?" Thomas asked with concern.

She nodded and fiddled with the too-long sleeves of the sweater. "Navy really isn't my colour."

He sighed in relief. If she was making jokes, then she had to be all right. "Be serious for a minute," he instructed in mock sternness.

"I am fine, beyond a sore elbow and a headache."

"Did you check the elbow?" Thomas directed the question at Clara, who stood at the foot of the bed.

Clara nodded. "It's sprained and will need to be in a sling for at least a week."

Thomas hesitated before voicing the question that had weighed on him since the moment Kasey brought the limp form through the door. "What happened?"

"I went out to help serve coffee at the canteen. I was walking back to the Jenningses' house when someone jumped me from behind. I didn't see any faces. He just hit my head, and the next thing I knew I woke up here." Alaina glanced around the room to make her point. "How did I get here?"

"Kasey brought you in. Said Kavan heard you fall into the water down at the harbour."

Alaina shuddered. "Didn't know I had such a close call."

"God still has work for you here," Clara whispered as she wrapped an arm around her shoulders.

Alaina smiled. "I'd have been happy to meet Him, but I will admit, I do want to see this mission through." She flashed Thomas a smile. "You can't get rid of me that easily, you scoundrel. Someone has to keep an eye on you."

"Do you remember anything else?" Thomas pressed earnestly.

Wincing as she frowned, Alaina suddenly said, "Hair tonic."

"Excuse me?" Thomas asked, bewildered. Perhaps she *had* suffered a more serious blow to the head than he first thought.

"I smelled hair tonic when I passed the alleyway by Newfield Road. Not like yours, Thomas. It was stronger. You remember Douglas, from Sheffield? He used one that you could smell the day before he even arrived in town. It's that strong." Alaina's laugh faded to a groan as she gripped her injured elbow.

Thomas ran downstairs to fetch a sling from the supply closet.

"Have you heard from Jennings?" Alaina asked as Thomas fit her arm in the sling.

"Nothing yet. Today was the day of that transfer. I hope he found a way to keep it from going through," was all Thomas said before admonishing her to get some rest.

"I'll stay with her," Clara offered as she and Thomas entered the office a moment later.

He opened his mouth to reply, but before he could, the phone rang.

"Nurse Clara; how may I help you?" Her voice was brusque as she answered the phone.

Thomas watched the frown spread across her face.

"I'll tell him," was all she said as she hung up. She frowned slightly. "A certain Myles Cumberland had a heart attack. He's at the hospital in Lewes now, but he's asking for you."

With slumped shoulders, Thomas picked up his bag and left the office without a word. Myles Cumberland was a middle-aged man who had been trying to die for the last ten years. Ever since his only son died in a train wreck, he had lost his will to live. Thomas had gotten dozens of calls to the man's bedside since the day he stepped foot in Newhaven nearly a year ago. The night air stung his face as he drove towards the hospital. There would be no sleep in sight for him that night.

CHAPTER 33

Together

11 May

THOMAS SOUGHT Kavan out at the harbour and found the young Irishman on the loading docks, preparing his transport ship for a run to France the next morning. The harbour lights were harsh in the gathering darkness, while the wind moaned softly as it snaked through the quay.

"Grahame," Thomas called out in greeting. "Can I talk to you for a minute?"

Straightening, Kavan absently stroked the scar that stretched from chin to ear on his left jaw in his usual habit while thinking. "Meet me at the Hope Inn in fifteen minutes. Order me whatever you're having."

Thomas offered him a nod before hurrying to the harbour public house. Claiming a window side table, he ordered two coffees—as usual, unfortunately, there was no tea to be had—and waited for Kavan to join him. The room was quiet that night compared to the usual hubbub. Light jazz music played from the gramophone in the corner, and the gas lights were low. He stifled a yawn. Myles Cumberland had finally died in the early hours of the morning, and Thomas hadn't gotten any sleep.

"Waiting for someone, Doctor?" a feminine voice asked at his elbow.

Thomas glanced away from the window and smiled at the newcomer. "Good evening, Emily. Yes, a friend."

Emily set the two mugs down on the table. She twisted her apron string around her finger and glanced over her shoulder before whispering, "I know what happened to your coffee when you were here a while back. I just wanted you to know I've handled both those cups myself tonight and didn't let them out of my sight."

"I appreciate it; thank you."

The young lady flashed him a smile before scurrying away to take another man's order across the room. Thomas spun his mug around carefully, watching the black liquid twirl as it gained momentum. He was relieved by the young waitress's assurances.

A figure with an ebony thatch of hair and blue eyes dropped into the seat across from him, arresting Thomas's attention. Kavan picked up the coffee mug Thomas slid across to him and took a long draught. His eyes were clouded with worry as he asked, "How's Alaina... uh, Miss Huntington?"

Thomas took a sip of his own coffee to cover his grin at the man's slip but grimaced at the taste of burnt ashes. "She's fine. Shaken up and has a sprained elbow, but she'll recover."

"Good." Kavan sighed in evident relief.

Thomas studied the Irishman intently for a moment. He had figured Kavan was sweet on Alaina, but he wasn't exactly sure how he felt about it now that he knew for certain. "What did you see last night?"

"A big man dumped her into the harbour and took off before I got a good look at him. I fished her out and got her to Kasey's. He brought her to you in the cab, and I went back to the dock to look around. What could she tell you?"

"Not much. She never saw the man's face. You said he was big though?"

"Tall and broad." Kavan took another swig in silence.

Thomas thought back to Emily's description of Sean. It certainly matched Kavan's, and Emily said that Sean hadn't been at the public house last night.

Kavan fiddled with his cup. "I did find this." Fishing in his pocket, he pulled out a piece of paper.

Thomas snatched it, reading it anxiously. He frowned at the unfamiliar letters and instantly wished he were better with foreign languages.

"Gaelic," Kavan explained at the puzzled look on Thomas's face. The Irishman quickly translated it. "Proceed with plan. Take all caution. West dock after canteen. The Piper."

Thomas smashed his fist into the table with disgust. Realisation dawned on him. The Piper knew Gaelic. Lotta had been telling the truth after all when she said he was an Irishman. In keeping with their agreement, Thomas and Clara hadn't disclosed her assistance to Jennings, but with this new information, they might just be getting somewhere. Thomas pounded his fist into the table again angrily. They were dealing with another Irish-German alliance just like with Price and Fallamhan. They were probably in cahoots. The question was: which Irishman?

"Whoever he is, he knew her schedule."

Thomas stood and dropped a few coins on the table. "This note might be the slip up we've been waiting for. Good work."

"Anything for you and the lady, Doc. She's something special." Kavan bobbed his head as his face flushed red.

"Don't I know it," Thomas agreed before tossing a good-bye over his shoulder to Emily and setting out towards Bridge Street.

13 May

As he locked the kitchen door of the clinic, Thomas caught sight of Emily hurrying down the road towards him. "What can I do for you?" he asked.

"I found out more about Sean," she whispered when she paused beside him.

Thomas's eyes widened. "I'm on my way to a house call. Can we walk as we talk?"

Taking the arm he offered her, Emily plunged into her narrative. "Hazel's twenty-four, and Sean is thirty-one. He's from Carrickfergus, and his last name is Aiken. He works on the west dock."

"Does he use hair tonic by any chance?" Thomas interjected.

Emily rolled her eyes. "The strongest I've ever smelled. The public house reeks for hours every time he comes in." She paused, a questioning look on her face. "Is that important?"

"You're a miracle worker." Thomas smiled. At last, they had something to go on.

Thomas drove out to the Jenningses' estate that evening. Now that he had digested the information from Emily and Kavan, he felt the need to finally disclose it all to Jennings.

Jennings listened intently as Thomas explained about the German spy with Irish loyalties. "So Clara was right," he mused after Thomas finished. "We're dealing with a network that extends far beyond little Newhaven."

As much as Thomas's pride hated to admit it, Clara had called The Piper's bluff months in advance. They just hadn't possessed the hard evidence to support her theory. If Sean was working for The Piper, there had to be others as well. That must have been why Hazel tainted his coffee; she had been working with him. One Irishman and his sweetheart weren't enough however. "We only have two suspects. There has to be more," Thomas voiced his thoughts.

Jennings exhaled heavily. "I was able to stop the transfer. With Price out of the picture, your mission, essentially, is done here."

Thomas jolted, shocked by the sudden closure of his life here in Newhaven. "I can't leave. I have to give six months' notice—"

"Slow down, Lindsey, and let me finish. You are all staying on to help with the Piper, Detweiler, and Fallamhan situation. We're going to see this through to the end. Together." In an undertone, he added, "Please God, we all live that long."

CHAPTER 34

In-Between

6 June

AS MAY FADED INTO JUNE, the town basked in the warm promise of summer. Clinic work kept Thomas and Clara busy, but after Price's death and the money transfer, they hit a waiting period, a season of in-between. While Jennings had kept them on to help with The Piper, there had yet to be any new information.

On a particularly slow afternoon while Clara was out, Thomas cradled the secret file he had compiled on her in his hands. He stood resolutely before the kitchen stove. Lifting the lid, he moved to stuff the papers inside when a voice behind him stopped his intentions.

"What are you doing?"

Clara.

He straightened; she was back earlier than he had expected. Holding up the papers, he explained steadily, "Burning this."

"What is it?"

He tilted them towards her, and she paled instantly at the sight. "Seems to me I promised to trust you. I'm a man of my word, and this is long overdue." With that, he shoved the papers into the stove, and they watched in silence as the sheets curled into burnt ashes as the hungry flames licked them into oblivion.

"You were serious," she whispered. "I don't know what to say."

"Then don't say anything. Sometimes the less we say, the more it means." He flashed her a kind smile before slipping out of the room.

~

As they prepared to close the clinic that night, Clara dared to ask a question. After Thomas's rare display of humanity earlier, perhaps he would be willing to give her an honest answer. "Will you tell me about the picture?"

He stiffened visibly. "My father," he whispered after a pregnant pause.

"Your... your father?"

He nodded. "With Joseph Cromwell. I need to find their connection." Pausing, he fiddled with the report he was holding. "My father was an agent under William Melville before the new Secret Service was started. He died of a heart attack during a mission in Calais, in 1905."

"But you don't believe his death was an accident." It came out more as a statement than a question.

He shook his head. "No, I'm convinced he was murdered. Someone wanted him out of the way. Now I have to prove it."

~

14 June

Thomas marched into the office as Clara carefully copied out the next day's house call list. "Jennings wants to see us at eight tonight," he said breezily, removing his jacket and rolling up his shirt sleeves. A drip of sweat tickled his neck as he loosened his necktie. Much better. The summer heat was growing unbearable.

"I'll be there at nine," Clara countered without looking up.

He frowned. "I beg your pardon?"

"It's canteen night, and the earliest I can get away is 8:50," she repeated, still without looking up.

"Can't you skip tonight?"

The suggestion brought Clara's head up with alarming speed. "I'm not shirking my duty, Lindsey. If it were an emergency, Jennings would have sent for us immediately. It can keep. I'll be there at nine."

The sparkle in her eyes, the set of her jaw, and the determination in her voice silenced Thomas from further questioning. He bit back a grin. For a woman so unflappable, there was something satisfying in being able to rile her just a little.

The canteen was a smashing success that night. Clara was bustled onto the small platform up front, and she tucked the violin under her chin, beginning to play. Cheers echoed and applause rang out after every tune. As she rollicked through "Danny Boy," "It's a Long Way to Tipperary," and "Keep the Home Fires Burning," her eye caught a glimpse of Lena, who danced with the grace of a butterfly. Her blue gingham dress swirled constantly as every man in khaki waited for his chance to dance with her. She was the epitome of energy and flamboyance.

Clara felt tired just watching her and glanced towards the back where Alaina served coffee and doughnuts. Though not nearly as stunning as the blonde on the dance floor, she gave an encouraging word and a warm smile with each cup of coffee she served.

When Clara tucked her violin in its case after finishing for the night, she noticed Lena chatting with a young man at the door. Unlike the majority of the men in the room, he wasn't dressed in a soldier's uniform. Seeing them slip out the side door, she latched her violin case closed and hurried after them.

The sun had just barely set, leaving the streets bathed in a dusky hue of grey shadows. Trailing the pair at a discreet distance as they moved towards Brighton Road, Clara abruptly stopped. She hadn't told anyone where she was going, and she was alone. Probably not her smartest move. Checking her pendant watch, she realised she was late for the meeting with Jennings.

Ten minutes later, breathless and flushed, she burst into the office where Jennings and Thomas were waiting. Apologising quickly, she explained her detour.

"Why didn't you follow them further?" Thomas questioned. "This could have been a major break."

Clara raised an eyebrow. "I figured I would be of better use alive then dead in a ditch, Doctor."

Jennings chuckled at the exchange. "Agreed."

CHAPTER 35

Impossible or Absurd

1 July

JENNINGS HAD his back to the door when Clara poked her head into his study. "Thomas said you were asking for me, sir?"

Turning slowly, the colonel motioned for her to be seated. Clara politely accepted the offer, but as she studied the man's face, her heart plummeted—it was the face of a man with grave news.

"I received word that the HMHS *Llandovery Castle* sank yesterday morning just off the coast of Ireland."

Her throat constricted, but she kept her voice steady as she asked, "What aren't you telling me?"

Jennings's sympathetic gaze met her questioning one. "It was a Canadian hospital ship out of Halifax en route to Liverpool. There are over two hundred dead with a mere twenty-four survivors."

At the mention of Halifax, the air left her lungs. "My contact?" she whispered. When Jennings nodded solemnly, her composure crumpled. "Oh, Jonathan."

"I wanted to tell you before you read about it in the newspaper," he said quietly.

"What was he doing on that ship? What about the girls?" Clara choked, swiping at the rapidly falling tears.

"He was on his way to the front; they needed more doctors. As for the girls, I am sure his parents will look after them."

Clara left the colonel's estate half an hour later in a daze. Her last "contact" to her previous life was now dead—a war casualty. *God, I don't know how much more I can take. I have lost everyone closest to me. I just want to find a place to call* home, *and I'm afraid I never will.*

In the coming days, news of the ill-fated hospital ship stormed the papers. Tempers ran high in flaming indignation, while Clara grew quiet and apathetic. She avoided reading the newspaper to prevent seeing a familiar name printed on the casualty list. That would make it all too real.

~

8 July

A week after the accident, Clara found an envelope on the front step of the boarding house. Nana evidently hadn't found it yet since it was devoid of teeth marks and slobber. The looping script on the outside was addressed to Clara, and she perused the short, typewritten note on her way to the clinic.

"In order to attain the impossible, one must attempt the absurd." Remember the windmills. Urgent.

The quotation was vaguely familiar, but she couldn't place its origin. But windmills? She mulled over the message the entire walk into town without coming any closer to its meaning or the identity of the sender. Sighing, she shoved the paper into her skirt pocket and pushed open the kitchen door. A meditative, quiet manner settled over her all day, seemingly much to Thomas's consternation. Periodically, the doctor would try to draw her out of her silence with a tactful question, but Clara never took the bait. When the clock finally struck five, she prepared to take her leave.

"Clara," Thomas's voice stopped her in the doorway. "If something is wrong, do let me help."

"I'm fine," she replied, flashing him a vacant smile. "Goodnight, Doctor."

It wasn't until midnight that the answer occurred to her. Shooting up in bed, Clara rubbed her forehead. *Of course. How could I miss it? Don Quixote.* Throwing aside the quilt, she rummaged through her trunk in the corner. Had she brought her copy of Miguel de Cervantes's classic tale? Austen, Dickens, Shakespeare, Alcott, Defoe, Bunyan. No Cervantes.

She rolled back gently on her heels in thought. The boarding house might have a copy in the parlour library. Shrugging on a dressing gown, she eased her door open and slipped into the silent hallway, careful to avoid the well-known creaks on the wooden staircase. In the parlour, she struck a match, lighting a small candle. Running her fingers down the spines of familiar titles on the shelves sent tingles down her spine, but there was no copy of *Don Quixote.*

Retreating to her bedroom, Clara paced quietly on the braided rug beside her bed. The quotation could be alluding to any number of events, but she instinctively figured it had something to do with Thomas. As brilliant as the man was, some of his methods were... questionable at best and illegal at worst. She snapped her fingers and paused her pacing. The doctor had a copy of *Don Quixote* in his office; she had seen it while she was browsing the shelves weeks ago. Exchanging her dressing gown for a lightweight skirt and shirtwaist, Clara donned a light cardigan and checked her pendant watch. It would be nearly one o'clock by the time she arrived at the clinic. Thomas would be asleep, or better yet, out on a call.

Praying it was the latter and not the former, she slipped her key into her pocket and crept back into the hall and down the stairs. No creaks gave away her escape into the balmy summer night. Nana lay on the front doorstep, guarding the door. Her brown eyes glanced up at Clara mournfully, but she didn't even offer a tail wag as Clara stooped to pat her head. The canine had never been the same after the death of her young master.

Once Clara was a safe distance away from the boarding house, she paused in the middle of the dark lane. Was she out of her mind? Sneaking into the clinic after hours? She wasn't technically breaking in since Thomas had given her a key, but couldn't this wait till later in the morning? She almost turned back, but a gentle nudge in her heart pressed her forward. She was about to put Cervantes's quotation into action and attempt the absurd.

Slipping the slender metallic key into the lock was simple. Turning it and opening the heavy, wooden door without a sound proved more difficult. Clara poked her head into the office and noticed the black bag was gone from its usual place. Perfect. Thomas was out. Striking a match and lighting the candle she kept on her desk, she ran her fingers along the book-shelves and plucked off the second to last book on the third shelf. Quickly flipping through the pages, she found another typewritten note.

Bell tower at parish of St. John as soon as possible. Come alone. CD.

Even without the signature, Clara knew the sender of the note. Snuffing out the candle's flame, she fled the office and retreated through the kitchen door, remembering to lock it behind her. The cobblestones clicked beneath her shoes, and the shadows danced eerily under the lampposts as she wove through Newhaven in the direction of Lewes Road. Piddinghoe was a half-hour walk away, and she mustn't keep Chantelle waiting.

Thomas wearily unlocked the kitchen door and trudged to the office. A glance at the eastern sky told him dawn was still a few hours off, and he hoped to put them to good use and catch some sleep. As he dropped his bag onto his office chair, he sniffed curiously.

Smoke. Or at least the faint detection of it. And was it... lavender?

His fingers immediately curled around the Webley at his waist holster. He turned on every light in the clinic and yet found no one hiding in the shadows. Someone had come in and left. *But why?* The doors were both locked, and no windows were forced. Coming back to the office, Thomas noticed a wayward book on Clara's desk.

Don Quixote.

He frowned. That hadn't been there when he had left earlier to deliver the Shepherds' baby. Thumbing through the pages, he found nothing of interest. His eyes drooped with lack of sleep, but his mind raced. Dropping into his chair, he propped his head on his arms. *Must... stay... awake...*

Lewes Road was deserted in the early pre-dawn hours. Mist swirled lightly across the ground, and a sliver of moonlight bathed the silent road. Clara pulled her cardigan closer around her slender frame. The parish church was straight ahead with its bell tower and cupola silhouetted against the star-dappled sky as the River Ouse gurgled a short way beyond. Slipping into the shadows of the stone archway of the bell tower entrance, she waited and let her eyes wander over the ancient stonework.

A light hand touched her arm, and she whirled around to see Chantelle's hazel eyes dancing in the soft light.

"You came," Chantelle whispered with a smile.

"I found the message. Is something wrong? Why are you here?"

Chantelle fished an envelope from the recesses of her black cloak and handed it to Clara. "For Thomas."

"Why couldn't you give it to him yourself?"

The girl ignored the question and handed Clara another envelope. "For you."

Clara took the second missive silently and stowed it along with the first inside her cloak. "Why me? And why did you mention the windmills?"

"You'll know when the time comes. Sometimes our worst enemies aren't the ones we expect to see, but the ones we don't." Chantelle held Clara's questioning gaze. "The lies we live and the secrets we hide."

Cryptic and entirely too much like something Thomas would say. Clara's forehead wrinkled into a frown. "I don't understand but thank you."

The brown curls bobbed in reply, and Chantelle turned to go. "Till we meet again. *Dieu soit avec vous* [God be with you]."

After watching the lithe figure disappear from the archway and into the shades of darkness, Clara followed suit. The mysterious deliveries burned in her hand, and a sense of dread enveloped her heart. She would deliver Thomas's in the morning, but hers? Shaking her head, she flew nimbly down the sleepy street towards the boarding house to catch a few hours of rest. Reading her letter could wait; she had no strength for any more unwelcome surprises.

CHAPTER 36

Coincidence

5 August

THE SCENT of heather hung in the air as the wind blew its perfume off the nearby downs. July had faded into August, and autumn would soon be knocking on their door. Clara inhaled deeply and smiled. Heather always reminded her of Robbie and of home. *Home.* The word brought a dull ache to her chest, but she shoved it aside. She wouldn't linger on the sadness today.

"I'm home!" she called merrily as she entered the boarding house. "And what a delightful—" Her voice died off as she poked her head into the parlour and saw Mrs. Forsythe weeping into her apron. Mr. Forsythe had his arm around his wife, and his own eyes were wet with tears. Clara backed softly out of the room and found Elizabeth in the kitchen, sniffling.

"Lizzie, whatever is the matter?"

Elizabeth wiped her eyes with her handkerchief before answering. "Telegram came today from Glasgow. Peter died in the battle at Buzancy."

Clara's heart dropped as her hand groped for the support from the nearby counter. Not only had the Forsythes lost their youngest son, but now their oldest too? And what of Peter's wife and children? "How awful," she whispered, tears burning the backs of her eyes.

Elizabeth continued kneading her bread with vigour. "And poor Marjorie left alone with five small children." Her voice cracked. "Oh, Clara, it could have been me losing my husband."

Clara hugged her friend tightly, but neither said another word. There was nothing to say. They both knew Elizabeth had spoken the truth. It was the reality every heart faced when they bid their soldiers good-bye. A return was never guaranteed.

"I wish I could go to Marjorie," Mrs. Forsythe softly whispered the next morning as Clara and Elizabeth helped her with the breakfast dishes.

"Why don't you?" Elizabeth asked.

"I can't just up and leave, lass. I may be grieving, but I'm not daft."

"Surely, you can. I'll manage it while you're away. School's out so I have the time," Elizabeth said confidently.

"And I'll help," Clara chimed in. "I'm sure Thomas would understand if I needed to work a few less hours."

"I don't know..." Mrs. Forsythe faltered.

Elizabeth touched the woman's arm and smiled warmly, her grey eyes shining with unshed tears. "I would want someone to do this for me, if it were Aaron."

The Scotswoman folded both young women into a tender embrace. "God bless you."

Two days later, Mrs. Forsythe boarded a train bound for Scotland. Clara and Elizabeth had accompanied her to the Newhaven Town station to wave her off.

"Thank you both," Mr. Forsythe said gratefully as the train disappeared in the distance.

Elizabeth flashed him a watery smile, and Clara said softly, "We're just doing our part to help win a war."

It was shortly after Mrs. Forsythe's departure that Aaron also left. After three months of convalescence and moderate light duty, his injured limbs had recovered enough for him to return to France. Elizabeth moped around for the first few days afterwards, but quickly threw herself into the management of the boarding house to keep her mind off her pain. Clara helped all she could, balancing her nursing duties, canteen commitments, and boarding house chores.

~

16 August

On Friday morning, Thomas sat at his desk, scribbling away on his records. There were a few more files he wanted to finish up before he started his rounds, and Clara was running late. Not that he blamed her. He had reduced her office hours so she wouldn't run herself ragged, something he knew she was fully capable of doing.

"Thomas!" Clara's urgent tone jogged his pen, and he glanced up from his writing to see the serious expression of his nurse in the office doorway.

"What's wrong?"

"Lena's gone." She paused to catch her breath, and at Thomas's raised eyebrow continued, "Her room is empty, and she left notice that she won't be needing it anymore."

"When did she leave?"

"Sometime during the night. We saw her at dinner, but Elizabeth found a note in her room when she checked it this morning. Lena was supposed to work this morning at the telephone office, but her manager said she hadn't come in."

"What about the train station?"

"I checked with the ticket officer, and Lena hadn't been there either. She somehow left Newhaven, and it wasn't by train."

Thomas laid down his pen and pressed his fingers together,

steeple fashion. The sudden disappearance of an agent was serious, and skipping town certainly didn't place Lena in a flattering light. However, he was impressed by Clara's thoroughness in the matter.

"Do you think she could be The Piper?" Clara queried.

A frown creased Thomas's forehead. "Lotta said The Piper is Irish, and the Gaelic note Kavan found seems to confirm that. Lena most certainly isn't Irish. She's from Lancashire. But she could have been the accomplice. She had the means, if not the brains."

"We have to tell Jennings."

Thomas nodded. "You go ahead. I'll start the rounds."

Clara vanished down the hall, and the kitchen door clicked a minute later. With a heavy heart, Thomas lifted his bag and trudged out to his car. *Lena Mitchell, what have you gotten yourself—and the rest of us—into?*

Later that afternoon, Clara reported back that Jennings was livid. Like Thomas, the man wasn't convinced that Lena was The Piper, but he was clearly unimpressed with the woman's behaviour in leaving town without official sanction.

"I called Kavan, and he said Sean Aitken is missing from the docks; too coincidental for them not to be related," Thomas added once she had finished.

"You mean, they're working together?" She thought about the man from the canteen who had left with Lena. She hadn't gotten a good look at him, but she supposed it could have been Sean. It was all starting to fit together.

"Probably. Sean is Irish and is allegedly the one who tried to drown my cousin." Thomas winced and hurriedly added, "Forget I called her that. Alaina would kill me."

Clara smiled. "Alaina told me months ago."

He stared in astonishment. "You knew all this time?"

She nodded. "But to your credit, I would have never guessed the courting couple was only a cover. You were both very convincing."

"Since I'd never dream of actually courting her, it's perfectly safe."

Clara laughed heartily, and Thomas frowned, clearly not understanding the joke. "Thomas, if you said that about any other girl, you would have a broken nose."

Thomas rolled his eyes. "Back to Sean. He isn't The Piper because he received a message *from* The Piper." He groaned and raked his fingers through his curls. "If only we knew who he was. He's done more damage than almost every other spy we've caught combined."

"How has he eluded capture this long?"

Thomas shook his head ruefully. "I have no idea."

22 August

Thomas took one look at the arm of the older man in his office and instantly wished Clara were back from her afternoon rounds; they didn't usually take her this long. He needed a second set of hands to tend the extensive burns. Footsteps sounded in the hall. Excusing himself for a moment, Thomas peeked out into the hall.

"Clara, is that you?" he asked quietly. When Alaina's head popped out of the kitchen doorway, he sighed.

"Sorry to disappoint you."

"Can you help me for a few minutes?"

"Sure." Alaina shrugged and followed him back to the examination room.

"I need to clean up—" Thomas was interrupted by Alaina's gasp.

Her face was tinged some sort of greyish green. Covering her mouth, she swallowed and turned her back. "Just tell me what you need," she said hoarsely.

The older man chuckled softly around a grimace of pain, and Thomas shook his head in amusement. "Iodine and bandages, third shelf." He washed his hands and set to work treating the burns that covered the man's entire forearm in blisters, raw flesh, oozing fluid, and peeling skin.

The older man groaned in pain. Alaina handed Thomas the implements and iodine as he called for them, all while keeping her eyes diverted from the scorched flesh in front of her.

After Thomas had finished tending his patient and sent him on his way with orders to stop in again tomorrow, Alaina fled the room as Thomas cleaned up. Her face was still pale when she returned a few minutes later.

"Feel better?" Thomas asked with a smile.

"Yes, thank you," and she lifted her chin, clearly attempting to save face.

He chuckled softly. "I appreciate the help. I had forgotten you had such a weak stomach."

"Confidential information, Lindsey."

"Of course. I wonder though, what would you be like in a true emergency?"

Alaina shrugged wryly. "Let's hope we never find out."

31 August

Mrs. Forsythe returned as the last of the summer's roses faded. The heather was in full bloom, and the nights began to grow slightly chilly. Clara and Elizabeth were glad to hand household duties back to the Scotswoman, more appreciative than ever of all she did after having tried to fill her shoes for three weeks.

Life eased back into a comfortable routine of normalcy, and

Clara enjoyed a late summer sunset one evening down at the Promenade. Frothy waves lapped the beach, reflecting in the setting sun. She shuddered as the distant echo of gunfire drifted across the Channel and the drone of the patrol planes thrummed overhead. The lines of war and beauty had begun to blur together —what a paradox. Much like her own life.

CHAPTER 37

The "Spanish Lady"

9 September

"THOMAS, can you pay a visit to the McIntyres?"

Thomas glanced up from the newspaper he was skimming as Clara entered the office. He read the pensive look written across her face. "What's wrong with the old lady this time?"

The elder Mrs. McIntyre's reputation as a hypochondriac preceded her. Thomas had lost count of how many times in his mere sixteen months as a doctor in Newhaven that he had been called to the old lady's bedside under the pretence that she was dying. How her daughter-in-law, Irene, had the patience to deal with her day after day was beyond him.

"Nothing. It's Irene I'm worried about."

Curious, Thomas set down his paper and studied Clara intently, waiting for her to explain.

"She has a raging fever that won't come down. She's struggling to breathe with a wet phlegm cough. There's blood coming out her nose and mouth, and her lips are going blue. I haven't seen anything like this before. And what's even more strange is that Timmy said her symptoms only started last night."

Thomas snatched up his bag and left the room without another question.

~

When he returned to the clinic an hour later, Clara instantly noticed his drawn face. She waited till he was sitting at his desk and had a cup of tea in his hand before broaching the subject. "How is she?"

"She's gone," he said roughly before swallowing a mouthful of tea.

Clara stared at him in abject horror. "Gone? So fast?"

"Anyone else in town with symptoms?"

Pausing, she did a mental inventory of patients. "Not that I know of."

"Could be some freak of nature."

"Or not," she said quietly.

He sighed heavily and nodded. "Keep a close eye out and let me know the minute you suspect something or see similar symptoms."

Clara promised she would and absently collected her belongings before heading home for the evening. Irene's sudden illness and subsequent death occupied her thoughts on the walk home and all through dinner. Saying nothing about her concerns to her housemates, she retired early that night.

Mrs. Forsythe knocked on her door shortly after eight. "Doctor's asking for you on the telephone."

Clara hurried downstairs to take the call.

"Sorry to bother you, but word came through Sam Johnson that a few folks in the flats on Lawes Avenue are sick, and Emily called a minute ago saying a man dropped dead in the public house earlier tonight."

She tried to absorb the rapid-fire information. "Are all the symptoms the same?"

"Yes."

In less than twelve hours, there were already two fatalities. "What do you think it is?"

The doctor's voice was heavy-laden with concern. "I don't know. I'm calling a colleague in London to see if they've seen anything like it."

"Could it be like what's going on in Spain?" she dared to ask.

News of a deadly "Spanish flu" raging through neutral Spain and spreading around the globe had been reported through the uncensored Spanish papers arriving in England. It was also a hotly debated topic in the British Medical Journal.

Thomas hesitated. "Pray to God it's not."

She cradled the receiver for several moments after Thomas had hung up. A cold hand gripped her heart as she trudged up the worn wooden stairs with lead feet. In the solitude of her room, she dropped into the chair at her desk and surveyed the moonlit landscape of the downs. Familiar words echoed through her mind.

Thou shalt not be afraid for the terror by night; nor for the arrow that flieth by day; nor for the pestilence that walketh in darkness; nor for the destruction that wasteth at noonday.

Burying her head in her arms, Clara lifted her heavy heart and abundant fears to her Heavenly Father. If things were as bad as she feared, nothing short of a miracle would save them now.

10 September

Thomas handed Clara a white muslin mask when she arrived at the clinic and gave her strict instructions to wear it when seeing patients. "I talked to Doctor Lawrence in London. He was a mentor of mine in university."

"And?" Clara asked hopefully.

Thomas shook his head. "It doesn't look promising. There are cases popping up all around the country, but the papers are too caught up with the war news to publish anything about it."

"What about treatment?"

"Aspirin or camphor," Thomas replied grimly as he raked his fingers through his curls. "Beyond that, I haven't the faintest idea. No one else seems to either."

Five more cases were reported that day, one of whom died, and Thomas filled out the death certificate for Lucy Collins, aged thirty-three. When he returned to the clinic, Clara wasn't there, but a hastily dashed note on his desk disclosed her location at the Evelyn Avenue flats.

For the first week after the mysterious illness hit, doctor and nurse worked around the clock, battling the medical threat that had invaded their small community and the world. Churches, cinemas, libraries, and other public gathering places closed across town. Trains were barely running. People were told to stay home. Yet, despite the precautions, the infection rate exploded and the number of fatalities kept pouring in. Many grew sick in the morning and were dead by teatime. Others lingered for days, the life slowly ebbing out of them.

Thomas had never seen the likes of this disease in his lifetime —a sickness with no known name and without modern precedent. He shuddered as he filled out yet another death certificate.

At the end of the second week, he murmured, "Twenty-two dead."

Clara glanced at him with understanding in her face. Twenty-two was not just a number, but the mothers, fathers, sons, daughters, and friends of people they knew.

Unable to give voice to the swirling thoughts and emotions warring inside of him, Thomas slipped out of the room to start on his next set of rounds.

The streets were deserted, and the number of familiar faces dwindled as the cemeteries filled with the victims of the "Spanish Lady." Showing no mercy to youth or vigor, the disease ravished the small seaside community, and nothing could stop it.

Kavan had sent word that he and Kasey were doing well. Emily had called Thomas to let him know the Hope Inn had been closed to the public, and she was with the Jenningses. The Forsythes, too, were well. So far. But for how long?

22 September

Thomas found Clara sitting on the rug in the office when he stumbled in slightly before midnight. A book splayed across her lap, and she cradled a cup of cocoa in both hands. Her eyes were rimmed with weariness.

"How is he?" she asked as he dropped with exhaustion into an easy chair.

Thomas thought back to the depressing scene he had left not ten minutes before. A young man in his early twenties, home on leave from the war, had choked to death on the fluid in his lungs while resting in Thomas's arms. The youthful face had been tinged with an ever-spreading blueish hue: heliotrope cyanosis. No words came. He only shook his head. *It's not enough that he survived the German guns, but now he dies at home on English soil.*

Clara slipped out of the room and brought him back some cocoa before resuming her seat, only on the sofa instead of the floor this time.

He had never been a drinking man, but given the ache in his heart, never had a drink held so much appeal. He would do anything to drown out the pain he was feeling. The endless crying. The wracking coughs. The blood. The corpses. He sipped the cocoa, barely feeling its scalding warmth. He glanced at the books she had been reading. *Gray's Anatomy* and William Ostler —his medical textbooks. Any distractions to get them through these dark days were welcome.

They sat in weary silence for several moments before she rose, announcing that she would start on the rounds. "Sit," she instructed as Thomas shifted to stand. "You haven't slept in three days. Get some rest." Slowly picking up her black bag, she moved towards the door.

"Wait," Thomas called after her, and she paused, waiting for him to continue. He felt raw and vulnerable. Perhaps it was the exhaustion. He struggled to form the words that swirled in his mind. "I just want you to know... in case something happens... I'm glad you were sent here last autumn. You were a Godsend, Clara Dankworth."

Clara simply stared at him, her face belying her disbelief at the statement he had just uttered. "Thank you," she stammered. "I'm glad I came here, too," she added before fleeing the room.

Thomas leaned back in his chair and sighed. He had thought those words for months; he was glad to finally have given voice to them. Finishing off the cocoa, he locked the doors—Clara had a key to get in if she needed to—and trudged upstairs to bed.

The phone would probably ring for him soon enough. He needed to catch a bit of shut-eye before it beckoned him back out into a war he knew he couldn't win.

27 September

Thomas had called neighbouring hospitals and the local military hospital begging for nurses, but the message was the same every time—none were available. He and Clara worked around the clock, but they couldn't keep up with the rapidly rising number of cases. As he trudged up the stairs to Hazel Whyte's second-storey flat on Lawes Avenue, Thomas stumbled and caught himself from falling backwards down the stairs. He gave himself a stern lecture and a mental shake. His body couldn't quit on him now.

Hazel's younger sister met Thomas at the door and ushered

him into the bedroom. Hazel's pale form was a far cry from the bubbly, free-spirited young woman she had been only days ago.

"Can you help her, Doctor?" the younger girl asked nervously.

Thomas didn't answer. One look at the patient told him she wasn't far from death's door. A spasm of choking racked Hazel's frame, and Thomas helped her sit up to try and open her airways. Blood trickled out of the woman's blue lips.

"Forgive me," Hazel gurgled through the rising fluid in her throat as she clutched Thomas's hand.

Thomas thought back to his poisoning nine months earlier and figured that was what she was referring to. He smiled at her faintly and said, "I do."

"Sean... I... sorry..." More choking cut off Hazel's words as her body convulsed and contorted, gasping for air, until she fell still.

Thomas released the young woman's hand and stood slowly. Pulling out his pocket watch, he slowly recorded the death certificate for Hazel Whyte—27 September 1918. Her younger sister had approached the bed and touched Hazel's hand.

"I'm sorry," Thomas whispered as her tortured eyes sought his face for understanding.

The girl broke into sobs and buried her face in the quilt.

He finished writing and squeezed the girl's shoulder before he left. There was nothing more he could do.

30 September

Clara found herself across town at a small house near the harbour, filling out the death certificate of a young widow. The woman's mother sobbed uncontrollably by her daughter's bedside. As Clara slipped out of the room, she found the woman's three children staring at her.

"Is Mummy going to get better?" the eldest girl, who appeared to be about nine years old, asked.

Clara shook her head briefly as the sound of sobbing emerged from the bedroom.

"No!" the girl cried out.

Clara caught the girl in her arms as the child wept her heart out. The younger two children drew near and wrapped their arms around Clara and their sister, evidently frightened by their sister's emotional behaviour. Clara's own eyes burned with tears that refused to fall.

She trembled violently as she stumbled out of the small flat's door some time later. Collapsing in a heap on the doorstep, she hugged her knees to her chest and buried her face in her woollen skirt as fierce sobs tore through her frame. The awfulness of reality had caught up to her, and the tears fell thick and fast. Would this tragedy never end? *O dear Lord, save us,* was all she had the heart to pray.

CHAPTER 38

As She Lay Dying

2 October

THOMAS STUMBLED into the clinic after his rounds as the clock chimed six. He rubbed his bleary eyes as he splashed cold water on his face at the kitchen sink. A wave of nausea rolled over him, and he placed a steadying hand over his stomach and exhaled slowly. *What a morning.*

Half an hour ago, he had knocked on the front door of a small cottage to check on a family, but no one answered. He had poked his head inside, but nothing in his medical training prepared him from what he saw. An entire family, dead, but not from the flu. The wife and two children's throats were slit, and the husband, a burly sailor, had a knife in his chest. Thomas had heard about this happening in other towns; the flu gripped some of its victims in such a way as to drive them to madness—slaying their families to relieve the suffering. Shutting the door on the horror, Thomas had promptly lost the contents of his stomach and hurried back to the clinic.

With a shuddering breath, he splashed more water on his face as he waited for the sick feeling to pass. That was when he noticed how quiet the clinic was. Eerily quiet. He entered the hallway and paused. "Clara?"

No answer.

She wasn't in the office, supply room or examination room. Upstairs, the spare room door was open, and the room was empty. Retreating back downstairs, he checked the sitting room—why in all of England hadn't he thought to check there before?—and found her on the sofa, her teeth chattering violently.

"Thomas," she croaked.

Thomas knelt beside her. "I'm here."

"I think I caught it," was her whispered statement.

Thomas whipped a thermometer out of his bag and slipped it under her tongue. He blinked at the reading, tempted to take it again. *It can't be that high. It can't be.* But he knew it was. Dashing out of the room to the office without a word, he dialled the boarding house, and Elizabeth's greeting floated over the line.

"Clara's sick. Can you come?"

"I'll be right there," and the line went dead. True to her word, Elizabeth knocked on the kitchen door twenty minutes later with a carpet bag in her hand. She raced past him up the stairs to where Clara was already situated in the spare room. Elizabeth watched silently as Thomas listened to Clara's shallow breathing through the stethoscope. "I'll stay with her. I know you have others to see," she said in a subdued tone.

Thomas blinked in surprise. A subdued Elizabeth was a new kind of Elizabeth. "If anything happened to you, your brother, not to mention your husband, would kill me."

"Don't worry about Richard. I'm a married woman, and I know Aaron would approve."

He nodded. "Keep her comfortable and try to get her fever down. I've written instructions down. Here." He thrust a paper into her hands and grabbed his bag. "Make sure you follow them. I'll be back soon."

However, Clara grew steadily worse throughout the day. Her fever raged, and a wet cough racked her frame. When Thomas checked her temperature that evening, he shook his head. No change. Wearily, he retreated to the door, but a pitiful groan behind him halted his steps. He hurried back to the bed, careful to avoid Clara's flailing arms. "Clara," he said softly.

Her eyes blinked open, but they were unfocused and confused. "Mama?" she croaked. "Mama, where are you? Don't leave me. Not again. I'm all alone. Don't leave."

Thomas's heart hitched at the words. He had never heard Clara speak of her parents or any family at all. He took one of her fevered hands in his and squeezed it gently.

She clung to his hand with both of hers. "Don't leave."

"I'm not leaving," he whispered, which seemed to calm her. He felt the agitation die in her as she slipped from delirium into a more natural sleep. When her grip slackened, he carefully slipped his hand from hers. Wringing out a fresh cool cloth, he draped it across her forehead. He wasn't leaving her, not yet. Not after those painfully poignant words nearly shattered his already heavy heart. He knew all too well what it was like to be alone. His thoughts were interrupted by Elizabeth's entrance.

She dropped heavily onto the floor on the opposite side of the bed. Her chin propped on her clasped hands on the quilt top. "Will she make it?"

Thomas glanced at her. "There's no guarantee, but I would move heaven and earth if it would do any good."

She swallowed and nodded. "Thomas, I..." A tear trickled down her cheek.

"Never mind, Lizzie. I was a fool, and I'm sorry," he said gently. His gritty eyes met her teary grey ones with sympathy. Letting her know that the past was forgiven was his peace offering, and she accepted it with a grateful smile.

The next two days were a blur in Thomas's mind. He left Clara in Elizabeth's capable hands during the day while he rushed all over town treating other patients, fighting the same battle for life. He had signed six death records since Clara fell ill, and he shuddered at the thought. Death had shown no mercy to health or youth—grandparents died alongside infants. It was a cruel thing to watch.

Every evening Thomas dragged himself back to the clinic. By the end of the second day, Clara's fever still raged dangerously high. Using every bit of medical knowledge in his power, Thomas waged war hand to hand with the grim reaper intent on taking her life, and yet, still she grew worse.

The fever rose, the cough persisted, delirium overcame her, and blood continuously trickled from her mouth and nose. No change.

Mentally and physically exhausted, Thomas collapsed in the easy chair beside the bed. Covering his face, his shoulders shook with shuddering sobs. No medicine could save the countless lives lost. He was powerless to change the outcome of this illness. The numbing fear of losing the ones he fought hardest to save, the ones he cared about the most, consumed him. "God... You know I'm not the best at this... I hardly know what to say." He bit his lip. "I know I don't have a right to ask this after I blamed You for everything, but would You save her? I've done all I can. You'll have to do the rest," he whispered.

Kasey's words echoed through the fuzziness of his thoughts. *You're not the Almighty... you're only a man. You can't control Him, and He doesn't answer to mere mortals. If the Good Lord allowed her to be taken, He had a reason. I know you think you can run your own life, but His hands are far more capable than yours, son.*

Clenching his fists, his heart hammered. He did not want to accept that. He didn't want to lose her—that wasn't part of the plan. Of his plan, at least. He studied the fever-flushed face asleep on the pillow. Clara's chestnut hair was tangled into a braid, but the curls around her face were plastered against her forehead. She embodied everything warm and familiar in his life. She brought colour to his world of grey. From the beginning of the epidemic, he had a vague sense this might happen. But preparing to get sick was one thing, preparing to die was quite another. Or in his case, watching someone slowly slip away before his very eyes.

Violent coughs wracked her frame, and he slipped an arm beneath her shoulders to raise her up. When the attack passed, he carefully wiped a fresh trickle of blood from her mouth with a clean handkerchief.

Elizabeth joined his vigil and lowered herself onto the rug on the opposite side of the bed. Neither said a word. She opened her mouth to say something but closed it again quickly.

"It's all right, Lizzie, say it," he encouraged gently.

"Do you think she'll make it?"

Barring a miracle, not a chance. Thomas swallowed the thought and didn't answer for several moments. When he did, his voice was hoarse and hardly above a whisper. "We've done all we can. She's in God's hands now."

Shortly after midnight, Elizabeth's head drooped in sleep against the quilt top. Thomas fought the urge to shut his eyes. *I must stay awake.*

As the clock struck two o'clock on the morning of October fourth, Thomas jolted awake with a start and shook himself. He quickly turned up the lamp. Clara's face had lost its flushed feverish look and had taken on a pasty pallor. His heart dropped. *No, no, no!* Leaning over her, he touched her forehead. It was damp and cool to the touch, and her eyelids fluttered. His heart leapt, and an unbidden tear slipped over his unshaven cheek. "You did it, Lord," he murmured with awe.

Against all odds, her fever had broken.

CHAPTER 39

For Whom the Bells Tolled

THE NEXT FEW days had Thomas signing even more death certificates, his mind numb to the grueling task. Clara was recovering. A few nights after the crisis, she regressed and gave him cause for concern, but her death certificate was not one he had to sign, and for that, he was grateful.

Clara wiggled the thermometer under her tongue as Thomas checked her temperature, as he did every evening.

He smiled with satisfaction as he took it out of her mouth. "Fever's still down."

Dropping her head back against the pillow, her eyes fluttered shut in exhaustion.

He studied her as he closed his bag. "What's the matter?" he asked quietly.

One brown eye peeked open. "I'm tired of fighting, Thomas," she whispered. "I just want to go home."

A pucker formed between Thomas's brows as a single tear trickled down her pale face. Not quite the speech he had expected from the woman who had just miraculously returned from death's door. Gently, he covered her hand with his.

Both her eyes blinked open at him.

"My mother used to say that it is God who strengthens us for the battle." He paused, giving her hand a light squeeze. "Few could have endured as long as you have. Don't lose hope yet."

A wobbly smile touched the ashen face on the pillow before her eyes drooped closed again.

Quietly, he left the room and leaned his forehead against the closed door. "Please don't let her quit now," he murmured.

Clara's recovery continued to creep slowly, and Thomas fielded questions as to her recovery daily. "They seem to have greater concern for the nurse than the doctor," he told her dryly when he checked on her one evening.

She only laughed. Relief washed over Thomas at the sound. Her voice had lost its sad, despairing edge from days before. She would make it. They all would. They had to.

A week after the crisis, Clara begged to return to the clinic. Thomas steadfastly refused, maintaining she wasn't strong enough, and that he didn't need another patient on his hands. She grumbled dismally, but he remained resolute.

"At least bring me the books and records, I can catch up on those," she wheedled.

Thomas hesitated. Though she was becoming more like herself with each passing day, he could still see the lingering exhaustion in her face. At last, he conceded with a shrug. "No harm in that, I suppose. I'll bring them up in the morning."

~

13 October

Clara leaned back against the pillows propping her up, surrounded by patient records that Thomas had brought up for her earlier. Dabbing her eyes, she bravely attacked the files.

Emma Jones...19
Anne Simpson...34
Mary Ellis...27
Jane Watson...38
William Ward...30
John Crawford...21
Mary Andrews...22
Joseph Andrews...11 months

Her eyes widened at the name. Mary Andrews and her baby were dead? Her mind flew back to the autumnal day almost a year ago when she had delivered that darling little boy to his young mother. Mary's husband was supposed to come back and meet the baby. Now they were both gone. The young soldier would never meet his little son. Sobs clogged Clara's throat as she gripped the pages. She was vaguely aware of Thomas coming in a few minutes later and lowering himself into the easy chair beside her bed.

Gently, he eased the paper out of her hand. "Perhaps this wasn't the best idea," he said softly.

Clara didn't look at him, but her sobs calmed gradually. "I didn't know about Mary." The whisper barely made it past her lips.

He grimaced. "It happened while you were sick. She and Joseph went the same night."

She shuddered. "What about Maggie?"

He shook his head. "She went two days later."

"When will it end?" she whispered, burying her face in the quilt as the tears continued to fall. When she could speak again, Clara wiped her eyes, her face flushed. "Sorry to take it out on you."

"I'm a doctor; it's part of the job description," he quipped lightly.

She rewarded him with a faint smile.

"Work through files as you feel up to it, but no nursing for you till you get your strength back." He rose and went to the door.

Clara sighed. "Yes, Doctor." She watched him hesitate in the doorway.

"I'm glad you made it, Clara," he said softly. "Hang in there."

CHAPTER 40

Rescue Mission

16 October

STRUGGLING up the back steps after a long day, Thomas made his way to the kitchen for a cup of tea. A dark head emerged from the office doorway, and Thomas shouted in surprise, swinging out his Webley.

"Only me," Richard cried, raising his hands in surrender. "I've been waiting."

Thomas lowered the gun, clutching his chest, as he leaned heavily against the wall.

Grabbing his friend's elbow, Richard led him to the kitchen and made him sit down. "You look terrible," he commented, handing the doctor a cup of tepid tea. "When did you last sleep?"

Three days now, or was it four days? Thomas waved off the concern. "Don't remember. Why are you here?"

"Rescue mission."

"I don't need rescuing. We're in the middle of a pandemic." He frowned, rubbing his bleary eyes and sipping his tea.

"Not you this time. It's Clara."

Thomas choked on the flavourless liquid. "What?"

"Walter overheard a man at Crouthers's office say he has plans for her. Didn't catch what, but he told me she needs to disappear for a while."

"Where to?" Thomas blurted out, then added hastily, "Don't tell me. It's better I don't know." He gave himself a mental shake; he was losing his edge.

Richard nodded. "But I still need your help. I drove a car here since most of the trains are down. But I heard the train in Portsmouth is still running, so I'll take her there."

"She's been sick and has barely recovered. She's in no condition to travel."

"Thomas, I don't know how long I have to get her out of here before Crouthers intervenes." Urgency radiated off Richard's rigid stance, and he reached out, clasping a firm hand on Thomas's shoulder. "She has to go now."

Thomas swallowed another mouthful of tea. He didn't like it one bit, but his friend was right. He sighed heavily in resignation.

"Tell her to pack light." Richard opened the back door, pausing to add, "I'll be back at midnight."

Thomas nodded, using the table to pull himself to his feet, and wearily moved towards the hall. "You had better keep her safe, Richard."

"You have my word."

Something in Richard's tone made Thomas glance back at him, and he saw a passing shadow in his friend's eyes, but Richard was gone before Thomas could say another word. He shook his head. He must have merely imagined it.

As promised, Richard arrived at midnight. In the foggy street behind the clinic, Thomas held out his hand to Clara, and she shook it warmly. The words he wished to say lodged in his throat.

Clara hesitated before ducking into Richard's car. "Don't topple too many kingdoms while I'm away," she whispered to Thomas.

"I won't. I promise," Thomas returned with a wry smile.

❧

Silently slipping into the back seat, Clara inhaled deeply. There was only one thing left to say. "Till we meet again, be it in this world or the next, God be with you, Thomas Lindsey."

The door closed, and as the car sped away, she watched him grow smaller through the back window. This was good-bye.

She shifted uncomfortably where she lay in the back of the car out of sight. Richard was silent as the last house disappeared, and the automobile laboured up an incline. The South Downs. Two hours passed before the car drifted to a stop.

"We're here," Richard announced.

Clara weakly pulled herself upright. "Where?"

"Portsmouth. We'll catch the train from here." Richard slid out.

Climbing out the door Richard held for her, Clara glanced about her. The street was quiet and dimly lit from the lamp posts. She donned the mask Thomas had given her, and Richard did likewise before picking up her small valise.

"This way," he instructed, taking her elbow and guiding her towards the door.

The Portsmouth station boasted only a handful of people as they entered. Clara sank onto a bench, exhausted, while Richard bought tickets. For the next several hours, the pair caught train after train. Losing count after Sheffield, she leaned against the cool window. Her memory jogged as she remembered her train ride nearly a year earlier. Newhaven had been all she could have asked for, and now she was on the run once again. Sighing, she mused over the memory.

The loving welcome of the Forsythe family, Lizzie's impetuous but fiercely loyal friendship, Robbie's bright smiles, the weekly canteens, and Thomas. She smiled to herself. They certainly had been at each other's throats often enough in the beginning, but they had worked things out eventually.

Richard tapped her shoulder. "Last switch up ahead."

"Which station is this?" she asked, clutching her seat edge as the train rolled to a stop.

"Chester."

"We've come that far? Where are we going?" she questioned in hushed tones.

"Conway."

She frowned as she mentally tried to recall her geography. "Where's that?"

"Northern Wales."

"Wales!" Her pitch raised to a muffled shrill through her mask. When Richard shushed her, she added more quietly, "Why Wales?"

"I'm taking you to Donovan and Maranda."

"Does Thomas know?"

"No one does. It's better that way so he can't slip up when they question him."

"Are you expecting that to happen?" Clara asked.

"You've been in the Service long enough to know the answer. We all expect the unexpected. For now, I need you to trust me."

"I've heard that before," she muttered as he led her through the crowded station.

"Haven't we all?" he teased lightly, but shadows lurked in his eyes.

"What will happen if they find me?" she asked softly after several minutes. "Would they kill your sister and Donovan?"

Richard hesitated. "Sometimes we lose a battle to win a war. Just trust me."

At the Conway station, Richard hailed a cab and ushered Clara inside. Pale morning sunlight bathed the lush green fields and the heathered hills rolling in the distance while the sparkling azure waves of the Conway harbour flashed by.

"It's lovely here," Clara breathed incredulously.

Richard smiled in agreement.

The cab stopped in front of a small cottage with a white fence surrounding it. The last of summer's roses still bloomed in the garden, their subtle fragrance mixing with the faint sea air. Clara breathed in deeply; she could get used to this.

Maranda answered Richard's knock. Her dark curly hair was swept back from her face with a hair ribbon and her eyes sparkled. "Richard!" she cried in delight.

Richard embraced his sister and planted a kiss on the top of her hair. "How is my littlest sister and favourite niece or nephew?"

Cradling her swollen stomach, Maranda laughed. "Perfectly well." Noticing Clara, she lifted an eyebrow at her brother. "Thomas's girl?"

Clara's eyes widened, and Richard chuckled. "I don't think it's official, but yes. Miss Dankworth, you remember my sister, Maranda Byrne."

Maranda's eyes twinkled as she enfolded Clara in a warm hug. "It's so nice to see you again!"

"I have to leave right away, Maranda," Richard interjected.

Maranda's face fell. "So soon? Can't you wait till Donovan comes?"

"Afraid not, little sister." Richard kissed her forehead and turned to leave but then paused. "And it's *cod coch*."

Maranda's face paled slightly under her already creamy complexion. "Understood."

Richard gave them a final nod and disappeared through the gate.

"You must be exhausted," Maranda said sympathetically as she closed the door. "Why don't you lie down for a while?"

The hundreds of miles caught up with Clara, and her shoulders sagged at the very suggestion; she had no argument. Following Maranda to a small, back bedroom, she shrugged out of her coat and unpinned her hat before sinking onto the bed.

Maranda smiled at her from the doorway. "Take all the time you need. Rest well."

"Thank you," Clara whispered with a shaky smile before the door closed, leaving her alone. She was practically asleep by the time her head hit the downy pillow. Hours later, she awoke, somewhat refreshed, and crept out into the kitchen.

Maranda smiled when she saw her. "You're awake! How are you feeling? Tea?"

"If it's no trouble."

"None at all."

Clara glanced about the little cottage. There were two doors leading into other rooms. The kitchen opened upon a lovely sitting room with chairs and a cosy fire.

Maranda handed her a mug of tea and motioned to the sofa. "Please sit." Shyly, she added, "I know we only met that once, but I feel like I already know you so well from Thomas and Lizzie's letters."

"Do they write often?"

"Lizzie writes every week and gushes about you in typical Lizzie fashion, while Thomas writes once or twice a month." She grinned. "He doesn't gush, but he does speak highly of you."

Clara flushed and sipped her tea with an averted gaze. They chatted amiably for several minutes about Conwy, their mutual friends, and Maranda's upcoming baby.

"Maranda," Clara asked slowly. "Why did Richard say, 'It is code red'?"

A small frown tugged the corners of the small rosebud mouth. "I didn't know you understood Welsh. It's a system Richard and Donovan developed based on the seriousness of an agent's concealment. Code Red is critical, and you're our first one with that honour."

Clara nodded thoughtfully. "I see. Do you work for the Service? Lizzie told me Donovan is..." and she bit her lip before finishing the sentence.

"An Irish rebel?" Maranda finished with a smile. "He is, and, no, we don't work for the Service. We have helped harbour a few agents though, and don't worry about Donovan. He's perfectly safe, I assure you."

"Oh, I wasn't worried. Lizzie said he's the dearest man next to 'her Aaron,' but she did impress upon me her shock that her sweet and gentle little sister could marry a rebel."

Maranda blushed and twisted the Claddagh ring on her left ring finger. "I guess it surprised me as well, but he was so sweet and loyal and always helping others—how could I say no?"

After their tea, Clara offered to help prepare dinner. They were nearly finished when heavy footsteps entered the house, and a warm voice called out, "Acushla!"

Maranda's face bloomed prettily, and her eyes danced. "In here, Donovan."

A tall, broad-shouldered man filled the doorway. His red hair had been arranged at the will of the wind, and his green eyes sparkled as he smiled at his wife. Petite Maranda practically disappeared when the muscular man took her in his arms.

"Donovan, you remember Clara Dankworth. Richard said it's *cod coch*." Maranda motioned to Clara when Donovan released her.

The Irishman's friendly eyes crinkled with a grin that spread across his face, and he engulfed the hand Clara offered him with his own. "You're most welcome here, Miss Clara."

"Thank you, Mr. Byrne."

He chuckled deeply. "Just Donovan. You're practically family with how much Lizzie and the doc talk about you."

Maranda nudged him as Clara felt her face flush, but she laughed anyway.

The little family in the stone cottage fell into a comfortable routine. Maranda seemed delighted with the company, and Donovan's friendly, carefree nature was impossible not to appreciate. *Even if he is an Irish rebel,* Clara mused to herself with a chuckle.

A few days after Clara's arrival, Donovan announced he needed to take a short trip to Ireland the next morning.

Maranda's brow wrinkled. "Are you sure it's safe?"

He pulled her close with a smile. "Yes, acushla."

"You'll take the letter?"

"Of course."

Donovan disappeared out the door, leaving the two women

alone in the little sitting room. Maranda went to her desk and began writing on a half-filled sheet of paper.

"You don't take letters through the post?" Clara asked, sipping her tea.

Maranda smiled at her as she looked up. "This is a special delivery to Thomas's sister." Her voice dropped. "She's been in hiding in Ireland for years."

This was a new piece of information. Thomas had never mentioned a sister or any family apart from his dead father. Let alone that he had ties to Ireland.

"Why Ireland?"

"It was the safest place for them. His sister and mother, that is."

Maranda wrote in silence for several minutes as Clara mulled over what she had said. How old was this sister? Was she like Thomas? Why was she in hiding? Leaving Maranda to her letter, Clara retreated to the garden. Little was still in bloom this late in October except for the rich heather surrounding her on the distant hills, the pungent fragrance filling her nose. A redheaded image came to mind. Dear Robbie. He had shared her love for heather. Inhaling the scent, she lifted her head skyward and smiled despite the solitary, salty tear that trickled down her cheek.

CHAPTER 41

And Then There was One

18 October

THOMAS WANDERED into the office with his cup of tea. The silence was grating on him. His fingers traced the edge of Clara's desk. Though the room rather resembled the size of a matchbox, it seemed hollow and almost too large. Wearily, he dropped into her chair. If he closed his eyes, he could smell lavender and hear her tinkling laugh. He fiddled with the loose papers that had piled up in her absence. At the bottom of the pile, he found a house call list. The last one before their world had turned upside down. The sight of her flowing script brought a lump to his throat. How was she doing? Had she suffered a relapse? Where even was she?

Some time later, Richard slipped into the office, surprising Thomas, who still sat at Clara's desk, staring meditatively at the floorboards. Light from the grate danced on the walls, casting eerie shadows. Thomas didn't glance up as Richard sat down in a chair opposite him.

Richard went straight to the point. "You all right?"

Thomas only took a swig of tepid tea and swallowed it untasted.

"I've never seen you like this."

"I'm a fool. With how long I spent trying to get rid of her, you'd think I would be happy she's gone."

"But you're not," Richard finished the thought. "It was for her own safety."

"I know."

Richard hesitated. "You really care for her, don't you?"

Did he? Thomas rubbed his forehead. Everything felt wrong, mixed-up. Death lingered in the air. Clara was gone. He wanted things to return to normalcy. But what even was *normal* anymore?

Richard seemed to take the silence for an answer. "Anything I can do?"

"I would rather be alone."

With a nod, Richard obliged him.

Thomas returned to his contemplative state until the clock struck nine. Trudging to the kitchen, he realised he had skipped supper. Opening the cupboards, he found them empty. Shopping had been the last thing on his mind, and Clara had managed that for him almost since the day she had arrived. His stomach roiled as he thought about it, so he locked up and retired upstairs to his room.

Sitting on the edge of his bed, he gazed out the nearby window, where moonlight illuminated the sky. Somewhere, Clara must be looking at the same moon. Deep inside his chest, a vague thought arose. A thought he could not voice or even put words to, and yet, it was a thought that tugged his heart in a way nothing had before.

Turning off the light, he collapsed into bed. He had taken to sleeping in his clothes, since calls came at all hours of the night these days. The haunting dreams of a little black-haired girl had morphed into dreams of a certain chestnut-haired, sparkling-eyed nurse who infused hope wherever she went and smelled of lavender. His last conscious thought was in the form of a prayer: *God, please keep her safe because I can't.*

The telephone rang, shattering the morning silence. Rubbing the sleep from his eyes, Thomas dragged himself out of bed to take the call, knowing full well it was probably another patient begging him to come and do everything he could to save a loved one.

Mid-morning, he made himself a weak cup of tea and sat at his desk in an attempt to catch up on the records in the account book. The office door clicked open.

"Where is she?" a low voice demanded.

Thomas met Reynolds's flashing eyes. "What do you mean?" he returned innocently as he leaned back in his chair.

"You know exactly what I mean, Doctor. Don't make me lose my patience. Clara Dankworth."

"She was sick and has been on leave."

"Where?"

"I don't know. I didn't ask her," Thomas said. It was true enough. "She needed a holiday—"

"Fool!" Reynolds raged. The two men leveled each other with their gaze. "I will ask once more." Reynolds's voice sliced the air. "Where did she go?"

"I don't know," Thomas returned coolly.

"You would never have let her go if you knew who she was."

"Maybe I did," Thomas countered, his face unmoving, although he really had no idea who she was. The woman seemed to have more aliases than he did.

Reynolds growled. "Crouthers wants her back immediately."

"Not possible."

"You're going to regret this, Lindsey," Reynolds threw over his shoulder before slamming the door behind him and setting the pictures rattling.

Thomas laid his gun on the desk and raked his fingers through his curls. Clara was in more danger than Richard had let on.

A short time later, a knock on the kitchen door startled Thomas from a doze. *I don't remember falling asleep*, he thought as he lifted his head from its resting place on the desk. Dragging himself to his feet, he trudged across the hall. The door opened on Alaina, her brown eyes weary and rimmed with dark circles.

"You look awful," he said as he pulled her inside and sat her at the table.

"You look just as bad," she replied sharply.

"I didn't mean..." he spluttered as the impact of his words hit him.

She smiled tiredly. "I know what you meant, comrade. No harm done. But you do look terrible. Are you sleeping?"

He sat down across from her, rubbing his bloodshot eyes before running a hand through his hair. It was getting too long. "I took a nap last night for the first time in... a while."

She glared at him. "You're going to kill yourself!"

"I'm down a nurse, and people are dying by the dozens. Elizabeth and others are doing their best, but..." Thomas shuddered and hid his face. "I've never seen anything like it," he whispered between his fingers.

"I know; I've been all over town as a nurse."

His head jerked up. "You? A nurse?" he asked in amazement. He hadn't even considered the possibility till now.

She nodded coolly. "You remember when you asked how I would do in a real emergency? Well, I guess we found out."

He nodded with an approving smile.

"Can I do anything to help you?" she pleaded.

Thomas hesitated and stole a glance through the open kitchen door to the office. A large stack of patient files sat on his desk. "You could go through the records and mark the deceased. I haven't had the time."

Alaina's face blanched, but she nodded resolutely. "Just show me what to do."

With Alaina and an already helpful Elizabeth working beside him, Thomas continued to put in his long hours, running all over town to visit the sick and comfort the dying. Elizabeth proved herself a capable nurse, and Alaina kept the books and records up to date in between nursing patients. Despite all their efforts, the death count continued to climb.

Thomas came into the office one evening and found Alaina sobbing at Clara's desk. He touched her shoulder so as not to alarm her.

"Oh Thomas, it was awful," she cried, looking up at him. "There were fifteen this week."

Thomas's heart dropped. He had lost count of the casualties, but it sounded worse when spoken out loud. A telegram from Dorset caught his eye on the desk in front of his cousin, and he snatched it up.

*FLU KILLED HARRY. GLENNA RECOVERING.
STAY SAFE. JANE.*

Her father dead; her mother alive. "I'm sorry, Alaina."

Alaina's eye caught the missive in his hand. "I didn't get to tell Dad I forgave him," she whispered and burst into a fresh fit of tears. "I tried to go home once, but I didn't have the courage."

Thomas squeezed her shoulder reassuringly. "You will. When the time is right."

CHAPTER 42

Healing Hearts

Late October

MEANWHILE IN WALES, Clara basked in the friendly welcome she had received at the Byrnes' little cottage. Every night, they would gather in the snug sitting room before the merry, dancing, hearth fire. Donovan told stories and kept up a steady stream of chatter in his lilting voice as Maranda's needles clicked from where she sat knitting in her rocking chair. Clara crocheted as her shaky hands allowed, and they would sing together. It was like... *home*.

One night before retiring, Maranda handed Clara a knitted, oatmeal-coloured cashmere cardigan.

"For me?" Clara blinked in surprise.

"Welsh nights are colder than those in Sussex."

Clara fingered the handiwork curiously. The pattern was strangely familiar. "Are you the one who made Thomas's sweaters?"

Maranda nodded.

"Thank you." She swallowed the growing lump in her throat. "I love it."

"You're family, Clara, and you always will be. We look after our own."

Clara's heart leapt at the words. Robbie had said almost the same thing to her once. Later that night, she snuggled under the covers and clutched the cosy quilt and crocheted afghan under her chin. Maranda was right—Welsh nights were much colder than those in Sussex. But, she was happy here. Breathing a thankful prayer to the Lord for bringing her to a haven of rest, the warmth seeped through her frame and lulled her off to sleep.

Rising early the next morning, Clara settled the afghan around her shoulders and opened her Bible. From a tender age, the importance of the Scriptures had been impressed upon her, and she had taken those lessons to heart. This morning, as was her custom, she thumbed through the familiar pages. However, the familiarity did not diminish the precious sweetness she found within the pages. After half an hour of reading, her heart warmed at the words:

And ye now therefore have sorrow; but I will see you again and your heart shall rejoice, and your joy shall no man take from you.

Her heart was heavy now, but it wouldn't be forever. True joy could only be found in Christ, and her circumstances could never change that. Fumbling for the chain around her neck, she traced the delicate design of the filigree cross. God had never failed her all these years, and He wasn't about to begin now. Smiling, she bowed her head and her heart in prayer for a long talk with the One who was always there to listen.

~

1 November

Thomas wandered aimlessly along the dark shore. Gentle waves of low tide raced over the sand, stinging his bare feet as the sea breeze teased his curls. Pausing, he faced France and reached into his pocket, letting his fingers brush the tattered blue ribbons he often carried with him. He gritted his teeth. It was over. Everything he had worked for all these years. He had lost everything.

Several agents had been murdered, he had no leads on a thirteen-year-old cold case, no control over what would happen next, a town full of those he considered friends dying by the dozens—and the woman he loved was in hiding. Thomas started. Where had that thought come from? But he could not deny it. He did love Clara Dankworth.

A shallow, bitter laugh escaped his lips. Kasey had been right —he was only a man. A powerfully inadequate man. The laughter died quickly, and he sank to his knees. The surf seeped through the knees of his trousers, but he barely noticed. Burying his head in his hands, he wept long and hard like he never had before. *I asked for answers, God, and found only more questions. What am I supposed to do?*

Someday you'll come to the end of yourself and find a problem you can't fix. Clara's sad voice pierced through his mind in the darkness. Why couldn't he have seen this coming?

Thomas had been fluent in religion all his life. Raised in a Christian home, he knew the Bible. He knew the way of salvation through Jesus Christ. He knew what God expected of him. But after the death of his father, he had dismissed the Almighty from his life altogether, convinced God couldn't be so cruel. For the last ten years, Thomas Lindsey had been in control of his own life—or so he had thought. Now, he began to realise just how futile his efforts had been. He hadn't been able to save Robbie. He couldn't save the dozens dying of the deadly flu. He couldn't even save Clara. Beneath the aliases and the lies, he finally saw himself for who he was: a broken man who couldn't fix himself. He was at the mercy of God. But instead of resenting the thought, he felt strangely warmed by it. Perhaps he didn't need to carry the weight of the world on his shoulders after all. God's hands were far more capable than his.

"Oh, God, have mercy on me," he whispered between his fingers that covered his face. In the next few minutes, kneeling in that wet sand, he bowed his heart before the King of Heaven who had sought him so patiently and so persistently all those years.

When Thomas rose from his knees some time later, a peace engulfed him that he had never felt before. His problems were the same, but he had found perspective for them, and he now knew he was no longer alone. Throwing his head back, he studied the twinkling stars. *I didn't deserve it, Lord, but thank You.* He slowly wandered back towards the promenade.

"Are you all right, lad?"

Relief washed over Thomas at the sound of the low, familiar voice. "I am now, Kasey. You were right."

The old captain stepped out of the shadows and studied the younger man's face intently. "About what exactly?"

"That I am only a man and would have to bow before the Almighty some day."

Kasey nodded knowingly. "Figured that's why you were here tonight. I waited to make sure you didn't do something desperate."

Thomas's face fell. "I can't say that it hasn't crossed my mind."

"As much as I wanted to come to you, I knew this was a battle you had to fight alone."

"I finally understood."

Stepping closer, Kasey wrapped the younger man in a strong embrace. "Those words do my heart good, son."

With a lump in his throat and tears stinging his eyes, Thomas returned the hug. So much like a father's. And his heart swelled with gratitude for loyal friends, the love of God, and a second chance.

~

4 November

Thomas leaned his forehead against the smooth top of his desk, shoulders sagging with exhaustion. How long had it been since he had slept? He couldn't remember. The office door creaked open, and the light tread of heels sounded on the wood floor. Alaina.

"Are you all right?" she asked softly.

He detected the undercurrent of concern in her voice and lifted his head slowly to meet her gaze. Alaina had planted her hands on the edge of the desk and leaned towards him slightly, her brown eyes clouded with worry. Offering her what he knew was a tired grin, he nodded.

The shadows did not leave her eyes, despite his reassurances. After a moment, her eyes widened in disbelief, and she leaned further across the desk to touch his hair. "You're going grey," she choked.

Thomas jolted and jumped out of his seat, rushing to the small mirror that hung on the wall across the room. Peering at his reflection intently, he ran his long, slender fingers through his dark curls. The mirror affirmed Alaina's discovery, and his shoulders dropped. He wasn't ready for this. "This war has made me an old man," he whispered hoarsely, not looking at her.

A gentle arm slipped around him, and Alaina leaned her head against his shoulder. "A wiser man, Thomas," was her soft rejoinder. "Once you dug past the aliases, the lies, and the cover-ups, you found who God intended you to be. And I'm proud of you."

Thomas glanced down into the eyes of his cousin. "You're the only one who would say that. You always told me the truth of the matter whether I wanted to hear it or not."

"Someone had to," Alaina quipped before adding in a softer tone, "But I know the others would agree."

"You think so?"

Alaina cocked her eyebrow at him in the mirror. "Know so."

Thomas slipped an arm around his cousin's shoulders and

rested his chin on her head. "You're a good sport, Alaina. Thank you."

CHAPTER 43

Disappearing Act

9 November

THE HEARTY Welsh air was better medicine for Clara than any pill box. Her strength returned in increments, and a healthy colour started to stain her cheeks. Her only secret complaint was Donovan's smoking in the house. But what the giant of a man lacked in outward polish, he more than made up for in greatness of heart. Never had she met a man more devoted to his wife or loyal to his friends.

However, despite her love for Wales, her mind often wandered south to Newhaven. She missed her friends who had become family there, and though it felt strange to admit, she missed Thomas, too. She bit her lip to hold back a smile. *Who would have thought?*

In the evening, Maranda and Donovan left Clara at the cottage, promising to return after they checked in on their neighbours.

Clara smiled to herself as she stood in the silence of the empty kitchen. She had read Psalm 27 that morning, and she replayed the words in her mind, letting them wash over her as she prepared a cup of tea in one of the dainty china cups Maranda took great pride in.

The Lord is my light and my salvation; whom shall I fear? The Lord is the strength of my life; of whom shall I be afraid? When the wicked, even mine enemies and my foes, came upon me to eat up my flesh, they stumbled and fell. Though a host should encamp against me, my heart shall not fear: though war should rise against me, in this will I be confident.

As the clock chimed nine, she stood at the front window, sipping the warm liquid and watching the faint moonbeams dance around the garden. She hadn't felt this safe or comfortable since she had left Halifax four years ago. *Thank You, Lord, for always being with me and for seeing me this far,* she prayed silently with a sigh of contentment as she fingered a button on her cardigan.

A moment later the world went black as a cloth clapped over her face, its sickly-sweet scent suffusing her nose. She heard the china cup shatter as it hit the floor before she slumped over, a dull *thud* cracking against the back of her head. Then all was dark and silent.

Clara's head throbbed with each pounding heartbeat, and her eyes refused to focus as she slowly emerged from unconsciousness. The floor was damp beneath her back, and she suppressed a shiver. Rubbing her eyes to clear them, she groped the air around her for a wall. Cold stone brushed her fingertips. Pulling herself into a sitting position, she observed her prison. With stone walls and a dirt floor, she knew instinctively she was in a cellar. But where and more importantly, why?

She touched the swollen knot at the base of her head and winced. Grateful to be wearing the cardigan Maranda made her, Clara wrapped it more tightly against her slender frame. Attempting to stand up, the room began to spin, and she fell back against the rough rockwork with a moan and clamped her eyes shut. "I don't know where I am or why, but be with me here, Lord," she whispered.

Some time later, a sliver of light shone into the room. Unmoving, Clara waited. The sliver grew larger, and a man's silhouette appeared in the door frame and slowly descended the stairs. She pressed further back into the corner as a slow sinister smile appeared on the stranger's face, and the cat's eyes glowed in the dim light of his torch. Reynolds.

He grabbed her upper arm, jerked her to her feet, and dragged her up the stairs to the door. Still clumsy from the chloroform and weak from her convalescence, Clara stumbled to keep up with him. As her captor led her through the hall, she stopped in astonishment.

Reynolds, seeming to anticipate the reaction, grinned slyly. "Recognise the place?"

She shuddered and trailed her fingers over the polished wood railings as he marched her upstairs. The silk curtains. The velvet carpets. The polished wood. Hollyside Manor. Her heart quaked, though she refused to show Reynolds how deeply she hurt. "Why would you bring me here?" she asked quietly.

"Just following orders." Reynolds shoved her through a doorway leading into a large apartment.

Thousands of books lined the oak shelves. An easy chair sat near the fireplace. Hollyside's library. How many happy days she had spent here as a child? Candles dimly lit the room, and a fire glowed faintly in the hearth, illuminating the plush carpet underfoot. The clock read six o'clock. *But what day is it?* She glanced at the windows. With the curtains drawn, she couldn't even tell if it was morning.

"She's here, sir," Reynolds purred, keeping his viper grip on Clara's upper arm.

Clara's attention snapped to the oak desk and the portly man who swivelled in the desk chair to face her. She inhaled sharply and stiffened. "You?" she asked in bewilderment.

"Surprised to see me, my dear?" Crouthers smiled sardonically and leaned back in his chair.

She blinked, her mind struggling to overcome the fuzzy effect of the chloroform and make sense of the situation. "I don't understand."

"It's quite simple really. But there is someone else you should meet."

A side door opened, and a man in his early thirties with honey-coloured hair nodded at her as he entered.

"Charles?" she whispered hoarsely.

"Nice to see you at last, little sister."

"You... you're supposed to be... dead," she stammered. She had seen the telegram with her own eyes, confirming him as an early casualty of war. What in all of England was going on?

"Well, here I am." Charles grinned at her. Not in a friendly way. Instead this grin held a sinister threat.

Clara refused to give way to the shudder threatening to course through her limbs. Summoning every ounce of courage, she glared at her brother and demanded firmly, "What is the meaning of this?"

"It's quite simple. There's a fortune awaiting me with only one thing in the way."

She studied him. "That one thing being?" She knew the answer before he confirmed it.

"You."

"I haven't a penny to my name and have been in hiding for ten years. Were you behind that, too?"

Charles's eyes flamed. "I knew Jonathan would never give up the papers. I had to wait for you to get away from his hold."

She frowned. "What papers?"

"Don't be coy. You know which ones."

"I don't," she insisted. "I never knew of them. For all I knew, the inheritance was yours. Take it all and let me go."

"I plan to, but I can't without those documents."

Clara surveyed the room. Crouthers. Reynolds. "Have you been behind this whole sham? To get the inheritance?"

Charles laughed mirthlessly. "Oh, there is more at stake than just an inheritance. True, I have debts to pay and need the money, but the Germans are willing to pay a high price for a world-renowned British heiress with a trust fund."

"The Germans..." Clara's voice dropped. "You're The Piper?"

"No, but you may have the pleasure of his company later."

Rage and confusion coursed through Clara's veins. Each one of those men she had trusted, and each had betrayed her. Her heart, her life, and her calling. She was nothing but a pawn to be used at whim. *Pawn, why does that sound familiar?* Then she remembered. *Lotta mentioned The Pawn. That's me. All this time, it's been me.* The intensity of the circumstances crushed her heart, and the room swam before her eyes. *Dear Lord, help me.* Then, she did something she had never done before—she fainted.

When Clara came to, she was back in the damp, cold, lightless cellar. Alone. In the stillness, a well-beloved voice whispered in her mind: *Never sacrifice the truth on the altar of ease.* Scalding tears coursed over her cheeks, and sobs wracked her frame in remembrance of the first time she had heard those words. When the last of her tears were gone, her eyes burned, and her face was flushed feverishly. Laying her cheek to the cool cellar floor, she fell into an uneasy sleep.

CHAPTER 44

The Pawn

10 November

FRANTIC POUNDING on the kitchen door echoed through the clinic. Thomas groaned as he lifted his head off his desk. He must have fallen asleep again. To his amazement, the clock chimed half-past ten in the morning as he ran his fingers through his hair and rubbed his eyes. Hurrying to the kitchen, he threw the door open upon a tall figure. Donovan. The doctor held out his hand in welcome, but instead the Irishman swallowed him in a bear hug.

The strangeness of the situation suddenly hit him. "What's going on?" he questioned in alarm as Donovan released him.

Shadows haunted Donovan's green eyes. "It's all gone wrong, Doc."

Thomas's heart plummeted as he ushered his friend inside. "Tell me everything."

Half an hour later, Thomas sped to the Jenningses' estate. Pushing past Kerridge at the door, he bolted up the stairs two at a time and burst into the colonel's study.

Jennings scowled as he looked up from his paper. "Lindsey, you better have a good reason—"

"Clara's missing," Thomas interrupted. "You seem to know more about her than you have disclosed. Do you know who could have taken her and why?"

The sage eyes narrowed on the doctor. "I need more details than that."

Thomas quickly filled the colonel in on said details, leaving nothing out, from Richard's taking Clara to safety, to the broken china cup the Byrnes had found on the floor. "Donovan said he and Maranda were away for less than an hour. Clara was gone when they returned, and her belongings were rifled through. She doesn't appear to have gone willingly."

"How long ago?"

"Some time between 8:30 and 9:30 last night. Do you have any idea where she could be?"

"My guess is Colchester," Jennings said slowly.

Thomas frowned. "In all of England, why Colchester?"

Another pause. Jennings's sage eyes probed Thomas's face, and he let out a heavy sigh. "Because, Lindsey, she... she is Clarissa Cromwell."

The air rushed out of Thomas's lungs, and he sank into a nearby chair, his legs shaking. The heiress of Joseph and Marian Cromwell? "How can you possibly say that? She's dead."

"Long story, but I assure you she is very much alive. At least for now. But we need to find her before it's too late."

"Who's behind this?"

"I can't tell you that, but we have a little time. They won't... dispose of her immediately. She still has something they want."

"She's The Pawn," Thomas muttered, remembering his conversation with Lotta Detweiler months earlier.

"Head to the harbour and tell the Grahames to meet us at the station. We'll see if there's a train running. But for goodness's sake, don't tell them about her identity."

Thomas rose in stunned silence. If Clara really was Joseph Cromwell's daughter, her father was the one who tried to save his father's life in Calais. No wonder she was interested in his photograph. Something jogged his memory. Clara hadn't been the only one interested in the photograph. It went missing after Lena had been in. Why would she have taken it? In that moment, he realised just how little he truly knew about Lena Mitchell. She had joined the Newhaven division shortly before Clara arrived, but before that, he had heard she was an overseas agent. She didn't seem to have heaps of brains and most of her information came from flirting with unsuspecting victims. Thomas wrinkled his nose in disgust. Pushing the string of thought aside since he had no answers, he hurried to obey Jennings's orders.

Back at the clinic, Donovan made a quick call to Wales to let Maranda know he would be delayed. He had left her in the care of her cousin.

Thomas dug through his bottom desk drawer feeling for his shoulder holster. Slipping it on over his vest and strapping an extra Webley to his waist, he shrugged into an overcoat as Alaina appeared.

"There you are, Thomas. I..." Alaina frowned at the guns. "What's going on?"

"Emergency mission. You'll have to excuse me. Sit at that phone and don't move. Wait for my call in a few hours."

"A few hours? Where are you going?" she asked, catching his coat sleeve as he tried to rush past her.

"Colchester. Now be a dear and do as I say for once." Thomas tore out of her grasp and disappeared down the hallway with Donovan on his heels, leaving Alaina in stunned silence.

Jennings, Kasey, and Kavan were already waiting for them when Thomas and Donovan arrived at the train station. Quickly purchasing their tickets, the men boarded the noon train.

Once in their seats, Thomas leaned over and whispered to Jennings, "Can you fill me in on this Cromwell business?"

Jennings hesitated before he answered in a subdued tone to avoid being overheard. "Joseph was a prominent Parliament member until 1908. Parliament was a mess at the time, and problems escalated while tensions rose. I never learned what or with whom exactly. Joseph and I were old friends, and he started to suspect foul play lay ahead. His daughter Catherine and her husband Jonathan were in Ireland at the time. Joseph asked me to get Clarissa out of Colchester and smuggle her to them." He paused. "Joseph, Marian, their butler, and a child everyone assumed was Clarissa were murdered that night."

"Why did they assume that?"

"Clarissa wasn't well known. Few people had ever seen her, so when the family doctor reported the victim as Clarissa, no one disputed it."

Thomas shook his head in bewilderment. "Then what?"

"I managed to have Clarissa's name changed, and she stayed with her sister's family in Halifax under the guise of being an orphan—Home Child, you know—until the beginning of the war. After her nursing training, she went abroad."

"What are they after?"

"Paperwork."

"A will?"

Jennings shrugged noncommittally. "Amongst other things."

"You're serious?"

"Of course. We're talking about documents that would make them very wealthy men."

"Then she's been a pawn all these years?"

Jennings nodded again.

"What's the harm in giving them what they want? It's just an inheritance."

Jennings's head snapped up. "It's more than an inheritance, Lindsey. With that paperwork in the wrong hands, we would lose the war with the amount of money and power that is at stake. Not to mention information with the ability to ruin some of the most powerful men in Britain. It would be chaos. The world would end as we know it." The colonel shook his head resolutely. "We can't give it up."

Thomas said nothing. He stared out the window at the dismal countryside rushing past, but he barely noticed it. Not only had he been working with a supposedly murdered British heiress, but she was now in the hands of the unknown enemy. It was her life or the world's freedom. He groaned inwardly and dropped his head in his hands. That was not a decision he wanted to make.

CHAPTER 45

Familiar Roots

CLARA AWOKE with a groan as she slowly stretched out her stiff muscles, wincing as she touched the knot on the back of her head. Apart from a few bruises on her face, she wasn't physically any worse for the wear.

Never sacrifice the truth on the altar of ease. That wise sentiment had echoed from the deep voice she had loved so well. Dear Father. The realisation of what it meant jolted her—the truth would cost her everything.

"Thank you, Father. I won't forget," she whispered, leaning her forehead against the stone wall. "And thank You, Lord, for parents who prepared me for what lies ahead years in advance."

A deep ache had replaced the angry tears, but grateful ones began to flow as she sat in the cellar of her beloved childhood home. Regardless of what the day brought, she was prepared.

When Clara was dragged back into the library for questioning hours later, another person joined them. Lena.

"What are you doing here?" Clara questioned.

"Lena was of great help in getting you here, my dear." Charles flashed her a smile as he slipped his arm around the blonde's slim shoulders.

Clara shuddered. What had this woman done? "What

happened to Mother and Father? Did you...?" She choked and couldn't finish the thought.

Charles had the audacity to laugh. "Of course not. He did," and he motioned behind her.

Swiveling her head, her gaze landed on Doctor Greshem from Folkestone, her former employer. Her hands flew to her temples. How could this be happening? It had to be a dream. A horrible dream.

Greshem nodded at her without a word.

Rage coursed through Clara as she addressed Charles. "You had them and Catherine murdered? And kept threatening me all these years? Why? To scare me?" Tears burned her eyes, but she refused to give Charles the satisfaction of them. "What do you want now?"

"You have two choices."

She snorted. "So many?"

"I want to know the location of those papers before sundown."

She eyed the clock. It was nearly noon; she had a little less than five hours. "You won't get anything from me."

Charles's gaze turned to ice, and a firm hand slapped her face, causing her to cry out in surprise. "Reconsider, little sister. You are nothing but a worthless pawn in my hand, and I always get what I want. I have waited this long, but I will wait no longer."

"But I—"

The next blow came harder, causing her knees to buckle, and Clara tasted blood as she fell to the floor.

"Take her away!" Charles roared.

Reynolds brought a tray of food in sometime later. The fare was far from tempting, but Clara was famished and her throat parched. Reaching for the nourishment, a thought stung her mind. *Poison.* What would stop them from poisoning her? Not enough to kill her but enough to make her miserable. Casting aside the tray, she retreated back into her dark corner and huddled her knees to her chest.

She vainly tried to remember back to the day Colonel Jennings smuggled her out of Hollyside Manor to Jonathan and Catherine in Ireland. Her mother had reassured her all would work out, and her father had hugged her tightly. It was a day she had attempted to forget for the last decade, but something jogged her memory. There was something important about that day she was forgetting. A wisp of truth hovering just out of reach.

Instinctively, her fingers found the cross hidden under the collar of her shirtwaist. She fingered it meditatively for several minutes and then unclasped it from her neck with shaking hands. It was too dark to see the silver and sapphires. Leaving the security of her corner, she slipped the necklace, along with one of her hairpins, onto the shelf above the secret trapdoor in the corner. Too bad it only opened from the other side. If someone did come through the tunnel, they would find it, and hopefully before the impending threat was carried out at sundown.

With a sigh, Clara withdrew to her corner and prayed. Prayed for safety. For courage. For peace. For someone to find her. Frankly, for a miracle. And at last, committing her soul to the keeping of her Saviour, she fell asleep.

She jolted awake from a dream, her head fuzzy. She remembered something. Shutting her eyes, she tried to conjure up the hazy image.

Ten-year-old Clarissa sneaking out of her room and peeking over the upstairs railing. Father handing Colonel Jennings a package with a few whispered words. The colonel nodding and shaking hands with Father.

Clara shook her head, and the image vanished. The next day, she had been smuggled out of Hollyside, and news of the murders had followed. Her lungs tightened, and her breaths came in short pants. That file must be the papers her brother mentioned. But after the night, she had never seen them again. Where did they go?

Reynolds arrived a quarter of an hour later and hauled her upstairs for another round of questioning. From the light coming in one of the windows in the hall, Clara knew sundown was not far off. As she strove to keep up with the man's long strides, her mind reeled for words. She wasn't about to give in to her brother and his minions, but what could she say?

Reynolds shoved her into the library, keeping her pinned with his viper grip on her upper arm. Crouthers still remained behind the large mahogany fortress of a desk in the corner, and Greshem stood with his back to her, staring into the fireplace.

Charles rose from the sofa where he sat with Lena as she entered. "Welcome back, little sister."

Standing straight and impassive, Clara shot a frown at Sean, who chuckled from the easy chair in the far corner. *Where did he come from? And just* who *is The Piper?*

"Stubborn to the end. Trying to be brave, are we? You'll change your tune shortly," Charles goaded.

Refusing to respond to his barbs, Clara remained silent and met his gaze with determination and peace in her heart.

Charles deliberately pulled a long knife from its sheath at his waist and approached her. Swallowing hard, Clara took a shaky breath. With the point of the knife under her chin, Charles raised her head to meet his eyes. The blade poked sharply, but she refused to acknowledge it.

"Your answer, little sister," he rasped. His eyes flamed with hatred.

She blinked but said nothing as the ticking of the clock drummed in her ears. Her gaze flickered to her father's chess set in the corner. She had never understood the game's mentality before, but now she did. The pawns were captured. They were expendable. The game was over. This was checkmate. She was out of time, out of options. All she could do was pray rescue would arrive before it was too late. Was that too much of a miracle to dare hope for?

CHAPTER 46

The Beginning of the End

AFTER A DETOUR to request backup from the police, the small group of men met in the Hollyside Manor grounds. Thomas studied the faces of each. Jennings, who had smuggled Clara out of this very house a decade ago. Kasey, the stalwart captain who loved her as his own granddaughter. Kavan, who shadowed her frequently to keep her safe. Donovan, the Irish rebel who had harboured her. Each one of them had a direct link to Clara and was determined to see her out alive.

"We have to positively identify that she's here before the authorities step in," Jennings whispered. "They are standing by, awaiting our signal."

"How will we get inside?" Kavan asked.

"Can't exactly charge the front door," Thomas said dryly.

"There's a tunnel into the cellar from the barn. The trapdoor is in the back corner of the third stall on the right. From the cellar you can get anywhere else inside," Jennings said quietly.

Thomas stared in amazement. *How did the man possibly know all that?* "I'll go," he stated without voicing his inner question.

"Very well," Jennings acquiesced. "When you come to a fork in the tunnel, keep to the right and use the first overhead trapdoor. Go too far and you will end up in the kitchen pantry. I want no unnecessary heroics. If she is there, bring her out. If not, look for proof that she could have been." He paused. "Be careful, Lindsey. These men will stop at nothing."

Thomas nodded and slipped out of view into a grove of silver birches leading to the barn. True to Jennings's instructions, he found the trapdoor in the barn, hidden under a few bales of hay in the third stall. Shoving them out of his way, he eased the wooden cover up and descended silently into the black abyss. His torch shone on smooth, compacted, dirt walls and a labyrinth of spiders' webs. Keeping his arm out in front to dislodge the silken strands, he forged his way through the tunnel, stooping to avoid banging his head on the short ceiling. The tunnel had obviously been made with those of a shorter stature in mind.

After three minutes, he reached the fork. Keeping right as Jennings had instructed, he watched intently for the first trapdoor above his head. The latch was in working order as he fingered it. Tucking his torch into his pocket, he braced his shoulder against the panel and lifted, grimacing as the hinges squeaked with age.

Thomas poked his head up through the hole and scanned the room. Black as night, dank, and frigid. Hauling himself the rest of the way into the cellar, he swept the light around in hope of finding his missing nurse. "Clara? Clara, are you here?"

Silence.

His heart thudded in panic. What if this wasn't where they had taken her? *Please, God, show me if she was here. I need a miracle.*

There were a few boot scuffs in the corners opposite the trapdoor. He checked the cellar door. It was locked. Pausing at the trapdoor, his light caught the shelf, and a startled gasp escaped him as his hand shot out to retrieve a shining object. Clara's cross. And a hairpin? Thomas grinned. *Thank you, Lord.* Pocketing the necklace and the pin, he ducked back into the tunnel and hurried back to the waiting rescuers. He showed them the necklace, and Jennings's eyes flashed in recognition.

Thomas frowned. *He knows more than he's saying.* Returning

the necklace to his vest pocket, he held up the hairpin. "She also left this. We can jimmy our way in with it."

"I'll alert the authorities that we have an international incident demanding the utmost caution," Jennings stated, then swept his eyes over the group. "Are we clear?"

The group of men nodded, and Jennings continued, "They likely have her in the library on the second storey. You will need to lure them out with the element of surprise, but I want them alive. They still have information we need."

Thomas made mental notes as Jennings explained how to find the library, and as the colonel slipped away, Thomas led the way into the tunnel. No one spoke as the line of men trailed through the dark, underground corridor and entered the musty cellar.

Shining his light around the room, he retrieved Clara's hairpin from his pocket. "We have to hurry," he whispered as he jimmied the lock and eased the door open.

Every man had his gun in hand. The coast was clear.

Thomas led the way through long, elaborate halls. No servants hustled about, and every curtain was drawn. Kasey slipped from the group to unlock the front door as they passed it and rejoined them swiftly. The mansion was silent apart from the faint murmur of voices from the second storey. Velvet carpet graciously muffled their footsteps as they mounted the stairs.

Thomas's pulse thundered in his ears. This entire mission was by far the most dangerous of his career. He just hoped they weren't too late. At the top of the staircase, he pointed every man to his assigned position. The element of surprise would be their best defence since they hadn't the faintest idea how many guns—or men—they would be up against. Every one of them had an order to hold their fire till he gave the signal.

Once they were each in place, Thomas dropped an antique vase from a side table over the railing. A loud crash sounded from the delicate china shattering as it hit the railing below, and he quickly ducked into his hiding spot in the alcove.

"What was that?" a muffled voice asked from inside the library.

"Well, go check," another voice instructed after a moment.

The library door squeaked open, and a blond man slunk out. Thomas recognised him instantly as Reynolds. The cat-eyed man surveyed the hall. Thomas didn't dare breathe. When Reynolds moved to the right, Thomas heard rather than saw the *thud* as Reynolds hit the carpet. Kavan's pistol stock had found its mark.

CHAPTER 47

The House of Cards

INSIDE HER LIBRARY PRISON, Clara stood with her back to the wall and Charles's knife poking into her neck. Hope flickered in her chest as the seconds ticked by after the commotion.

Charles watched the door impatiently. "What's taking that imbecile so long?" he muttered. Stowing the knife in its sheath, he shoved Clara towards the sofa where Lena reclined and tossed the blonde woman a pistol. "Keep her here, Lena. Let's go, men," he instructed, heading for the door with Sean, Greshem, and Crouthers behind him.

There was an eerie silence, followed by the sudden ringing of gunshots and bellowing roars from the hall outside.

Lena jumped up. "Come with me," she whispered hastily.

Clara stared at Lena, unable to believe what she was hearing. Lena had voluntarily worked to hand Clara over to her captors, and now she wanted her to trust her blindly? It had to be a trap. "Why would I do that?"

"Because Charles has every intention of killing you, and I have every intention of preventing him. Come."

Indecision raged in Clara's heart. *Please, Lord, don't let this be a trick,* she prayed silently before following Lena through the door opposite them.

Struggling to keep up with Lena's rapid pace, Clara darted through several rooms, all of which she recognised from her childhood with a lump in her throat. The final door was thrown open upon a narrow hallway, and Lena made an immediate right, leading them to the servants' staircase. The young women flew down the stairs and into the kitchen. Dashing out the kitchen door, they pelted across the grounds in the direction of the barn. Shadows lengthened across the lawn in the gathering darkness, the grey clouds making it difficult to determine whether or not the sun had set.

Lena broke the silence with an urgent whisper. "Run to the front. It's you they want. Find the authorities and meet me in the barn."

Clara stopped. "The barn?"

"Hurry! I'll have The Piper!" Lena hissed and then bolted away, disappearing through the barn door.

Clara sprinted back towards the estate. Still weak from the fever and lack of food, her breath came in short pants, and she stumbled several times. *Don't let me fail now, Lord. Help me see this through.* A second-storey window shattered above her head, and the sound of gunfire echoed in the otherwise quiet night. As she burst through the front door, she ran straight into Colonel Jennings.

"Clara, what happened to you?" Jennings asked, catching her elbows to keep her upright.

"Lena. Barn. Piper," was all she could splutter in an attempt to catch her breath.

Jennings barked orders to several policemen, and they followed Clara out to the stable. As they entered the dimly lit building, Clara broke the silence. "Lena?"

"Back here," Lena called from the third stall on the right.

They found the blonde holding a gun in one hand and a knife in the other. A tall man in a reefer coat and a black fedora pulled low over his face stood rigidly opposite her in front of the open trapdoor with his hands raised.

"May I introduce you to The Piper, also known as Fallamhan," Lena said with great flourish.

The words jolted Clara. *What? Both were the same man? But who...?*

"Remove your hat, sir," Jennings demanded in a voice laced with steel.

When the man hesitated, the sound of several pistols being cocked seemed to change his mind and the black fedora gave way to a crop of brown hair and green eyes.

Richard Morgan.

His eyes widened in surprise as he stared at Clara. "You were supposed to be dead by now."

She gripped the stall wall for support. "It was you? Why?"

He pursed his lips into a grim line. "I have a country that needs me, and I couldn't let you get in the way."

Clara cringed as he muttered a strong oath. Her mind whirled in disbelief at the change in events. Never had Richard fallen under suspicion. How could it be possible? Everything he said had been a lie. He had betrayed them all.

Lena surrendered her pistol to Jennings as the policemen took over. In a low tone meant for only Jennings and Clara to hear, she said, "You should know he was behind Robbie's death. There won't be evidence, and I can't say he's the one who actually pulled the trigger, but he gave the order, and that's the truth."

Jennings's jaw tightened in visible anger, and he gave a curt nod before moving to join the policemen.

But the news sucked the air from Clara's lungs, and Lena gently led her away from the stall. "Sorry to bombard you with the truth like that," the blonde apologised.

Clara's mouth felt dry, and she hardly recognised her own voice. "All this time it was Richard. We thought... that is... you..."

"I know, and I can explain."

Clara motioned to the weapon in Lena's hand. "Why the knife?"

"I cut the brake lines just to be safe," the young woman answered, pointing to the Bearcat parked in the center aisle of the barn.

"You're a mechanic?"

A smile curved Lena's lips, and a flash of merriment danced in her icy blue eyes. "Among other things. My main occupation is as an actress."

Clara felt as if the floor had just disappeared beneath her feet. "Everything in Newhaven was all an act?"

Lena nodded with a wry smile.

"But why? If Crouthers was in on the plan, why would he have stationed you there?"

"I don't work for Crouthers. I work under Jennings in foreign intelligence."

Clara's jaw dropped in amazement, but she couldn't help it. This woman was talented, and there was no end to her surprises. "But your disappearance—"

"I know, it left a poor impression, but I didn't get a chance to tell Jennings before I had to leave. I knew I had to get to the bottom of this and hoped you would all show up in time."

"All this time I thought you hated me, and that Richard was on our side," Clara said slowly. *Things aren't always what they seem.*

Jennings rejoined them a moment later and shook hands with Lena. "Well done, Miss Mitchell; you far exceeded your reputation."

"Thank you, sir."

Clara motioned for a private word with the colonel. Out of earshot from the others, she wrung her hands. "Sir, might I recommend that Thomas not see Richard. They were friends, and... I don't know how Thomas would react when he finds out." That was an understatement. Thomas tended to overreact to everything.

Jennings snorted. "My dear, he would do what any decent man would do to another man who was threatening someone he cared about. He would throttle him. Friend or not." He patted her shoulder reassuringly. "Don't worry. I will discuss Richard with him later privately. For now, the authorities are taking charge of him. We need him alive for his trial."

Clara thanked him before he strode back to the manor. Watching the police haul Richard away, she sighed heavily and rubbed her temples as the truth slowly began to sink in.

Lena touched her elbow, and Clara started. "It's starting to rain," the woman said slowly. "We should head inside."

Clara blinked in surprise. She hadn't even noticed the drizzle around them. They scurried across the lawn towards the manor and ducked inside just in time to see several officers escorting Crouthers, Sean, and an unconscious Reynolds down the stairs.

What about Charles? And where's Greshem? Clara frowned. Once they were gone, she glanced back up the stairs and noticed Jennings with... Thomas? Her brown eyes widened with unspoken questions as she met his gaze.

Thomas bounded down the stairs and grasped Clara's elbows. "Are you all right? Did they hurt you?"

She stared at him in shock. "What are you doing here?"

"Long story, but are you hurt?" His gaze flitted over her as if assessing any damage.

She shook her head numbly. How did one answer that question? Her entire life had been turned upside down and crumbled at her feet. Never had she dreamed the truth would be harder to believe than a lie. "I'll live. But my question stands: why are you here?"

"I was worried."

Against the backdrop of betrayal, those simple words changed everything. Thomas Lindsey had shifted from the cold, calculated machine of a man into a frank and caring one. The gentle man she had only seen hints of now stood in the flesh before her.

He glanced back up the stairs as Jennings called to him. "I have head back and finish, but you're sure you're all right?"

"I'll see to her," Lena promised.

Thomas glared at her, suddenly realising her presence. "I don't know how you fit into all this, Mitchell, but—"

"She's on our side, Thomas. Don't worry. Do what you have to do and then we'll talk." There was more going on than either of them had ever realised.

As Thomas and Jennings disappeared from view upstairs, Clara sagged against the sturdy banister, overwhelmed.

Lena grasped her arm. "Come."

Clara let herself be led down the hallway to the parlour and sank into the amply cushioned davenport. The silence was deafening until the grandfather clock across the room bellowed five o'clock. Her mind swam with memories. The easy chair still stood in the corner where her father used to read the Bible to her every night. The lakeside painting her father had bought her mother for their twenty-fifth anniversary still graced the wall above the mantle, and her mother's silk curtains flanked the windows.

Clara smiled as she remembered the long hours she used to spend laying on her stomach reading in front of the fire. Her thirst for knowledge she had inherited from her father, as he encouraged her to learn as much as she could. Oh, how she hoped her parents would be proud of the woman she had become. The woman that their training and God's grace had made her.

Thomas hastened up the stairs and bumped into Jennings, who was smiling knowingly. "I know what you're thinking, but I don't want to hear it."

A low chuckle escaped Jennings as Thomas bent to examine a body. As he rolled the dead man over, Jennings's amused look morphed into a mild curse, causing the doctor to glance up in surprise. The colonel's usually steady sage eyes blazed, and his eyebrows sank into a fierce frown.

"What is it?"

"Not what," Jennings growled. "Who."

Thomas eyed the body again. From a strictly medical perspective, the man had died of several gunshot wounds to the torso. Nothing of significance stood out to him.

"Charles Cromwell," Jennings said in a low voice, meant only for Thomas's ears. "We were told he died years ago."

Thomas's head spun. Nothing was making much sense at the moment, but Jennings clearly had no doubts as to this man's identity.

The older man sighed heavily as if in pain, and a weariness stole over his countenance, making him appear to have aged a lifetime in a few short hours. "And so the unravelling begins."

In the parlour, silence lingered as Clara was lost to retrospection.

After a time, Lena tentatively broached conversation. "I'm sure you can imagine my surprise when I learned that one of my colleagues was the alleged victim of a ten-year-old murder case and a British heiress."

Clara started at the words. "How long have you known?"

"Only a few months." Lena paused. "What will you do now?"

"I have no idea."

When Jennings and Thomas joined them several minutes later, the entire story tumbled out, piece by piece.

"And to think I said you needed brains and not just looks," Thomas spluttered, slapping his forehead at the end of Lena's account.

Lena smirked at him then slipped from the room. The next part of the narrative wasn't meant for her ears.

When Jennings asked Clara about her abduction and subsequent confinement, she recalled every detail she could remember with quiet resolution to avoid losing her slipping composure.

"What about the papers?" Thomas cut in.

"I have never seen the contents," Clara answered. "But you have, haven't you, Colonel?"

Jennings nodded slowly. "I wondered if you would remember, but I don't have all of them. Your father knew something was amiss and split up your section of the paperwork. Crouthers knew Jonathan had them but not that I did. And he never took into consideration that there was a third set right in front of him."

"What do you mean?" Thomas asked with a frown.

Jennings's sage eyes held the younger man's gaze steadily. "You."

"Excuse me?" Thomas spluttered.

"Clara, do you remember the name of a man your father always spoke of, but whom you never met?"

Clara frowned at the strange question and replied, "Kian Meredith. Why do you...?" Her eyes widened as she saw a look of disbelief fall over Thomas's face. "You're Kian Meredith's *son?*"

Thomas stared at her, aghast. "You knew him?"

"Like Jennings said, I never met him, but my father spoke highly of him." A slow smile curved her lips. "Legends never die, Thomas."

"And unless I am greatly mistaken, your father entrusted the papers to you before he died," Jennings said to Thomas.

"I've never looked through the strongbox," Thomas said slowly, adding to Jennings, "How long have you known?"

"I knew you would follow in your father's footsteps. You're a lot like your father. I had my reasons for pulling some strings to get you to Newhaven."

Thomas raked his fingers through his hair and rubbed his forehead, clearly overwhelmed.

"Astounding," Clara whispered.

The room was silent, save for the rhythmic ticking of the grandfather clock and the murmur of voices in the hall.

"What exactly just happened here?" Clara asked, rubbing her forehead. Every fibre of her being felt as if she were dreaming.

Jennings rose and laid a hand on her shoulder. "I believe, my dear, you helped save the world, but it's a story the world can never know. Both for its own safety as well as for ours."

~

After the meeting, the trio returned to the scene of the crime. Kasey, Kavan, and Donovan had given statements and were helping clean up the mess, while Thomas retrieved his doctor's bag from its hiding place outside and took inventory on injuries amongst the group. Kavan had a broken finger, and Donovan had been shot just above the elbow. Thankfully, it was just a flesh wound.

"Where is Charles?" Clara asked suddenly.

Thomas shot a glance at Jennings. *I told you she would ask.*

"Charles is dead," the colonel said slowly. "Shot in the gunfight."

"And Greshem?"

Jennings cleared his throat after Thomas threw him another look. "Also dead."

Beyond biting her lip, Clara gave no other indication of what she was thinking, and she moved as if on instinct to wrap Donovan's arm so Thomas could splint Kavan's finger.

"Alaina's at the clinic. Could I call her?" Thomas asked her in a low tone, nodding towards the telephone after he was finished.

"Go ahead."

Lifting the receiver, Thomas asked the operator for the Bridge Street Clinic, and Alaina's voice floated over the line a moment later. "I was wondering if you would ever call, you scoundrel. These chairs are awfully uncomfortable."

He smiled with relief. "I'm glad you listened to me for once and stayed put."

"What are you doing in Colchester?"

"I'll explain when we get back in the morning." When Alaina fell quiet on the other end, he added, "Something wrong?"

"Not wrong. Only, I was terribly worried," was the quiet rejoinder.

"We're mostly all right. Any news or emergencies?"

"A call came from Wales. Tell Donovan he has a little girl waiting for him."

Thomas smiled into the phone. "Brilliant."

"Hurry back, rascal." Then the line fell silent.

With a chuckle, Thomas turned back to the group that waited expectantly for him. A smile lit his face as he clapped Donovan's good shoulder. "You have a little girl waiting for you at home, my friend."

A cheer waved around the room.

"Guess I better get back to my acushla," Donovan said, a happy grin plastered across his face.

"We wouldn't think of keeping you. I'll walk you out." Thomas led his friend out of the room and down the hall towards the grand front door. "Keep that arm in a sling for a few weeks and make sure the wound stays clean. Trust me, I will be telling your wife."

Donovan chuckled as he reached for the door handle, but Thomas stopped him. In a low voice, he said, "Near as I can tell, it was your bullet that saved me from taking one from Charles. Thank you."

"I'll always have your back. You know that," the older man promised, clapping the doctor's shoulder.

They shook hands before Thomas shoved Donovan gently towards the door. "Bring them both down to see us in a few weeks."

"Count on it, Doc!"

CHAPTER 48

A Year Ago November

11 November

WHEN CLARA AWOKE the next morning, it took her a minute to recognise her surroundings. The events of the previous night flooded her mind, and she shuddered. Straightening the shirtwaist and skirt she had slept in, she perched in the window seat of her childhood bedroom, the happy memories of childhood rushing over her.

The rose scent of her mother's hair. The sweet camaraderie shared with her elder sister, Catherine. Her father's booming laugh. Charles teasingly tugging her braids. The expansive gardens. Cuddling in her father's arms every night as he read the Bible and listening to his low, reverberating voice rumble in his chest as she pressed her ear close to listen. Her mother gently brushing her hair while telling her stories before she fell asleep.

Gentle tears rained over Clara's cheeks as she leaned her forehead against the cool window. Hollyside Manor was as lovely as it had been ten years ago—very little had changed—but it held a trove of bitter reminders she longed to forget. Far in the distance lay the rolling plains of Dedham Vale. An ache in her heart longed to wander the hills and survey the River Stour, to lose herself in the wonder and enchantment as she had as a child. Before the nightmare. Perhaps, before they went back to Newhaven, she would get the chance.

What will I do with the manor? With both of her elder siblings deceased, the manor was hers by legal right... although, there was the matter of her being legally dead. But Newhaven beckoned her. It was the closest she had felt to home in years. Shaking her head to clear the reverie, Clara slipped out of her room. As she descended the stairs, she trailed her fingers down the polished wood handrail. Though she had grown up in that home of plush carpets, velvet cushions, and servants, she now felt oddly uncomfortable around them. Times had changed. She had changed. Circumstances had forced her to make do and do without. Though she had embraced a simpler—and more dangerous —way of life, she was happy. A sense of purpose flooded her soul. The Lord was calling her back to Newhaven, and she was content to go.

Outside in the gardens, the late-autumnal breeze teased her ruffled hair. Clara loosened the braid and finger-combed her long locks before weaving them back into a plait. She paused at the banks of the whispering brook that cut across the estate and sighed. Then, lifting her face to the sky, she inhaled deeply. *Thank You, Lord.*

"I thought I saw you slip out here," Jennings's fatherly voice called from behind her.

Clara smiled at him as he joined her. "Just taking a little walk down memory lane."

"What are you going to do with it?" Jennings asked, gesturing to the expansive manor behind them.

"Haven't the faintest."

"You don't plan to stay here then?"

She shook her head. "I'm going back to Newhaven."

"Are you certain?"

"Very certain. I had a long talk with the Lord this morning. Newhaven is calling to me, and I feel a peace in returning. I can't stay here alone, and there's nothing left for me back in Halifax."

"I had hoped you would say that." Jennings smiled with approval and reached out a hand, giving her shoulder a paternal squeeze. "You are far braver than I ever gave you credit for, my dear."

"I never thought I would find home again, but for now, Newhaven is it." She sighed with contentment.

The colonel nodded. "It's a fitting name, you know."

Clara's merry laugh tinkled softly through the air as the play on words struck her. "Very fitting, indeed. Only now, I'm not running anymore." She had faced the past, the shadows, the nightmares. They would always be a part of her story, but the page had turned. A new chapter awaited her.

They returned to the house in time to find the others already awake. The plan was to return to Newhaven by the afternoon train, all except Jennings, who was going to London. He would see to the scheduling of the trials and promised to call with the latest developments.

Lena had also decided against returning to Newhaven. "I think I'm going to head home to Lancashire for a while. I have left enough of an impression on Newhaven with my grand exit and excellent character, or lack thereof." She shook hands all around before Jennings escorted her to the train station. "Good working with you both," she said, shaking Thomas's hand and hugging Clara. "I'll write you sometime."

Later, as Clara studied the blurring scenery out the train window as they whirred southward, she smiled as she remembered her first trip to Newhaven. For an entire year she had called the idyllic, seaside town her home. In a single year, so much had happened, so much had changed.

In the gathering dusk, they stepped onto the platform at the Newhaven Town station—back where it all began—and clanging church bells met their ears.

"What's going on?" Clara wondered aloud.

A newsboy bolted past with the evening papers, and Thomas stopped him to buy one. The doctor's hands trembled as he scanned the newspaper. "The Germans surrendered in France this morning. The war is over." His voice was hollow with shock.

Distant cheering blended harmoniously with the church bells, but none of the returnees breathed a word. There was no victory shout, but tears coursed down more than one face.

"Thank God," Clara whispered at last. "Sometimes I was sure it would never end, but after four long years, it has. And we made it, by God's grace, we made it."

"It's news I've prayed to hear for years, but now that it's here..." Kavan shrugged, at a loss for words.

"Let's spend a moment thanking Him," Kasey said huskily.

Forming a circle in the middle of the station platform, four grateful souls lifted their hearts in solemn joy.

"Lord," Kasey's voice rang out reverently. "We come before You and thank You that this long nightmare has ended at last, and that You have brought us safely through. We are missing some of our number," and here his deep voice cracked. "But we commit them to Your keeping. We thank You for seeing us through, for giving us friends who have become family. And as we forge into the future, Father, may we never forget the lessons You have taught us through the fires of war, or the ones who gave all they had because of it. In Jesus' name, amen."

Gentle *amens* rippled through the circle, joining the distant cadence of ringing church bells filling the air with solemn celebration.

CHAPTER 49

His Final Mission

14 November

THOMAS STOOD with his arms akimbo before the landscape painting hanging on his bedroom wall. With a deep breath, he lifted the heavy frame off the nail and laid it gently on the bed. Carefully peeling off a loose section of wallpaper revealed a hidden wooden panel. Prying it open, he lugged a small strongbox from inside before quickly closing it again and smoothing the paper back in place. With a deep breath, he rehung the picture. As he fingered the box, memories of his father rushed back to his mind, eliciting an aching throb deep in his chest.

"I miss you, Da," he whispered. Tears pricked his eyes, and he muttered to himself, "Get a hold of yourself, Lindsey. It was fourteen years ago."

He probed the picture frame with deft fingers, feeling for the catch, and retrieved a key from the hiding place. Just like he had in Edward Price's study. *It's time*, he thought with a determined nod as if to convince himself. Sitting down on the edge of the bed, he twisted the key. The lid creaked as it opened on its hinges.

A faded photograph of the Meredith family lay on the top. It was the only family portrait they had and was taken shortly before

Kian's death. Thomas smiled as he ran his finger lightly over the smiling faces of his mother, father, sister, and cousin. Kian's leather diary followed along with several documents relating to his agent work under William Melville. At the bottom of the strongbox was an oilcloth-wrapped package. Thomas unwrapped it slowly. The inheritance papers. He set them aside to show to Clara later and focused his attention to the other documents in the box where he found a scrap of paper crumpled in one of the corners. He smiled at the familiar bold scrawl of his father.

I entrust to you the inheritance papers for Clarissa Cromwell. Find her and keep her safe if ever you can, my boy. I know not whether Joseph's plan will succeed. The little girl may disappear or meet her death. But keep these documents safe from the enemy, for without them they cannot succeed. Be strong in the Lord, and in His strength you will not fail.

He drew a shuddered breath and wiped a salty tear off his cheek. After collecting himself, he carried the box and papers downstairs to the office where Clara was filing patient records.

She cocked her head as he entered. "Did you find your answers?"

He set the box down on his desk. "My father entrusted this to me... and there is something in here for you." He saw her gulp, but she nodded her head and cautiously joined him at the desk.

Letting out a puff of air, he opened the lid and showed her the picture of the Merediths and Alaina. Clara touched the face of a little girl with curly dark hair tied up in ribbons. "The ribbons... they belonged to your sister?"

Thomas met her questioning glance and nodded. "She gave them to me when I left to join the Service..." His voice cracked. "They are a reminder of my promise to never forget her."

"She looks like a sweetheart."

"She is." He cleared his throat and held the oilcloth package out to her. "The papers."

Clara reverently took the package and thumbed through the documents. Her only display of emotion was in biting her lip.

"Read this," he said quietly, offering her the note from his father.

She read it in an instant and stared at him. "My father knew something was wrong years before anything happened. He was protecting me."

Thomas nodded, and a long pause ensued. "I am not the man my father would be proud of."

She reached out and squeezed his hand. "Then maybe it's time to become the man God intended you to be."

He had told her on the trip back from Newhaven about that stormy night on the beach, and she had given him one of the brightest smiles he had ever seen. "I hope to," he said simply. "It seems we were destined to have met, Clara Dankworth. Without your answers, I would have never found mine."

"It was no accident that landed me on that train platform a year ago, Thomas. That was Providence," she said sincerely.

He nodded in agreement then gestured to the papers in her hands. "I am certain you will want to take those to Jennings right away."

Clara shook her head. "I think you should be the one to deliver them." When he frowned, she held out the package to him and added, "Fulfill your father's mission, Thomas. That was your dream."

Thomas accepted the package in silence, the lump in his throat too large for words. Seven years ago, he had embraced the life of an agent to follow in his father's steps and ensure justice. He had accomplished both—delivering the package would give him the closure he had earned. He might never know how his father really died, but he could finally let the past be the past and trust God with the future.

∼

15 November

A knock came at the back door of the clinic shortly before closing time. Clara opened it upon the impish-faced, hazel-eyed Chantelle, who bounced inside and hugged Clara impulsively.

"Chantelle, what's going on?" Thomas cried in alarm, walking in on the joyous reunion.

Chantelle whirled and hugged him next. "Kasey brought me. My job's over now that the war's done, and I thought I would see England in the daylight instead of always at night."

Thomas held her shoulders and gazed at her intently. "Are you sure you're done?"

"Only until I join the Service permanently."

Clara's forehead puckered at the statement. "You weren't a real agent?"

"Oh, she was a real agent," Thomas said with a smile. "Just not on the books. She worked primarily in France as my personal ferret. She even escaped gaol twice."

"Goodness," Clara cried in surprise.

Chantelle explained that her father, Captain Jean Durand, had been good friends with Thomas before he was killed in the Battle of Charleroi. She and her mother, Anne, had fled from France to her mother's family in Liverpool. Anne and Chantelle, along with several other family members, were on the ill-fated *Lusitania* when it sank. Chantelle was the family's only survivor. She had run away from her great-aunt in Brighton to join Thomas, who had promised Captain Durand he would look out for his daughter should anything happen to him.

"It's been a full-time job," Thomas cut in dryly.

Chantelle laughed merrily. "I wanted to join the Service back then but was too young, so Thomas let me work under him off the record."

Clara sent Thomas a pointed look. "Another off-record case?"

Thomas shrugged. "It worked out in the end."

"Impossible man."

"But he's a dear," Chantelle replied, digging an elbow into Thomas's ribs.

"Are you going back to Brighton?" he asked.

Chantelle shook her head. "There's nothing left for me there. I would rather stay here; at least until I go back home to Reims."

"I guess it won't hurt to introduce you then, but no telling anyone about what you've done, understood? I'll have Alaina get you a new identity card."

"Another name? I was just getting fond of this one," Chantelle moaned.

"I'll tell her to keep Chantelle and change Delvaux then."

Chantelle wrinkled her nose and sighed.

"Such is the agent's life," Clara said brightly, looping her arm through Chantelle's. "Who shall we meet first?"

"The Forsythes." Chantelle coloured at Thomas's questioning glance. "I accidentally met Robbie once when you were late one day." Softly, she added, "I'd like to meet his family and give my respects."

"The Forsythes it is," Thomas agreed, blinking back the moisture from his own eyes as a pang of sorrow surged through his chest. As Clara and Chantelle passed through the doorway and out of earshot, he whispered, "You were a good chap, Robbie, and I will never forget you. Upon my word."

"Did you open the envelope I gave you?" Chantelle whispered to Clara as they walked.

Clara shook her head. With all that had happened, she had forgotten about it. "You said I would know when the time was right; what did you mean by that?"

"You'll see."

Later that evening, in the privacy of her bedroom at the Forsythes', Clara cautiously retrieved the hidden missive from the false bottom of her trunk. Sinking on the edge of her bed, she toyed with the envelope. She didn't want any more surprises. *Lord, whatever it is, give me the strength to bear it.* Slitting the envelope, she pulled out a single sheet of paper, written in Chantelle's handwriting.

Find the truth.

A frown tugged at her forehead, and she set the note aside, completely bewildered.

~

6 December

Ever since Clara and Thomas had returned from Colchester, they worked in companionable silence. Neither said much nor referred to the spectacular rescue. On Friday afternoon, Clara sat at her desk with her chin propped on her hands while Thomas scribbled away on patient records.

"Worried?" he asked.

Clara started from her reverie. "A little."

The colonel had been travelling back and forth between Newhaven and London for the last three and a half weeks. Jennings's position and influence, coupled with the seriousness of the treason, had managed to secure a nearly immediate court-martial date for the prisoners.

"Jennings said he would call as soon as he had an update." Thomas tapped his pen rhythmically against his desk in an agitated fashion.

Another pause.

"Thomas, did you know Richard had Irish ties?"

"Not a clue," Thomas growled.

Clara knew he hadn't recovered from the stinging betrayal received at the hands of his best friend. She fell silent as she thought about Richard. His double-agent ways burned her heart, and then she thought of his role in Robbie's demise. *Because dead men tell no tales.* She mulled over the coarse-sounding words they had found on Robbie's body, but they were true.

The phone rang, breaking the silence. Clara shuddered as Thomas answered, "Doctor Lindsey."

Pause.

"Jennings," he mouthed to her. She edged over to his desk, and he held out the receiver so they could both listen.

"We're both here. Proceed," Thomas said.

"The trials are over." Jennings hesitated. "Mostly successful."

The air left Clara's lungs as Thomas choked, "Mostly?"

"I'll be down in the morning. Come to the manor around two, both of you." He paused before adding, "We can talk then."

∼

7 December

"Well?" Clara asked quietly as she and Thomas sat in Jennings's study the following afternoon, after Thomas had handed the oilcloth package into the colonel's capable hands.

Jennings's face was grim. "Sean Aiken received life imprisonment for the attempted murder of Alaina and his work as an accomplice in espionage." The colonel studied the two faces in front of him before continuing, "Greshem and Charles are obviously out of the picture."

Thomas huffed and ran his fingers through his hair, tension lining his face.

Clara twisted her skirt fabric around her finger. Three down, three to go.

"Reynolds and Crouthers were tried for and found guilty of both espionage and treason. Their executions were carried out this morning."

She shuddered—war was an awful thing. Even though it was over, now they were faced with the aftermath. Justice would be served, but she felt sick just the same.

~

A wave of nausea roiled Thomas's stomach, and he clutched the arm of his chair. Something wasn't right. "And Richard?" he asked hoarsely.

Jennings's expression grew even more solemn. "I couldn't have him tried for Robbie's murder without evidence. However, he was tried for espionage and treason, but before his sentencing, he attempted a gaolbreak with the help of some other Irishmen... He didn't make it." He fumbled with his pocket, tugged out a letter, and held it out in Thomas's direction. "He left this for you. He was due in Ireland today. It seems he tried to give freedom one more shot. Guess he knew how things would end," was all the man said.

Thomas stared numbly at the white envelope before him and mechanically reached for it, the bold scrawl on the outside familiar to him. It was over. He jumped when a hand touched his shoulder. Understanding radiated from Clara's eyes when he glanced up at her.

"Go," she whispered. "Take the day off."

He didn't have the strength to argue. He only wished it were all a dream.

Stopping in the doorway, he turned back and gave Jennings a nod. When his gaze landed on Clara, the words he wanted to say in thanks remained lodged in his throat. She smiled sadly and nodded. He knew she understood, even without the words.

Thomas retreated from the manor, and leaving the car for Clara, he trudged towards the downs. Passing the boarding house and the cemetery on Lewes Road, he dragged himself onwards. Grey clouds hung low overhead, threatening rain, and a gentle gust of wind toyed with his coat flaps. Veering off the road, he began his ascent of the nearest down. At the top, he dropped into a heap on the withered grass and surveyed the landscape. Lewes sprawled out in the north, and the hills beyond were bleak with the shroud of late autumn. Winter would soon be upon them.

Keeping his back to Newhaven, he sat with unseeing eyes, his thoughts racing.

When he finally fished the letter out of his pocket, his fingers brushed against a cool metal object. Still holding the letter in one hand, he pulled out Clara's necklace and ran his finger over the filigree etching. He had kept it in his vest pocket ever since the rescue. Though she seemed to have forgotten about it, he knew he should return it—and tell her how special she had become to him. He sighed. *Someday.*

Sliding the necklace back into his pocket, Thomas turned his attention back to the letter. He wondered when Richard had written it and more importantly... *why.* Closing his eyes against the rising feelings of anger and betrayal, he drew a shaky breath, unsure of what to expect.

True to his promise to Clara on the night of the rescue, Jennings had quietly disclosed to Thomas that Richard was Robbie's killer, or at least the one responsible for the boy's death. After some intel from Lena, it appeared Thomas had been right. Robbie had accidentally overheard Richard in Crouthers's office, though the lad obviously didn't think it was important. From there the narrative grew fuzzy. Whether Richard had stalked Robbie back to Newhaven to silence him or had sent someone else, no one could verify. Regardless, intercepting the note from the Secret Service hadn't been the main goal. But exactly what happened that night, they would never know.

With a quick prayer for courage, Thomas broke the seal, and a single slip of paper fell out. Hands sweating and heart pounding, he read the familiar bold strokes.

Thomas,

If you are reading this, then Jennings made good on his promise to deliver it to you. I never had any hope of giving it to you myself as I knew from the moment you arrived in Colchester that my luck had run out.

Time is short, as I will either be dead or in Ireland when you read this. I know you have a thousand questions, but I can't answer them all. So I shall tell you only what is most important.

I never told you I was Irish. After my mother's death by influenza when I was six years old, my father hated me and my Irish heritage. That kind of prejudice against me as a child drove me to vow that I would never tell another soul of my Irish connections. I kept that promise with the exception of Donovan. However, he did not know of my double loyalties so don't hold it against him.

I had so entwined myself in a web of deceit that I knew there was no hope of my escape. I cannot find regret for what I have done—Germany promised money, and Ireland needed that money as much as it needed me. However, I do regret that it hurt you in the process.

I used you, Thomas, but you were a good friend. That's more than I can say of myself. I know I have no right to ask this, but please look out for my sisters and don't hold my wrongs against them.

I wish things could have ended differently between us.

Forgive me,
Richard Morgan

～

After Thomas left, Clara fiddled with her skirt pleats and thought of how Gwen Morgan would take the news of her stepson's death. How horrible to have to read about it in some sensationalised newspaper, but they couldn't write and tell her beforehand without implicating themselves. According to Maranda and Lizzie, Josiah Morgan had died in a coal mining disaster in 1913. She knew none of the Morgan siblings were close to their parents, but she wasn't exactly sure why, as none of them talked about it. Thomas only said Josiah Morgan had been a bully of a man and Gwen Morgan a mouse of a woman. Clara didn't know what drove Richard to do what he had done, but to her surprise, she found the impossible to be true. She almost pitied Richard Morgan—betrayal and all.

Swallowing hard, Clara extracted Chantelle's note from her pocket and showed it to Jennings, being careful to avoid mentioning how and from whom she had received it. "I don't understand what this is talking about, but I'm tired of secrets and half-stories. I need to know the truth, whatever it is. I cannot keep living a lie."

The sage eyes studied her curiously for several moments, softening as they did so. "It's time you knew." He paused. "Do you remember Abbington?"

"Yes, of course. He was our butler. A perfect gentleman in every way. He would have a tea party with me every time I begged him to when Catherine was busy." Clara smiled thoughtfully. "I hadn't thought about it in years."

Jennings rose from his seat and paced the room in deep concentration. Gravity etched across his strong features. "Clara, Abbington... was your father."

Her jaw dropped. "What?" After all the tragedy and betrayal, she wasn't even a Cromwell?

"Lucy Abbington and Marian Cromwell gave birth to daughters days apart, but Mrs. Cromwell's was stillborn," Jennings explained. "When his wife didn't make it through the delivery, Abbington decided to let the Cromwells adopt you into their family. He didn't want to give you up, but he couldn't raise you alone. So he did what he thought would be best for you."

"That's why he spoiled me," Clara mused through the silent tears. "I always thought it was because I was the youngest, but really... I was his daughter."

Jennings nodded. "Greshem was your family's doctor at the

time, and one of the only ones who knew about the secret switch."

Both sat in silence for several long minutes. Clara's mind swirled with her own thoughts, fears, and memories of the past ten years. She didn't know what to think and felt nearly orphaned all over again. "Thank you for telling me," she said at length. "And thank you for everything you did over the years."

Jennings nodded with a grave smile.

"If you don't mind, sir, I would like for Clarissa Cromwell to remain dead to the world. It's time for me to move on. For good this time."

Understanding gleamed in his sage eyes. "Your secret is safe with me."

CHAPTER 50

One Last Surprise

18 December

THE CURTAINS at the clinic were drawn, and the gaslights low as Alaina marched into the office where Thomas sat perusing the newspaper at his desk.

"I'm going home," she announced.

Glancing up from his reading, he studied his cousin's face. With all the places Alaina had lived in the last twelve years, he wasn't exactly certain which one constituted the title of *home*. He cocked an eyebrow at her.

"Weymouth," was the answer to his unspoken question.

"But you said—"

"I know, I said I would never go back, but I've said a lot of things I didn't mean." She sighed, her brown eyes begging him to understand. "Father's dead now," she added in a low voice, "and I'd like to see Mother again. Jane sent another telegram saying she hasn't been well after her bout with the flu."

"Then go with my blessing," Thomas said with a small smile. He had grown used to having his cousin around, but he knew her mother needed her. It had been too long. "Give Aunt Glenna and your friend my greetings."

"We'll have to keep our good-byes short if we want to avoid exposing the façade. I know for certain I'll start blubbering, and I would rather not at the train station," Alaina finished with a strained laugh. "It would be déjà vu."

Thomas smiled ruefully. He remembered the day he had said good-bye to her when he left home to become an agent.

Alaina studied him. "You love her, don't you?"

"Who?" Thomas tried to appear nonplussed.

She skewered him with a pointed look. "Love isn't a sign of weakness, comrade. In fact, it's an admission of strength. That you care about someone besides yourself. That you need help."

"I'm not sure it would ever work out," he cut in. "It's a risk that could ruin everything."

"Of course, it's a risk!" She patted his cheek. "But you've spent your whole career taking risks, and all your life you've tried to save everyone else. Maybe it's you who needs a little saving now."

～

20 December

When Thomas escorted Alaina to the train station, her words still burned in his ears. "I guess this is good-bye," Thomas said slowly as she rejoined him on the platform after purchasing her ticket. He held out his hand professionally. "Always a pleasure working with you, Alaina."

"You too, you old rascal," Alaina returned, giving his hand a squeeze.

"What about the Service?"

"Oh, Colonel Jennings is giving me an extended leave, but if something comes up, he said I can work just as well from Weymouth as from Derby. Home is calling, and I must go, at least for a little while. I'll miss you, comrade. Do try and stay out of trouble."

"I'll do my best," Thomas promised with a chuckle.

The conductor's "all board" hampered further conversation. After giving Thomas's hand another squeeze, Alaina scampered aboard the train, throwing promises to write over her shoulder. Her face appeared at a window near him several moments later, but Thomas could see the traces of tears as she gave him a brave smile and a small wave.

Returning both, Thomas watched the train pull away from the platform and let out a breath he hadn't realised he had been holding. Alaina was gone, and he would miss her. A smile tugged his lips into a grin at the thought. With all his cousin's abruptness, stubbornness, impish smiles, and fiery, copper curls, he would miss her.

"Come back soon, cousin of mine," he murmured along with a silent prayer that her reuniting with her mother would be successful. Turning on his heel, Thomas made his way over to the sheltered portion of the platform when a tap came on his shoulder. Whirling around, he found himself staring into the rich brown eyes of none other than Clara Dankworth. He hadn't noticed her earlier.

"Doctor Lindsey, I presume?" Clara quipped with a smile.

Thomas rolled his eyes but couldn't restrain his grin. He remembered well their first meeting thirteen months earlier and held out an arm to her. "Seems we have been here before. Come along, nurse. We have work to do."

Taking the offered arm, Clara laughed softly as she flashed him an amused smile. "Right beside you, Doctor."

Later that day, they worked on patient records in companionable silence until Clara asked abruptly, "When was the last time you saw Bryn?"

Thomas jolted but continued writing for several minutes. Apparently convinced he wasn't going to answer her question, Clara returned to her work.

"Almost seven years," he said slowly.

"You must miss her terribly."

He nodded and rose suddenly from his desk, crossing to the window. Stuffing his hands in his pockets, he sighed. He watched Sam and Emily traipse by, arm in arm. It wasn't hard to see how they felt about each other. Emily's eyes sparkled as Sam told her an animated story. Thomas was happy for her, for them both. Perhaps some good would come out of the wretched war after all. Turning back to Clara, he whispered, "She was ten when I left. She would be almost seventeen now."

"I'm sure she's a lovely girl," she comforted.

"It would be just my luck for her to have found some nice Irish chap to marry. She's likely forgotten all about me," Thomas lamented, rubbing his forehead.

Clara cocked an eyebrow at him. "Thomas," she said firmly. "I see no danger of that. You are by nature unforgettable."

His mouth twisted into a rueful grin, a soft chuckle escaping him.

"Besides," she went on, "from all I know about her, I have full faith she will come running to meet you with open arms and then you'll be begging to breathe."

Thomas's grin widened, the picture amusing and pleasing him. He turned from the window and returned to his desk.

"I received a letter from Lotta, or Merryn as she goes by now," Clara added after several minutes.

"Oh? Where did she escape to?"

"Manitoba, Canada, of all places. Do you think we should tell Jennings about her now?"

Thomas leaned back in his chair, thoughtful. "I don't know. I rather think Arthur Jennings is already keeping enough secrets to last him a lifetime."

~

23 December

Donovan was true to his word and brought Maranda and their baby girl down to Newhaven from Conway. The group met in the Forsythes' cosy parlour. Clara was cuddling the little bundle with Maranda beside her when Thomas arrived.

"We named her Marissa," Donovan announced proudly.

"Is that a family name?" Clara asked, taking her eyes off the infant and glancing up at the Irishman.

"Sure is." Donovan grinned and winked at her. "A combination of Maranda and Clarissa, after two of the bravest acushlas I know."

Clara's radiant face bloomed into a smile and unshed tears shone in the depths of her brown eyes. She sought confirmation from Maranda, who put an arm around her and hugged her. "Kian told Donovan years ago," she whispered softly. "Your secret is safe with us."

"I couldn't agree more," Thomas added quietly from the doorway. That won him three smiles and a baby being suddenly deposited in his arms. He studied the infant with a smile.

"She likes you, Doc," Donovan commented as Marissa's tiny hand grasped the doctor's finger and hung on tightly.

"Must be that charming grin," Clara said teasingly, and that won her one of the aforesaid grins. Sometimes the greatest of gifts came in the smallest of packages.

Thomas spent the remainder of the day at the boarding house. As he sipped his tea, he glanced around him and smiled. No man could ever be a complete failure with friends like these.

A knock sounded at the front door, which Donovan jumped up to answer. "Christmas present for you, Doc," the Irishman called.

Curious, Thomas approached the front door. Stopping on

the steps, his jaw slackened in shock. A grey-haired woman stood at the front gate, smiling at him. "Mam?" he whispered. Thomas rushed down the steps, engulfing her in his open arms. Dark head bent over grey as their tears mingled.

"How did you get here?" Thomas asked, holding his mother's shoulders and gazing into her sparkling eyes.

"Never mind that yet. There's someone else," Alys Meredith whispered, stepping back from him.

A dark-haired young woman at the gate caught his eye. The little girl of his dreams. She flew to him, throwing her arms around his neck, and he twirled her around the yard, straining her to his heart. He heard her sobs and realised he was weeping as well. Cupping her face with his hands, Thomas kissed her forehead. "Am I dreaming again, Bryn?" he murmured against her hair, hugging her again.

Bryn squeezed him tightly with a sad little laugh. "Not this time."

There was only one thing of which he was perfectly sure—his heart was finally home.

With a smile, Clara watched Thomas spin his little sister around the yard. The Christmas surprise had worked better than she could have imagined. Donovan flashed her a wink, which she returned. Her heart swelled with warmth as she studied the little group. The Forsythes who had lost so much, the Byrnes soon to be on their way to Ireland, the Merediths reunited.

I came here friendless and alone, and now I have friends I wouldn't trade for all the wealth of England.

God had blessed them richly, the war was over, and for now, they had peace. As for what lay ahead... well, there were still problems, unanswered questions, and a war-torn world to rebuild, but if they trusted God with their pasts and their present, they could trust Him with their futures. Because He was faithful, and that was enough.

THE END

Author's Note

In January 2020, I was in the throes of working on a nightmare project and needed a distraction to save my sanity. So, in a random document on my computer, I started to write drabbles about the adventures of a doctor and nurse spy duo during World War One. I had no plot, no plan, nothing. Just an eccentric collection of thoughts from an overwhelmed and overburdened heart wondering if there was still good to be found in the world. I never intended to finish this story, but God had other plans.

After I had tucked the smattering of scenes away for a few months, I was prompted to give NaNoWriMo a try. I had never attempted writing a novel in a month and had little idea of what to expect. Although November is the traditional month for NaNo, I decided to do it on my own time, and in June 2020, I pulled out my ramblings and wrote the book you now hold. Well... in its infancy. It was a little over 73,000 words, but I had done what I thought impossible.

The Lord gave me a heart for this story and taught much through it. As much as *The Lies We Live* is the story of the "War to End All Wars," behind the scenes it is also the story of a woman in her twenties facing a world that had crumbled in ashes at her feet: full of lost relationships, broken hearts, shattered dreams, and betrayal. She was desperate to fix it but wasn't sure how. She wanted to be the girl she used to be but couldn't go back. Too much had changed—she had changed.

Yes, that girl was me. I came face to face with the lies I believed about myself—the lies I lived. I saw the identity I had crafted for myself, instead of the identity I was born to live in Christ. I listened to the voices of those who told me I would never amount to anything, and I believed them. I felt tremendously overwhelmed and under qualified every step of writing/publishing this story and shed many bitter tears. But like Thomas and Clara, I had to learn who I was behind the aliases and the masks. Truthfully, I'm still learning.

That month reignited something in my heart for storytelling. I had lost sight of the passion and the heart God had given me for writing. But that summer of 2020, when our world changed as we knew it, I found what I had been missing, so I kept writing. In that time, I have drafted more novels, short stories, and novellas, but this was my first step, and it taught me much. In the midst of my own struggles, I wanted to craft a story of hope, of light, of redemption, of brokenness. Because, maybe instead of trying to become who we used to be, we need to become who we are meant to be.

I want to thank you for picking up this book and taking a chance on me, dear reader; it truly means the world! If you enjoyed this story, I would be most grateful if you would consider leaving a review on Amazon and/or Goodreads. Reviews are EVERYTHING to authors and a wonderful way to spread the word. You can also find me over on social media where I love connecting with readers and talking about all things bookish. Thank you in advance for your support!

With much love,
Morgan

Acknowledgments

Writing can be a lonely profession, since only the writer can actually write the book. But there is far more to publishing a book than just writing. John Donne said it best: "No man is an island entire of itself; every man is a piece of the continent." Without the help of so many others, this book would never have made it into your hands. It truly does take a village, a community, and I think the world of mine!

Noah: You were the first person to ever read this story. As your big sister, I assigned it to you as an English project. You got an assignment out of it, and I got feedback. A real win-win! Your adoration of Robbie has been greatly appreciated, and readers may thank you for championing against his demise, although sadly it was necessary for the story.

My parents: You were the next in line to read this story and offered helpful insight. Thank you both for your unending support, enduring my odd hours, smiling at the "Do Not Disturb" sign on my door, and keeping me plied with strong cups of tea and scones! Love you!

My beta readers: Taryn, Micaela, Jocelyn, Stephanie Lynn, Catherine Thompson, Rick, and Kysa. You lovelies were gems to work with! You gave me so much encouragement and valuable feedback. I would have been lost without you, and you helped shape this story into something better than I had dreamed.

Victoria Lynn: I hardly know where to start! Ever since I stumbled upon your corner of Instagram, I never left. You're a woman of many talents, and you brought my ideas for The Lies We Live to life as an editor and in designing my original cover (which I still love!). It was a dream come true working with you! You have been one of the best cheerleaders, encouragers, and inspirational figures!

Katja Labonte: Thank you for your lovely work in proofreading! It was a pleasure working with you (littleblossomsforjesus.blogspot.com), and I'm grateful to have you in my community of friends!

Hannah Linder: Working with you was a dream come true! Thank you for capturing the world in my mind so perfectly in the cover. You're amazing.

Catherine Posey: Formatting intimidates me, so thank you for answering my numerous questions and for doing such a beautiful job!

Amanda Tero: You were the first indie author I ever heard of, and in a way, the one who inspired me to take the indie route myself. I had so many questions about... well, everything, and you've been incredibly helpful and patient in answering them! And I've enjoyed getting to know you better over our nerdy texting conversations!

A shoutout to my amazing Instagram community: Caitlin Miller, Alissa J. Zavalianos, Faith R. Mathewson, Kellyn Roth, Cheyenne van Langevelde, Tabby RH, Valerie Cotnoir, Ella Meyer, Katja Labonte, Anna Augustine, Drew Taylor, Kate Willis Hopman, Erin Phillips, Brian McBride, Livy Lynn, and so many more. You have all been a light and provided huge doses of inspiration and encouragement in more ways than you will ever know. Plus, you are all amazing writers, and I consider it a privilege to journey alongside of you.

To those who championed me through every step of the publishing journey, thank you! Even if you couldn't beta or ARC, you shared the word with others and encouraged me! I can't thank you enough for this. You are gems. I can't even begin to name you all, but you know who you are.

The last thank you is the most important—Jesus. Who is the Truth and the true Author and Fixer of every broken heart. None of this means anything without You!

Character List

Thomas Lindsey (26) – MI5 agent and doctor in Newhaven
Clara Dankworth (21) – MI5 agent and nurse in Newhaven

Forsythes
Alistair – father; runs the Forsythe Grocer in Newhaven
Agnes – mother; runs the family boarding house
Peter (30) – eldest son; his wife Marjorie and with five children live in Scotland; he is a soldier in France
Susan (28) – eldest daughter; Red Cross nurse in France
Duncan (26) – second son; his wife Flora and their daughter live in Scotland; he is a soldier in France
Jessie (24) – second daughter; works on the British railway
Robbie (15) – youngest child; the only one still at home; former Boy Scout now serving as an informal messenger for the Newhaven Spy Ring

Richard Morgan (31) – MI5 agent; Thomas's personal ferret for information and his best friend
Elizabeth Morgan Tilney (23) – generally known as Lizzie; her husband Aaron is a soldier; she lives at the Forsythes' boarding house; works as a school teacher at the Boys' School and is a

volunteer for several societies aiding the war effort; Richard's half-sister and Maranda's sister

Maranda Morgan Byrne (19) – youngest of the Morgan siblings; married Donovan, a friend of both Richard and Thomas; lives in Wales; Richard's half-sister and Lizzie's full-sister

Lena Mitchell (25) – MI5 agent working in Newhaven as a telephone operator; stays at the boarding house; notorious reputation for flirting

Crouthers (55) – leader of the MI5 branch the Newhaven ring is part of; works in a secret office in London

Walter Reed (24) – Crouthers' secretary; mans the bookstore working as a front to the secret office in the back

Colonel Arthur Jennings (52) – former war veteran and retired solicitor; lives in Newhaven with his wife Hannah; heads a branch of the Secret Service

Kerridge (70) – the Jennings' butler

Edward Price (48) – Newhaven's prominent society member and town banker; supposed of being a German sympathiser; the Newhaven Ring is tasked with exposing him

Myra Evans Price – Edward's deceased wealthy wife

Emily Price (15) – Edward's daughter, who suffers from a hunchback condition; Thomas's informant

Captain Kasey Grahame (75) – an Irish American sea captain who moves supplies for the army between Newhaven and France; also smuggles contraband information and spies

Kavan Grahame (28) – Kasey's great-nephew who works with him

Alaina Huntington (24) – MI5 agent in Nottingham; friend of Thomas's who is in charge of identity paperwork

Chantelle Delvaux (16) – Thomas's ward; an unofficial French spy

Konrad Reynolds (30) – cunning double agent for MI5 and the Germans

Hazel Whyte (24) – Hope Inn waitress
Sean Atkins (29) – Hazel's Irish boyfriend

Morgan Taylor Giesbrecht fell in love with fictional realms at a young age and quickly began writing tales of her own, full of hope, authenticity, and intrigue. She's a hobbit at heart (but not in height) with deep roots in the past, who loves the occasional adventure, accidentally talks in a British accent on occasion, and has the dry humour to match. When she isn't writing or reading a book on her never ending to-be-read list, she can be found drinking copious amounts of tea, watching murder mysteries or period dramas, hanging out with family and friends, reorganising her bookshelves, or playing Christmas music year-round. British Columbia, Canada is the place she calls home, be it by ocean or by mountains.

Find her on Instagram at: @authormorgantaylor
Or on her website: www.morgantaylorgiesbrecht.com